What reviewers are saying about the stories in
Dark Side

The Dark One -- Angela Knight

"Those brave enough to read this erotic tale will be surprised and delighted. An intriguing read from start to finish."
-- *Sharyn McGinty, In the Library Reviews*

Chain of Thorns -- Willa Okati

"I would highly recommend this tale of dominance, submission and redemption."
-- *Anita, Fallen Angel Reviews*

Waiting For You -- Elayne S. Venton

"Waiting for You by Elayne S. Venton is like a rare chocolate liquor bonbon; rich and decadent and filled with a surprise guaranteed to burst over your senses with orgasmic intensity."
-- *Keely Skillman, eCataRomance Sensual Reviews*

BloodWolf -- Sierra Dafoe

"A superbly written novel that combines horror and eroticism in a way that will leave the reader reeling."
-- *Terrie, Romance Reviews Today*

Night Creatures -- Elisa Adams

"Ms. Adams has written a twisted vampire tale of intrigue and sensuous longing - dark cravings... It beckons the readers to turn the pages, enveloping them in explicit hungering."
-- *Janalee, The Romance Studio*

D1524182

www.ChangelingPress.com

Dark Side

Angela Knight
Willa Okati
Elayne S. Venton
Sierra Dafoe
Elisa Adams

Publisher:
Changeling Press LLC
PO Box 1046
Martinsburg, WV 25402-1046
www.ChangelingPress.com

Printed in the U.S.A.
Lightning Source, Inc.
1246 Heil Quaker Blvd
La Vergne TN 37086
www.lightningsource.com

Anthology Editor: Margaret Riley
Cover Artist: Angela Knight
Cover Layout: Bryan Keller

The individual stories in this anthology have been previously released in E-Book format.

The Dark One

Angela Knight

Chapter One

Kaska of Artane slowed his stallion to an easy amble. Prince Britar's fortress lay a full day away, and he'd ridden poor Warbringer hard this past month. He knew the Prince awaited the intelligence he'd gathered as a spy in neighboring Trovan, but laming his horse would serve no purpose.

Particularly with war on the horizon.

Besides, the last time Kaska had come this way, he'd had to battle the local brigands. Two fell to his blade before the rest fled, but that left five. And they might be in the mood for revenge. *I don't care to ride headlong into an ambush.*

"Whoreson bastards!"

A woman's roar of fury brought Kaska's head up. He drew Warbringer to a prancing halt.

Swords clashed, interspaced with male taunts and laughter. The laughter had a distinctly ugly note. The woman swore again, an edge of grim desperation in her voice.

The thieves had found a new victim.

Kaska set his heels to Warbringer's flanks and thundered up the road toward the sound. Rounding the bend, he saw five men fighting a lone female traveler they'd managed to unhorse. He recognized the dented, rusted armor and unshaven faces; it was indeed the same band of thieves.

But their victim was no common woman. Her armor and sword marked her as a follower of the Maid of Light -- a female warrior. She was tall for a woman, with a lithe, muscular build and pretty breasts barely contained by her intricately embossed breastplate. Long black hair swirled around her face as she spun and hacked at her tormentors with a slim sword designed for a woman's hand.

Dark Side

One of the brigands already lay dead at her feet, but four others remained, odds too great even for one of the legendary Battlemaids.

A grin of sheer, savage joy spread across Kaska's face. With a howl, he drew the blade sheathed across his back and kicked Warbringer into a thundering charge.

The nearest of the brigands whirled too late. Kaska took his head with a single stroke.

Another of the men jumped at him, hacking for his thigh with an axe, but Kaska spun Warbringer aside and thrust his blade into the thief's chest. The man tumbled off the lethal point, gurgling out his life.

Meanwhile, the third brigand fell to the Battlemaid's sword. His head tumbled from his shoulders.

The fourth man looked from Kaska to the thieves' would-be victim, calculated the odds, and took to his heels.

Kaska snatched a dagger from his thigh sheath and hurled it at the coward with an expert flip of his wrist. The man went down, the blade buried to the hilt between his shoulder blades.

Scarcely breathing hard, Kaska turned to the maid. "Are you well?"

"Well enough." She studied him, her dark eyes level. There was a sharp and elegant beauty to her face, with its broad, high cheekbones and square little chin. Her lush mouth could inspire a monk to carnal fantasies.

"My thanks, warrior," she said at last in a low, husky voice, pushing the long black hair out of her face. "There were too many of them for me to best alone." She considered him, appraising the width of his chest and the strength of his sword arm. Female appreciation lit her gaze, mixed with a warrior's caution.

She had reason for that caution, for he meant to challenge her himself. He worshiped the Dark One, and his god relished nothing as much as the moans of a defeated Battlemaid.

Imagining the tight grip of her virgin ass, Kaska felt his cock swell behind his loincloth.

Give her time to rest, and then…

Of course, the maid might well kill him instead, but looking at her long legs and full, sweet breasts, Kaska thought it a chance well worth taking.

As he opened his mouth to warn her of his intent, all color left the Battlemaid's face. Her eyes rolled up. Kaska threw himself from Warbringer's back as she collapsed in a heap.

Two long strides carried him to the maid's side. Dropping to one knee on the dusty road, Kaska began an anxious examination. He found no wounds on the front of her body, so he rolled her onto her stomach.

The maid groaned and lifted her head. "Wha --"

"Seems one of your cur attackers landed a blow after all," he told her grimly. "There's a stab wound in your back just under your backplate, over your left hip."

"Aye," she said, letting her head fall. "One of them had a dagger."

"'Tis not deep, but it bleeds still," Kaska said. "I can treat it, if you permit."

"Aye," the maid said, breathing now in shallow pants. "My thanks."

Kaska nodded and rose to retrieve his pack of battlefield medicines from Warbringer. *Well,* he thought as he walked to his horse, *I won't be challenging her any time soon. Not with that wound.*

Later, perhaps. When he'd examined her, he'd noticed she had a truly delicious ass.

He wanted it.

Matia of Ruza took another swallow of ale and held it in her mouth while her mercenary rescuer slid his needle into her skin. Pain lanced through her flesh as he tugged the stitch tight, but she managed to keep the groan between her teeth.

To distract herself, she looked up at the limbs of the great oak they sat beneath. The grass felt cool under her thighs. "So, Kaska, may I ask whom you serve?"

He hesitated, probably deciding how much to tell her. "Prince Britar of Renat."

She relaxed slightly. "The goddess must have guided me to you, then. I'm on the way to the Prince's fortress myself."

"Oh?" Another stinging stitch.

"The Daughters of the Maid in Trovan wish to offer him their support in his campaign against the usurper Svec. I am to offer him my sword."

Kaska hesitated again, the thread pulled tight. "He will be glad to hear it."

"The Elder Daughter at the Maid's convent told me Britar is a good man. Directly descended from Kral the Conqueror, which would make his claim superior to Svec's. Should he choose to press it."

"Aye."

"What manner of master is he?"

"I have found him just."

Obviously, Kaska was not a man to chatter of his leader's business. Matia nodded in approval. "I suppose I shall discover that for myself," she said. "Thank you again, warrior. Had you not come to my aid, I'd be raped and dying by now."

He grunted and slid the needle in again. "I have no doubt you'd have made them pay dearly. You're good with that blade."

"Not good enough to best them all." Grimacing, she took another swig of the ale and closed her eyes at the pleasantly yeasty taste.

A big, warm hand gave her shoulder a gentle pat. "That's it, my girl. Your wound is closed and cleaned."

Matia opened her eyes to watch as the warrior walked past to kneel by the riverside and wash her blood from his hands. He wore little but a loincloth, boots, and bracers. His armor must be tucked inside his packs.

Despite her Battlemaid's vow of celibacy, she'd have to be blind not to admire all that hard male strength. Muscle worked up and down Kaska's tanned, scarred back as he bent, bunching in his ass and brawny thighs. His long braid swung back and forth across his spine as he moved, reminding her of a panther's tail.

For a moment, she let herself imagine how he'd look with all that dark hair tumbling around his shoulders.

His face was as comely as his massive body, with eyes a piercing blue against his tan. Deep dimples rode at either side of his mouth when he smiled, and his cheekbones were broad and regal. That nose would have been too big on another man's face, but on his, it balanced a jutting chin and thick, dark brows. His mouth was her favorite of his features, wide and sensual, with even white teeth and lips that looked soft.

All in all, he made Matia regret becoming a Daughter of the Maid.

"Can you ride?" Kaska asked, turning to face her.

She considered the question cautiously. "If you help me on my horse, aye."

He nodded, his blue eyes lingering on her face in a way that made something heat deep in her belly. "'We'll travel to the fortress together, then."

Kaska's gaze rested on his companion's lovely face as he silently cursed his luck. He could not lay a single lustful finger upon her. Not only was she injured, she'd sworn to serve Prince Britar. Challenging her would deprive his leader of one or the other of his badly needed warriors.

The Dark One would not approve, Kaska thought, with a sigh of regret.

Then the wind picked up the long, black strands of her hair and tossed it around her slim shoulders. Her luscious ass rolled in the saddle with each stride of her stallion.

By the Dark One's Double Cocks, he wanted her.

Kaska's eyes narrowed in consideration. *We won't be in Britar's service forever. I could claim her after the Prince releases us. And in the meantime, I'll keep an eye on her and see she comes to no harm before I steal her from her goddess.*

Of course, eventually she would discover he worshiped the Dark One and realize what he intended. He'd be lucky not to take a dagger between the ribs for his temerity.

But, as he watched her throw back her head and laugh at some sally of his, Kaska decided claiming the little Battlemaid for his own was more than worth the risk.

Chapter Two

As Prince Britar took them to war in the months that followed, Matia discovered she'd found a valuable ally in the big mercenary.

The Daughters had schooled Matia in the arts of combat since she'd been five years old, and she had killed more than her share of thieves and murderers in the mountains of Trovan. Yet war was an altogether different matter, a scarlet-splashed hell of chaos and screams and gut-sickening terror. It was Kaska who kept her alive as he watched her back and helped her keep her courage in the bloody confusion. He held her head when she puked up her guts after her first battle and got drunk with her after the second.

Until, with Kaska by her side, Matia found herself falling into a cool, focused trance that allowed her to fight and kill and think of nothing at all. Much as the big mercenary did, judging by the way those beautiful eyes went cold and empty when he fought.

By her fifth battle, she was veteran enough to save Kaska's life, beheading a coward who'd been about to drive a sword in his back. Her new ally turned as the man fell, saw the weapon lying by his feet, and gave her that flashing smile again. She grinned back in pride.

So it was that Kaska and Matia became Shieldmates. Soon they were sharing a tent, platonic as brother and sister.

Until the day he told her he was a follower of the Dark One.

* * *

They were ranging ahead of the army as they often did, acting as advance scouts, when Matia reined in her white stallion and stared. "Sweet Maid shield us," she whispered.

A great stone circle lay off to the left of the road, paved with fine black marble. In the center of the ring stood a towering statue of the same gleaming black stone.

At first Matia thought it depicted some warrior and his captive, until she looked closer and saw the standing figure was naked, with two massive cocks. The first looked thicker than her forearm, while directly above it was a shorter one. At the figure's feet crouched a nude woman, her wrists chained, her head bowed in submission.

Directly in front of the statue, a huge column lay on its side. Carved of the same black marble, it was shaped like an erect phallus.

"It's a shrine to the Dark One," Kaska said quietly.

"Aye," Matia said, swinging down from her horse. "The Daughters told me of such, but I never expected to see one."

"Did you not?" he asked, in an odd tone.

Feeling wicked, Matia went to the edge of the stone circle, but didn't step into it. She was quite sure she wouldn't care for the Dark One's revenge, should she offend him. "This must be where the Dark Warriors make their sacrifices."

"Aye," Kaska said, still in that strange tone. "They strip their pretty captives, bind them well, and bend them over yon altar. Then…"

Matia turned to look at him, feeling the rise of wicked heat. She knew it was dangerous to have such an erotic conversation with her Shieldmate, yet she could not resist. "Then?"

Instead of answering, he swung from his horse and strode to her side. "Are you a virgin?"

Matia laughed. "What a question. Nay, before the Daughters allowed me to swear my Oath, I had to take one of the men from the village. The Elder Daughter said it was best if I knew what I gave up."

He flashed those straight white teeth in a rogue's grin. "So how was it?"

"Less than memorable." She shrugged. "But you needn't fear you sully innocent ears, assuming anyone who has killed as many men as I could be called innocent. So, oh wise and wicked Shieldmate, what do the Dark Warriors do to their captives next?"

"Very well," Kaska said. Something dangerous glittered in his eyes. "Next the warrior plies a whip over his captive's naked rump to make her dance for the god. He torments and pleasures her by turns, until she is wet and begging."

Matia swallowed as her own wetness rose. "And then?"

"Ah, then..." He watched her face like a wolf. "The warrior carries her off to another chamber, where he greases her tight, virginal anus until she is slick and ready. He's hard by then, hard and more than eager. Usually that's when she starts to beg, knowing what comes next, but her pleas for mercy only inflame him more. He presses the thick, rounded crown of his cock to the sacrifice's tiny rose pucker, and begins to slowly force it inside."

Matia knew she should be shocked, yet she felt only rising desire. Her nipples rose tight and hard within her breastplate, and her swollen sex ached, slick with lust.

"He takes his time raping her ass," Kaska continued in that deep, velvet voice, "claiming her for the god in leisurely strokes while her whimpers of pain turn to moans of pleasure. Finally, he spends, roaring his thanks to the Dark One."

Never in the six months they'd been Shieldmates had he said anything so blatantly carnal to her. Heart pounding, she wondered what pleasures a woman would find as Kaska's sacrifice.

She'd felt the heavy erection behind his loincloth just last night, while they wrestled in mock combat. Imagining the sensation of that massive cock forcing her last virgin orifice, she licked her lips.

"How do you know that?" Matia managed when she could finally speak. "I thought the Dark Warriors' ceremonies were secret."

His gaze did not waver. "I am one of the Warriors, Matia."

"You --" Stunned, she gaped at him. Her hand fell to her hilt. If he challenged her...

Kaska's harsh laughter rang out. "Have no fear of me, Shieldmate. We serve the same master, remember? I'd not deprive the Prince of your sword." His lids dipped, concealing the glittering, hungry blue of his gaze. "But if I'd met you on the field of battle, the Dark One would still be savoring the nightly sacrifice of your cries."

Praying the heat she felt didn't show, Matia tossed her head. "More like your god would be savoring the acid gall of disappointment."

His smile merely broadened.

"Ah!" she said, her arousal losing its heat as she remembered the amused looks the other warriors had given them. "No wonder the others laughed behind their hands. A Dark Warrior and a Battlemaid -- now there's a pairing rarely seen." Anger stabbed her, and she glowered at him. "You should have told me."

Kaska shook his head. "I feared you'd turn from me," he said. "I did not care to lose you as a Shieldmate."

Her anger cooled. Matia nodded, realizing she had no desire to lose him either.

He'd come to mean far too much to her.

They'd barely started back toward camp when they saw the woman on the road.

Matia's eyes narrowed as she recognized the girl's wheat blond hair shining in the sun. Vlasta, one of the camp followers.

But why was she walking *away* from the camp? Matia drew rein as Kaska did the same. "Well met, Vlasta," she called, keeping her tone pleasant. "Aren't you going in the wrong direction?"

The girl glanced up, saw the Dark Warrior, and stopped in her tracks. The blood drained from her face, leaving her sheet white with guilt.

"Why are you going in the wrong direction, Vlasta?" Kaska asked in a menacing rumble.

Vlasta squeaked once like a panicked mouse and turned to flee.

She might as well have saved herself the effort. They caught her in six galloping strides. Kaska snatched the girl off her feet, and she shrieked in pure terror. When she tried to fight him, he dropped her belly-first on his saddle and planted a big hand in the small of her back, pinning her flat.

"She runs like a spy," Matia growled as they drew rein with the woman struggling futilely across Kaska's thighs.

"Indeed she does," he said grimly. "Let's see if we can discover if she is one in truth."

They only had to strip her naked.

Matia found the small map of Britar's encampment rolled in a tight tube and sewn into the hem of Vlasta's skirt. It listed the number of his forces and the siege weapons they'd built -- deadly information in enemy hands.

"Who do you work for, and what have you told them?" Kaska snarled. The girl, bound and naked, shrank from his wrath.

"You'd best confess, wench," Matia told her coldly. She had no sympathy for a sneaking little bitch who'd betray them all to ambush and murder. "Kaska is a Dark Warrior, and you know what his kind do to captives. Especially..." She eyed the woman's nudity. "...spies."

Vlasta turned wide eyes on him. He gave her his best evil leer. "No!" she gasped. "I'll tell you everything."

And she did. Matia watched Kaska's grim face and wondered if her Shieldmate was disappointed. Her threat about the Dark Warriors' taste for rougher interrogation has not been empty.

It was as they'd suspected. Vlasta confessed that King Svec had indeed sent her to join the whores of Britar's camp. For months, she'd watched and collected information about the Prince and his men, and now she was headed home to her master.

Vlasta swore she'd had no other chance to reveal what she'd learned, and Matia believed her. The bitch feared Kaska's feral smile too much. Besides, she'd been frightened enough to give them the name of another of Svec's spies, a mercenary both Matia and Kaska knew. The man was such a thoroughgoing bastard, neither was surprised to learn he was also a traitor.

Exchanging a look, Matia and Kaska silently agreed they'd attend to him later.

"Now," Matia said, looking at Vlasta as she lay bound and naked in the grass, "what shall we do with her?"

"Hand her over to the Prince." Kaska bent and picked the spy up as though she weighed no more than a bread loaf. "But in the meantime, I mean to make a sacrifice of her ass. It's been months since I've had a woman."

"What?" Startled, Matia stared after him as he carried the spy toward his horse. "Where are you going?" she demanded, striding in pursuit.

"The shrine is just around the bend," he told her, tossing his captive across Warbringer's saddle. "A bit of sacrifice should jar any remaining truth from the wench's tongue."

Heart pounding, Matia mounted and rode after her Shieldmate. A Battlemaid had no business watching one of the Dark One's rituals, yet she was reluctant to leave Kaska alone while she rode back to camp. What if Svec's men attacked him while he was... occupied?

So she rode with him, heat flaring through her as she watched what he did to Vlasta.

One of those big hands busied itself between the cheeks of the spy's pert ass, stroking some kind of oil deep in the hole he lusted to fuck. Kaska shot a look at Matia over his shoulder. "Being a whore, she's not the virgin I prefer," he said in a coolly offhand voice. "But this oil will tighten and sensitize her." He curled a lip. "She'll not forget my cock, I vow."

His captive squirmed, her expression mingling arousal and fear. His hand looked very big and dark against the pale flesh of her backside as he continued to torment her.

Matia turned her eyes away and licked her lips.

When they reached the Dark One's Shrine, she tried to idle by the horses as Kaska headed toward the cock altar with the spy across one brawny shoulder. He glanced back at her. "Come, Matia. Watch. Though you're a warrior indeed, this is one pleasure of conquest you'll never know."

She shook her head silently, telling herself she had no desire to witness such a wicked sacrifice.

But after he bound Vlasta to the altar with the shackles set in the stone around it, he started to strip off his loin cloth. That's when Matia discovered it would not be so easy to stay away. Bold as he was, Kaska had never let her see his cock.

So, heart pounding in guilt, she moved cautiously closer.

The sight of her Shieldmate naked was itself enough to make her nipples peak. He looked even bigger, broader without his armor, his shoulders wide as a broadsword's length, his long legs powerfully muscled.

His rod thrust, thick and curving, flushed dark with his lust. Beneath it nestled his balls, covered in the same thick ruff that decorated his powerful chest. Vlasta whimpered in fear and anticipation as he stepped behind her.

Matia half expected him to fall on the spy and begin thrusting like the bull his cock suggested, but she'd underestimated him. Instead, Kaska stroked the wench's pale, vulnerable ass, caressing the pink petals of her labia and fingering her bud until they began to glisten with reluctant passion. She moaned, tossing her head, fine blonde hair swirling around her pretty face.

A fine sweat broke out across Matia's upper lip. Her breastplate felt uncomfortably tight.

Kaska locked his crystalline blue gaze with hers. "There is a legend among the Dark Warriors," he said, in a voice as rich and smooth as heated mead. "When the Dark One made women, he gave them two openings. One, he told the first brothers, was for pleasure and the getting of children. But the other was forbidden to the common run of men. Do you know why?"

Matia licked her lips. "No."

Kaska's smile was dark and knowing. "Because he wanted to make sure his Dark Warriors would have tight virgin holes to enjoy after a conquest. To this day, the symbol of victory in our language is derived from the image of a kneeling bound woman." Using both big hands, he spread his captive's pale cheeks. "Look at her. So lovely, so female. So helpless. She knows she's going to take my hard cock in her ass, and there's nothing she can do about it. It's my right as her conqueror." Extending a big forefinger, he touched Vlasta's tightly furled anal bud. Slowly, he began to press. She moaned as it sank in.

Kaska looked up and smiled into Matia's eyes, his own burning and bright. "The oil tightened her nicely. She's going to be a delicious fuck."

"Please, warrior!" the spy whimpered. "Spare me! Your cock will surely rip me open!"

His dark smile widened. Matia remembered what he'd said earlier: *her pleas for mercy only inflame him more.* "Spare you? Would Svec's men have spared any of us, had you succeeded in your treachery?" He put the thick head of his cock against her puckered opening.

Guilt and lust made Matia's heart thunder as she stepped closer to watch. Kaska entered very slowly, the tiny pink anus stretching desperately to accommodate his size as the spy gasped sobbing breaths. The muscles of his powerful belly laced as he forced more and still more of the thick rod into her depths. His eyes blazed with savage pleasure even as he gritted his teeth with effort, nostrils flared like a wolf's.

Matia knew she should turn away, yet she couldn't. She'd never been so aroused, certainly not with her own stripling lover all those years ago.

"Delicious," Kaska rumbled, when his hips were finally snug against the spy's. He looked up, meeting Matia's in unmistakable promise. "Though not so tight as another captive who begs in my dreams."

She stared at him in shock.

He drew out slowly, and his prisoner moaned, this time in shamed pleasure. "Tell my little Shieldmate how it feels to take my cock in the ass, Vlasta," he growled.

"It -- oh! -- It hurts!"

Kaska drove in a thrust that made her yelp. "I think she's guessed that. But how does this feel?" He began to withdraw.

Vlasta panted. "Good," she whimpered. "Oh, it's good."

"Aye," he growled, "it is." He rammed in to his balls again.

Matia watched in frozen fascination as Kaska claimed the spy for his god with brutally ruthless digs. But as he rocked in her, the tone of Vlasta's cries changed, taking on a note of helpless hunger. Finally she began to lift her hips for his entry, until she was thrusting onto the cock that reamed her. The little spy shrieked out her climax just before Kaska's bellow of triumph.

For a long moment, Matia could do nothing but stand frozen on the rim of the stone circle, shaking with arousal and guilt. Finally, unable to bear it any longer, she turned to stumble toward the horses.

"Matia," Kaska said in a soft, dark rumble. Automatically, she turned to look at him.

He'd withdrawn, and was holding his limp victim's cheeks apart. Her abused anus pouted, red and swollen from the hard fucking he'd given it, glistening with oil and pearly drops of male cum. "After we take Trovan's capital," he said, "the Dark Warriors in Britar's army will serve every pretty woman just like this." His gaze sharpened on her face. "Every one of them, Matia."

She whirled and fled toward her horse.

* * *

They rode back to camp in tense silence, Kaska holding his limp, naked captive in front of him. Matia could barely sit her stallion, remembering the way her Shieldmate's massive cock had spread the girl to splitting.

And, goddess forgive her, in the depths of her heart Matia envied the spy her brutalized ass.

Once back in camp, they met with Britar, then helped the Prince fall upon the traitor mercenary their captive had identified. Britar lost no time running the man through.

Vlasta herself he gave to Kaska as a slave.

Matia would have expected her Shieldmate to keep the little blonde for his own use, but when they left the Prince, he found another Dark Warrior in Britar's service and sold Vlasta to him. The fellow gave Matia an odd, amused look as he took her away.

Matia had a feeling she knew exactly what the man found so amusing.

Kaska had said he would have challenged her when they met, had they not served the same master. But what would happen when they left the Prince's service?

She suspected the answer to that was obvious.

He'll challenge me.

In their tent that night, Matia watched him as he worked with his knife, carving a piece of fine ebony wood. As his long, strong fingers turned and shaped the thing, she realized it was a dildo.

And she knew full well what he meant to do with it.

"I cannot let you simply take me, Kaska," she told him softly. "Not and keep my oath of celibacy to my goddess. I will kill you if I must."

He looked up at her, his eyes very blue. "I know."

Chapter Three

The night slid past as Kaska worked on the dildo, his cock hard and aching as he imagined Matia bent over the Dark One's altar. His Shieldmate said nothing more as she sat on the other side of the tent, watching him with brooding eyes and drinking from a skin of mead. Finally she put the skin aside and lay down on her pallet, sliding quickly into sleep.

By the Double Cocks, he hungered for her.

But taking her would be no easy thing. True, she was smaller than he and no match in strength, but her skill and growing ruthlessness had allowed her to kill men every bit as big.

More than that, though, he feared hurting her. He couldn't stand the thought of that.

Kaska took another deep draft of his own skin of mead and eyed her backside as she lay curled in sleep. When had she become more to him than a virgin ass to plunder?

Though the Dark One knew he still dreamed of that burning pleasure.

With a soft sigh, she rolled onto her belly, thrusting her tight little rump in the air. Her loin cloth slid aside with the motion, baring her tanned cheeks. Her skin looked like satin. His fingers itched to touch it.

Why not?

Still, Kaska hesitated, knowing he'd likely had too much mead.

Then she rolled her slim little hips and moaned. Lust surged through him. Before he knew it, he was across the tent and sliding a knee onto her pallet.

With shaking hands, Kaska flipped her rump cloth up, baring her sweet backside completely. Her thighs flexed, thrusting her ass up at him. He smelled a hint of female musk.

Unable to resist, he reached between her slim thighs and stroked a finger along her velvet labia. The seam of her lips was richly wet.

His cock kicked violently against his loincloth. He licked his lips and pushed one forefinger deep inside her.

Double Cocks, she was tight. That lover of hers must have been thinner than a nun's toothpick.

Swallowing, Kaska slid the finger out, then in again, slipping easily in her thick, rich cream. She whimpered in pleasure.

He hardened even more. Unable to resist, he withdrew his hand and spread her firm cheeks. Holding his breath as guilty excitement rose, he touched her anus with the finger she'd dewed with her arousal. Slowly, he began to slide it in.

Her tiny anus resisted, then opened suddenly to let him in up to the knuckle. She was so deliciously tight, Kaska had to bite back his own groan.

With his free hand, he drew his cock from his loincloth and began to stroke himself as he explored Matia's tight, virginal ass. He knew no other man had touched her this way.

Sliding his finger in and out, watching the way her rectum pulled and sucked at it, Kaska imagined her bound and waiting for his cock.

"Kaska," she whimpered.

He froze, abruptly cold sober as guilt seared through his lust. *What in the Dark One's name am I doing? I have no right. She doesn't belong to…*

Matia lifted her hips with a low groan, driving his finger even more deeply into her ass. "Kaska," she whimpered. "Oh, Kaska, harder."

Me, he realized, stunned. *She's dreaming of me!*

Maddened, he straddled her hips and pressed his erection against her ass, not entering, but teasing himself with her silken flesh. She moaned. He began fingering her ass in earnest, rubbing her clit with his thumb while he stretched her with long strokes, first one finger, then two, then three, jerking hard at his cock while he watched her anus struggle to take him.

She pumped her hips, taking his fingers and groaning.

"Are you awake?" he asked softly.

Matia only sighed, her breath carrying the scent of mead. *Double Cocks, she's drunker than I!*

He should stop. He should...

Her anus suddenly tightened and pulsed around his invading finger. She groaned in wanton pleasure, tossing her head until her hair whipped across her pillow.

She came, Kaska thought, surprised and unbearably aroused. Her first anal orgasm. "It won't be your last, girl," he growled, and began to work his own cock in a frenzy of lust.

Withdrawing his fingers, Kaska held her cheeks apart so he could look at her swollen anus as he climaxed. He made sure he hit that tiny pink virgin target with every single jet of sperm, until his cum ran down her crack in a white stream.

When it was over, Kaska cleaned her thoroughly and staggered back to his own pallet. He fell asleep to dream dark dreams of enslaving Matia and bending her over the Dark One's altar.

He woke the next morning with a roaring hangover and a case of gnawing guilt. Though he watched Matia anxiously, she showed no sign of remembering the night. He had no intention of reminding her. He had the ugly feeling she'd call him out.

It was probably no more than he deserved, but he had no wish to fight Matia in a killing rage. He was too likely to lose, or worse, have to hurt her to win.

That's when he knew.

When did I fall in love with her?

* * *

Taking Trovan's capital city three weeks later was no easy matter. King Svec fought like a cornered fox to keep Libuse, for he knew if he lost it, his throne, too, was gone.

But Britar would not be denied, and soon Kaska and Matia entered the city in the company of the Prince and his five thousand men. Svec tried to flee, but they all thundered in pursuit. He died in his futile bid to escape.

Libuse, like the country around it, offered Britar no more resistance after that. The people of Trovan had suffered so long under the tyrant's yoke that Britar's just hand came as a vast relief. The new king and his army settled in for a little welcome peace.

But for Matia and Kaska, the peace only provided more opportunity for the tension between them to grow.

When she learned the Prince planned to pay off his mercenaries, Matia knew her time had run out. Kaska would challenge her the moment they were free, and she had no desire to fight him. Distasteful as the idea of running from a duel was, the thought of killing him was worse -- yet surrender simply was not an option.

So without telling her Shieldmate where she was going, she took her leave of the Prince, mounted her stallion, and started back to the convent.

Matia was barely an hour outside the city gates when she heard the thunder of hooves coming from the woods beside the road. She turned Stormheart and drew her sword as her soul cringed. She knew there was no more point in running. Kaska would chase her to the edge of the world.

Warbringer burst from the forest in a surge of velvet muscle, Kaska on his back, his expression grim. She watched him draw rein with dread in her heart. "I can't let you leave, Matia."

She sighed. "Kaska, don't make me do this."

He studied her face, his gaze level and intent. "Is it the sacrifice you fear?"

Matia shook her head. "Nay. In truth, if it were not for my oath, I would take pleasure in submitting to whatever you choose to do. But..." She made a helpless gesture. "I have given my oath to the goddess. I will not break it, no matter how my body burns for yours."

"I love you, Matia." The glitter of his blue eyes demanded her belief. "I'll give up the sacrifice. Indeed, I'd give up my god himself to keep you. Just stay."

Her spirit leaped, then collapsed into a tight, miserable ball as she realized how hopeless it was. "Ah, Kaska, my heart is yours. Perhaps it has been from the moment you saved me from those thieves. But what would either of us be if we threw away our oaths?"

"I will not give you up, Matia." His gaze went grim. "Even if I must steal you from your goddess to have you."

She winced, though she'd expected no less. "I will not be so easily taken, Kaska."

"I know." He drew his sword, swung a leg over Warbringer's neck, and slid neatly off his mount to land in a battle stance. "If I lose, kill me. Better that than living without you."

Matia dismounted more slowly, dread clutching at her heart with sickly claws. Kaska was not the kind of opponent she could fight casually; it would take everything she had to best him. It was possible she could wound him seriously enough to allow her escape, but such a wound could also kill him.

She ached to simply throw down her weapon and let him do with her as he would, but she knew she'd come to despise herself for it. If he defeated her cleanly, there would be no stain on her conscience. The goddess would be satisfied.

But nothing less was acceptable. If she fought him, she could not hold back.

So as she lifted her sword and stepped to meet him, her belly laced itself into a sick knot of fear.

They began slowly, each too familiar with the other's skill for overconfidence. Matia circled Kaska, intensely aware of his size, the muscled power of his tall body. It had always been so comforting having him at her back. She wondered now how much of her courage had been born of the knowledge that he'd die to protect her.

Now, facing him, she felt the sweat of dread roll cold down her spine.

Kaska did nothing to signal his first attack. His grim expression did not tighten, his eyes did not narrow. He simply blurred into furious motion.

She parried more by instinct than conscious thought. The jar of his broadsword against her slimmer blade jolted all the way to her shoulders. She was so rattled by the impact she almost didn't parry his next attack in time. It was all she could do to hold onto her sword as his slammed into it.

Matia scuttled back as he charged, throwing attack after attack at her, each more thunderous than the last. Steel rang in the brutal percussive music of combat as she labored to block his blistering swordplay.

She knew she should mount her own attacks, but he simply didn't give her time. Her skill might be equal to his, but his speed, reach, and sheer brute strength were far greater. She did not dare let any of his blows get through.

Then came the attack she'd known would come -- hard enough to knock her sword so far from her torso, Matia knew she'd never be able to parry his next attack in time. She winced, waiting for the pain of steel sliding into flesh.

Instead his broadsword slammed into her blade again, almost knocking it from her hand. And she finally saw his strategy.

He wasn't attacking her. He was attacking her sword.

Matia cursed beneath her breath. It was a solid technique if you meant to take a smaller opponent alive. His broadsword was so much heavier, it might well shatter her thinner blade. Even if her weapon held, he could catch it and flip it out of her hand. If that failed, he could simply wear her down until she'd be unable to mount a proper defense.

Suddenly she remembered what he'd told her months ago, after she'd fought a man almost as big as he was. "When you battle a man my size, lose no time going for the kill. Otherwise, you cannot win."

It was painfully clear he was right.

Dark Side

She saw his broadsword flashing toward hers. Instead of trying to parry, Matia circled her weapon around his and drove straight for his upper arm. He saw it coming and twisted aside, but still she felt her blade cut into flesh.

Despite herself, she winced.

Kaska flicked a glance down at the long slash across his biceps. Though it was not deep, blood poured from it. "I wondered how long it would take you to catch on," he grunted. "Didn't I tell you not to take chances with an opponent my size?"

She would have liked to snap a reply, but she didn't have the breath.

He swung at her torso. Matia didn't dare miss that parry. Her muscles protested at the savage impact as she beat him off and retreated.

Her arms ached, and her sword felt like a length of solid lead in her hand. She'd thought to inflict shallow wounds designed to incapacitate through blood loss, but now she realized that plan wouldn't work. Her body would fail long before his did.

She'd have to maim Kaska with her next attack, or she was lost.

Panting, Matia watched him, blinking as sweat burned its way into her eyes. She didn't dare lift a hand to wipe it away.

He dropped his guard ever so slightly. Matia reacted, lunging for the opening on sheer instinct before her brain had time to process what she was doing. At the last instant she realized that she was about to drive her sword into his chest. Heart leaping in terror, she jerked up her blade, trying to miss...

Kaska brought his sword around, neatly entangled hers in its quillions, and jerked. The weapon flew from her hand.

She watched numbly as her sword pinwheeled into the brush beside the road. "Trap," she wheezed in realization.

"Yes." A muscled arm circled her waist, jerking her against his body. His skin steamed with heat and sweat, contrasting with the cool steel of his blade against her throat.

Dragging her head around, she looked up into his eyes.

"I claim you for my god, Matia," he said softly. "And myself."

Then his mouth came down on hers in a kiss that stole the last of her strength with its passion. She sagged into his arms as joy boiled up, guilt in its wake. "Kaska," she moaned.

"Hush," he said, scooping her into his arms. She could feel his muscles tremble with effort, and felt a pale satisfaction. At least she'd made him work for his victory. "You defended your oath, Matia. I'm fortunate you had no wish to kill me, or this might have ended differently."

He walked to the roadside and went to his knees, laying her on the cool grass. Panting, she looked up at his handsome face as she tried to catch her breath.

"You said earlier that you found pleasure in the thought of me sacrificing you to the Dark One," he said abruptly, his blue gaze searching hers as he sat back on his heels. "Did you mean it?"

Matia swallowed, remembering the way the spy's asshole had gaped as he fucked her. "Yes. When I watched what you did to Vlasta, it made me burn." She paused to gather her courage. It was hard to admit just how the raw sight had aroused her. "I have never felt that way."

His smile was white and very male. "Good."

Then he flipped her onto her belly.

"What --" She jerked up her head as he gathered her right wrist in one hand and reached into one of his belt pouches for a length of rope. "What are you doing?"

"Binding my captive," he said, wrapping the cord around one wrist before serving the other the same. "If you have no objection to dancing for the Dark One, it will be my great pleasure to see to it."

Matia closed her eyes and shuddered with need as he proceeded to rope her ankles with the same ruthless skill.

Then he flipped her over onto her back. His mouth dropped down to hers again, and he kissed her, hard, deep, hungry, a kiss of conquest and ownership.

"How many nights have I dreamed of this moment." His gaze burned hot with weary triumph. "How many nights have I watched you as you slept, staring at your high, round breasts, your long thighs. Watching you roll over, seeing the way your muscular little butt curved in sweet invitation. And I'd grab my cock and fist it hard, dreaming of this..."

"You...pleasured yourself thinking of me?"

He laughed, the sound a little wild as he pulled her up into his arms. He lowered his head again. "Oh, aye. Many nights. Especially once I realized how you dreamed of my possession."

Helpless with desire, Matia opened her lips and let him take her as he would, accepting each deep thrust of his tongue, moaning as he bit delicately at her mouth. All she could think about was the image he'd created -- Kaska, masturbating as he planned to take her captive and ream her with that huge cock.

When he rose and bent to throw her over his shoulder, Matia wasn't hypocrite enough to struggle.

She rode back to Libuse draped over his saddle as he caressed her bottom and thighs. Matia shivered in pleasure with every brush of his fingers, too dazed with lust to do anything else. Finally she roused enough to ask, "Where are you taking me?"

"There's a Temple of the Dark One here. The Brethren in Britar's service have appropriated it for our own use."

At that she shivered again. It was said that any woman who went into the Dark One's temple came out as a warrior's slave. She considered, briefly, putting up a fight. Then he caressed her again, and the feeling of his hand on her skin sent such lightning arching through her, Matia knew there was no point.

Kaska had enslaved her long ago.

Chapter Four

The Dark One's temple lay in the Temple Quarter, a brooding, black marble building with thick stone columns topped in rounded capitals. Gazing at them, she realized they resembled nothing so much as erect cocks. Still, it was a surprisingly sedate building, for such a den of sex and blood.

Kaska swung down from the saddle, then reached up for her. As he met her gaze, he asked suddenly. "Are you sure? Once I begin the sacrifice, I fear I'll be unable to stop. My need runs hot, Matia."

Indeed it did. She could see it blazing in his eyes and bulging against his loincloth. Swallowing, she whispered, "I want to experience your passion, Kaska. In full."

Male triumph flashed in his eyes, and he grinned savagely. The next minute she was in his arms, and they were striding into the Dark One's temple.

As he carried her through the great building's halls, it quickly became all too obvious just what kind of god the Dark One was. Near the entrance the black walls were sculpted and brightly painted with scenes of battle; depictions of warriors hacking their way through the ranks of lesser men, splitting skulls and ripping bellies. In the center, they stormed a great city and rode triumphant through its gates.

From there on, the walls depicted raw sexual conquest; bound women writhing under the cane, having their nipples tortured, being fucked and sodomized, submissively sucking hard warrior cocks.

Then they stepped into a massive central room with a huge statue of the Dark One at its heart. Carved in black ebony, he stood naked and massively muscled, his twin cocks thrusting outward, one set below the other. In his right hand he carried two severed male heads. In the other, he held two ropes, each tied loosely around the neck of a naked female captive. The first knelt beside him, staring up at him in supplication as she lifted her bare breasts to him in offering. The second crouched with her head down and her curving ass in the air, holding her rump spread with her hands, looking over her shoulder at him with a pleading expression.

Yet the idol's attention seemed focused on the altar before him, where a living woman lay, bound bottom upward.

Charmar, one of Kaska's Dark Brothers, slowly drove a double-headed dildo in and out of the woman's anus and pussy. Her buttocks were striped, as though he'd just finished whipping her. Yet she moaned in shamed pleasure with every stroke of the dildo, writhing helplessly in the grip of an approaching orgasm.

"Well met, Charmar!" Kaska called.

The Dark Brother looked up and grinned at the sight of Matia slung over her Shieldmate's shoulder. "Well met, indeed. I see you finally took the little warrior. And wonder of wonders, neither of you lost a limb in the process."

Kaska nodded. "The Dark One was with me." His tone was serious. "I was afraid she'd force me to hurt her."

"Good fortune indeed. I'll admit I didn't see how you'd ever capture the little Hill Cat in one piece." He drove the dildo deep, and his victim gasped out a strangled cry. "That's it, my captive," he crooned. "Come on the Dark One's cocks."

She screamed and climaxed, her eyes squeezed shut, her face contorted.

"Finally!" Charmar pulled his knife and cut her free, leaving the double dildo in place. Dragging it out at last, he pulled her to her feet, then guided her over to kneel at the statue's feet. She looked dazed and well-fucked. "Say the words as I've taught them, little prisoner."

Swaying, the naked redhead licked her lips and looked up at the Dark One's idol. "Your Dark Warrior, Charmar, has taken me captive, but it was my own torment and pleasure that made me his slave. With my every moan and scream, I will thank you for giving me to such a master."

Charmar grinned up at the idol. "My gratitude for your lush gift, Dark One. I hope my sacrifice of her gave you as much pleasure as it gave me." Catching his captive's head by the hair, he pushed it into the idol's stone groin. "Show him your submission now, Amria."

Obediently, the girl opened her mouth and sucked first one and then the other of the thick marble cocks. Then Charmar pulled her to her feet. "Come, slave. It's time to get your ass split." Picking her up, he swung her over his shoulder and rolled his eyes at Kaska. "I vow, I'm hard as the Dark One's marble rods. She rolled her rump most delightfully under her flogging." He grinned suddenly, eyeing Matia's butt as she hung over Kaska's shoulder. "Yet I find myself envying you."

Kaska laughed. "Go ream your slave, Charmar. I'll take care of Matia." He didn't even wait for Charmar to leave the room before he lowered her to the cock-shaped altar, cut her bonds, and started tying her spread-eagle to the rings that hung from its side.

Once she was securely lashed, he went to work on her leathers, cutting away her breastband and loincloth until she lay naked. The air was cold on her nipples, and she shivered. The Dark One's idol stared down at her, its carved features wearing an expression of lustful enjoyment.

The look on Kaska's face matched it. "My gratitude, Dark One," he said softly. "At first I didn't understand why you'd send me such a prize, knowing I'd be unable to take her for so long. Yet the pleasure of this moment would have been so much less had I enjoyed her a year ago, and I would never have known the courage that lies under these ripe breasts. Surely you have never gifted a warrior with a captive so lovely...or so tempting."

His blue eyes narrowed. "Tonight I'll thank you properly for your gift, Dark One."

Breath caught in a combination of desire and anxiety, Matia watched as he untied a large pouch from his belt. From it he drew a familiar length of wood, topped with three strands of braided silk, each no more than three feet long. She licked her lips, recognizing it.

He'd made the thing about the same time he'd made the dildo, whittling the butt and braiding the silk in the tent they shared. She hadn't bothered to ask what use he intended for it.

She'd known. And she'd dreamed hot dreams about it.

Kaska stripped off the loin cloth that was all that hid his glorious nudity. His cock sprang free, bobbing and violently flushed with hunger. "It's time to dance for the Dark One, Matia," he said softly, in a voice like dark velvet as he lifted the wooden butt.

She licked her lips. "I am ready."

"I know." He snapped his wrist. The braided cords swished out to curl around one of her stiff pink nipples in a stinging bite. With a gasp, Matia arched her back. A second snap, this one hitting the other hard point. "Kaska!" she cried, writhing.

"That's it," he rasped. "That's a dance to make even a god hunger."

With that he began to torment her in earnest, cracking the light little whip at each breast in turn, painting fire over her skin. The lashes were so thin and delicate they didn't break the skin, but the sting was ferocious, and she twisted and moaned.

All the while, Kaska's cock rose hard and red, bouncing with every snap of his arm.

As Matia writhed, her attention fell on the idol's stone face looking down at her. Its black eyes were no longer empty, but burning red. As her stiff, pointed nipples swelled under Kaska's whip, she sensed a presence in the idol, something powerful and dark and alien. And very, very male.

Kaska paused to admire her breasts with a conqueror's satisfaction. "The night I worked on this whip, you were wearing that loose cotton tunic of yours, sitting between me and the fire, kneeling as you polished out a spot of rust on your armor. The firelight silhouetted your pretty breasts, and they bounced as you worked. I braided the lash and imagined the way they'd jiggle when I whipped your nipples."

Then, lips curving into a dark smile, Kaska proceeded to make them jiggle indeed with a series of skillful snaps that took

Matia's breath away. Only her warrior's discipline kept her from
screaming as he tortured the pointed red peaks. Yet each sting of
pain stoked her arousal higher.

At last he tossed down his whip and moved to stand
between her thighs. Before she knew what he was about, he
lowered his head and thrust his face against her mound. Matia
jerked. A hot, wet tongue pushed between her lips, stroked the
tender flesh.

Then, as her nipples stung from his skillful torment, Kaska
began to suck and nibble her sex. Each lick teased the pleasure
into a breathtaking spiral of delight that rung pleading groans
from her lips.

At the same time, his big, rough hands stroked her thighs,
her belly, her hips. Finally they found her aching breasts and
soothed them with gentle caresses. Soon she was writhing with
pleasure so great, even the burn of her abused nipples was
nothing but a luscious counterpoint.

It seemed the idol's eyes glowed even brighter.

Kaska gently inserted a big finger into Matia's cunt. It
slipped through the hot cream of her arousal, stretching the
swollen, eager flesh in time to her helpless moans. Twisting his
hand, he began to screw in and out with a penetration that kicked
her delight even higher.

Then he slid in a second finger -- but this one went up her
ass.

"Ah, Matia," he purred. "How sweet and tight you are."

He stroked deep in a burning possession that only hinted at
what she'd know from his cock. Matia arched her back and
screamed with the first waves of orgasm. Kaska caught her clit in
his mouth and sucked hard, simultaneously thrusting his fingers
in and out of pussy and ass until she convulsed. Locking her gaze
with his, he jammed deep and hard inside her, holding his fingers
there as she shook and screamed.

In the aftermath, Matia was barely aware of being untied,
lifted, turned bottom upward, and retied. This time the whip

Kaska pulled from his pouch was much heavier, and his target was her helpless rump.

The first hard blow bit even through her languid pleasure, and she howled in shock. But her Shieldmate showed her no mercy. Again and again he struck, painting first one cheek and then the other with molten stripes.

Still, even in the chains of heat Kaska forged for her, Matia remained a warrior. She knew pain, knew how to embrace or ignore it or use it as she pleased. And so she turned the tables on her Shieldmate to inflict her own kind of torment while he flogged her burning ass. Deliberately, she slowed the instinctive plunge of her hips, turning it into a seductive roll that kept time with his lash.

Kaska had said he loved her backside, and she made sure he had a good look, lifting it high as she flexed her thighs, knowing the pose would spread her labia. She heard him growl in lechery. Slowly, she lowered her pelvis, though the whip stung her skin like a wasp as if to spur her on.

Deliberately, she began to grind up and down, side to side, feeling the tip of the lash strike faster and faster as he plied it in a frenzy of lust. Though pain danced along her nerves, Matia shuddered with pleasure, imagining what he was thinking, imagining his hunger.

A fitting sacrifice indeed.

She blinked, breaking rhythm, as the dark male voice rolled through her mind.

In all the years since my race came to your world, I have never seen a captive embrace her fate with such eager heat. Nor have I fed so well on a sacrifice.

It was the god.

You might have, Matia thought, a little dazed, *had any other captive had such a captor as Kaska.*

An unusual warrior, the Dark One agreed. *I find myself admiring his self-control. See how you tempt him...*

Suddenly she saw a gloriously naked woman lying belly-down over the Dark One's cock-shaped altar. With a sense of shock, Matia realized it was herself. She could see her own ass, spread by her posture to reveal her labia, visibly wet with lust. Her anus looked impossibly small and pink, tightly puckered.

In his mind, Kaska was imagining watching that hole slowly dilate as he drove his cock into it -- the way the strong muscles would fight him at first, then yield slowly as he worked his way deeper. He could almost hear her gasps...

She could see the memory of other lush prisoners, lying bound and helpless in a variety of positions as he fucked them, celebrating his victories in tight assholes.

To Kaska there was no pleasure like chasing down and capturing some lovely maid, binding her tight and well, then savoring each slow, grinding thrust into her anus while he brought her to reluctant orgasm. Yet never had he felt such hunger, such violence. Kaska wanted to ram Matia's asshole, fuck it mercilessly while he listened to her helpless cries of pain and desire.

He'd fantasized about taking her for months, even as his love for her grew. Now his mind was such a confused tumble of lust and tenderness, he was afraid he'd draw blood in his madness. She could feel the whip vibrating in his hand as he fought his darker impulses.

"Do it, Kaska," she cried. "Take your pleasure..."

His control didn't so much break as explode. An instant later she felt the whip crack hard against her anus, and she yelped in true pain. Twice more he struck her there, then again and...

She heard the whip hit the opposite wall with a clatter. Out of the corner of one eye, she saw him stride to his pouch and pull out the double-shafted cock that symbolized the dark god's. He smeared it with butter, turned -- and drove it into both her cunt and ass like a twin-blade knife.

It should have hurt, but such was the lust he'd built in her that the shafts slid in smoothly under his strength. At the same time, he sought Matia's clit with the thumb of his free hand and circled it as he ground the double dildo in and out. She whimpered at the brutal pleasure-pain.

She'd never felt so hot for a man.

"Enjoy her cunt and ass, Dark One," he growled. "I promise you, I will."

The shafts slid faster and faster in and out as her clit flamed. The dildo in her cunt was delicious, but though the cock in her bung was much smaller than Kaska's, it still felt huge, overwhelming, a brutal, tunneling presence.

"The one in my ass," Matia moaned, her thighs constricting with the first waves of orgasm, "it feels like a broadsword..."

"Good," Kaska said. "You need the stretching -- because you're going to get something a lot larger than this." And he rammed it in.

She came.

Dimly she heard the god say, his rumbling mind-voice amused, *I think it's time to lubricate you for your new master...*

Deep in Matia's ass, the shaft representing the god's cock began to spurt gush after gush of thick oil. A lecherous miracle -- the dildo was solid wood.

Matia was scarcely aware of being untied, lifted, and deposited on her knees before the Dark One's idol. "Say the words, Matia," Kaska rasped, as though fighting for control.

She blinked hard and tried to remember what Charmar's slave had said. "Dark One..." She had to stop to clear her throat when her voice cracked. "Dark One, your warrior Kaska has defeated me in battle, bound me, and sacrificed me on your black altar..." Those weren't exactly the slave's words, but Matia didn't care. "But it's my own lust for him that has made me his slave. With my every cry of submission and delight and anguish, I will thank you for sending me to defeat at his hands."

"Dark One," Kaska said hoarsely, "I do not know what I have done to deserve Matia, but my thanks for guiding me to her."

You're welcome, the god said, in rumbling amusement.

She bent forward without being told and took the idol's smaller cock in her mouth. Rolling her tongue around it, she sucked the cold marble as though it were hot flesh, caressing the thicker cock below it with her fingers. Then Matia drew back and lowered her head for the second flesh blade. She had to tilt her chin to accommodate it, but she took it as deep as she could. Finally she sat back.

"I hope you suck my cock that well, slave," Kaska growled, as he reached down and pulled Matia to her feet. He swung her onto a broad, hard shoulder and turned toward one of the doors off to the side. "My thanks, Dark One!"

For a moment she could only lie limp, watching the gleaming, sweat-slicked muscles work in his back as he carried her. Her ass burned ferociously from his whip.

She would be sore tomorrow, probably from injuries she did not yet have.

"By the Dark One's Double Cocks," Kaska grumbled. "Never have I had so much difficulty controlling myself before the Dark One's altar. It was all I could do not to ram right up your little ass after that flogging."

Matia smiled. "I know."

"Gloat now, slave," he said, giving her a stinging slap on her well-whipped rump. "You'll sing a different tune when you feel my big shaft splitting your virgin pucker."

"Where are we going...conqueror?" She gave the last word a note of mocking servility.

"Why, the Fuck Chambers...captive."

Matia realized what he meant as he carried her into a long hallway lined with closed doors. Even through the thick wood, she could hear gasps and cries of pleasure, surrender and pain.

"The Dark One's Warriors are busy this night," she muttered.

"The rewards of conquest." There was laughter in his voice. "Speaking of which..." A door banged open under his kick.

Chapter Five

The room was not large, but it was opulent.

Kaska carried her to a strange platform in the center of the room. On it was a wooden bench set before a small idol of the Dark One.

He put her down and told her to kneel on the padded projection that ran between the bench legs. Urging her thighs apart, Kaska circled each of them with a tough leather cuff before roping her hands behind her back. Then he bent her over so she was draped across the bench's padded seat.

Barely long enough to support her hips and lower torso, the bench was inclined so that her rump was lifted higher than her head.

Matia suddenly noticed two thin chains hanging from a pair of rings in the idol's hands. Each chain was no thicker than a lady's necklace, and ended with a narrow metal wire looped in a circle.

Kaska picked up the loops and caught her nipples in them, pulling the metal circlets tight enough to bite. The chains were so short they pulled her stiff points out from her breasts, exerting a pressure just brushing pain. Matia didn't dare struggle; she knew the chains would jerk her breasts brutally. She was completely immobilized.

Ready to have her ass violated by Kaska's big cock. Even in her nervous anticipation, she couldn't help but admire his burnished masculinity -- the broad, sculpted muscle of his chest, pelted in curling dark hair, the bulging strength of his arms, the long powerful legs -- and his cock, a thick, rosy truncheon of flesh visibly throbbing with his heartbeat. His balls were drawn up tight to his shaft, swollen with the seed he was so hungry to pump into her.

And his eyes... Matia didn't need his god to tell her what he was thinking. She'd never had a man look at her like that, with blue eyes flaming with such unrepentant lust and anticipation. The bones of his face stood sharply etched under his tanned skin, as though with starvation.

And she was the only meal that could sate him.

Matia was glad for the bench. Without it, her powerless knees would have dumped her on the floor.

"Are you afraid of me, Matia?" he asked softly.

"Yes." It was something she'd never thought to admit to a man.

He smiled.

Slowly, Kaska moved toward her. She jerked in her bonds, wincing a little at the resulting yank to her nipples. He stretched out a big hand, brushed his fingers down the sensitive small of her back. Matia shuddered, her mouth dry as sun-burnt leather.

"Luscious Matia," he whispered. "Do you know how hard I'm fighting to keep from ramming my cock up your ass?"

She nodded, unable to speak.

His rough fingertips drifted down to her bottom, then ghosted down the sensitive cleavage, not pushing between, just teasing. They traveled lower until they slipped between her trembling thighs. Dipped between her lower lips, gently sampling.

"You're wet, Matia," Kaska said. "And you're shaking. Are you remembering what I did to Vlasta?"

"Yes," she croaked.

"What were you thinking when you watched me take her?"

The feeling of those fingers pumping inside her pussy was slowly driving her mad. "I was thinking...how big you were. How you stretched her. I thought she wouldn't be able to take your width. I wondered if you'd stop if she couldn't..."

"And?"

"I think...I think you would have made her take it. You would have made her love it. Even that."

He smiled. "But can you take me?"

"It doesn't..." She had to stop to whimper. "It doesn't matter whether I can or not. You will."

His smile grew darker. "You're right."

With that he abandoned her dripping pussy and sought the hole the Dark One had so thoroughly oiled for him. She felt him part her. For several long moments he did nothing, just staring until she could feel her very anus start to burn. Then, finally, he spread his fingers and put his thumbs on either side of her anus. Exerting pressure, he forced her rectum open. Again he studied it as she quivered in helpless anticipation.

At last he slid his thumb inside, rotating his hand to screw it in. He gave it several slow, leisurely thrusts. She squirmed as her bung began to burn in protest.

"Do you feel like a slave, Matia?" he asked suddenly.

"Yes, master," she moaned.

"You aren't. I have no wish to enslave you," he told her. Then his smile darkened. "Except in this room."

He pulled out his thumb and ruthlessly pulled her open as far as he could, then caught his cock in one hand and aimed it for her tortured bung. He entered her like a burning sword, a slow, endless, hot impalement. Matia jerked, only reduced to stillness by the pressure on her captive nipples.

"By the Dark One's Double Pricks, Matia, you're tight," he growled.

And he was bigger than anything she'd ever felt, slowly stuffing her to bursting. So slowly.

Kaska took his time with his anal conquest, only working his way forward by molten fractions as though intent on enjoying each bit of rectal territory he invaded.

Matia had never felt so fucked, so overcome by male strength and male flesh. His cock burned like a column of solid fire inside her. She could only surrender.

Yet even after her muscles relaxed, Kaska moved no faster, keeping his invasion slow and relentless as he slid inside, stretching her wide.

"That's it, Matia," he purred, when he was all the way in at last. He bent to find her clit with his rough fingers. "Yield to my big cock. Taste the pleasure of enslavement, the dark delight of submitting to your master's rod. And here, I am your master."

"Yesssss," she moaned.

He drew out, sending pleasure scalding its way up her spine. She whimpered. "You've been dreaming about this for months, Matia, about the pain and ecstasy, about being vanquished and tied and reamed..."

She gasped, "Yes..."

"And I've been dreaming about it too." He began to thrust, slowly at first, then faster, deeper. "Dreamed of laying you on the cock altar, of seeing you dance for the whip, of bending you over and forcing your virgin ass with hard strokes. Just...like...*this.*"

He was fucking her now far more brutally than he'd taken Vlasta, as if too heated for any thought of mercy. But Matia didn't care. His stroking fingers teased pleasure from her clit, and his every withdrawal was a dark delight to match the pain of his inward thrusts. She lifted her hips for him, savoring it all, ecstasy and agony in equal measure.

"Am I hurting you, Matia?" he growled.

"Yes..." she whimpered.

"And you love it anyway."

"Yes!" She could feel her thighs begin to twitch. "Oh, yes! Harder, Kaska!"

"Yes!" And he began driving hard, fucking her ass deeply and mercilessly, until all she could do was buck and scream. Her orgasm rolled over her in burning waves that matched each pitiless thrust, and she convulsed, her scream spiraling into a screech.

"Now..." he gasped, "now I'm going to...pump...you...FULL!"

Dimly, Matia felt him ram to his full length. With a roar like a hunting Hill Cat, he began shooting jet after jet into her violated rectum.

When at last they could breathe again, he freed her from the bench with hands that shook. He went in search of clean water and cloths and cleaned them both, his hands tender on her flesh. Then, spent, almost limp from the violence of their passion, they staggered together to the bed that stood on one side of the room and tumbled into it.

"Are you all right?" Kaska asked hoarsely, as he drew her into his powerful arms.

"Aye," she sighed. "Oh, aye."

Despite the weals on her ass and the ache of her anus, she tumbled into a blissful sleep to the sound of his heartbeat.

Big, rough fingers traced the lines of fire striping her backside, jolting Matia awake. She lifted her head and blinked at the morning sunlight pouring through the window grate. "Oh, gods!" she groaned, and dropped her head.

"I have hurt you." The note of guilt in Kaska's voice made her lift her head again and frown at him. He was anxiously studying the weals he'd left with his whip. "What demon possessed me?"

Matia yawned hugely and turned over, wincing a little at the fierce ache. Hot as it was, it was somehow satisfying. She smiled. "I think its name was lust, M'Lord. And it had its lovely claws just as deep in me."

He sat up, combing his big hands through his hair, a deep frown on his face. "Where did I leave my saddle bags? I think I have some salve that should..."

"Oh, come, Kaska," Matia said lightly, dropping a hand on his powerful shoulder. "Think you I've never had a flogging? Sweet goddess, the Elder Daughters took a whip to me every time I missed a parry. And I must say, I enjoyed yours far more, as they never brought me to climax afterward."

He studied her face, grim doubt in his eyes. "I was rough with you."

She grinned. "Aye. And 'twas most exciting. I rather enjoy driving you to such extremes."

"Matia..."

She sighed, for his expression had not lightened one jot. "I am a warrior, Kaska. I rather like being taken as one. As much as you enjoyed taking me, I might add."

"But..."

With a sigh of exasperation, she rose, flung a leg over his hip and settled down across his thighs. "It strikes me, master, that your slave's cunt has yet to know your cock. And..."

Now his gaze burned fierce into hers. "I told you, you're no slave, Matia. You are my Shieldmate. And, if you wish it, my wife."

She smiled slowly and let her hands trace the ridges and hollows of his big, muscled body. His nipples rose to tight peaks as she thumbed them. "Oh, aye, Shieldmate. I do wish it, most sincerely."

As his great cock stirred and rose against her belly, she bent to taste his firm mouth. "By the Dark One's Double Cocks, Matia," Kaska groaned, "I do love you."

At that, a wild heat rose in her. "And I love you, Kaska, master of my heart."

Then, angling his cock into the air, she rose and took him deep in her creaming cunt. Her ass stung as she sank onto the big shaft, but she barely noticed. She was too entranced by the feeling of his thick, satin width so deep in her.

Slowly, moaning in pleasure, she began to grind down on Kaska's cock as his hands lifted to tease her nipples.

From the corner of one eye, she thought she saw the black marble eyes of the Dark One's idol.

They glowed bright red.

Riding her lover, Matia smiled.

Angela Knight

Angela Knight has worked as a comic book writer, a newspaper reporter, and a novelist. Her stories have won several awards, including the South Carolina Press Association award. Her first writing love has always been romance. In 1996, she discovered the small press publishing and realized her dream when her first Romance was published in Red Sage's Secrets 2 anthology. Angela is now multi-published, as both an author and a cover artist, and enjoys success under several names, but that success would be hollow without the love and support of her friends and family. It's no surprise Angela Knight considers herself a profoundly lucky woman. You can visit Angela's website at http://www.angelasknights.com.

Chain of Thorns

Willa Okati

Chapter One

Ever since the Earth exploded, nothing had been the same. Nothing at all.

* * *

How did I survive?

Riven still didn't know the answer to that question. They'd only had a little warning, less than a day from start to stop with the whole thing. Massive ships appearing out of nowhere to ring the globe, each of them bent on blasting it out of the way of their war. A force had come behind them, their enemies, though for a few hours the panicked peoples of Earth looked on them as friends.

At least, until they began scooping folks up off the streets and into their own ships. No warning, just *zip*, and they were gone. Must have been a few thousand stolen before the bigger ships got fed up, frustrated, whatever, and let loose with some kind of uber-bomb which shattered Terra Firma like a clay pot.

Riven wasn't in a position to hear much by way of rumor, but he suspected everything on Earth lay destroyed. All life, all plants, everything in the seas. Stripped to barren chunks of rock. Nothing worth fighting over any more, and the battle between the two armies had moved on.

They'd taken Riven with them.

He'd been one of the first ones snatched up by their so-called allies. Walking to class, juggling a sheaf of graded essays and his laptop. He'd had no warning except for a sudden tingling much like static electricity, and then he had just been -- gone.

Then, here.

Wherever *here* was. Even after the weeks he'd spent in the place, Riven wasn't sure. At his best guess, he'd been put into some sort of holding pen with hundreds of other men and women, all races, all orientations, all stolen from their lives.

Food came on a monotonous, regular basis, three times a day. Filling, if bland, bread, vegetables, and water. Bells sounded for them to run laps around the huge cargo bay where they ate, drank and slept. Lights went out, then came on eight hours later, training them into a sleep pattern. Riven supposed these aliens thought they were taking good care of their captives. He'd even bet they believed themselves to be generous. Benefactors.

After all, better imprisoned than dead, right?

Riven wasn't so sure. Wouldn't it have been better to have things over in an eye-blink than to live on, not knowing from minute to minute when something worse would happen? His fellow prisoners, also apparently chosen without rhyme or reason, argued about it when they weren't otherwise busy talking, playing cards or games, or finding shadowy corners to fuck in. Not like everyone didn't know what they were doing. Still, Riven supposed you couldn't stop the human imperative.

Not him, though. There were other gay men on board, but he'd stayed celibate. Ready. Keeping himself clean and fit for whatever happened next. He knew the other prisoners called him a snob, and figured he thought himself too good for their company.

Not so. Riven just preferred to be careful.

He felt... safer... that way.

* * *

"Your attention, please!"

Riven jumped as the voice blared over a communications unit hidden somewhere in the walls of their holding pen. It had a curious accent to it, as if English were a language it had learned from listening to the prisoners, and its tongue wasn't used to shaping the consonants and vowels. It repeated itself in Spanish and French, with the same strange twist to its speech. Understandable, but only just.

No matter. Riven hunched balanced on the balls of his feet, ready to spring into action. He'd been waiting for days now. Maybe at last, they'd find out what was going on.

"Citizens of the planet known as Earth, by now you realize you now belong to us," the voice went on, emotionless, as if it read the words from a paper or screen. "We have saved you from destruction. For this, you owe us your lives. You are ours, and we will do with you as we see fit."

Riven heard a woman scream behind him, and a clamor of voices started up. He remained silent, poised to jump. He'd suspected something like this would come. If not sooner, then later. Their 'saviors' would exact a price for rescuing them.

All saviors did.

So maybe he was cynical. Unfortunately, being cynical also meant he was almost always right.

"We are in need of -- servants," the voice said. "There are many of us who need slaves upon their vessels as they go on to fight in our glorious war against the K'thartin. Many of you will be chosen for transfer to those vessels. Others will be returned to our home planet for different purposes."

Riven's lip twisted. Servants, huh? The deal sounded a lot more like enforced slavery to him. Thanks to all his lessons in historical perspective, he ought to know.

At the end of their cargo bay, a door slid open. "Do not panic," the voice droned. "You are now being separated into those chosen for battle and those who will return to our home. Your new home. We are armed, but will not use force unless necessary."

More cries and wails went up. "You are panicking," the voice said, with a note of something like curiosity. "Why do you alarm yourselves? We are not the enemy. We are kind to our spoils of war."

Spoils of war? Riven choked down a laugh. What a way to turn the phrase!

The door opened all the way now. What came through it defied description. Flunkies, more-or-less humanoid shaped, emerged one by one, all different colors of the rainbow, decorated with tentacles and tendrils where arms and legs should be. They slithered toward the prisoners with the swift, menacing aim of pythons, carrying electrified sticks no doubt intended to stun the unwilling into compliance.

Yeah? Well, fuck them! Riven stood up, holding his head high. He might go down, but he'd go down proud, with his chin raised. No multi-limbed B-movie nightmare was going to cow him into submission. He was a man, a proud man, a gay man, who knew who and what he was. They might beat him, but they couldn't *beat* him.

No matter what they said, and regardless of what they did, he was a human being. Come what might, he'd be treated like one, and damn the consequences.

Just as he'd thought, the creatures moved throughout the bay, zapping those who fought against them or drew back and away in fear. They weren't looking to fight, then -- they just wanted obedient lumps of meat. Watching, assessing every move they made, Riven noticed each alien carried pouches full of red and blue tags. Almost as if at random, they slapped a tag onto each man and woman, with far more red tags than blue applied. *Slave. Slave. Slave. Warrior. Slave. Warrior. Slave. Slave.*

Riven stood at the far edge of the hold, almost separated from the cowering crowds, but at last one of the aliens oozed to a stop in front of him. Purple-skinned and bare of clothing, its exposed genitalia, surprisingly humanoid in shape and size, told Riven it was male. Corded, tough-looking muscles warned him the thing would be a strong one. Eyes betraying a startling intelligence ran up and down the length of his body, gauging its strength and abilities to the last fraction.

"I'm not your cow," Riven said, low and flat. "Go ahead and tag me, or zap me if you want, but I won't bend over and take it without a fight. If you even know what I mean, especially with a man like me, you know what you're in for."

The alien blinked. "Ahh," it said -- no, hissed -- through its mouth, cluttered by too many teeth for clear speech. "You are one of those, then."

Riven frowned. "One of whats?"

"Husssh." The alien reached out one tentacle, a long, thin appendage, and laid the tip against Riven's temple. It tapped his skin in a gentle rhythm reminiscent of a heartbeat, leaving behind a sticky residue. "Yesss, you are one of those," it said, sounding thoughtful. "And one of *those*, too. There are not many of you among this lot. According to the data we have, you are considered physically pleasing. You measure up to every basis for comparison in our databanks. A handsome man."

Riven's skin darkened with embarrassment. "I take care of myself."

"As we can tell." More tentacles extended, stroking down his chest, across his biceps and thigh muscles. Probing with a feather-light touch at his penis and across his ass, turning a deeper shade of indigo as it did so. "You are a lover of other men, true?"

Riven glared at him. "You ever hear of *my body, my choice*? I knew what I was when I was a boy. A young human. I haven't changed my mind since. If you're expecting me to turn around and be something else for you, you're in for a whole new battle." He'd fought too long and hard on Earth to be accepted for what he was. Damned if he'd let aliens, slimy, tentacled aliens, try and stop him from being gay and proud.

The creature let out a long, wheezing chuckle as it withdrew. "Far from it, human. We have another use in mind for you." It searched inside its pouches, pulling out an entirely new kind of chip. Green, shaped like a diamond. It pressed the patch to Riven's shirt, pushing down to make sure it stayed in place, then curled up all but one of its 'arms.'

"You are a prize, but still, you have much anger in you," the thing mused as if to itself. "Best to keep you sleepy, then, until the time comes when we present you to your new Master."

"Master?" Riven demanded. "I have no 'master.' I --"

"Husssh." The alien ignored him. Reaching for its stun-stick, it tapped a button to activate the thing. Riven saw blue sparkles of electricity dancing at its end. Part of him wanted to yell and run, but the other part knew what would happen if he tried.

He stood tall and proud as the alien brushed him with its wand. He kept his eyes open even as his limbs collapsed from underneath him and he felt his body hit the floor, spasming with the force of the jolt. He might have lost this battle. But by God, he'd win the war.

He would. They couldn't keep him down...

Yet even as he thought it, the world went fuzzy and black.

* * *

"... this, this is the one," a hissing voice said in Riven's ear. He felt a vague, slimy stickiness as tentacles stroked his cheek. "Does he please you, my lord? Is he the sort you have been searching for?"

"Perhaps," said another voice. Crisper, clearer. Riven struggled to open his eyes and see who -- or what -- spoke, but found he could not. His body still lay locked in the rictus of paralysis, unable to budge the slightest muscle. He fought hard as he could, but was unable to do more than quiver.

"A fighter, as you said," the second voice observed. "Wise of you to use the highest setting on your stunner."

"Yesss," the alien said. "I thought so. He might have made a scene."

"We certainly don't want anything of the sort, at least not yet," the second being murmured, sounding amused. "Remove his clothing. I want to see all of him."

Take his clothes off? Like hell! Riven struggled again, this time producing a twitch of his fingers. The alien sighed. "Perhaps I should find you another, Massster. This one will not be easy to train."

"Ah, but you see, from what I have read, therein lies most of the fun." Yes, the second being was getting a kick out of this, no doubt about it. "Go ahead and strip him of his clothing. Use lasers to cut away the cloth. Gentler and simpler."

Riven twitched, images of smoking beams filling his mind. Instead, a cool light flowed over his skin. He felt a blast of cool air hit him as his shirt and jeans parted neat as you please, leaving him bare on -- what? A table? A bed? Something hard and flat. God, if only he could see!

"Most impressive," the second being said, measuring him up as if he were a slab of meat. "He has a fine cock. Large, but not too large. I see he has fallen prey to the operation known as circumcision. It is a pity, but not so much of a flaw I would cast him aside. Marvelous balls, heavy and pendulous. A matching set. Most are a bit larger on one side than the other. I have made a study of this, you know."

The definitely-alien creature wheezed out a laugh. "I am aware. Your taste for the humans isss well known."

"Are you mocking me?" the second being snapped, voice sharp. "Impudence costs you, soldier, and remember although I have chosen you for this task, you are still a soldier. Would you care for a taste of military discipline?"

The tentacles shrank back from Riven's skin. "No, Master, no. Please, no."

"A much better answer." Something warm and soft pressed against Riven's chest. Not sticky, not slimy. A little hard and callused, but almost... human. Riven battled to open his eyes. Sight. He had to see!

Something else moved through his hair, ruffling it with a soft, deft touch. "So very pretty," the being said in approval. "Soft, even after so long unwashed. I look forward to seeing its glory when cleaned."

"You will take him, then?" The alien's voice was fearful. "Have I pleased you?"

"Well enough," the other being allowed. "I can sense here -- " The digits brushed his head. "-- and here --" Touching his heart. "-- he has it in him to want what I have to offer. He'll make a fine slave. A good pet for a master who treats him with a firm but kind hand. Yes, you have done well."

The alien let out a whistling breath that sounded suspiciously like relief. "I tried my bessst."

"I'm sure you did." The hard, warm thing caressed him again. "I am pleased. I wonder... does he know? Is he awake, aware enough to hear our talking? Does he suspect what lies in store for him?"

"His fingers have been twitching this whole time," the alien pointed out. "I do not believe it is like the actions of a lesser mammal in sleep."

"So he knows." The being laughed. "Can you reverse the effects of your stun for just a moment? I would like to see the look on his face, when he opens his eyes and looks upon me for the first time."

Yes! Yes, you bastard! Riven struggled, this time moving his arm.

"I can, but I would advise putting him under again just after, deep under," the alien warned. "Otherwise we will never get him onto your shuttle without causing him damage as he fights."

"As you will." The warm digit caressed his cheek. "Go ahead, then. Just a bit of wakefulness for my new pet, so he may see what lies in store for him."

Riven felt a light, featherlike tap against the top of his head. His eyelids, struggling to budge, sprang open. His lips fell apart, angry speech spilling out: "You almighty son-of-a-bitch. You think I'm going to lie here and let you talk about me like I'm a hunk of tenderloin? I'll fight you with everything I have."

"No doubt you will," the being said with a laugh in its voice. It circled around the hard surface Riven lay on, coming into his field of vision. Fully into his sight. Despite himself, Riven drew in a deep breath.

"Oh, God." He managed to raise himself on his elbows. A face he hadn't seen in years -- no, it couldn't be. Could it? "Eduardo?"

No. Couldn't happen. Had to be a disguise. A human wouldn't be in league with or in a position of power over these aliens. But damn, he could tell no difference between the alien's assumed face and the real thing. No visible difference between this creature and the Ma... the man named Eduardo who Riven had once known.

Lean and whipcord strong, dark hair swept back over an angled, foreign face, and full lips meant for kissing. For kissing him. Bending over, the alien brushed their mouths together, running his tongue across Riven's own, moving across him with a hunger indicating what would be coming soon.

"I drew this face from your memory," the being whispered. "The face of one who was very dear to you. Do you like it?"

No! Riven jerked back. "Get away from me! I won't," he rasped. "You called me a pet. You're not my master. I don't play the bondage scene. I won't -- I can't --"

"Ah, but you can, and you will," the Eduardo duplicate said, running one nail across Riven's cheek and brushing a thumb over his lips. "You will, and I have read you well enough to know, deep down, you love it."

"No," Riven swore, glaring with all his might.

"Yes," the duplicate insisted. He turned to a side. "Put him back under. See him carried to the room I have fitted out in my shuttle."

"Yes, Master." Riven felt another tap to his head, and once again the utter torpor flowed over him in thick waves. Unable to so much as flicker an eyelash, he could only listen, and fear.

"A fitting gift for a war hero," the 'man' said. "A human of my very own. Make him sleep, now. Let him sleep until I have him bound and chained."

"As you wish." Another tap, and the world went black. Another battle lost -- but still, not the war.

Riven's last thought as he went under was, *If you think you're going to have a meek little mouse, you have another think coming, whatever you are. I'll fight you. I'll fight you till my dying breath...*

Chapter Two

Dark. Quiet and dark.

Not knowing how his body was manhandled from one ship to the next, stored in cryogenic gel, kept in a storage locker, and swept light-years away from where Earth had once been, Riven hovered in a clear glass container, and, unawakened, slept on and on.

As he slept, it seemed as if he entered the world he dreamed of. A memory, relived once again, so real it could be happening…

* * *

God, it was good to be eighteen years old and going on a fishing trip with some buddies! Riven and his friends had waited for the first good, warm spring day for this, and finally it was there.

Older friends had bought beer for them, and they'd loaded up at least three coolers with drinks and sandwiches, not forgetting a knapsack filled with stuff for the real point of the trip: condoms and lube. Oh, yeah, they'd taken fishing poles, too, but they forgot to bring any bait.

They didn't care. They hung bits of baloney on their hooks, balanced the rods so they hung over the side, then turned to one another. No one was around to see them. They'd chosen their spot after debating for hours, deciding on an old "fishing hole" one of their grandfathers had known about. There weren't any fish to speak of, but there *were* thick, sheltering trees around the water's edge, and no one on the lake could get a peek in.

Abandoning all pretense of fishing, they began to reach for one another, skinning tank tops off smooth, tanned shoulders and unzipping the flies of their shorts or pulling down bathing trunks. Groping, stroking, and rubbing, the sun beating down on them and the water rocking with their hips.

Riven had been all for moving the fun to the bank. He didn't like the way their boat tilted and almost bounced on the water when they moved too fast, and his hormones were firing on all cylinders. Three of the five on the trip were already going at it full-bore, cocks out and hard, playing like adults. He wanted a taste of the action, and more.

For his first trip out with guys who all admitted they were gay, had decided they were all hotties, and wanted to have a little fun, he didn't want to be the one left out. A day like this was a dream come true. Something out of one of the pornos he kept hidden under his dorm room bed so his somewhat frighteningly straight roommate wouldn't find them.

He just didn't want to fall overboard.

The other guys laughed at him. For them, danger was part of the thrill. Knowing they could get dumped over the side at any time just added a little spice.

One of them, a swarthy Spanish exchange student, laid dark hands on his tight thighs, palms up, and mocked Riven. "Are you so afraid of a little water? Do you think you will melt? Forget the lake. Come here and let Eduardo show you what he can do to change your mind."

Eduardo had long, talented fingers able to draw anything from a still life to a detailed architectural diagram. Riven didn't know him too well, but he ached to have those fingers wrapped around his cock, pressing hard and eager against the seam of his shorts.

Swallowing down his fears, he obeyed the command. Heart in his throat, he'd crawled over the length of the boat, passing the other three boys, having fun of their own together with loud kisses and hands shoved down to fondle gleaming, swollen cocks. Unable to stop himself, he stared at the sight.

"It is beautiful, is it not?" Eduardo asked. "I can show you something better. Come. Come to me. Come."

Riven swallowed and moved on. He reached Eduardo after what seemed like an eternity.

The brown-eyed boy smiled at him, pride in his eyes. "You see? I knew you could do it."

Riven grinned back, nervous. "Do I get a reward?"

"All good boys get a reward," Eduardo crooned, reaching for Riven. His hands were warm and dry on Riven's bare forearms as he pulled him close. His lips felt soft and hot, tasting of salt and yeasty beer when he pressed their mouths together. Riven moaned into the kiss, opening his mouth for more.

Eduardo laughed at him again, but gave him more. A smooth, gliding tongue tangled with his, fighting a mock duel in their mouths. A hand against the back of his head, holding Riven firm, making sure he couldn't move. It frightened Riven a little, knowing Eduardo had complete control, but at the same time, there was something so sweet about just giving in. Knowing the other boy wanted him enough to just *take* him. And willing, God, yes, he was willing.

Eduardo began to let his free hand rove over Riven, thumb circling his nipples, tracing the thin line of hair on his chest and trailing down the waistband of his swim trunks. God, Riven had been so hard his cock stood straight up against his belly, already wet, aching for attention.

"What is this?" Eduardo murmured into their kiss. "A surprise, just for me?"

Riven moaned.

"Such a pretty cock," Eduardo crooned. "You are a virgin, yes?" At Riven's shy nod, the Spaniard grinned, teeth white in his dark face. "Then you must let me show you something good. This, you will like."

Eduardo caught Riven's hand and pressed it against his own erect phallus, letting Riven feel the bulge, the heat, the need. "All for you," he breathed. "Every drop of this comes of watching you, so innocent, so ripe for the plucking. Will you fall into my hand like a sweet fruit from the vine? Say you will be mine. Speak the words."

Riven's head leaned back on his neck as Eduardo's expert hand worked his cock. "Yes," he said in between gasps of air. "Yes, I'm yours."

Eduardo's smile was bright. "Good boy. Now, let me show you even greater delights, as a reward. Undo my trunks."

Riven had gulped, swallowed hard, and moved his fingers to Eduardo's waistband --

Shifted his feet too far in the wrong direction --

Stumbled --

Capsized the fishing boat.

Riven shouted, splashed, and gurgled as he went underwater, startled by the cold blue closing over his head and swallowing him whole. The water proved much deeper than any of them had suspected, and there was an undertow. It caught him in the riptide, dragging him along, floundering with arms and legs. Not knowing what to do.

So this is what drowning feels like, he thought. He would die, caught under the still waters which had been holding him up. But, as he ran out of air and his brain became fuzzy, he'd decided it wasn't too bad. He'd been at the peak of pleasure, and the end was coming on quick enough. After all, what better way to go?

A hand snatched at his swim trunks, and then strong arms caught him about the waist. A hard yank and he slipped out of the tide and into smoother waters, too startled to blink. He felt himself being dragged toward the surface, a bright circle of light growing whiter and whiter until he broke through it, coughing and spluttering, about as romantic as a dog caught in the rain.

Eduardo held him tight in his darker arms, thumping his back with balled-up fists while Riven got out the water he'd swallowed. As he moaned and choked, Eduardo rubbed soothing circles on his skin, treading water to keep them both upright.

"You were only under for a moment," he said, his dark eyes serious. "Longer, and you would have been in great danger. This was not your fault, I realize, but you must not take such risks again. Move when I tell you to move, and do as I say. Do you understand?"

Riven blinked water out of his eyes. He almost felt like crying -- he'd ruined it all -- but Eduardo just laughed at him and petted his shoulders. "I know what you are thinking, and we will not let this spoil anything," he ordered. "There is still fun we can have together. Look!"

Tucking Riven under one arm, he made for the bank, where the other three boys were stripping off what little sodden clothes they had left. Pulling Riven up onto the shore with him, Eduardo reached for and grabbed a handful of condoms and packets of lube. He gave Riven a seductive smile. "The sandwiches and drinks are lost, but leave it to those others to rescue the good stuff, eh?"

Riven shivered from the cold and from arousal, despite the aching of his muscles and the stinging of his eyes. No matter how tempting Eduardo might be, the last thing he wanted just then was sex. He wanted hot soup and to be wrapped up in his bed, underneath the blankets.

"No, no, such a long face! This expression will not do." Eduardo put one finger under Riven's chin and tipped it up. "You said you were mine. I do not take such promises lightly, Riven. You will rest a bit in the sunlight, recover, and then you will please me. I will help you return to where we left off. See how good I am to you already?" Stroking Riven's face with his fingers, Eduardo slid down the length of Riven's body, took Riven's limp cock into his mouth, and began to ply it with a more than expert tongue.

Riven lost his virginity on the sunny shore, in more ways than one. More than once, as Eduardo sucked him, or when the Spaniard's cock slid deep into Riven's throat, he'd felt he was once again drowning.

* * *

But it was only a dream... a dream... a dream...
So real, though.
No wonder.

Drowning. That was what this felt like, now. Riven floated, lost in a sea of something warm and wet. Almost like being back in the womb. Fears prickled at his mind, but the soothing glide of the gel he floated in calmed him.

Must be something narcotic in it, he thought, his head fuzzy. *Don't forget. Must remember. I'm a prisoner now. Being taken to meet my new 'master' in his chambers.*

He wondered why he had remembered Eduardo and one sun-drenched collegiate afternoon with such clarity. He'd seen it all in his mind's eye as if living the moment out, as if all were real and happening once again.

Bastard! He's tapped into my memories. Stole my -- stole Eduardo's face and made himself a mask to wear.

Riven struggled to fight, to kick. He managed only the most sluggish of movements before hearing laughter, and feeling a light tap to the chest. Then, with the same sickening wave of vertigo as he'd felt before, he went under to the dark. Under, where he lost himself, and knew nothing else.

Chapter Three

"You are waking up... yes, now you are waking up... yes, just so. Good boy."

Riven shifted and moaned under his breath. His muscles ached as if he'd just run twelve miles instead of the ten which pushed him to his limits. A deep soreness burrowed into every joint and sinew, aching and burning. He cried out again, unable to help himself. Something held him pinned fast, upright, like a butterfly on a corkboard. The restraints forced his body tight against a cold metal wall. Manacles and chains?

"Hush, yes. I know it is painful. The soreness will ease soon. Consider it an aftereffect of the transport material I used to keep you still while you were brought here."

Brought here? Here where? Riven's mind swam. Memories mixed together, blending in a cloud of confusion. He'd just been on the river with Eduardo and the guys -- no, he'd been in a holding pen -- no, in a cold room with his clothes stripped from him.

Good boy.

Something in him prickled at the name. No one had called him any kind of nickname in years, least of all something you'd call an actual pet. He was Riven McDaniel, a man who'd made his way in a world set against him by nature. He didn't do pet names. Endearments were for those weak enough to need them.

Cool wetness, something like water, trickled down his cheeks. Grunting in displeasure, Riven tried to raise a hand to brush the liquid away. To his dismay, he found himself unable to move more than an inch.

Wait... yes... they had stunned him. He must still be feeling the effects. "Just give me time..." he slurred. "Wait until this wears off. I'll fight you."

"I have no doubt you will want to," a voice replied. "From my readings, I understand fight or flight is a natural response to strange surroundings. But you shall do neither. I have taken steps to reassure myself you do not. You will learn your place, pet. Slave." Fingers caressed his hair, carding through it. "I am a kind master to those I choose, but I will be obeyed."

Riven fought again. He could feel restraints around his wrists and ankles now, just tight enough to keep him bound. Was he standing up or lying down? He couldn't tell.

"So much struggle," the voice chided. "Why not accept what will be, will be? Truly, you would save us both a great deal of trouble. Go on, use your delicious mouth to call me Master and please me enough to earn a reward, like a good slave."

Riven spat. "No man is my master," he said through a throat seeming to be filled with gravel. "I'm no one's slave."

He heard a sigh. "Let it be on your head, then. Well, we have time. And there is, no doubt, a certain pleasure to be found in training pets how to obey."

Riven shook his head hard. At least he could move a bit. "No!"

"Yes," the voice said, quite calm. "You have not earned it, but as I said, I am a kind master. I will permit you to open your eyes, so you can see me, and look your fill."

Automatically, Riven tried to blink, only to discover his eyelids sealed shut. A shiver of panic ran through him. But was being blinded so bad? He didn't want to look at the owner of the too-familiar voice. He stilled himself, refusing to answer yes or no.

He felt a slight prickle of pain on his chest. "This is but a taste," the voice warned. "When I ask you a direct question, I expect a direct answer. Do you wish to open your eyes and see the world around you?"

Riven fought against the urge to spew out curses, and tell the voice just what it could do with itself, and how. But the thought of opening his eyelids, sealed shut against his cheeks... Finally, he nodded. One stiff, sharp jerk.

"There, you see?" the voice approved. "Was obeying me so hard?" More wetness dripped across his eyes, along with something soft being rubbed across them with a touch light as a butterfly's wing. Riven felt something like glue dissolving, being washed away.

His eyes sprang open.

He had been brought to a small room made of metal, cluttered with a wild assortment of dangling harnesses, X-crosses, and, bizarrely, puffy blobs that looked like beanbags, all shapes and sizes, every blinding color of the rainbow. In front of him stood a man -- no, *the* man, the Eduardo look-alike, the one he remembered from before. The alien who'd gotten him as a gift. He swallowed hard, staring. Just as beautiful as before, his face warmed by an encouraging smile, this alien was the sort of man who, if Riven hadn't known better, he would have tried to strike up a conversation with in a bar or gym. Proportioned just right, with silky hair and an angular face, his physical form was everything Riven had ever dreamed about.

He parted his lips, words of admiration springing unbidden to his tongue -- then stopped. What, was he crazy? This creature was his jailor. Riven, his prisoner. God knew what the alien planned to do with him.

The alien drew back. Riven could see it held a soft cloth in one hand, smeared with the remnants of blue gel. "There," it said, smiling at him. "Any better?"

Riven glared, refusing to answer.

"I see." The alien laid down his cloth and reached to a small table at his side. Picking up a small wand, he tapped Riven in the center of his chest. The same prickle of pain ran through him. "I have studied your Earth rules of dominance and submission," he informed Riven. "They fascinate me. Since I discovered such a culture existed, I have wanted a human toy of my own. My research tells me a direct question from one's master requires a direct answer. Until you learn to obey, I am willing to keep shocking you. All day long, if such is required. Now, I will ask again: being able to see, is it better?"

Riven's chest stung. The pain, sharper on this second blow, stung as if he'd been attacked by a flock of bees. Despite his better intentions, his head jerked in a nod.

"Good!" The alien looked pleased. "Soon, you will not require pain to remind you of my requests. You will know them all by heart, and it shall be your pleasure to obey."

"It won't," Riven gritted.

The alien put aside his stun-stick and sighed. It sat on a cushion in front of Riven and looked at him with infinite-seeming patience. "How little you know yourself," it mused. "The heart of a true pet beats within your chest, yet you deny it. I know this. I have looked inside you."

Riven tugged at his arm restraints. No good; they held fast. "You're wrong."

"A Master is never wrong." The alien gestured to itself. "And I am your Master, whether you like it now or not. Accept my words, slave. The sooner you do, the easier it will be for both of us."

"Never."

"Ah, Riven…" The alien reached out his perfect copy of a human hand to trail across Riven's chest. "Perhaps more drastic measures are called for," it said after a moment's thought. "You are a hard nut to crack, as I believe the saying goes."

"How would you know Earth sayings?" Riven burst out. "You're not one of us. You're one of those tentacled things, hiding inside a human shell. Don't pretend to be like me."

"I did this for your easement," the alien said, blinking. "Would you rather I appeared in my natural form?"

Riven glared.

"It was not a hard thing," his captor went on. "Our race is able to shift forms as we please. I looked inside your mind to see what shape would please you best, and fashioned myself a shell to capture your fancy. Unless your body lies, and I think it does not, you find this form appealing." The being slid its hand lower, to Riven's cock. Riven realized with a sudden burning shame he was still naked, and although he couldn't feel much, he'd gotten hard.

"My body's reactions don't mean anything," he said, attempting to will his cock soft while the rest of him stayed ready, fighting the wrist and ankle cuffs with all the strength he had. "It's just a chemical reaction. Hormones. Nothing more."

"Why do you lie to yourself?" The alien's hand curled around Riven's cock, stroking with gentle pressure. To his shame, Riven felt the first tingles of an impending orgasm at the base of his spine. "It is not just your body, Riven. Your mind desires this too, though I see now it is at war with itself. You have -- yes, you have fought so hard to be your own man you have forgotten your true nature. Your need to be dominated."

"I don't," Riven gritted out.

"So much confusion." The alien rubbed its thumb around the head of Riven's cock. Sensations were flooding back to the lower part of his body -- brought on by the creature's touch? -- and he realized he was leaking pre-come. "Your body plays the traitor against your declaration, no matter what you will or do not will. It likes what I am doing. You like my touch, too, if you will but admit so to yourself. Hush, peace. I am giving you a gift." It smiled. "A welcome aboard, as you will. A free orgasm. After this, you must earn the right to come. But once, just for once, you are free to find your pleasure."

Its voice dropped into a husky whisper. "Do you like to fuck, Riven? To feel flesh spread and part around this wonderful organ? To savor the sensations as you slide deep inside a hot, warm and willing body? Or perhaps I should ask, did you like to fuck before you cloistered yourself like a holy man? I can sense you have not pierced another for a long, long time." The alien's other hand slid between Riven's back and the icy wall, slipping between his ass cheeks and probing delicately at his hole. "And here, too, it has been ages. You are tight as a virgin, unplundered for ages." It grinned. "A condition soon to change. If you are good, very, very good, I might sometime allow you to fuck me as I ride you. But as to the other, I will take your self-imposed celibacy as is my right. Every night, until you scream for mercy, and for more."

Riven found he was panting, and drops of sweat had sprung out on his forehead. His skin felt damp. Stupid body! It responded to all the things the alien said, lusting after the beautiful shape it wore. It wouldn't listen to his mind, telling it not to fall for what the being said.

The gentle touches would be his undoing, or perhaps the stroke-and-twist of his cock, which had not stopped since the alien began to touch him. "I can feel the pressure building up inside you, Riven," it whispered. "You fill with seed, like a flower -- a dandelion -- ready to burst with a single breath of air. Perhaps, like this." The being bent, and exhaled a long, steady stream of warm breath over Riven's cock.

Riven couldn't help it. With a sharp bark, and a deep groan, he felt his cock spasm and jerk. Felt the bright bullet of orgasm hit him like a lightning bolt, sending shockwaves of pure bliss to his brain. His come spurted out in heavy gouts, covering the alien's hand.

When it was over, he hung from his restraints, panting for air. The alien sat smiling up at him, licking his fingers as if Riven's seed was the best thing it had tasted in years. "You are delicious," it said with a smile. "Ah, Riven. Give me a chance. I have shown you how good I can be to you. From now on, you will learn how to be good to me. You will love it, I promise you. Your memories tell me you yearn to submit to a master's hand. Now, I am your master. All will be well," the being said, stroking Riven's cheek.

It smeared a dab of semen across Riven's lower lip. "Taste, and see how good," it encouraged. "How long has it been since you let yourself go, let yourself be what you yearned to be?"

Riven turned his face away. The come burned on his lip, but he trembled. The orgasm had been so powerful, stealing his breath. The knowledge that he couldn't stop it, no matter how hard he tried... He drew in a ragged breath. God. What if he was what the alien claimed? A natural? A submissive, a slave in need of a master?

The being drew back, seeming to be well-satisfied. "You see?" it asked. "There is great pleasure to be found here. More than you would have experienced otherwise, on Earth. I think you were meant for me, and I for you."

Riven shut his eyes, letting his head drop in despair.

"There, there, now, be at peace." The alien stood and petted his shoulder, stroking, burrowing in with strong fingers which knew just how to work the muscle. "You have taken the first step, Riven, and it was not so painful, was it?"

"The first step," Riven said, ashamed of how his voice trembled. "There's more?"

"Oh, so much more," the alien replied. It smoothed its hand down Riven's arm. "I must mark you as my property, slave, but fear not. I will prevent it from being a taste of true pain, and then you will have your fill of pleasures beyond your most exotic dreams. It must be done, to keep you safe and to let others know to whom you belong, but the process of marking is also a means to sexual thrills beyond compare."

"Marking?" Riven's head came up. "What do you mean?"

The alien laid a finger across his lips. "Lesson the second, as I understand it," it said. "A slave does not ask direct questions, or call into discussion his Master's decisions. I know best, here. I will be gentle as possible with you, but you must, must, must learn. I will have it no other way."

Stroking his cheek, the being withdrew. "I go now, to fetch the tools I need to decorate your body as I have said. But Riven, before I go, I will give you one more gift. My name." He smiled. "Well, an approximation of my name, at least. In my native tongue, it is unpronounceable to you. But it means 'phoenix.' It is what you may call me, when you speak to me on summons. Master Phoenix."

Phoenix leaned forward and brushed a kiss across Riven's lips. "Be still, now, and gather your strength," he advised. "I'll be back within half of an hour with the implements I need. Rest, and prepare yourself. Lesson the third is soon to begin."

He tapped the stun wand. "Remember what I have already taught you, Riven. Obey and you will know bliss upon bliss. Disobey, and I will be forced to teach the lessons until they are learned. Do you want to be schooled thus? The pain increases with every blow from the wand. Think on my words, and then tell me what you want. Truly want."

Riven gave another tug at the straps holding him upright, feeling himself shake and tremble. Flashes of Eduardo commanding him, and how happy he had been to do what the Spaniard said, crossed his mind, along with remnants of the bliss from his orgasm, combined with revulsion at being the property of an alien. He shook, unable to form words.

"Yes, I see." Phoenix petted his hand. "It is hard, I know. This is your life now, though. It can be a very good one, Riven. Be still, and think until I return. Know I will never push you past what you can bear, and I will treat you with as much kindness as I possibly can, if you obey my orders."

He stood, and began to walk out of the room. "Think hard, Riven," he called back. "Think long and hard."

Riven trembled in his straps. He struggled not to laugh. God, how a man's life could be turned upside down in a heartbeat! Think, Phoenix had ordered. What the hell else could he do?

He wouldn't have been able to help it, anyway.

Because he had to admit, even if to himself, being taken -- commanded -- worked until his body gave up despite his mind -- it felt *good*. So very good.

He was sure Phoenix knew it, too.

Who was he, now? Was he still Riven McDaniel? Or had Phoenix changed him into something else altogether? Something his traitorous inner self didn't mind at all, despite how he might argue against it?

Riven sagged against the wall. He'd thought he'd known who and what he was. Now, he wasn't so sure.

Waiting for Phoenix to return with his implements, all he could do was question what had come, and what would be...

Chapter Four

Forever. Phoenix had been gone forever. God, when would he come back? Riven hung in his restraints, struggling to stop himself shivering from cold and dread. He knew Phoenix would be back. It wasn't his nature just to walk away and forget a project like Riven. On the other hand, though, the alien had said he went to fetch 'implements.' What did Phoenix mean? Was he going to mark Riven? Tattoo him, pierce him, scar him? Riven's body rippled with a full-body shudder at the thought.

Oh, God. His cock… it was getting hard.

Sickened, he closed his eyes, still a little tacky from the gel, and tried to will the start of his erection away. Thoughts of being altered forever by Phoenix's 'implements' shouldn't give him a hard-on. Shouldn't make him ache for a hand around his cock, just as Phoenix had held him before, stroking him to climax. He wasn't a kid anymore. He couldn't just come again and again on command, 'master' or not.

But no! Phoenix wasn't his master. Riven might be the alien's slave, whether he chose it or not, but he wouldn't call Phoenix 'master.'

He wouldn't do anything Phoenix wanted, if it wasn't for the alien's wands. Riven twitched. The electric wand, and each gentle tap to the chest hurt so much. Words could be forced out of him whether he meant them or not. He thought he was strong enough to stand up to torture, but the way Phoenix did it, with his soft words and his other hand caressing Riven's arm, his thigh, his prick… it made him hard, even though it hurt like hell.

Phoenix knew it, too.

Nauseated at himself, Riven began to retch. He brought up nothing, heaving dry until the spasms ended in a fit of coughing and finally stopped. How long had it been since he'd eaten? Phoenix could have kept him in storage for months, absorbing nutrients through his cocoon of blue gunk, stomach otherwise empty. It would make sense. No fuss, no muss.

Now he'd been freed, though. He sensed Phoenix enjoyed getting a little messy. The way he'd licked Riven's come off his hands had been startling in its sexiness. No man on Earth, no date or hook-up Riven had ever been with, had tasted his seed with such hunger. As if it were made of honey and wine, better than ice cream, sweeter than syrup. Phoenix must have known so, too, if he'd looked inside Riven's mind as he'd claimed. Must have known Riven had always dreamed of someone savoring him thus, just as he'd tasted others.

Although the thought repulsed him, Riven found himself wondering what Phoenix tasted like. If he could alter his form, maybe he could alter other things, too. Regular come had a salty-musky-bitter taste to it, but maybe Phoenix's seed *would* taste like sweet things, treats he'd crave devouring. He'd only ever known one man who tasted a little different. Sort of like fruit, a little sweet and tart on the tongue.

Eduardo. Eduardo, whose form Phoenix had stolen for his own.

God, Eduardo. Hadn't he been thinking of him -- dreaming? -- just before Phoenix had woken him up? Eduardo, who Riven hadn't thought of in years. Eduardo, who'd been... no, no, he wasn't a master, and Riven hadn't been his pet, no! He hadn't been. They had just... played at it. Pretended. But had it been dream, omen, or dragged up by Phoenix's meddling inside his head?

It was all too much for Riven. Thoughts of the dark, sloe-eyed boy he'd known in college filled his mind. If he closed his eyes, he could almost smell the spicy cologne the exchange student had worn, along with the salty sweat of his skin. He could feel sunlight beating down on his shoulders through an opened dormitory window, and the chill of linoleum under his knees.

If he just closed his eyes, he could... no, he *would*... remember it all, every bit of it.

He couldn't help it. Sagging in his restraints, Riven went slack. Whether his own body took control or Phoenix did something to his mind from a distance, he found himself falling asleep, hard and fast, like tumbling down a well, and opened his inner eyes in a dream of perfect memory.

* * *

Riven swallowed hard, clenching his hands. His palms were sweaty. Shit. He hated sweaty palms on other guys, and now his had to go and get all damp just when he least needed it. At least his pits were okay. Still dry, and he got a whiff of Sailor's Delight deodorant when he moved his arms a little. A bit like sandalwood, a bit like cedar. Expensive as hell, but he loved the way it smelled.

He saved the stuff for special occasions because it permeated his shirts, making him smell as if he'd been sitting in a room full of light and incense. The other day, hadn't Eduardo said he liked Riven's fragrance? He'd been wearing it then, on the fishing trip, on a whim, a little joke on what they were doing.

It hadn't felt like a joke when Eduardo had him up on the riverbank. Both of them with their shorts down around their ankles, bellies rubbing slickly together with spunk, swollen cocks scudding against one another and their taut stomachs until it was too much and they came and came, bursting apart in one another's arms.

After it had been over, and the threesome with them had finished their circle suck, they'd all lain down naked and let the sun bake them for what felt like hours.

Sleepy, no one had said much of anything, except Eduardo, who bent over to whisper in Riven's ear, "Come visit me, some day soon. I would very much like a visit from you. I will teach you more things, if you wish. You will visit me. Say you will."

Riven had shivered in delight, answering with a whisper, "Yes, I will."

So. He'd waited a few days, not wanting to look too eager, but just about to pop every time he thought of the Spaniard. Finally, when he couldn't take it anymore, he'd just -- done it.

Gotten out of bed at two a.m., showered, cleaning every inch of his body with cedar-scented soap and shampoo, and rubbing sandalwood lotion into it so he'd be soft and smooth. He'd toyed with the thought of shaving himself, to be utterly hairless and slick, but wasn't sure where the idea had come from, so in the end he'd put down his razor.

Three a.m., the sun still hours from coming up, he'd headed for Eduardo's dorm. A little trick he'd learned from some party-going friends of his about campus codes came in handy, and he punched in the master key combination to the locked front door. It snicked open. Then, it was just a matter of sneaking past the resident assistant's room and up the side stairwell.

Up in the hall, it had smelled like raw maleness. Sweaty, pungent, a little stinky, laced with aftershave and toothpaste and sneakers. Eduardo's room was on the very opposite end of the hall. Lucky guy, he had a single. Much smaller than the others, but no roommate to deal with, not like Riven. His own roomie had thrown a basketball at his head as he moved around, getting ready, even though he'd tried to be quiet as he could. By a stroke of luck, he hadn't asked any questions, just tossed his weird camouflage comforter over his head and burrowed face-first into his pillows. If he'd sat up, all buzz-cut and attitude, demanding to know what the hell Riven was doing getting all "prettied up" after midnight...

God. It figured he'd end up sharing a room with a homophobic prick. Riven didn't even dare hang up any pictures or take his videos out of hiding, for fear of Trey's reaction. He'd never hear the end of it, at least until Trey kicked the shit out of him or demanded to be moved out. It'd be a huge scene. His parents would be called in. His mother would cry and ask God what she'd done to deserve this. His father would have taken him home, and beaten the hell out of him a second time.

If they knew what he was about to do... what he had done... what he hoped to do...

Swallowing hard, Riven lifted his fist and rapped on Eduardo's door. A little light shone underneath the crack, and he hoped it meant the Spaniard was still awake, not fallen asleep with the lights on, or left them burning while he went out. He could take a lot of blows to his pride, but the courage he'd needed to answer Eduardo's summons, even though he wanted to with every fiber of his being... God, what a paradox. Riven shook his head, confused.

No answer. Riven bit his lip. One more time? Careful, so careful not to wake anyone else up, he tap-tap-tapped at Eduardo's door again.

This time, he heard the soft padding of footsteps behind it. Light blinked out at the peephole, and then the lock slid undone. Eduardo swung the door open, stepping aside from its arc inward. His eyes were fixed on Riven. He smiled, a bit predatory, a bit welcoming. "Come in," he said, barely above his breath. "Quiet, now."

Riven ducked his head and went inside, Eduardo shutting the door behind them in silence. He began to head for a chair, to sit down, maybe to whisper a quiet conversation with the exchange student, but found himself caught instead in a pair of strong, lean arms turning him around without allowing any argument. Eduardo held him fast, pulled tight against himself, body to body, their faces inches apart. His strong, lean fingers cupped Riven's ass, stroking with gentle fingers.

Embarrassed, Riven looked down again. He could feel his cock springing to life through his jeans and boxers, and knew Eduardo must be able to feel it, too. He could feel Eduardo's hard-on through his thin-washed jockey shorts, hard, insistent, pressing against Riven's own.

"So shy," Eduardo murmured. "So shy, after all we have done together. But ah, so much remains to explore, no? You came to me, as I ordered. Good, obedient Riven." With a small laugh, Eduardo lifted one hand to Riven's chin and tilted his head up, until their eyes met. "It was because of my summons you slipped in here, like a thief in the night?"

Riven trembled. Part of him, a small, prideful part, didn't want to own up to it. Didn't want to confess just how much he'd needed to see Eduardo again. To feel the warmth of his praise. But the greater portion of him, which ached for the Spaniard's sensual approval, made him nod, not saying a word.

"You are good at this already." Eduardo placed a finger across Riven's lips. "Do not speak until or unless I bid you open your mouth," he ordered quietly. "We must not be discovered. You may nod."

Riven had bobbed his head, bashful but eager to please. Eduardo laughed under his breath and ducked his head for a kiss, pressing his lips to Riven's so soft, sweet and gentle it almost stole the air from Riven's lungs. He would have followed after Eduardo, chasing his kiss, but Eduardo's hand under his chin kept him in his place.

"Not unless I say," the Spaniard whispered with a frown. "Obedience, Riven. I know much more than you do, and I can teach you so many things. I do not, though, have the time for questions and arguments and why-why-why? You want me."

Eduardo pressed their groins together, moving with a slow and lazy circle of his hips. "This I can feel. You can tell I want you, too. We may have many good times together, Riven, if you agree to do what I say. Only what I say. Only me. Will you?" He had kissed Riven again, a sweet taste of heaven. "Will you? Say you will. You may speak."

Riven stared at him with love-starved eyes. Eduardo, so proud and strong, so dominant, holding him tight and *demanding* his obedience and the right to savor his body. How could he say no? He'd have to be crazy. He wanted this more than anything in the whole world. "Yes," he said, voice very, very low. "Yes, I will."

"Mmm." Eduardo buried his face in the hollow of Riven's shoulder, biting, then suckling to raise a hickey. "My mark, on you," he murmured against Riven's flesh. "No one else will see it if you keep your shirt buttoned, but now you know you belong to me."

"I do?" Riven whispered, dazed.

"You have said it. I asked, and you said, I *will*. You are mine, Riven. Now, turn out the light." His slender, talented hand slipped down to wrap around Riven's hard, dampened cock, thumbing the tip in a circle. "There are other things I would teach you before the morning comes. Before anyone wakes, we will shower together, in one stall, and I will teach you still more."

"What if --" Riven had managed to say, struggling through the mist as Eduardo stroked him to even greater fullness. "-- what if someone catches us?"

Eduardo laughed. "Does that not make it even more appealing, such a thought?" he asked. "Perhaps I will have you on your knees on the tile, the water spattering down upon us both as if we were in a Madrid thunderstorm, in an alley. Perhaps some foolish athlete will stumble in with his shampoo and see you, kneeling before me, worshipping my cock. Hm? Do you think he would be horrified, or would he perhaps be jealous?"

"I thought you said no one could find out --"

"Not unless I wish for them to. This image, it entices me. Tell me: how would you feel?"

Riven exhaled. "Me? I would be jealous."

"I know you would." Eduardo touched his lips. "Silence, now. I have given myself an appetite to have your lips wrapped around me, and to feel your tongue bathing my cock from tip to root. Come, now."

Eduardo moved his hands to press down on Riven's shoulders. "On your knees, beautiful boy. Yes, just so. Next time we will have a pillow for you, to spare your bones, but now, I cannot wait. Tug my shorts down and help me take them off. Throw them aside. I care not where they land. Now, yes, now, lean forward and open your mouth wide as it can go to take me in, for I am not small, and I have grown large with wanting you."

In the following hours, Riven learned more about sucking cock than he'd ever dreamed was possible. Eduardo could last for what seemed like hours. His jaw and throat had gotten sore, but Eduardo had always stopped, pulled back, and massaged life back into them until he could go on. He'd whispered promises and naughty things. "This is your first lesson, lovely Riven. The first time we were together was for pure pleasure. Now, I teach you how to pleasure me with your mouth. Next, it will be your hand, and then your cock, and then I shall show you what it feels like to have your sweet little virgin hole plundered, to feel my cock pushing deep inside you, splitting you in two. You will feel so tight around me, sweet Riven. And you will do as I say, when I say it. Say you will, Riven. Say it."

Riven, drawing back from Eduardo's cock, had always whispered it to him. "I will…"

* * *

Riven began to come back to himself, struggling up through the mists of sleep. His head hung heavy on his neck, feeling as though a heavy weight were dragging it down. He couldn't seem to raise it. An aftereffect of sleeping on the alien ship? Maybe.

Eduardo. God. How long had it been since he'd had such a vivid dream? So real, as if he'd been there, living it all over again. Tasting the dark bronze cock in his mouth, heavy, throbbing with an internal pulse, damp with pre-come flavored almost sweet from all the fruit the Spaniard ate, musk, and maleness.

What he'd give to be there again, on his knees, on a hard dormitory floor, his hands gripping two slimly muscled thighs, his head bobbing forward and back as he suckled and withdrew, learning to use his tongue and suction both. Feeling more alive than he ever had before.

When Eduardo had come, he'd clutched his hands in Riven's hair and cried out, a soft, wailing moan of triumph, as if he'd accomplished a great task. Just the sound of it had Riven's own cock jerking and spasming, pouring out gouts of heavy, salty seed and ruining his jeans which he'd never even gotten to take off while Eduardo stood like a naked Spanish god before him. Bronzed and beautiful.

Eduardo had petted him, shaking a little from the force of his orgasm, and crooned soft words to him. Things like *so good*, and *just as I said*, and *you obey me well*.

Obey.

Obey.

Riven began to shake. God. Had it... Was he... Had he been... Oh, fuck, fuck, fuck, no wonder Phoenix thought...

But that wasn't him. Not anymore. Eduardo had been a one-time college thing, and it had ended. More than ended. He hadn't ever played those games with anyone else since then. He hadn't wanted to. He was his own man, damn it, and no one's plaything. He'd learned his lesson and learned it well.

Only trouble was, it seemed like now, in this impossible situation, this improbable scenario, the alien wearing Eduardo's body wanted Riven the way Eduardo himself had. Wanted to teach and train him to obey orders. Seemed to think he would get off on it... again.

Planned to mark him as a slave, not for a sunny fall in college, but for all time. For the rest of his life.

Whether he wanted it or not.

Riven began to shake, his muscles spasming. No, he chanted to himself. *No, no, no, no, no!*

A thought crossed his mind. A picture, clear as the dream had been. Himself, kneeling before the beautiful alien, being allowed to grip those slender hips and knead them with his hands while he suckled at a cock tasting of sugar, champagne, and sweet fruit. Feeling hands card through his hair, eager for more, pushing him on, but rewarding him at the same time for being such a good slave...

Riven shook hard as a ripple of pleasure overwhelmed him. *Oh, God*, he whimpered to himself, feeling his erection hard against his stomach, sticky with drops of pre-come. *I'm sick. The alien bastard is going to come back any second and mark me. You know what marking means, Riven. No escape. Not even if there was an Earth to go back to. You'll belong to Phoenix forever.*

Another ripple rocked him from head to toe. Pure bliss. *I can't like this*, he moaned to himself. *I'm my own man. I am, I am, I am...*

"Yes, you are your own man," Phoenix's voice replied as he stepped out of the shadows. "But you are also my man, now. What will it take to teach you these things are not incompatible?"

The alien slid forward, inhumanly smooth in his gliding walk. In one hand, he carried a selection of wands, and in the other, a palm full of jewelry. Heavy hoops and chains, a vast tangle of them, spilling through his fingers. His smile hungry, broad and white like a tiger's, or a shark's, Phoenix came to a stop in front of Riven. "But you'll learn. In time, my Riven, you will learn…"

Chapter Five

"Come along. I will make you more comfortable, shall I?" Phoenix reached up to unlatch one of the manacles holding Riven to the wall. As his nimble fingers worked, Riven tensed. Now? Was now the moment? Could he bolt and run?

"Where would you go?" Phoenix asked as one hand came free. "These are my private quarters on a ship filled with those who took you in the first place. If you ran into any of them, they would but return you as you might a lost -- what would it have been, a puppy? Should you manage to escape them, and to hide from the link I have forged between us -- an impossible thing, I should mention -- once we land the ship is decontaminated with a substance toxic to your kind."

Clink, clank, and the other shackle almost loosened. "Really, Riven, there's nowhere to go," Phoenix said, his voice kind, reaching down to stroke Riven's cheek. "You must accept your fate. You know you want to. It is all a matter of understanding who and what you are."

The shackle came free. Riven lowered his arms automatically to find the wrists were still bound together. But they were in front of him, and if he bunched his fists together to take a swing --

"You cannot render me unconscious," Phoenix informed him, bending, exposing the back of his neck as he undid Riven's ankle shackles. "My skin is much tougher than yours. Soft to the touch, yes, and hairless, as you prefer in your deepest thoughts, but you could not break it with an axe if you had the means to try." He glanced up. "Well? I know what you desire, Riven. I see your mind. Touch it. Touch me. Go on. I give you permission."

Damn him. How had he -- alien mind meld sci-fi shit. Riven cursed, earning himself nothing more than a chuckle, and a tap to the knee.

Dark Side

"Do you forget how well I know your language? We will
have to work on your choice of vocabulary, slave," Phoenix said
with a smile in his voice. "Or perhaps teach you how better to use
such words. Salty language is ripe with possibility, when not used
in anger. But why do you hold back? You yearn to touch me. Go
ahead. Stroke my neck. Feel and see I am good."

Riven shut his eyes tight. The problem was, he *did* want to
feel Phoenix's skin. See if it felt like it looked, soft as a woman's
and slick as a seal's hide, tough and smooth as good, supple
suede. He opened his eyes as his fingers reached out despite his
better intentions, brushing the back of Phoenix's neck.

Ahhh...

Riven couldn't help letting a sigh escape him. Phoenix's skin
was... he had never felt anything like it. Better than anything he'd
thought it might be. Warm, alive, responding to his touch with a
thrill of goose bumps, Phoenix arching his back.

Phoenix laughed, delighted. "So that is what it feels like to
be tickled in this form! Delightful. You must do it again
sometime."

Tickled! Riven drew his fingers back as if stung. The
comment hurt, though he didn't know why.

The ankle shackles came loose with a sharp click of metal.
Glancing down, Riven saw his legs were still chained together, but
with enough give to allow him to walk... or kneel, raise his legs
over a man's shoulders, maybe even turn and present. He had to
give it to Phoenix. The man -- *no, alien, damn it, alien!* -- knew what
he was doing with his hardware.

"Come," Phoenix said, as if he were coaxing a kitten to a
saucer of milk. He put a hand on the small of Riven's back,
nudging him forward. "I have prepared a place for you. You have
been standing for so long. You must lie down."

Riven blinked. He didn't see -- oh, wait, there, a lumpy,
beanbag-like thing on the floor. Some kind of alien chair, made for
their natural shapes? Phoenix laughed at his thought and, gentle
but firm, eased Riven down into the creases, dips and hollows of
the bag. It molded to the shape of his body, warm and inviting.

Every sore muscle, from his aching arms to his strained legs, was cushioned by the stuff he lay on, supporting his limbs and almost making the pain vanish.

Riven caught himself before he could arch and stretch in contentment. *No. You're a slave, remember? Comfy bed aside, this is still your jailer you're dealing with. Don't let your guard down!*

Phoenix regarded him sadly. "Ah, Riven, things could be so much better if you would let go and give in. I try so hard, but you persist."

Riven glared up at him, stubborn in his silence -- a wrong move? Phoenix had said a good slave should be quiet, ordering him not to ask direct questions or speak unless instructed.

Well... he just didn't *feel* like saying anything. Nope. Wouldn't give Phoenix the satisfaction. Riven crossed his arms over his chest as much as he was able to and narrowed his eyes in defiance.

Phoenix tilted his head. "There was a poem in one of the books we took," he said without warning. "You bring it to mind. *Tyger! Tyger! burning bright, In the forests of the night!* You are like one of your Earth kittens hissing over the carcass of a dead mouse. What you knew is gone, Riven. There are balls of yarn and sweet herbs and fresh meat for you, if you choose to accept them."

Riven turned his head.

"So, you think you will not be swayed by pretty words." Phoenix sighed. "Riven, what I am about to do, I fear my actions will make you hate me all the more. Know I do what I do for your sake. To protect you by marking you as mine, belonging to me among my kinsmen, my slave and my pet. Our kind does not care for humanity outside of what useful purposes they serve. They would not understand the affection I feel for you."

Riven managed to keep from turning in surprise. Affection? For him? Phoenix had a hell of a way of showing it. Stealing him, making him property -- and he was supposed to believe it was affection?

"More care and concern than you can yet know." Phoenix stroked Riven's cheek, fingers gentle and soothing, his thumb stroking over one cheekbone. Gentle, but too strong to resist, he lowered Riven's arms until they lay at his sides. "You will protest this, so I must make it so you cannot move."

He ran his hand over the side of the beanbag-like bed. It froze into place, cementing Riven into position, his arms unable to lift up and his legs spread just a bit, exposing his bared cock and balls.

Oh, fuck. "I can't move!" Riven blurted, staring at Phoenix with wide, panicked eyes. Not even his neck would turn. He could close his eyes, and open his mouth, but no more. "Let me go, let me go!"

"Riven, Riven, Riven..." Phoenix sounded saddened. "I would if I could. I fear your attacking me in your current state of confusion when I begin the work I must perform to keep you safe once we arrive at my home. Here, no one will harm you. There, unless you are marked, one who does not care for you as I do might try to steal you away for hard labor. I mean you for a life of pleasure, in my bed and out of it. I want to have you as a pampered, precious pet. I have used the term 'slave,' true, but no more. I see it brings unpleasant connotations to your mind. From now on, I will call you pet. And like any good pet, you must be collared."

Collared? Oh, no --

Riven's eyes darted to a long, low table where Phoenix had laid his double handful of jewelry and wands when he'd entered the room.

"Do not fear them." Phoenix stroked a lock of Riven's hair away from his cheek. "They are not meant to hurt you, not in any way. I would even make this pleasurable for you, pet." He reached out and seized a pink wand. "Here, let me show you."

Riven braced himself for a shock of pain as the tip touched his shoulder. To his astonishment, a rosy glow of warmth and healing rolled through his body, suffusing him from head to toe with a feeling of lazy, sleepy bliss. He felt a little tingly, as if he'd gone numb, but in a good way, floating on the outer wakeful edges of sleep. Phoenix tapped him again on his other shoulder, his stomach, and both his thighs. By the time the alien had finished, Riven was awash in a sea of contentment he just couldn't help.

Neither could he stop a lazy smile when Phoenix stroked his arm, petting him as he might a dog. "There," the alien crooned. "Better, is it not? In future, I will give you this wand as a reward, when you have pleased me. Not too much or too often, lest you become spoiled or addicted, but it is very like eating lotus, I am told, or smoking the cannabis. It has the added benefit that you will feel no pain, nor be able to panic under its influence. Again, Riven, I do this for your own good."

Riven flickered a glance up at Phoenix. There went an unwelcome mention of pain again. Just what was Phoenix planning to do to him?

Phoenix leaned down and pressed a chaste kiss to Riven's forehead. The sweetness of it suffused him, as would a ray of sunlight. "We begin," he murmured. "All for your own good, Riven. I will explain as I go."

"Can… I can talk…?" Riven asked, wrapping his tongue around the sounds with effort. Words proved slow to form, but they came.

Phoenix ran a finger down the bridge of Riven's nose. "You may ask questions if they are urgent, or tell me if the drug wears off and you are in pain," he said. "But as for the rest, silence. You need to hear what I have to say, sweet Riven. Silence, pet."

"Stop calling me --"

"Hush, now, hush." Phoenix laid his finger across Riven's lips. A sense memory of Eduardo doing the same thing flashed across Riven's mind. He almost kissed it from sheer force of a habit he'd thought long dead before he caught himself. Phoenix smiled at him, eyes alight with amusement, and reached for a second wand, this one striped and marbled with many colors. He twisted some rings set into its base.

"First, I will make your skin like mine. Soft and hairless, supple and sweet to the touch. I enjoy the contrasts of hair, hardness and softness, but there will be times when I require certain toys and devices which may cause you pain with hairs catching or chafing against you."

Phoenix tapped Riven's chest. A wave of warmth rolled down his length, along with a vague prickling sensation. "It is easy, see? Already done. And to clean you off, all I need do is blow."

Bending over Riven, Phoenix expelled a long stream of warm air from his mouth, far more breath than any set of human lungs could hold, smelling of cinnamon and cloves as it whistled down his body. It felt as if he'd buried himself in leaves, and someone were brushing them off. Straining to look, Riven saw his chest was soft and pink, and could just catch a glimpse of hairless cock, half-erect.

Phoenix reached down to caress it. "You like what I do to you," he said, running his fingers across the length. "You are so responsive, pet. But to ensure you do not come before I say you may, a little prevention..."

He reached for his pile of jewelry, sorted through it, and produced a golden cock-and-ball set of rings. Riven sucked in a breath as the cold metal touched him, clicking into place. *Oh, God...* His cock sprang to full life. Phoenix adjusted the rings, his fingers lingering as if to tease, a smile playing on his lips. It was torture, but of the most exquisite kind.

"There," Phoenix said, lingering over his words as if they tasted good. "Now you are ready for more pleasure still."

He ran his palms down Riven's bare chest. "First, I will tattoo you. Put my mark and those of my clan upon your skin."

Riven's eyes widened. Tattoos -- needles! Pain! He struggled against the drug and the bonds holding him steady, but his muscles were lazy with the effects of the pink wand and held fast by the bed he lay on. Phoenix ran a hand through his hair, letting the ends of it curl around his fingertips. "It will not hurt," he soothed. "This is not the sort of tattoo you are used to. I need no rapidly firing needles to set a mark into your skin. All I need," he said, holding up the wand, "is this."

Lowering the device to Riven's chest, he began tracing a pattern across the skin. Riven couldn't see, not much, but he got a vague glimpse of bright colors and something almost Celtic. Loops and whorls, interlocking rings and rococo edges, covering him from nipple to nipple and running down his chest. Wherever the wand ran, a path of fire followed, but not one of pain. Purest pleasure, instead, warming him further and sending bolts of bliss straight to his groin. His cock strained against its bonds, a drop of pre-come appearing at the tip.

"Oh, how good," Phoenix murmured. He stopped his work for a moment to bend over and lick the drop off, his tongue swirling around with amazing skill. Riven groaned despite himself, aching to be able to arch up and -- and what? Fuck the alien's mouth? Sick. He was sick to want any kind of touch from the alien.

But it all felt so good!

"There, you see?" Phoenix lapped at his cock again, devouring another pearl of pre-come. "You are coming around, Riven. Soon, you will understand it all."

At last, too soon, Phoenix lifted up and away. "No more," he said, voice full of regret. He stroked Riven's lower belly. "I desire you, Riven, as one man wants another, but I will not take you until you trust me fully. Earning your trust may take days, or even years, but I will be patient in my teaching. You are my pet, and you will understand I train you for your own pleasure and benefit in addition to my own before I take you and make you mine in such a way."

Riven stared up at the beautiful alien. A twinge of something -- regret? Couldn't be -- tugged at him. The being's lips shone cherry red. A small smear of come decorated his bottom lip. With a swipe of his tongue, Phoenix licked it off, and made a small purr of contentment. "You taste delicious, pet. I adore the flavor of pure man, untainted by anything but the sweet juices I have fed you while you rested before coming to me here. They have made you strong, and made you taste like wild fruit, rich and tangy." He sighed, and tightened the cock ring just a little. "No more, though. It tempts me more than is wise, pet."

Riven's cock jumped in its bonds. Straining back toward the alien's mouth. Phoenix's eyes warmed. "Yes, this at least knows what it wants, and is not ashamed. The rest of you, it is learning."

He laid down his wand, and reached again for the pile of jewelry. Shuffling so he could sit in comfort at Riven's side, he sorted out handfuls of thick, chunky hoops and studs and things Riven couldn't put a name to.

Riven's eyes widened in panic. They looked self-piercing, sharp needles on the ends of each hoop sliding into the other side to make a circle.

Phoenix glanced down at him. "Riven, why do you fear? You already know this will not hurt. The tattoos did not sting in the slightest, and if you could but feel, they have already healed over. But your heart, how fast it beats, pitter-pat, like a rabbit, and how your blood rushes through your veins. Perhaps you should sleep for this."

Riven would have nodded frantically if he could have. Instead, he settled for pleading with his eyes.

Phoenix gave his head a little shake. "To please you, pet, I will let you rest while I finish the decoration of your body. But once you are settled into your life and your position, we will take these out, let them heal, and do them again with you awake to appreciate the process."

He picked up a soft blue wand and laid it at Riven's side. "First, though, I will lay these out, so you can see where things will have gone when you awaken."

Riven could feel the cool metal as Phoenix began laying hoops on him. One on either nipple. Several along his ears. One on his navel. One poised playfully at the tip of his cock while Phoenix measured studs along the length of it, something like a silver dolphin on the underside, and a peculiar open-ended hoop pressed against his perineum. Chains came next, thin, delicate chains Riven sensed had the strength of titanium, designed to link the whole together. A leash could be clipped either to a chain between his nipples, or the ring around his cock.

"Beautiful," Phoenix whispered, stroking Riven's chest with the tips of his fingers. "You, too, will grow to love them as I do, seeing this metal of my own working glistening against your flesh. But you fear me so, still, and thus you must sleep..."

Phoenix raised the blue wand, and traced it in a soft, feather-light line across Riven's head, from temple to temple. Almost immediately, Riven felt himself falling away, tumbling back into the recesses of a dark and cozy cocoon within his mind.

"Sleep," he heard Phoenix command, as if from a distance. "Sleep, and dream of other times, so when you wake you will understand me better."

Riven felt the slightest of tingles as the first of the needles pierced his flesh. To his dismay, a shock of excitement sizzled down to his groin. Despite the tingles in his cock, he found he was unable to help himself from closing his eyes in sleep.

Phoenix would find out soon enough, if he didn't already know. It wasn't the first time Riven had been pierced for someone else's pleasure, though he'd long since let the hole heal up.

Long ago and far away, with Eduardo...

Chapter Six

Riven lay on his back in the middle of Eduardo's bed. Eduardo could coax anyone into anything, and he'd managed to have his standard-issue dorm cot put into storage. He'd moved a double-wide futon of his own into its place. Plenty big enough for two guys long of limb to stretch out in and lie beside one another, cuddle up close, or even wrestle, getting tangled in the sheets. Or doing other things, things grown-ups did. Riven felt almost light-headed every time he presented himself to Eduardo, knowing he would be in for another lesson, and better still, another reward.

Tonight, Eduardo had taken a notion to decorate Riven. He had a set of markers, the kind made to smell like the sweet fruit he loved so much, and he'd bared Riven from head to toe, laying him out flat like a sheet of paper to doodle on wherever he pleased. As he drew, cool air from a window fan swept over both of them, causing them to shiver in the otherwise humid room.

"Lie still," Eduardo said with a slight thump to Riven's hip. "I do not want to get this crooked."

Riven tried to angle his head. "What are you drawing?"

"A little of this, a little of that." Eduardo drew back a little and stroked his chin. "The human body is a difficult canvas. A caveman would call this primitive."

"I'm sure it's beautiful…"

"It is well enough. I like it. Circles and scrolls, tracings of your muscles, vines and leaves. All different colors. You look like a rainbow, my Riven."

"Mmm." Riven smiled, lifting one rainbowed arm to curl his hand beside his cheek. "What if I don't want to lie still?" he asked, still a little shy of making requests. Eduardo didn't much like it, but he seemed to be in a playful mood.

It didn't extend too far, though. Eduardo sat up, capping his marker with a severe frown. "Do you think to toy with me?" he demanded. "I said I wished to draw, and you play the sex kitten."

Riven shrank back into the futon's hardness. Eduardo would never hit him, but to feel his disapproval was worse than a blow. "Isn't... isn't sex what this is all about?" he faltered.

"When I say it is," Eduardo informed him. He gathered the rest of his markers and tossed them onto a desk. "I no longer feel like playing, Riven. Perhaps you should dress and run along home now."

"No! Please, no."

Eduardo's head turned. "What did you say?"

Riven trembled. "Please?"

Eduardo turned on him, suddenly savage. "Perhaps you want to play in some other fashion. Am I correct, Riven?"

Almost not daring to move, Riven nodded.

"Would you serve me? Service me? In the showers, where we might be noticed? On your knees because I have told you to go there, sucking my cock until your cheeks bulge with the weight of it?"

Another shiver ran down Riven, delicious tingles down his spine. "Yes." He breathed out the word. "Yes, Eduardo."

Eduardo regarded him with narrowed eyes. "Perhaps I will take you up on your offer some time," he said, careless. "For now, get dressed. Think on what you have done by disobeying me tonight. Come again tomorrow. If I choose to forgive you, I will open the door. Otherwise..." He shrugged. Turning on his side, away from Riven, he snapped off the light. "Find your clothes, and make your way home, boy. I have played enough for one night."

"Eduardo..." Riven reached out one hand, tentative, brushing the Spaniard's bare hip.

Eduardo jerked away from him. "Go home, I said! Tomorrow -- well, we will see what we will see."

* * *

The next day, Riven didn't allow himself to wash off the sweat he'd gathered from his hurried, almost tearful walk home. Neither did he let himself wear short sleeves and cut-offs which might show where Eduardo had made his marks. Those were private. They belonged to him and Eduardo. Instead, he dressed in a turtleneck and jeans, sweated his way through the day out of heat and nervousness, and waited for the night.

Under cover of darkness, he made another quick-step rush back to Eduardo's dorm, keying in the entrance code and rushing past the resident assistant's room. He didn't care if the boy noticed his entrance or not. All he could think about was getting to Eduardo, to see if he'd been forgiven, or if he was still *persona non grata*. If the Spaniard still didn't want him... God, the thought made his heart hurt.

Moist with perspiration, he'd knocked soft as he could on the door. Four times in quick succession, a signal to Eduardo it was him, waiting to see if he'd be allowed in. Sometimes, even when Eduardo wasn't angry, he chose not to answer. On those nights Riven went home disappointed and aching from a hard-on even fumbling masturbation didn't ease. He needed Eduardo's hands on him to let it all go, to reach the pinnacle of white light. Surrender and bliss.

He knocked again, too anxious to wait for Eduardo to answer the first summons, but then forced himself to wait, head down. He thought he heard footsteps. Could he be sure? Was Eduardo coming?

The lock clicked open. Riven exhaled in a great, noisy burst, relieved beyond words. He didn't look up as the door swung wide, but he could see Eduardo's bare legs, the dusting of hair covering them, up to his thighs and... oh, God... his naked cock, already erect.

"So you decided to obey," the Spaniard said, his voice like melting honey. "Have you learned your lesson? Will you do what I say from now on? Obey my whims?"

Eager, Riven nodded.

"Speak, if you will."

"I'll do anything," Riven had said in a rush. "Whatever you want me to do. Just don't kick me out again. I need you. Need you so much."

Eduardo's warm hand had curled around his arm, fingers petting him. "You have pleased me," he said gravely. His other hand came down to stroke the length of his own cock. "Good boys deserve rewards, I think. Do you wish for a reward?"

Water sprang to Riven's mouth. Could he speak?

"Answer me."

"If... if you think I've earned it," he whispered. It was the right answer. He could almost feel the light and warmth of Eduardo's approval sweeping over him in a wave.

"Good boy," Eduardo praised him. "I am naked, and you smell of sweat and other things. Do you remember the shower I spoke of? It is not long after midnight, and people might enter to see us in a stall together. Do you dare come with me and please me there? Answer."

Riven nodded, eager to please.

"Then come." Eduardo took him by the hand and ushered him out into the hallway, naked himself, but unashamed. "We are to be quiet. Let there be nothing heard but the water falling on our heads; let it hide the sounds of your worship; let us move in utter silence. I will undress you, and we will throw those stinking clothes away in the lavatory wastebasket. Then, we will go into a stall and pull the curtain closed. Do you agree? Speak."

Riven nodded, licking his lips. "Yes, Eduardo. Whatever you want."

Fingers tipped his chin up. Eduardo was smiling, his eyes heated with pride and affection. "You obey me so well, when you possess the sense," he said. He took Riven by the arm. "Come. Come with me, be naked, and fall to your knees. If you are good, very, very good, I will take your cock in my own hand when we have finished, and I will stroke you to completion."

Riven shivered. Eduardo's hand on him... love and light... it couldn't be any better. He nodded again, quivering with eagerness.

"Let us go, then." Eduardo tugged him along. "I want your mouth around my cock, performing all the tricks I have taught it. I want you to swallow my come down as if it were nectar, and lick your lips afterwards... and then, we will see if I am pleased enough to favor you in return."

Riven trembled as he let himself be led. "Yes," he whispered. "Yes, Eduardo."

* * *

"Speak. You may speak."

Riven hung back a little, his hand in Eduardo's. They could clasp fingers together there, in the gay section of town. No one would notice or give it a second thought. He'd thought he would die of pleasure when Eduardo had told him so. To be seen as loved in public! His happiness had known no bounds... until he had found out where they were headed.

Instead of inviting Riven into his room or the shower for a BJ or a hand job, Eduardo had appeared dressed in T-shirt, jeans, and a white grin in the middle of his bronzed face.

"Come," he had said, urging Riven along. "I have had an idea. You will love this. Come!"

Riven had followed, obedient to Eduardo's whims. He'd learned his lesson. He followed the Spaniard through winding streets and alley shortcuts, not complaining at the long walk through the campus and town. They'd come to this red-light district at last, and pulled up to a stop in front of a small brick building with bars on the windows and a flashing neon sign: "Tattoos/Piercing."

Eduardo let go of Riven's fingers and turned, hands on his hips, looking annoyed. "What is it? I have told you to speak."

"I... I can't get a tattoo," Riven whispered. "The markers were okay, but --"

"You would get one if I ordered you to," Eduardo informed him. "A pity, but neither of us has the sort of money inking requires. No, I have something else in mind. A hoop through both of your earlobes, and one through each nipple."

Riven stared.

"Well? What is it now?" Eduardo's smile turned a little cruel. "Are you afraid of the pain?"

Riven swallowed. He ducked his head, not daring to meet Eduardo's eyes. "Yes," he whispered, his voice so low he wondered if he had been heard. "Yes. I've seen shows. They use needles. I'm not good with needles. I can't even give blood."

"There is a weakness we must train out of you. I know of many good uses for needles in this world, among which are putting some permanent reminders on your body to tell you each time you look at them, feel them, touch them, who you belong to." Eduardo slunk closer, lifting the collar of Riven's T-shirt in both his hands. "We both know you are mine. This will prove it to me."

"But... it'll hurt." Riven felt himself go crimson with shame.

"Foolish boy. You fear it now because you have not learned to appreciate a little pain. Perhaps I have been too gentle with you." Eduardo tugged Riven's T-shirt a little tighter, giving it a bit of a twist. "We will remedy your fears soon. Sooner, now, with this. You will be pierced because I say it shall happen. You will not flinch nor cry out. Bear the pain like a man and you will see. You will find the white light you love so by obeying me and riding the sting like an ocean wave."

Riven swallowed again. He could trust Eduardo... couldn't he? "Will you hold my hand?" he whispered.

"Do not be foolish. I expect you to please me once we go inside here." Eduardo put his hand on the small of Riven's back, giving him a sharp little push. "Inside, now. Tell the woman what you want. I will pay; I have a little money. Tell them you want me in the room with you, though I will stand across the way and watch. Do you understand?"

Needles. Pain. Piercing his earlobes, Riven thought he could handle, but his nipples? He knew how sensitive those were, thanks to Eduardo. Riven felt the blood thundering through his chest in terror at the thought. But as the impatient smile on Eduardo's face threatened to change into an angry frown, he nodded once, forcing himself to jerk his head, and stepped through the entrance of the body-mod salon...

* * *

"You are special to me, Riven." Eduardo spoke smoothly and coolly as if he were rubbing Riven's back, rather than drizzling cool oil down the cleft of Riven's ass. He had covered his futon with solid black sheets incapable of showing stains, whether spunk or blood, and had taken pleasure in telling Riven so.

Then, Eduardo brought out handcuffs and linked Riven's ankles and wrists together, securing them with a chain to a hook he had mounted in the wall. Riven balanced on his elbows and knees, his genitals high and exposed, though his hard-on had gotten so full it slapped against his belly.

"You will not come until or unless I say so," Eduardo went on. His slim, nimble fingers began to massage the oil between Riven's cheeks. One fingertip circled Riven's virgin hole. "Such a tight pucker," he said on an exhaled breath. "You have never let anyone touch you this way, have you? No one but me? Say it. Tell me the truth I want to hear, or I will be angry. Speak."

Riven shivered. "No one. No one but you."

"Good." Eduardo seemed satisfied. "I would be able to tell. This velvet glove has never been worn before. But oh, how it responds to me." One slick fingertip probed again, then pushed its way inside. Riven winced with the stinging pain as he was breached, but breathed as Eduardo had taught him.

Yes... yes... God, yes... he could feel the peace starting to build. A cock ring, cinched tight, would prevent him from coming, but only with his body. Eduardo had been right when he'd talked about pain being pleasure, and pleasure being pain. Riven should have known to trust him. He knew so much more now, and --

"Ahh!" Riven bucked and let out a low wail as Eduardo's questing fingertip found some spot deep inside him and pressed down. Jolts and skyrockets of bliss shot to his brain and his cock, throbbing in its bonds.

Eduardo chuckled. "Little slut. I knew you would like it. Now, you will like this even more. Breathe for me."

Obedient, Riven inhaled and exhaled as he felt a second finger join the first, stretching him open. It hurt like hell, but at least things were slick with the oil Eduardo had brought. The scent of olives and sunshine filled the air as the Spaniard moved his fingers in and out, every so often scissoring them open to broaden the passage.

"Are you ready?" he whispered after a moment, his voice playful. "Can my Riven take three fingers? If he can, he may be ready for my cock soon. I cannot wait to plunge deep inside your tight slickness, and let you know what a real man feels like. Speak. Tell me what I want to hear."

Riven's hands clenched into fists -- not in anger, but from impatience, struggling to find the white light amid the pain. "Your cock," he panted. "Not three. I want your cock inside me."

"Impatient, are you? But ah, you know what I like to hear." Eduardo withdrew his fingers with one last brush across his sweet spot.

Riven almost whimpered at the loss. He'd been so close to finding a place where he was warm and safe, loved and accepted, approved of and appreciated... the white light, where everything was perfect because of what Eduardo did to his body. He raised himself a little higher, shameless as a cat in heat, asking for it. He could feel his channel, stretched open, needing something to fill it. "Please," he whispered. "Eduardo, please."

"You spoke without permission." Eduardo dealt a stinging slap to one ass cheek. "I would be displeased, but I am inclined to be generous tonight, since it is my cock you beg for. So prettily you ask."

Riven felt the futon shift as Eduardo moved into place behind him, smelled more of the sweet olive oil, and heard the slick sounds of the Spaniard anointing his own cock with the slippery substance. Then, the blunt, wet head of it pressed against his entrance. Pressed, and nothing more. "There is one more thing," Eduardo whispered, his hands roaming over Riven's back. "I would hear you say one more thing before I fuck you into the light and show you what it means to be mine."

Sweat ran down Riven's chest, stinging in the still-raw piercings of his nipples. His head spun. "I don't... I don't understand."

"One word," Eduardo coaxed. "You know what you are to me. I would hear you call me what I am to you. Think hard, Riven. The word will come to your lips."

With a gush of air, it did. "Master," Riven said in relief. His cock gave a mighty twitch, struggling against the ring binding it tight. "Master Eduardo."

Eduardo gave a satisfied hum. "You see? I knew I could teach you all you needed to be perfect for me. You have pleased me, Riven. Now I will please you, and myself in the bargain." He pushed forward, the huge thickness of his cock thrusting inside a blinding pain and an exhilarating bliss all at once. Not stopping for Riven to adjust, he seated himself to the root.

Riven squirmed, biting his lip to keep from crying out, struggling to find the good place he'd been hunting for. Pain... pleasure... pain...

Finally, he found it, as Eduardo said, "You are perfect, Riven. So very perfect for me..."

He began to plunge in and out of Riven's channel, the friction agony and ecstasy at the same time. Riven's mind blurred into pure white light with the bliss of giving in and the wonderfulness of Eduardo's cock in his ass, the Spaniard's hips pumping and his hands clutching at Riven's back.

Yes... yes... yes...

* * *

Riven opened his eyes. He could feel the weight of metal on his chest, cold against his skin. So. The piercings had been done. Phoenix lay beside him, arm underneath Riven's head, supporting him. "Riven," the alien murmured, putting a hand to Riven's cheek. "You are beautiful this way. Kiss me now. Kiss me, and let me taste you, sweet pet..."

Riven's lips opened of their own accord underneath Phoenix's.

But all the same, a tear slipped out and ran down his cheek.

Chapter Seven

Soft fingers traced a path down Riven's cheek. "You cry," Phoenix said quietly, dabbing the tear away. "Why do you weep, Riven? Have you been dreaming again of the past?"

"How -- how did you --"

"When I first took you in, I read it here..." Phoenix touched Riven's temples, then laid his hand over Riven's heart. "And in here, I think you would say. I knew you had been a pet before. You had a pure desire to please buried deep inside you. I thought if you remembered your long-ago relationship with your former master, it might make you happy. Might make you see me in a different light."

Phoenix licked the tear away from his fingertip. "This tastes of pure sorrow. Have I done you a wrong, in unearthing what you had buried so long ago?"

Riven shut his eyes tight. After a moment, he gave a shrug. His mouth opened and closed, but no words came out.

Phoenix studied him intently. "I see," he said, pulling Riven's head down to his chest. No heart beat where it should have, but Riven found the embrace comforting in an odd sort of way. Holding him thus, Phoenix rocked him for several long moments. He hummed under his breath, a strange arrangement of notes. It took Riven a minute to realize it was music. Probably something composed by one of his kind.

Lifting a hand to comb through Riven's hair, Phoenix began to speak. "You are already obeying me, or did you not realize? It came naturally, yes?"

Riven shuddered and gave a small nod against Phoenix's chest.

"You see? You want to obey. It is your nature. Not just because I have made myself over to look like this Eduardo you remember with such clarity. It arouses you. I feel your heart beat faster at my embrace, at my words. Your cock fills, nudging against my leg. The thought of being owned is not repellent to you. You crave it. You need to have a master who directs your steps. The difference between myself and this Eduardo is not so much my being alien to your world. It is this. I will be a *good* master to you."

Riven felt the tears trickling down his cheeks. "Beautiful," Phoenix crooned, "You are so beautiful, broken. I will rebuild you, my Riven. Make you a strong and pampered pet. You will live out your life in luxury, with iced fruits and slaves of your own to see to any needs you have. You were my reward for service on the battlefront, did you know? I have retired, and mean to live out the rest of my days in peace and quiet, on our home planet, where battle has not yet touched -- we struggle to prevent what happened to your Earth from happening to other worlds. In your case, we failed. I grieve its loss, too. Do you believe me? Nod yes or no."

Riven gave a short, jerky nod against Phoenix's chest. The hands petting him, soothing him, and the voice, cradling him in its embrace, all spoke of sincerity. Phoenix had been good to him so far. Why not believe him? What did he have to lose? And what he stood to gain, if he could just take one final step of belief...

"I read you," Phoenix murmured. "There is something you want, pet. What is it? Do not be shy. Tell me what you desire, and if it is in my power, I will make it so."

Riven choked. "Can't -- can't. Not yet."

The fingers resumed their stroking. "You need to put the final pieces of your heart at rest," Phoenix crooned. "You must visit the dream world once again, and see how things ended."

Riven cringed against Phoenix's strong chest, hands clenching at him.

"No, I have decided, you must. See how it ended, and know this: I will never, not ever, do to you what Eduardo did. No matter what temptation, no matter what the cost."

He stroked Riven's temples. "Sleep, now," he murmured. "Sleep, and be at peace. Know even while you relive these things, I hold you safe in my arms…"

And Riven, unable to stop himself, drifted into dreams.

* * *

The visions came as they had before, like the stinging slaps of a paddle.

"You like this, yes?" Eduardo panted, wielding the long strips of leather he had tied to a sturdy handle. Again and again the lashes came down on Riven's back as he lay spread-eagled, chained to the futon. Unable to move or resist. Hard despite himself. Relishing the pain even as he felt blood trickling down his sides and wanted to tell Eduardo, *Stop, stop, stop.*

He hadn't known what a safe word was. Would Eduardo have listened? He could see the blood, and knew what he was doing. The lash came down again, harder. "Faggot," Eduardo spat. "Filthy little queer. Unnatural pervert. You and all your kind tempt me beyond what I can bear, with your tight asses and gleaming chests. You make me do this. You've earned it, slave."

Riven's body wanted to curl up and protect itself. He wanted to shut his ears to the awful words. Eduardo loved him. He'd said so. He *had.*

"*El Diablo!*" Riven heard a thunk as Eduardo cast the crop aside, then a rough, ripping sound as the Spaniard tore open his zipper. He heard the sounds of jeans coming down and being kicked off. Then the futon dipped under extra weight as Eduardo climbed on top of it, behind Riven's ass, lifted high in the air by means of pillows stuffed beneath his hips.

Fingers traced over the dozens of searing marks on his back, slipping in the blood. "You see what you make me do? You must be broken. I will break you, Riven. You will be what I want you to be, because I say so."

Riven had nodded, eager. He would have spoken on his own, but a soft gag prevented him from letting any words out. As Eduardo parted his ass cheeks and thrust the head of his cock, barely lubricated, toward his dry hole, Riven bit down on the material filling his mouth. *Oh, God, oh, God, oh, God --*

But he deserved it. Even if he no longer found the white light, it was his place.

It was all he was worth, and Eduardo was his whole world.

* * *

"Kneel!"

Riven, bare of any stitch, scrambled to his knees on a filthy red-light district bath-house floor. Eduardo had a dangerous-looking stick in his hand, and he knew from experience the Spaniard wouldn't hesitate to use it if he were disobeyed. He spread himself, balancing on his kneecaps as he'd been taught, thighs wide apart. His genitalia hung between his legs, limp and un-aroused. His scrotum had drawn tight up against his body in fear.

"Pah!" Eduardo dealt him a blow with the stick. "You are worthless, Riven. When I call your name, you should be hard and ready for me. It matters not where we are. Walking outside, on those ridiculous fishing trips, in this bathroom. You displease me with your body's lack of willingness."

Another blow. "You will be taught better manners, by whatever means I consider necessary." *Crack!* "And you will prove it. Do you dare look up at me? Eyes down! I have invited guests, tonight. You will perform for me, and then for them, as they please."

Riven's heart beat like a rabbit in his chest. *No. Please, no.*

Eduardo lifted his head. "Come!" he barked.

One by one, they filed in. Some were dressed in jeans and T-shirts, some in leather vests, and all were in pants that showed off the outlines of their goods. Some were pierced, some tattooed. Some male, some female. All carried a whip, crop, or paddle of some kind. All ran their eyes over Riven as if he were a piece of meat, either a delicacy to be savored, or something rotten. No one touched. They formed a ring around him, fencing him in.

"This," Eduardo said, voice cruel and cold, "is a poor slave. See his cock? He disobeys me, his master, with his foolish fears. I have marked him with scars on his back and rings on his chest. He is mine. Mine to play with as I see fit. Yet he does not seem in the mood, does he?" Eduardo reached for a handful of hair and tugged Riven's head back. "Does anyone have a gag upon them? I would not have anyone hear what we do tonight."

A burly man, twice their age, dug a rubber ball gag out of one pocket. It looked old, used before, but Eduardo took it and stuffed it into Riven's mouth, fastening the straps. From his own pocket, he took a cock ring and fitted it onto Riven's penis and balls, tightening it past the point of pain. Riven's mouth opened around the gag in a silent cry.

His words seemed to be a signal. Blows came raining down, all of the men and women in the circle getting a strike in with their weapon of choice. "You see," Eduardo said, after delivering his own knock against Riven's head which left him dizzy. "You will obey. You will please me, and you will please them. All of them. Before this night is through, I will see you broken."

Eduardo unzipped his fly and took out his cock, swollen purple, hard, and massive. Aimed it at Riven's mouth. "You cannot suck," he said, his voice silky. "You must find another way to please me. Please us. Go on, then. Do it!"

Riven raised his manacled hands, shaking hard as an aspen in the wind, and laid them on Eduardo's cock. He shook with fear but did as he'd been taught, jacking him with a fist he tightened under punishment until it suited Eduardo. He wanted to jerk the damn thing off Eduardo's body, but God, those men and women, they'd kill him. Where had Eduardo found them? Was he going to be for anyone to take, whenever they wanted, from then on?

Never again, he swore, straining to brush his distended lips against the tip of Eduardo's cock and feeling hands tighten, painful, in his hair. *Never, never again…*

* * *

Riven hid in his room for a week afterwards. Not going to class. Covering himself with the comforter whenever his roommate was around. Eduardo had a key, and seemed to know when Riven would be alone. He came to Riven's room instead of demanding Riven come to serve him. He always brought a tube of ointment, some fresh bandages, lubricant, and condoms.

"You brought it on yourself," he crooned one day, working antibiotic cream into one of Riven's new marks. "I would not have taught such a hard lesson, Riven, if you had not deserved it. A good slave does what he is told. You had to learn. You see my point, do you not? It was for your own good."

Riven shuddered beneath the touch and said nothing. He hadn't been given permission to speak.

"Good, good," Eduardo murmured, reaching for more of the cream. "Whenever you look at yourself in a mirror, you will remember the lesson you were taught. Obedience, Riven. Obedience at all times. When I ask you to be ready, your body must be ready. I can be gentle, if occasion calls for it, but you must do my bidding when I call. You are my pet, my slave. You do as I tell you, when I tell you."

He put the ointment aside. "My touch, it still excites you, does it not?" He slipped a hand beneath Riven to rub at his cock. Cradled in soft cushions, it responded automatically to his touch. "Ahh, yes," Eduardo breathed. "That is what I like to feel. You have pleased me."

It's not me, Riven wanted to cry out. *It's just my body. It doesn't know any better.* But Eduardo had brought a crop with him…

"This hungry little hole, it wants to be fucked, does it not?" Eduardo parted Riven's cheeks to probe at his tightly closed anus. "I will use the slick, this time, and we will both enjoy what I do."

No. No. No!

Riven heard other noises -- a tube of lubricant clicking open, and Eduardo shucking his pants. Crawling up behind Riven, Eduardo smeared a thin layer of the slippery stuff over his hole, and, from the sound of it, a hefty dollop on his own cock. "Speak," Eduardo said, rubbing his fingers across the sores and lesions and cigarette burns on Riven's back. "Say it, my slave. You want me. You want my cock in you. Out loud, slave. Out loud, as I have taught you."

Riven swallowed around a dry, dry throat. "Yes, Master," he croaked. "Fuck me, Master. Make me yours again. Please."

"Good boy." Eduardo thrust two fingers into Riven's hole, pumping them in and out. "See how good I am to you? I even prepare you, first."

It hurt. It ached. It burned. But Riven's cock began to strain against the soft plastic ring Eduardo had insisted he wear all the time, not just when they were together.

Eduardo's slippery hand came around and pumped him, ignoring Riven's soft cry of pain when he bumped a bruised scrotum and scraped against raw thighs. "You will love this," he promised. "Rough and fast. I will ride you like a stallion, Riven. When I am done, you will thank me for the honor. Do you understand?"

Riven shut his eyes. At least Eduardo couldn't see his face. "Yes, Master."

The tip of Eduardo's cock began pushing into his hole. "There is my boy, yes. Good, Riven, good..."

* * *

Over it was over it was over oh thank god thank god dear god what do I do now he's gone oh god he's gone...

Riven sat in a corner of the shower room, hunched into a little ball. The water beating down on him had gone cold a while ago. How long he'd been in there, he didn't know.

Eduardo's gone he didn't even say goodbye he left me he left me all alone oh God...

Riven had gone to the Spaniard's room earlier, dressed in a black turtleneck and tight black jeans, just the way Eduardo liked him, hiding all the marks. He'd knocked, their special knock, the code for "Master, please Master, let me in."

No answer.

He'd knocked again. Still no answer. The rap sounded hollow, as if it echoed against a great emptiness. Panic began to fill Riven's chest. Eduardo -- where was Eduardo? Had those other leather-clad men and women taken him, too? Forgetting his manners, heedless of whether someone might hear, he raised his fist and thumped hard, leaving a smear of blood behind from his scraped knuckles.

A boy stuck his head out of the room next door. Tousled-haired and cranky from being woken up, he made a face at Riven. "What the fuck's goin' on, man?"

"Ed -- Eduardo," Riven stammered. "Do you know where he is?"

"Exchange freak? Gone."

Gone. Gone gone gone gone gone...

"What?" Riven stared at the boy, as if he could make it not true.

"Yeah. He made a big show out of it. This big bunch of leather freaks came and moved him out. Damn, some people are sick. They just about licked his boots, you know? Hell if I know what's gonna happen. He said somethin' about quitting school. He found something better." The boy rubbed at his eyes. "So yeah, he's gone. You gonna pound on an empty door all night or can the rest of us get some sleep?"

"No -- no." Riven let his hand fall to his side. "I'm sorry. I didn't mean -- I didn't know."

"Yeah, well, you do now." The boy had made a sour face. "Man, I'm glad he's gone. Damn horndog never did anything but fuck, anyway. Day and night."

He had others, others when I wasn't there, when he said I belonged to him, just him.

"I'm sorry," Riven had said again, his voice flat. Without another word, he'd turned and left. Gone back to his own dorm, to the showers, and stripped off every stitch. He'd fallen underneath the spray in the "spread" position until his muscles forced him back on his ass. He clutched himself around the knees, rocking back and forth.

Gone. Gone gone gone gone gone gone gone...

"Hey, what are you -- Jesus, man! Hey! Someone!"

Riven heard the yelling as if from a distance. It didn't matter. Nothing mattered. He'd never find the white light again.

Never see Eduardo. He should be glad -- God, he knew he should -- but he felt so empty inside. Like he'd been scooped out.

Hands were on him. Gentle hands, tilting him forward.

"What happened to him? Was he in a fight?"

"I don't think so."

"Then --"

"Look, go to my room, okay? Get the emergency number for the campus counseling center. And call 9-1-1. Some of these are infected."

The resident assistant. He was there? Riven gave a little moan and folded further into himself. A wet hand came down on his shoulder, trying to avoid the bruises, but there just wasn't anywhere unmarked to touch. It drew back. After a moment, Riven became aware of a guy around his age in a sopping pair of boxer shorts and a T-shirt, crouching in front of him.

"Are you -- are you my new Master?" he croaked.

The RA drew back. "Am I what?"

Riven leaned forward, hands desperate, scrabbling for the boy's cock through his molded shorts. "He left me. Let me please you. I'll do anything. Just don't go away, please don't go away!"

"God!"

Riven found himself being pushed back.

Someone turned off the water. Riven gave a huge shudder, folding into himself. Rejected again. For what? Wasn't he good enough?

Not good enough. Couldn't keep him.

Didn't want him. He hurt me.

Needed him. His smile. His arms. His touch.

Don't know what to do.

Help me?

Help me?

* * *

"Riven. Riven, wake up. Please, my Riven." Thumbs stroked at the corners of Riven's eyes, dabbing away the tears. "Your weeping cuts at my very soul. Had I known this would be so painful for you, I would never have put you through such an experience."

Riven opened his eyes. Not-Eduardo's face gazed down at him, warm brown eyes full of compassion and sorrow. Those so-familiar, yet unfamiliar hands petted him. "Only a dream, Riven. A very vivid one, seen as if you relived it, but nothing more than a shadow from your past."

Riven opened and closed his mouth.

"I dispense with the rule stating you may not speak unless instructed to. It only causes you more pain." Phoenix dropped a kiss against his temple. "Such is not my purpose, Riven. So very far from it."

"I said," Riven choked, struggling for air, "once I'd been through all the doctors, and all the therapy, I said never again. No one would ever have me as their pet or their slave again."

"And yet here you find yourself. No wonder you fought so hard, so long." Phoenix rocked him. "I have done you a great wrong, Riven. I looked inside your heart and saw there was the willingness to serve, and the desire to please. From my reading, I assumed you would be glad to become a pampered pet. But no, I was wrong. You are your own man, and you have fought hard for it."

Phoenix sighed. "I have so much to learn. I must study, from books, and from you, if you will teach me. I own you, Riven. Your world is gone, and you have been labeled as my property. I cannot change your status. But you... I see now you must be won to be mastered. Am I right?"

Riven shivered.

Phoenix's hands kept stroking him, gentle, as if he were a kitten. "There are many things planned for refugees from your world," he said after a moment. "Some, who went to crueler masters, will be used for hard labor. Some for breeding. I can feel within you even as I say the words how wrong you feel this is. You are like us. Not dumb animals, as many of my kind would assume. You have minds and wills of your own."

He paused. "There are three words repeating in your mind. Safe. Sane. Consensual. Please, will you explain to me what you mean by this?" Phoenix's arms tightened around him, but gently. Not to pin down, but to huddle close.

Riven licked his lips. "It's what I was taught," he said, voice halting. "By those doctors I told you about. They said there was nothing wrong with me. It was Eduardo. Relationships like ours have to be sane, safe, and consensual. He made me a real slave, not a partner who agreed to play games with him. He broke me."

Phoenix ran his hand across Riven's shoulder. "This Eduardo, he was an evil man. I have known many of my own kind with the same bent. They must tear one down in order to lift themselves up, and far too often they are glorified for it. Not I, Riven, not I. Safe, sane, and consensual. These are good words."

He nestled his chin into the crook of Riven's neck. "See how much you have already taught me? As I have said, I cannot change this fact: you belong to me. But your face is one I have dreamed of, with its beauty, as well as your body, marked though it may be with this Eduardo's scars. I wondered at them as I laid my own protective sigils on your skin. I should have asked. Will you forgive me?"

Riven shut his eyes tight.

"Perhaps in time." Phoenix resumed his rocking. "It is in my heart to love you, Riven. To be a partner with you. I know you crave the white light. You thirst for approval as a flower does rain -- yes, there is rain on my world, and there are flowers, too, in abundance. I have gardens you might dally in as long as you please. Knowing what I know now, it is also in my heart to wait until you are ready. Will you grant me this much -- a chance? Let me show you how well I can love you, different though we may be, and I will show you what it means to have a true dominant and submissive partnership. As I learn, I will teach you. And learn I will, from all who are safe and sane and willing to teach." He pressed his cheek against Riven's. "All I ask for is a chance. Will you give it to me?"

Riven lay still for a long moment. *So much to take in.* His world, gone. His body, owned. But... by someone who seemed to care for him. Care enough to be patient, and willing to accommodate his fears and desires. Was it possible he could be what Phoenix wanted? Could Phoenix be what he craved?

Slowly, ever so slowly, he nodded his head. His lips stayed closed until he remembered he was allowed to speak. "Phoenix," he said, tasting the name. "Yes. Yes, if you'll do one thing for me."

A light hand caressed his hair. "You have but to name it."

"Two things, then."

"Name them."

"Please, stop talking like *him*. Talk like me. Learn what sounds natural from the way I speak."

Phoenix pondered for a moment. "I'll try. Is this better? Not so formal?"

Riven felt his muscles, tense to the point of pain, begin to relax. The entire cadence of Phoenix's voice had changed, grown softer and warmer. "It's good. And... please... don't *look* like him. You can read my mind. Read what it is you think I'd like, and look like that. Not Eduardo. Anyone but him."

"Oh, Riven." Lips touched his cheek. "There's so much for you to teach me. But together, we'll learn, won't we?"

Riven trembled. Still, he nodded. This was his life, now. He could sense Phoenix would keep his word. Sometimes you could just tell. "Do you like me?" he asked, vulnerable as any boy. "Really *like* me?"

"I love you. I wouldn't have chosen you otherwise." Phoenix turned their heads so he could reach for Riven's mouth with his own. His tongue slipped out and traced Riven's lower lip.

Riven's eyes fluttered shut as he lost himself. Phoenix's kiss was like being reborn. A glimmer of the white light passed behind his eyes, a sense of warm surrender, like falling into the sun-heated ocean on a summer's day, innocent and free, willing and wonderful. He drew back. "Phoenix," he whispered. "Thank you."

Riven opened his eyes -- and gasped. Eyes, still warm and brown, looked back at him, but the face had changed utterly. Far more beautiful, like a fallen angel, aquiline and fine-boned, it had full lips swollen from their kiss, smiling at him. His body, too, had changed. Fragile, yet strong.

"Does this please you?" Phoenix asked, leaning forward to bump his forehead against Riven's. "You can overpower this form, if you ever need to. Do, if I overstep my bounds. I will never come to you otherwise. Together, we will find the purity, the white light you have sought. Absolute pleasure. We can find it together. I'm sure of it. Just... say it one more time, Riven? Say the words, so I'm sure of them."

Riven gazed up at the slender man. His cock began to stir and fill. "You're beautiful," he whispered. "Yes. Yes, Phoenix. We'll do it together."

"Then will you take a gift from me?" Phoenix leaned over to the pile of jewelry and sifted through the shining mass. Finally, he drew out a long, long, long chain, decorated with blunt-tipped silver roses and thorns. "To decorate you. Not to mark you as mine, but to augment what already makes you handsome as one of your gods in my mind."

Riven stared at Phoenix for a long moment before nodding. Phoenix's return smile felt like sunshine, warming him all the way through.

"Lie down," the alien directed. "On your back. I won't use the device on the cushion this time. Your piercings have already healed. You can take them out, if you want, until you're ready, but will you make me happy by leaving them in? In, and decorated with this..."

Phoenix slid the chain through both heavy hoops on Riven's nipples, then around his throat, where it dangled like a necklace. Another length of it dangled down his back, and one came forward, reaching down to his cock and balls. That one he left loose. "We'll fasten this when -- if -- you're ever ready," Phoenix said, letting it swing free. "Not until you trust me. I'll do all I can, everything in my power, to make that happen."

Looking up at the beautiful creature who had already stolen his way -- a little, just a little -- into his heart, Riven nodded. "Yes," he repeated himself, feeling his lips curve into an almost unfamiliar smile. "Yes. Kiss me?"

Leaning down, Phoenix did. And like the bird for which he was named, the past burst into flames, burning to ash. Something new and wonderful broke from the pyre.

Nothing would ever be the same again.

No. It would be better.

Willa Okati

Willa Okati is one hundred percent in love with all things vampire and supernatural. However, she's an even bigger fan of stories that feature beautiful men exploring their desires for one another. Casually known as the "blue-haired, tattooed wench" among Changeling folks, she lives for the fun of acting just as young as she feels. She'd love for you to visit her website at http://www.willaokati.com, join her reader's loop for fun and chatter at willa_okati@yahoogroups.com, or look for Willa at http://blog.myspace.com/willaokati. Happy reading!

Waiting For You

Elayne S. Venton

Chapter One

Ty probed her eyes with a hot gaze as he tightened the knot that bound her wrist to the tubular bed frame.

A chill snaked down her naked body. Careful to hide the uncertainty running through her mind, Reeva stared at her lover's determined expression, his dark brows furrowed in concentration, lips pressed in a firm line, eyes slightly narrowed and staring deep into her soul. Perspiration beaded between her breasts.

Heaven help her, she'd never given any man this much power over her body. Why had she submitted to a mercenary like Tybirius West?

Because he made her pulse pound in her throat, that's why.

Unable to use either hand now, she clenched and unclenched her fists. She swallowed hard when his brown hands skimmed down her pale legs, asserting just enough pressure to let her know he meant business, until his warm palms settled around her ankles.

Here we go. Butterflies swirled in her belly. Her heels squeaked across the vinyl mattress pad as he split her legs in a wide V. Instinctively, she squeezed her vaginal muscles, closing off access to her feminine core. When he raised a brow at her stiff legs, she gradually relaxed.

This was crazy! She expected wild, mindless sex from Ty befitting his forceful personality, not this slow, calculated imprisonment of her body. The hindrance of her freedom unsettled her, but that wasn't the only reason her heartbeat thumped faster. Her darkest fantasies featured sex with her captor, and Ty treaded dangerously close to sordid desires that both frightened and enthralled her.

"I'm not going to hurt you," he rumbled in a low voice, wrapping a plush cuff around her ankle.

Maybe not, but the uncompromising gleam in his eyes shot anxiety through her. Her warrior instincts screamed at her to resist him while the curious sexual being inside her flushed body demanded she lie still. When he stretched the cuff's strap down to the frame, she kicked out reflexively. Surrender didn't come easily.

He caught her foot centimeters from his face, unfazed by her reaction. No harsh retort. No disapproving stare. Only a slight shake of his head. He lowered her leg and set her heel on the sleeping pad.

Guilt oozed into her mind. No fair backing down now. She'd agreed to have sex by his rules. Not that he'd given her much choice. He said he knew what she secretly desired, and he'd prove it.

Okay, she'd give him one chance his way.

With a soothing murmur, he slid his palm up her calf and pressed her knee flat. The way he looked at her stirred the fluttering feeling in her belly. "Reeva," he whispered huskily, followed by velvety kisses sweeping along the inside of her thigh. "Relax."

Higher and higher he glided his lips, dusting kisses closer to the moist heat gathered between her legs. Time slowed as he neared the top of her leg. Each succulent caress of his lips lingered now, gently stroking and sucking her sensitive flesh, leaving a tingling trail behind.

Wet heat flooded her sex. Stars, he fired her blood! She slowly inhaled as he neared her swollen pussy.

His tongue snaked out and slowly swirled a wet circle in the dip between her leg and mound. His warm breath puffed over her dark red bush.

Go on. Lick my pussy. Ever so slightly, she shifted her hips toward his mouth. *Now. Right there.*

But he wasn't so easily enticed. He skipped over her dewy lips and trickled sensuous kisses down the other thigh.

Oh, no, oh… How she ached for his mouth on her heated center. A soft groan escaped, unbidden.

He raised his gaze and gave her a lazy, confident smile. "Patience, Reeva." His hand glided down her calf to her ankle once more.

A puddle of languid desire, she lay her head back on the pillow and let him immobilize her.

Once he tethered her to his satisfaction, he stood at the side of the cot, arms crossed over his chest, silently looking his fill. She rolled her head to the side and watched desire deepen the hue of his eyes from frothy chocolate to sultry brown. During the last few months aboard the starfighter, she'd caught brief snatches of him observing her the same way, and it always left her mouth dry.

Now that the battle had been won and they had several hours' transit time before they reached the nearest space station, she'd finally learn the depths of his passion.

Sadness banded her heart. She'd never met anyone like him. A born leader the troops called him, and after fighting by his side, she had to agree. Fearless, driven, relentless, and a risk taker. He amazed her. Now and then, he scared the hell out of her.

The air circulator hummed louder and a cool breeze swept over her, teasing her skin. Mesmerized by him, she waited, her gaze dropping to the impressive bulge in his combat pants. Liquid heat pooled between her legs, scenting the air with musky perfume. *Come on and show me what you've got*, she told him with her eyes.

His lips twisted into a self-assured smirk, and he studied her longer, waiting for who knew what.

"You'd better not walk out the door and leave me like this," she snapped, breaking the long silence.

A wicked grin spread across his face. "Sweetheart," he drawled, "I'm not leaving you for a long, long time." He tugged his sleeveless shirt over his smoothly shaven head, flexing massive biceps, forearm muscles and pecs. Hard-packed abs rippled as he flung the shirt to the floor.

Boldly, her gaze roamed. Her mouth watered as she scanned his dark, solid, delectable body.

He plopped a heavy combat boot on the side of the cot and flicked the buckles open. The loud snap cast tremors down her spine. With the boot tongue loosened, he dropped his foot to the floor and toed it off, his gaze never leaving hers. Thrusting the other boot up onto the bed, he repeated the process. He rolled his socks off his long feet, tucked the thick wads of synthetic cotton into the boot tops, and nudged the boots beneath the cot. The heavy leather fell to the side with a dull *thunk*.

Sliding his large calloused fingers into his waistband, he popped open the closure, and then shoved the durable fabric down his heavy thighs. Goliath, the squadron's nickname for his giant black cock, sprung out, tall and proud. Reeva swallowed, wondering if she could handle him.

Ty stepped out of his pants and kicked them aside. He sank one knee onto the side of the cot. "Are you ready for me, beautiful Medusa?" Bracing one arm above her head on the pillow, he leaned down and kissed her on the forehead.

Leisurely, he brushed feather light kisses over her temple and cheek, pausing over her mouth and then passing over it to press another tender kiss on the opposite cheek. He skimmed his other hand up her ribs, cupping his warm, broad palm beneath the swell of her rounded breast.

Reeva stared at his dark face, studying the tiny bumps on his freshly-shaven jaw, her pulse tripping twice as fast as her carefully measured breaths. His nostrils flared whenever he neared her parted lips, tempted to be sure but holding back. His control surprised her. She expected a rough taking, no holds barred. After all this bondage, she looked forward to something a little kinky, in fact. Instead, the only concession to touching her in a sexual way played out by stroking a gentle arc with his thumb across her breast. The simple caress fired her blood faster than she anticipated.

But dammit, she'd waited a long time to feel him move inside her. Why didn't he get to it?

"I'm ready, Ty," she breathed, rolling her hips upward.

"Hmm." He abandoned her breast and slowly slid his palm down her belly. His moist breath puffed above her ear. "I'll be the judge of that." His rough fingertips spanned her bushy mound. He dipped his middle finger between her swollen lips and stroked the dewy inner folds.

Oh, sweet torment! She sucked in her breath as one thick finger slid deep inside. "Mmm. Wet," he whispered against her parted lips. A second finger joined the first, flowing in and out in a sensual glide.

Her nipples drew taut. Keen on crushing him to her chest, she tugged up on her bindings. The movement jiggled her breasts.

"Very nice." He planted a kiss on the inner curve of her left breast. "Let me see that again." He fingered her deeper, his knuckles bumping the outer edges of her cunt.

Eyelids fluttering closed in ecstasy, she bit her lower lip to hold back a groan. Once more she struggled against her restraints, not out of frustration but because, astonishingly, squirming in helpless captivity fired her blood.

Ty laved a wet ring around one taut nipple.

Electricity splintered through her breast and bolted straight into her core. "Gods! Stop teasing me and fuck me, West."

He chuckled at her impatience. "An hour ago, you threatened my life if I tried to 'jump your bones' without a little warm up. Make up your mind, Medusa."

"I'm feeling warm enough, thank you."

He trailed moist kisses down the side of her throat. "When you get hot, let me know."

Chapter Two

Major Reeva Medusa woke from her combat nap with a start.

The stars in the expansive black sky above her had barely moved across the sky since she'd closed her eyes. No menace loomed over her -- always a good sign. Hand on the laser pistol strapped to her leg, she lay motionless in her cramped rocky hideout and listened for the disturbance that roused her. Strange predatory creatures inhabited the planet Earth, including humans, perhaps the most dangerous of all. She hated to be caught unaware.

Owls hooted, coyotes barked, and wings fluttered through the dark desert night, undisturbed. The lizard that had been sitting on top of a nearby rock remained. Her thudding heartbeat slowed. Nothing around her had disturbed her sleep. She swiped her damp palms over her snug pants. She'd been dreaming about Ty again.

How had she ever let him talk her into being tied up like that? In previous relationships, sexual dominance depended on her and her partner's mood, but it never progressed into bondage. Ty challenged her to push herself beyond her comfort zone. Surprisingly, his bondage game really turned her on. There was something to be said for being the center of attention. She'd never been so thoroughly pleasured.

Too bad their steamy affair only lasted a few weeks. Combat wreaked havoc with relationships. A warrior's agenda -- fight hard, play when you can, if you can, and move on to the next assignment.

Muffled voices in the prison yard below snapped her back to the present. Camped on this rocky ledge since sunset studying their defenses, she hadn't seen anyone enter or exit except for a changing of the guards. Grabbing her night vision binoculars, she stretched up high enough to see over the top of a rock and spy below.

The target seemed almost too easy to access. One squat building set in a narrow canyon, its exterior designed to meld into the rock wall behind it, contained one door, no windows, and no visible signs of high-tech surveillance. One guard patrolled the perimeter. Their main defense relied on the force field surrounding all entry points, invisible to the naked eye but not her infrared scanner. No wonder her commander sent her in alone. She'd infiltrated enemy strongholds ten times more secure.

She panned back to the two men conversing out front. No problem. She could handle two at a time. A smile played on her lips when her mind twisted her words into a sexual connotation. *Focus!*

Oh, no. Shock zapped her in the chest. It couldn't be him. Not here. She increased the zoom on her binoculars. Da-amn. The clear view of the tall, powerfully built warrior shot aching desire right between her legs. Heat rose up her neck. Blood pounded in her ears. No. *No. NO.* Why was Tybirius defending an *enemy* outpost?

The Bujirian laser rifle cradled in his arms snuffed out the joy of seeing him again. Traitorous mercenary! She blew out a breath of frustration. Ty put a major snag in the rescue operation, not only because he knew all her tricks and her weaknesses, but because her brain turned to mush in his presence.

He glanced up, as if he sensed her hiding among the rocks high above the cliff face. One look at his rugged face and the old sizzling attraction blazed. Moonlight reflected off the bulky contours of his bare chest and arms. The baggy desert camouflage pants he wore barely disguised the heavy musculature of his thighs. What she wouldn't give to run her hands over his brawny body again and feel his cock grow hard against her belly. She mentally shook her head, agitated by the impact he had on her.

Her fingers tightened around her night-vision binoculars. Forget the past. The Tybirius West she knew no longer existed. He'd gone rogue, become the enemy. She'd take him out without regret. If she caught him by surprise, he wouldn't have a chance against the power of a Medusa.

She could take these guys out with her eyes closed.

Well, not literally. She relied on her hypnotic eyes to immobilize the enemy. For thousands of years, Earthlings considered her kind a myth, but that was before interstellar travel. Many learned the truth the hard way. Those who provoked a Medusa discovered a single glance into one's concentrated stare constricted their muscles, holding them in place, sometimes forever.

Controlled properly, her supernatural hold on any prison guards she encountered would last long enough for her to free the hostages and get out. That was the beauty of this plan. No firepower required. All she needed to do was to get close enough to look the adversary in the eye.

The darkness made using her hypnotic eyesight more difficult, but daylight brought unbearable temperatures. She must strike soon.

Ty slapped the guard on the back and returned to the building. "It's now or never," she whispered to the lizard sitting on a nearby rock. The creature raised its head and blinked at her as if it understood. After taking a long swig of water, she hid her night goggles and other supplies in the rock crevice. If all went well, she'd be back to retrieve them in the blink of an eye. Okay, in the blink of her victims' eyes.

Painting on a harried expression, she wound down the steep gravelly cliff side as noisily as possible.

"Oh my gods! Civilization!" She stumbled toward the force field as if she didn't know it existed.

"Halt!" the guard called out.

Reeva wobbled to a stop. "I need help!" she called across the dark distance. "Today's electrical storm knocked out my track vehicle's GPS system. I'm lost. I've been following your faint signal for hours. Please." She held out her palms in supplication. "All I need is a directional microchip and I'll be back on my way. Can you help me?"

He tucked in his chin and grumbled beneath his breath. Hopefully, he wasn't using the mic hooked over his ear to call in additional troops. Although she could handle a group, her ability to immobilize others worked best one on one.

"Hands high above your head. Move slowly until I tell you to stop," he growled. Using his firearm as a pointer, he directed her left, exactly where she suspected the force field was thin enough to cross.

Reeva stepped gingerly over the rocky ground. Static ruffled her hair as she passed through the force field.

"Stop," the guard ordered gruffly.

Reeva obeyed. The guard flashed a light over her, taking a moment to admire her snug sleeveless shirt and combat shorts before he strode forward, weapon raised, obviously intending to take the pistol from her side. He probably planned a thorough pat-down too. *Not in this lifetime, scumbag.* She watched him approach, step by confident step.

"Do you like what you see?" she asked, frustrated that his roaming gaze didn't rise above her chest. A sharp soldier watched the enemy's eyes.

Eyebrows arched, he glanced up. *Mmmpht.* Done. One lifelike statue -- man caught mid-stride. Not one of her best works of art. She shrugged and pushed him over so he'd be less noticeable, then raced past him. Flattened beside the door, she waited to see if back-up had been called.

Sure enough, the metal portal slid open. Another guard stood inside, weapon ready, poised in a defensive position beside the open door. His gaze scanned the prison yard. Before he discovered the immobilized guard sprawled on the ground, she raised her hands in surrender and stepped into the entry light where he could see her. The shift in position lifted her shirt above her belly, and his eyes widened at the nest of hissing snakes tattooed on her belly. Unlike his guard-buddy, he obviously understood its meaning. He took a step back. Still, his fearful gaze darted up to her face. That's all it took. The guard stiffened into a flesh and bone sculpture.

Reeva darted around him. Recessed lights high in the ceiling dimly illuminated the hallway ahead. Clearly though, no one else was in sight. She scuttled down the hall, hugging the wall, following the boisterous sounds of a large crowd. At the corner, she snuck a quick look for more guards before inching forward toward the steps descending below ground.

The noise level grew louder. Colored lights flashed through an oval hole in the wall. Her footsteps faltered. The screams and groans coming from below she expected, but laughter? Hell, it sounded like an orgy down there.

More cautious now, she peeked through the open casement. She blinked and took another look. Wasn't that Nick Starlight, the most decorated hero in the Septar Triangle? And Charlene Tory, the brilliant warfare strategist, rubbing up against him?

A screaming siren rent the air and the crowd below froze. Blinding white light flooded the hallway where she stood. "Aah!" She thrust an arm across her face. Her eyes burned and watered.

"Surrender, Major Medusa."

Reeva spun toward the voice. *Oh, shit. Tybirius.* She couldn't see him, but she recognized his deep, commanding voice. He'd spoken those exact words to her on several, very sultry, occasions. *You will obey my every command. You will not question my orders. You will learn obedience, Reeva, and be rewarded beyond your wildest dreams.* Desire crashed over her in waves. Oh gods. Oh gods.

His boot heels thumped nearer.

Squinting into the glaring light, she pulled her weapon, and froze. She couldn't fire. At this range, the laser would burn a hole right through her lover's gut.

Cold-blooded murder wasn't her style, and she couldn't see if he held a weapon on her.

Crap! Where had her warrior instincts fled? Neutralize him!

He stopped nearby. She could smell his musky scent, sense the size of him, hear him breathe, but she couldn't see him, dammit! Before she could formulate a new plan, a hot pain stabbed her in the belly. "Wha --?" She clutched her stinging midriff. He'd shot her!

Her legs wobbled. Colors swirled behind her eyelids.

Sonofabitch! Why had she ever mooned over such a cold-hearted man?

Just before consciousness faded to black, strong hands gripped her shoulders.

"About time you showed up," Ty whispered against her ear.

Chapter Three

Reeva's naked body tingled as the numbing drug wore off, leaving her feeling bloated and weighted down. In reality, she hung in the air suspended upside down by a harness. Wide bands wrapped around her thighs and waist, and another circled below her breasts. Short vertical strips stretched between them. Another strip rested between her breasts and then separated into two shoulder straps that reconnected at the back. Metal links connecting the front pieces pressed into her skin while the back links angled away, held by whatever suspended her in mid-air. Her legs were drawn up behind her, the right ankle cuff secured to her right wrist and the left ankle cuff secured to her left wrist. Worse, a dark mask covered her eyes so she couldn't use them as a weapon.

She was screwed. Or soon to be screwed. Goose bumps danced down her arms.

Stupid, stupid, stupid! She should've anticipated a trap. If she shut down this operation, someone -- possibly Ty -- would lose hefty profits, and a clever outlaw never took chances.

Cocking her head, she envisioned her surroundings. The gurgle of falling water echoed around the humid chamber, giving her the sense of a large space. A cavern with a stream? Based on the outpost's location, built into a canyon wall, she must be underground.

Several pairs of boots clanged down nearby metal steps. Reeva lifted her head, letting them know she wasn't an unconscious rag doll.

"Ah, she's awake," a familiar, yet unidentifiable, male voice announced. A smooth hand skimmed up her bent leg. "And bound as you promised."

Reeva nudged him away with the outside of her knee. "Why are you doing this to me?"

"Stuff the innocent act, Major Medusa," he said, stroking her butt cheek. "We know you're here on assignment."

Reeva ground her teeth. "You're wrong."

A short distance away, Ty chuckled. "Don't argue, Reeva. It's a waste of breath."

The sound of his deep, rumbling voice made her heart pound. Accustomed with following Ty's direction as both a member of his battle group and as his lover, she automatically complied. The twinge of defiance that jumped to the forefront of her mind stalled when she heard him step closer.

Until she discovered their agenda, she'd keep mum.

Ty tugged on her bindings, most likely making sure they were secure. "You must've had a hell of a trek." He probed her tender shins with gentle fingers. "I used a med-stick to promote healing on those nasty scrapes. The soreness should disappear in a few more hours. I tied your ankles back so we don't accidentally bump your shins when we fuck the hell out of you."

We? A hot flush spread across her chest and up her neck. Did they both plan to take her at the same time? Her earlier naughty thought about handling two at once smacked her between the eyes.

Ty slipped his hands beneath her arms, pulling her upright, which eased the strain on her back. "Let's make her vertical. She's no good to us with a sore spine."

"All right," the mystery man replied. Cables whirred as they adjusted, raising her shoulders and dropping her hips until she could hold her head up without straining her neck muscles. She still leaned forward at a slight downward angle, but at least all the blood stopped rushing into her head. A series of clicks locked the cables in place.

"You know, whatever you do, I'm going to end up kicking your ass, Tybirius."

The other male snorted. "Licking his ass, more likely."

"Who is your obnoxious sidekick?" she asked, lifting her lip in derision.

"You remember Kit Passo, don't you?"

The hot weapons specialist from the planet Moria? The memory of an attractive humanoid warrior with thick black hair flowing to his shoulders and lightning bolts tattooed on his forearms flashed through her mind. His white skin had a bluish cast that offset his deep blue eyes. He reminded her of a vampire.

Although Kit's every thought revolved around sex, she liked him. His overblown ego amused her, and she'd secretly wondered how he *really* performed in bed. On top of that, in a battle crisis, he worked miracles. She hated to think he'd defected too.

"Hello, Major. You look scrumptious all trussed up and ready to be fucked."

That sounded like Kit, cocky and horny. "What are you doing in the company of a mercenary, Passo? I thought you were dedicated to the New World Freedom Foundation."

"I'm taking a break." Approaching her from behind, he stepped between her knees, slid his hands over her shoulders and cupped her breasts. A prickly sensation trailed the flowing contact.

Reeva held her breath. A Morian's touch could bestow great pleasure or sting to kill.

"Ni-ice," he said, caressing her breasts and rubbing his rigid erection against her backside. "It's about time we got together." Passo licked the outline of her ear. "I can't wait to sink my cock into your pretty ass."

A spasm of pleasure in her cunt caught her by surprise. Reeva jerked her head aside.

Passo chuckled at her defiance. "I never understood why you didn't fawn over me like the Earth women. I'm a legend among their kind, you know." He circled her nipple with his fingertip, leaving a burning tingle behind. The nub instantly peaked. "It doesn't matter. I've finally got you where I want you."

"Stop acting like a shithead, Passo," Ty snapped. "This is for her, not you."

Passo grumbled and defiantly bumped his rigid penis against her ass. "Right." He took a small step away from her and then dug his thumbs into her back and kneaded the tense muscles in her lower back. "You're going to love this, Reeva."

Ty gently squeezed her shoulder. "If you feel any pain in your wounds, let me know."

Despite the soothing backrub, anger sizzled along her nerves, mostly anger at herself for stumbling into this situation. "You shouldn't have wasted your time fixing me up since we're all about to be blown to pieces," she snarled. "If I don't disengage the explosive timer, your enterprise is going to be a pile of rubble."

"Thanks for the warning." The velvety cadence of his voice made her burn for him. A kiss brushed her temple in a spine-tingling caress. "But I know you better than that. You're bluffing. You wouldn't risk the lives of everyone here by blowing up the complex." His lips drifted over her mouth in a gentle whisper. "Would you?"

She clenched her fists. Only Ty would suspect she'd lie about a bomb threat.

The moist heat of his breath cascading over her lips melted her bones. To counter the sensation, she tugged at the cord binding her wrists to her ankles. "I've hardened since you left."

"Ha! Making mistakes is what I heard."

"Lies," she snapped. The recent gamut of lost battles by the Alliance had more to do with the enemy's strategic and technological advances than her minor slip-ups.

"You're my captive, aren't you?" he asked with a smile in his voice.

She clenched her teeth. Okay, she may have been a little distracted lately.

Had she subconsciously dropped her guard to ensure her capture by a man she couldn't get out of her mind? More than once in the months since she'd last seen him, she'd imagined Ty pinning her against the wall, her arms held high, her breasts heaving in surprise. With a victorious smirk, he'd slip his big cock into her sopping pussy, pushing hard, stretching her, filling her. She'd groan, loving every minute of it, pretending she didn't.

Then he'd fuck her good, plunging in and out, banging her ass against the wall until she panted hard on the cusp of orgasm.

Oh, gods. She clenched her thighs together, pushing away the building desire, and her legs bumped up against Passo. She'd forgotten his presence, overlooked the relaxing caresses at the base of her spine.

Ty grasped a hank of her short, curly hair and slowly pulled her head back as far as it would go. "It's all right, baby. I've missed you as much as you've missed me."

She swallowed, her heartbeat thundering in her chest, wanting him to stoke the smoldering coals inside.

No! Not now when they fought on opposite teams. "Let me go, Ty."

For the briefest moment, he hesitated. "Not yet." He plundered her mouth, his tongue probing deep and retreating.

Her breath caught in her throat. No one fired her passion as quickly as Ty. He had a way of making her forget everything except him. It took a lot of willpower not to respond. She considered biting down, but dammit, his scorching kiss broke all her resistance. Warm languid heat melted her resolve. Without thinking, she moaned into his mouth, heady with need.

The fingers that had been tugging her hair now massaged the back of her head, pressing her mouth against his lips. Tongues entwined. Blistering heat scorched every nerve. She wanted to snuggle up tight and lose herself in hot, raw sex. Her moans grew louder, more desperate. It was a dangerous thing to do, giving him more power than he deserved, but she couldn't stop the longing in her heart from flowing up her throat.

"Yes, baby, yes," he murmured into her mouth while one hand caressed her breast. "Let us fuck you."

"Mmmm," she moaned, her body aflame with desire.

Wait. What did he say? She pulled free from the stupor fogging her brain.

While Ty broke down her defenses with hot kisses and possessive squeezes on her right breast, Passo's hands had slipped down her buttocks. The Morian's tingling fingers probed between the plump cheeks, not deep, but enough to make her clench her ass muscles tight.

"No!" She tried to swing away without much success. "Stop!"

Ty grabbed her shoulders to hold her still and planted love bites up and down the long slope of her neck.

"Don't!" Her breasts swelled with heated lust, aching for his mouth, defying her cries to leave her alone.

His mouth lifted, allowing the cool air to soothe her flushed skin. "This is what you wanted, Reeva." She gasped when he smacked a hand on her buttocks and pulled her trussed body toward him. "You don't want me to stop. You enjoy being tied up." His thumbs dug into her hip bones.

"We're not playing games here!" Despite her outrage, excitement raced through her.

"Yes, we are." He pressed his rough cheek against her cheek, his breath steaming her ear. "If you were my enemy, you'd be dead by now."

Every muscle in her body locked. What did that mean? "What do you want from me?"

"This is all about what *you* want, sweetheart." His hand slipped between her legs and cupped her sex. "Fulfilling your fantasy. One cock plowing your juicy cunt while another one fills your ass. A luscious Reeva sandwich."

The image he painted flung a quiver of longing straight through her.

Yet the inflection in his voice didn't sound natural. He spoke as if he read from a script, and he didn't like his role. Still, he played the part very well.

She breathed deeply when Ty rubbed his long fingers over her pussy, massaging her until the lips felt swollen and dew-kissed. Kit Passo skimmed his magic hands up her ribs and squeezed her breasts together, the vibrations from his fingers pulsating to the tips of her nipples. Oh, gods. Heaven. She hadn't had sex since she'd said good-bye to Ty two months ago, and she missed him -- it -- like a drug addict without a fix.

The idea of two men making love to her at the same time sent a thrill down her spine. Four hands, two mouths, two hard dicks. Mmm, yes.

Her heartbeat skipped when Ty slipped his fingers between the creamy folds and sunk two digits deep inside. She closed her eyes and let herself enjoy -- for just a moment. Oooooh, help.

What was wrong with her? Ty spoke nonsense -- fulfilling her fantasy. Pffft! She had a job to do here. Prisoners of war to free. How the hell had Tybirius gotten mixed up with the Bujirians anyway? The Old World terrorists sought to eradicate aliens from Earth along with their human allies, without a care for the innocent lives they destroyed along the way. She'd thought Ty possessed a higher moral code. Obviously, she'd been wrong.

Doing her best to ignore Passo kneading her breasts, the leisurely slide of Ty's fingers, and the quiver in her belly, she dug her fingernails into the palms of her hands. "Why do you keep saying this is what I want? I never said --"

"Yes, you did." Ty's thumb dipped between the slick folds searching for her hot button. She couldn't prevent the twitch in her legs when he found it. *Stars above.*

"On Centron Six," he said, drawing a shudder from her when he rolled his thumb back and forth over her clit. "When our escape was hampered by a meteor storm and we were forced to hide out in enemy territory until it passed. I remember every detail of your secret fantasy."

"Oh, that." She still remembered her surprise when he told her he wanted a harem of females catering to his needs. Feeling inadequate, she'd countered with a whim of two males fucking her into exhaustion. "Silly banter to ease the tension."

"In my experience," he said softly, "when someone faces death, honesty tumbles out unheeded." He nipped her earlobe. "So don't tell me now you were kidding. You want this."

She pressed her lips together. No sense in denying the obvious.

Still, why did he bother pleasuring an enemy captive? What kind of tactic was that? "Fulfilling one's fantasy is a unique form of punishment, Tybirius. Are you planning on escalating the pleasure threshold into pain? I've endured worse."

His thumb stilled. She heard him sigh. "Kit and I are here for you, Reeva. As a matter of fact, I specifically requested your presence. The commander told us when to expect you." He brushed a kiss over her lips. "I've been waiting for you, Reeva -- impatiently."

Chapter Four

"You knew to watch for me?" The sting of betrayal whipped around her heart. An ambush set by her commander? "I don't believe you."

As far as she knew, the commander recently discovered the desert outpost and sent her in to shut it down, quickly and quietly. The mission was top secret. No one but Commander Cytra and she knew about it. Yet, spies lurked everywhere at command headquarters, and Ty had connections there. He could have learned her agenda.

Ty brushed the back of his fingers over her cheek. "This 'prison time' is your recreation period, established for high profile warriors too stubborn to take time off."

"Innovative idea, huh?" Passo injected, rubbing his long shaft along the crack in her butt.

Were they kidding? A playground for burnt-out heroes? She cut short the snort of disbelief. The high spirits of the distinguished officers she'd seen when she arrived popped into her mind. Maybe Ty spoke the truth.

The 'prisoners' had appeared to be enjoying themselves, jumbled together in a mass of intertwined limbs and joined body parts. Plus, she couldn't overlook the fact that she'd refused to take leave after the fiasco on Neptune. The commander had insisted she engage in a simple operation on base territory.

Could Commander Cytra be in on this game?

She frowned. If Ty spoke the truth about this place, he didn't need to bind and blindfold her. She'd willingly part her legs for him, and Kit too. He was grasping at straws. "That's the craziest cover-up for an enemy camp I've ever heard." Ty was trying to lower her defenses, that's all. "I suspect you and your Bujirian friends hope to recruit the New World Alliance's top military personnel by seducing them. Well, think again. After your captives have their fun and turn your offer down, what do you intend to do with them?"

"The others are not my project. You are." The gentle strokes over her clit resumed.

Ty must've mistaken her tightening muscles as a signal to increase his leisurely thrusts. Oh, that felt *so* good. Her limbs trembled. She had to get it together.

"This is what you dream of, isn't it?" Passo asked, squeezing her taut peaks. "Two men worshipping your body."

Yes, but it was a fantasy. What she really wanted -- "Oh!" Ty hit her G-spot.

Apparently misreading the hard jerk of her body, Kit gently rolled her nipples between his thumb and forefinger. "Like that?" The shockwaves from his prickly touch surged into her core, colliding with the burning aftermath of Ty's tap on her clit.

Her core contracted, flushing cream onto Ty's fingers. Behind her blindfold, she squeezed her eyes tight, and released a gut-deep moan. It was foolish expressing the depths of her arousal, but she couldn't help herself. She'd always been a boisterous lover.

Ty located the sweet spot again, and rubbed it mercilessly.

Mmm. She could imagine the leer on Ty's face when she shuddered with desire. "Conquering my body will not break my determination to free everyone, Ty," she ground out between clenched teeth.

"The only thing you need to free is your inhibitions, Reeva. Once we fuck the tension out of you, you can go back to combat."

What in the world? "You're going to let me go?" Oddly, disappointment shrouded her.

"If that's what you want."

"You're a liar."

"He's telling the truth," Passo said.

Frustration rose in Ty's voice. "You'd rather believe I work for the Bujirians than I'm here to make you happy?" Barely-there kisses tickled her neck.

"Happy?" The man had no inkling how to make her happy, and it was simple really...

"Satisfy you. Scratch your itch. Whatever."

If only she could read his eyes, dammit! She *wanted* to believe her mission was a giant hoax to lure overzealous warriors into mandatory leave. But, come on... how crazy was that? "Not a single Alliance warrior has damaged this place?"

"Some have created major havoc, but so far everyone has been convinced to enjoy their time here."

She shook her head. "That's scary. Or reassuring. I'm not sure which."

He gave her shoulder a gentle squeeze. "You can trust Kit and me, honey. We're the good guys."

"Have the bad guys ever shown up?"

He chuckled but it sounded forced. "If the best of the New World Alliance can't shut this place down, then no one can, right?" His hand dropped to her shoulder and his fingers pressed hard. *A warning?*

"Now for the time being, relax. Enjoy. I thought you'd prefer Kit and me over two strangers. At any rate, that's how I wanted it to be." His lips caressed the underside of her jaw. "I miss fucking you until you're wet and slick and begging for more."

Oh, Ty. Why here? Now? This wasn't how she imagined making love to Tybirius again. Then again, if Ty sinking his hard shaft into her pussy while Kit fucked her ass was the only way out of captivity... It wasn't an unpleasant way to gain an advantage.

Okay, so technically, getting fucked by the enemy constituted a fumble in her mission. It was a temporary setback. When the men were physically drained, and least expected a backlash, she'd regain control of the situation. Let them believe she accepted their ludicrous story. She'd do anything to get this blindfold off her eyes!

"If you're both going to fuck me, I want to watch you do it."

Ty snickered. "I don't think so, love. Beneath that calm acceptance, you're angry with me. It's too soon to trust those dazzling green eyes of yours."

Damn, he'd always been able to read her better than anyone else. "You promise to free me?"

The intonation of his voice dropped, as though he were sharing a dark secret with her. "The New World Alliance needs you."

"Fine," she said through clenched teeth, wondering what this fantasy enactment was really all about.

Ty's thick fingers brushed her hair back from her face, the strands damp from the heavy humidity. His calloused fingers grated over the edges of her mask. "Ask us to fuck you."

She knew exactly how he wanted her to ask, with a hint of excitement rather than a huff of resignation. He'd demand that she ask him over and over again until she said it like she meant it. She'd been down this road before. Ty always forced her to accept her darkest desires, no matter how much she hated voicing them. In the end, she felt freer. She treasured him for that.

"Ty. Kit." She drew in a deep breath and let it out slowly. "Please fuck me."

"It'll be our pleasure." Ty swept a soft kiss over her lips. "Lube her up, Passo."

The warmth of Kit's body eased away from her back, leaving behind a damp patch the length of her spine. Bare soles scuffled across the floor.

A shiver quivered across her shoulders. She wanted to rant at Ty, tell him how crazy he made her, how she couldn't stop thinking about him… them.

When she opened her mouth to speak, he snarled at her. "No more talking." Strong fingers gripped her jaw, holding her still while he kissed her long and hard.

For a nanosecond, she fought his control, but as always, she submitted. It was a choice, not a weakness. During combat, she demonstrated skill, strength, and willpower equal to any man.

During sex, she embraced the strength of her partner. His power over her made her feel feminine.

At the moment, two males prized her. How flattering. How arousing.

After running his hands over the curve of her ass, Kit parted the full cheeks. A finger coated with a glob of lubricant briefly circled her sphincter and then two digits pressed inside. Reeva gasped loudly into Ty's mouth. The static shock from Passo's fingers darted up her spine, forcing her back into an arch. Warmth flushed across her chest.

"Easy, honey," Passo crooned, slowly thrusting in and out. More lube squished between his plunging fingers.

The sudden gentling of Ty's kiss distracted her. The firm grip on her jaw eased. His hand slipped along her nape and up into her bouncy curls. She relaxed, sinking against Ty's hard chest, submerged in the passionate strokes of his tongue.

She squirmed against the tingling vibration Passo incited inside her. The anal sex she'd had in the past had turned her on because it turned the male on, but this... Mmm. She'd never *yearned* for someone to fuck her ass before.

Her mind processed Kit Passo as the one stimulating her body, yet Ty's sensuous kiss transformed the tactile pleasure into heartfelt passion. He tasted like raspberries, which charmed her because the big he-man preferred flavored water to the heart-jolting energy boosters she and other members of their old team drank.

She moaned and sought the deep, sensual glide of Ty's tongue. He countered with a guttural rumble coupled with a tighter grip on her hair.

"Ready?" Passo asked. Without waiting for an answer, he plucked his fingers free and a smooth rounded cockhead butted against her well-lubricated hole.

Her sphincter puckered in readiness. She was more than ready. A breath later, Kit wrapped his arm around her waist and shoved hard.

"Aaah!" Reeva broke the kiss, panting for breath. He'd driven deeper than she expected. The stab of pain subsided quickly but the shock lingered.

"Are you okay?" Ty asked softly.

She nodded, forcing her tight butt muscles to rest. In a matter of moments, the long easy strokes of Kit's cock stirred her anew.

"Ty says you like getting fucked in the ass." When she moaned in response, Kit kissed the back of her shoulder. "You're my kind of female, Reeva."

The gentle gurgling of the nearby waterfall soothed her while Kit slid in and out of her slippery ass. The soft slap of his moist thighs on her butt cheeks spiked her arousal. Bound and taken from behind... mmm... one of her favorite games.

Although the burn around her hole cast a warm glow over her buttocks and into her pussy, it would take a while to make her come this way. She needed something more for a supernova orgasm.

"Ty --" she said on a sigh when he smeared wet kisses below her jaw line.

"Tell me what you want." He practically growled it.

"Y... you." In the ensuing silence, she wished she could see the expression on his face.

"Reeva --" His mouth drifted lower, between her breasts, and then lifted away. With a low rumble in his throat, he flicked his tongue at a nipple.

Her whole body jerked. Her inner muscles clenched at the lightning strike in her cunt. Shock after shock speared through her body as he licked and laved, kissed and sucked her nipple until it drew so tight, the lightest sweep of his moist tongue made her whimper.

"Mmm. What a nice stiff, reddened nipple you have, Reeva." Ty's lips floated over her skin to her other breast. "Let's see if we can make a matching pair."

When his warm, wet mouth closed over her other nipple, she groaned in ecstasy.

Meanwhile, Passo thrust at a steady pace. His arm around her waist loosened and his hand slipped down her moist skin toward her mound. Sparks flickered from his fingertips into her skin, making her inner core contract in a hot, pulsing rhythm. *Holy universe!* How many of Passo's enemies had died in a state of erotic bliss?

Sexual hunger clawed at her belly. She clenched her inner muscles in an attempt to slow the sensual heat rushing through her body. A futile exercise. She burned with desire. Now there was nothing to do but go with the flow.

What a shame.

Ty slowly bit down on the taut nipple he'd been stroking with his tongue. He gripped the other nipple between his thumb and forefinger and gently squeezed.

"Ohgods... ohgods." Her breasts swelled. The spiky pain in the tips burst into a lava flow of desire. She rocked back against Passo, eager to ascend to the next level of pleasure. She wanted to scream at him to fuck her ass harder, but she refused to voice her lusty cravings. Her body language spoke loudly enough.

"Easy, love," Ty ordered, releasing her aching nipple.

His fingertips brushed over the moist tip. Reeva sucked in her breath at the fiery tenderness. He clamped both nipples between his fingers now while he planted kisses on either side of the strap running down the middle of her body. "The snakes tattooed on your quivering belly seem to be hissing at me, Reeva." He nipped the spots where she knew each snakehead flicked a tongue at him. "I bite back, baby."

Oh, yes. She knew that very well.

His forehead bumped her belly when he dropped lower. She heard the soft thud of his knee on the floor and the slide of a foot as he knelt before her.

Without a word, Kit grasped her nether lips and spread them wide for Ty.

Sizzling embers danced along the edges of her pussy. The musky aroma of her sopping sex scented the air. The muscles in her ass tightened as her cunt clutched at the empty air. "Oooh, please."

"Luscious," Ty uttered in a low sexy growl. His hands slipped around to the back of her thighs and he drew her forward in her harness swing. A breath later, he thrust his tongue between her parted lips.

Cream gushed through her core. Stars, they'd just begun and her pulse raced like a streaming comet.

She pictured his dark face pressed close between her pale thighs while his lips roamed around her ripe pussy, teasing her with slow swirling licks. Heat bathed her face at the soft sound of his sensuous slurping. When a low moan slipped through her lips, he gently raked his teeth over the fleshy inside of her spread open pussy, making her quiver. For every drop of liquid heat Ty lapped up, another dribbled from her core.

Lost in the sensation of his mouth devouring her and Kit's smooth strokes deep into her ass, she urged them on through low urgent whispers. "Lick me. Fuck me. Yes. Oh, yes. Mmm, more." Tomorrow would be too soon for them to stop.

Ty licked an erratic path up to her clit, waggled his tongue over the little nub until it puffed up for him, and then he laved his way back down again, leaving her aching with desire. She gasped when he stabbed his tongue inside her the same way he kissed her whenever he wanted a serious hard fuck.

At this rate, a climax wasn't going to take long at all. And then she'd be free.

The sound of Ty feasting on Reeva's sopping pussy must have kicked up Kit's pulse too because he started plunging harder.

The first nip of a building orgasm speared deep inside. "That's it," she slurred through heavy breathing. "Make me come."

Ty's nose bumped her clit and she gasped at how plump and sensitive the nub felt now. Like a homing device, his tongue slid upward and pressed up the sensitive clitoris. Reeva hissed through her teeth. One heartbeat and his mouth closed over the new object of his desire.

She twitched when he began sucking on the small, fat nub. "Ooooooh yeaaaah." A tiny orgasm struck her core. She imagined her clit as a swollen little penis and she wanted to fuck Ty's mouth with it. "Suck it... Suck it." She rocked her hips, using Kit's driving force to press her cunt against Ty's hot, wet mouth.

She swore she came with each tug of his lips. Then again, the climax seemed to be swelling, drawing her core tighter and tighter. Behind her, Kit groaned loudly as her ass muscles closed around him. Her nails bit into her palms. Her jaw hurt from clenching her teeth. A flash flood swirled wildly low in her belly, gathering speed.

"Ohgods, ohgods, ohgods... don't stop!"

Dammit, Ty pulled away! For several long seconds, he left her hanging on the verge of total meltdown. "Tyyyyy!"

Chapter Five

"Is this what you want, baby?" Ty slowly slid his big cock into Reeva's cream-soaked sheath.

Tears leaked from her eyes as he pushed forward bit by bit, stretching her to the limit as he always did. The searing strain increased ten-fold with two cocks stuffed inside, separated by a thin membrane. Her breath puffed out in rough pants. "No, I can't. Please --"

"Yes you can. Relax."

Her nerve endings screamed in both pain and burning pleasure. It hurt, but it felt incredible too. Her pussy pulsed around Ty's thick shaft, trying to draw him deeper despite the aching fullness that threatened to tear her apart.

Ty's muscular arms wrapped around her back and Kit's arms circled her waist. They began a seesaw of thrusts, both of them grunting and digging their fingers into her flesh. With her wrists tied to her ankles, there was nothing Reeva could do but go along for the ride.

And what a ride it was.

One moment she thought they'd split her in two and the next her whole body flushed with sexual heat. They fucked her and fucked her, pushing and pulling, in and out, in and out. She could no longer tell whose heavy pants belonged to whom. Grunts and groans resonated around the room. The tight knot in her belly returned, aching to unravel.

Yet, she didn't want it to end. With each powerful drive into her body, her slick belly slapped against Ty's hard abs, driving her arousal higher and higher.

Kit tightened his hold and panted near her ear. His labored breathing revealed how close he was to orgasm.

She was close too. Moist heat seared her neck. A bead of perspiration rolled down from her temple to her jaw and dropped away. Her breath expelled in short bursts that burned her lungs. If they withdrew now, she'd die.

Slick, musk-scented skin slapped her, front and back. She rocked in the dangling harness as ecstasy vibrated through her pussy.

"Yes, yes." Their rhythm flowed like an undulating river, smooth and powerful. Forward, back. In. Out. Each pounding thrust a burning intrusion that lit her nerve endings on fire. "That's it... right there... nnnnn... fuck meee..."

Kit's hands slid up from her waist and grabbed her breasts, the back of his hands nudging the heat of Ty's chest further away. Her nipples peaked instantly from his energizing touch. He massaged her plump globes, squeezing and pushing, and teasing her nipples with quick brushes of his fingertips.

Mmm, she was going to melt into a puddle of cum.

Ty latched his mouth onto her neck and suckled hard. The pressure of his fingers bruised her shoulder blades.

Blood pounded in her temples. She clamped her lips together as her orgasm pinched tight. "I'm going to come," she exclaimed in an expulsion of pent-up breath.

Both Kit and Ty slowed the slick sliding of their rigid shafts while her limbs trembled. The coil twisted inside clamped tighter and tighter. If her hands were free, she'd be pounding a wall or the floor or the nearest chest. "Yes, yes..." She gathered a deep, halting breath, her heartbeat racing...

Both men shoved hard and deep, stuffing her with thick pulsing cock. A dull pain jabbed her cunt as they stretched her to the max, pushing her climax aside for a moment. She groaned loud and long.

"Sorry, sweetheart." Kit's sharp indrawn breath hissed by her ear. "Damn, you feel good. Soft, hot and tight."

Ty gave her a quick kiss on the mouth. "Must... fuck... you," he groaned, sliding in and out in small increments.

The slight movement shot streaks of arousal to her core.

"Gonna come soon," he wheezed. "Come... with me, baby."

Her whole body quivered. "Yes," she huffed, surprised how quickly the discomfort subsided within her drenched, throbbing pussy. "Ooooooh... mmmnnnn..." The coil twisted inside, clamping tighter and tighter with each increasingly forceful thrust of Ty's cock.

The hot band of steel began to unravel, faster and faster, spinning wildly in her belly and lower. She rocked against her lovers faster and faster. Almost there... The straps supporting her floating body squeaked and dug deeper into her skin. She didn't care.

Ty slammed into her, making her arch her back.

Kit cried out. Hot sparks shot into her breasts from his firm grip. "Fuck her, Ty. Fuck her."

Her lips parted and she panted hard. Any second... Her breasts throbbed with arousal. Her clit burned. She was going to die --

"Oh. Gods! Tyyyy!" Whoosh! Raw desire hurled through her, searing her core. "Aaaaaaah!" Whatever she did, whatever she said, fled from her mind as blinding pleasure crashed over her. Her body shook like a bolt of electricity hit her, she knew that much. The tumultuous release stole her breath.

Throwing her head back, she came and came, twitching wildly, drenching Ty's cock with her creamy juices at the same time she wrenched Kit's cock in a tight vise within her ass. Her breath heaved from her lungs in a rapid tattoo in synch with the hammering of her heart.

Kit shouted loud and long as he jerked against her ass, spurting his cum inside. The warm flow felt strange, yet titillating.

Waves of excitement crashed through her cunt, drawing out her orgasm, which refused to quit while Ty pumped lazy strokes that kept her on edge. After one particularly hard contraction around his plunging cock, he yanked her tight against his body, pulling her free from Kit's embrace. Passo's warmth abandoned her back and his cock slipped out with a wet, sloppy *pop*. Now she belonged solely to Ty. Euphoria swept over her. The quick staccato heartbeats thumping in Ty's chest matched her own.

Harsh breathing from all of them echoed around the room.

With a feral growl, Ty jabbed deep. "I... want you... now." His arms banded around her, straps and all, while he lunged one last time. His bellow hurt her ears.

She was so drenched with her own cream it took her a moment to feel his hot seed gushing toward her womb.

Ty's shudder rattled the harness straps holding her up. His tight hold squeezed the breath from her.

A string of quick orgasms rippled through her, surprising her with their intensity. She barely noticed her long moan until she heard it fading away. Gods, that felt good!

Ty eased his hold, but didn't let her go. Moist warm breath burst past her temple and flowed over her hair.

Hanging limply, her cheek resting on Ty's damp shoulder, she concentrated on slowing her pounding heartbeat, one long drawn out breath at a time.

Her butt hole ached. Every section of the stiff harness bit into her skin. Yet, serenity seeped into her pores. The idea of a quick retaliation against Ty and Kit sounded ridiculous now. She didn't want to move. On the other hand, she didn't fully trust them. Even though she'd only caught a glimpse of this stronghold, she knew there was more to this place than met the eye. Exploration required freedom.

If Ty didn't let her go in two minutes, she'd shift into warrior mode.

Her pussy contracted one more time around Ty's firmly embedded cock. Then again. Gods, she could fuck them both again in a flash, except her heart might explode. She blew out a long breath, forcing her pulse back to normal.

The pungent smell of sex swamped her lungs.

"Holy Mother of the Universe," Ty muttered.

"She was one fine fuck, wasn't she?" Kit asked. After having him so close, now his voice sounded far away even though he remained close enough to stroke the damp skin of her butt. "I should've never let you take her away from me."

The sudden stiffening of Ty's chest muscles made Reeva smile. As she suspected, Kit embellished the facts when it came to his conquests. "You never had me before now," she said breathlessly.

"I could have," he said, sounding smug, "but six months ago, Ty threatened to kick my ass if I touched you before he had a chance to get to know you better."

Beneath her blindfold, Reeva's eyebrows lifted. *Oh really?*

Ty's hands slipped off her body. Her head bobbed a little when he straightened. "Did we give you everything you wanted, Reeva?" he asked a little gruffly.

She wanted more than sex from him, but she didn't dare say so. Fucking a potential enemy was one thing, loving him was another. As for Passo, it was no wonder females spoke so highly of his sexual mastery. Those fingers were magical. She'd welcome him into her bed anytime except her heart belonged to Tybirius. Or rather, it had.

"I've had better sex," she scoffed, remembering her first bondage experience with Ty, how he'd brought her down from her sexual high with lingering kisses and gentle massages on her reddened wrists and ankles. The gruff warrior had shown a tender side, one she'd probably never see again.

Ty slipped his cock free of her wet sheath. "With whom?" Anger bubbled beneath his words.

"With a man who knew how to make a female feel special."

"Pfft. She's going to get mushy now," Kit complained. "I'm out of here, West."

The bang of a heavy lid and the rustle of clothes followed his pronouncement. Soft padded feet clomped up metal steps and stopped. "You have a fine ass, Reeva." His tone sounded a bit awed. "I hope to explore it again soon. If you'll let me." Without waiting for an answer, he hustled the rest of the way up the steps.

Then silence lay thick within her prison walls.

"Who?" Ty snarled.

"Let me down," she said calmly, pleased he sounded jealous, but anxious for freedom.

The hum of a laser knife cut through the bindings securing her wrists and ankles together. She winced when she straightened her legs and pins and needles stabbed into them. She reached up to remove the mask over her eyes, but Ty caught her hands and pinned them behind her back. "Patience."

Reeva kicked backward, catching him in the shins. "I'm finished with this game." The contact twisted her body and she swung wildly from the harness.

"Behave, Reeva." He grabbed the band running down her torso and stilled her. "Or I'll teach you a lesson in obedience you won't forget."

His threat shouldn't have affected her, but too many memories rushed forward, drowning her in a warm sea of arousal. The last time he taught her a lesson in obedience, her butt cheeks burned while cum dripped from her lust-swollen pussy.

"You don't scare me, Ty."

He yanked her close, the movement jarring her body. "I'm not trying to scare you, sweetheart." A heartbeat later the tension on the straps eased and her feet landed on a smooth cold floor. When her weak knees wobbled beneath her weight, Ty banded his arms around her, securing her arms at her side. Her soft curves melded against the hard contours of his chest and legs.

His lips bumped her temple. "I'm still hard as a Plutonian rock. You do that to me. If I let you take off that blindfold, I'm afraid you'll cast a Medusa gaze at me, setting my cock in a permanent, throbbing erection."

Reeva snorted. "If you don't let me go right now, I will." Unfortunately, her powers only worked on muscles, not blood engorged cocks.

"Have you ever tortured anyone like that?"

"No, Ty. None of my other lovers pissed me off enough to consider it."

She heard him hiss through his teeth. "I'd like to beat the memory of every other male from your mind."

Her lips parted in surprise. She waited for him to expound on his thoughts, but in typical Tybirius fashion, he kept his deeper feelings to himself. She sighed in resignation. "Are you going to release me from the harness like you promised?"

A long silence met her question. "You wanted two men to fuck you. I hope you're satisfied."

"Ty --" The big dolt. He'd taken her fantasy more seriously than she did. He was the only one she wanted.

"Now I need you to do something for me, Reeva."

Uh-oh. "What?"

Chapter Six

"Have faith in me." Arms locked around her, Ty gave her a quick squeeze and then kissed the top of her head.

Despite her warrior instincts warning her to be wary, reassurance bloomed. Ty had never led her astray before, even when he'd been offered a light-speed starfighter if he'd turn her over to an adversary who coveted her Medusa power. For a mercenary, his loyalty astounded her.

"I'm waiting for you to uphold your end of the bargain," she said impatiently. "Get me out of this thing."

The back straps twisted when he unhooked the harness from the cables. "You have a choice now," he said softly. "You can leave." He unsnapped the straps around her chest and thighs and pulled the harness from her body. She took a deep breath, taking pleasure in the ability to breathe without constraint. The harness thumped at her feet. It sounded as if Ty kicked it away. "The commander will give you a new assignment. He won't be upset that you failed to free the 'prisoners' here. I'm sure he has another warrior to send in your place." Disgust laced his words.

Reeva stood deathly still, taking in everything he said, analyzing his words, tone, and actions. Ty was not happy with Commander Cytra. Why? If this outpost was a retreat, then Ty shouldn't care if the commander sent more visitors. If it wasn't an Alliance hide-away, then what exactly was the *retreat* a cover for? And did the commander know about it?

"The other choice?" Although she itched to yank off the mask, she clasped her hands behind her back, giving Ty the benefit of the doubt for the moment, especially since he absently rubbed the grooves dug into her waist from the binding straps.

"Or you can stay here for a while. With me."

She *wanted* to believe his outlandish story about this place, but how could she trust a man who'd captured her and manipulated her body and mind?

"Trust is a two-way street, Ty. Take off my blindfold."

He drew her arms from behind her back and held her hands in his. His thumb caressed the back of her hand. "I have instructions to keep your blindfold on."

"From whom?" she asked angrily.

His grip tightened when she tried to pull her hands free. "From the commander. He doesn't want you creating mayhem while you're here."

She narrowed her eyes behind the mask. "If this is truly a retreat for the New World Alliance, I'll behave." It wasn't a promise to refrain from using her powers, but it was all she was willing to give him at the moment.

"Good enough." He flipped up the mask.

She blinked reflexively, but thankfully, the room was dimmer than she anticipated. Cozier too. Although the walls were made of rough-cut stone, large, textured, shell-white tiles lined the floor. Purple neon lights zigzagged between the squares. Behind a glass wall, greenery flourished in large pots bordering a steaming natural pool, highlighted by rosy-colored sun lamps. The water she'd heard since her arrival flowed down the rock wall into the pool.

Though the room was pretty, it was Ty who stole her breath away. The stern expression didn't hide the vulnerability, or the hunger, in the depths of his eyes. How could she stay mad at him when he looked at her like that?

"I need you, Reeva," he whispered. "In more ways than you can imagine."

She tore the mask off her head. "You swear this is not an enemy outpost?"

A tick flinched next to his eye. The burn in her gut flared again. Something was definitely amiss. "Commander Cytra controls everything that goes on here."

He cocked his head at the uncertainty in her eyes.

Well, what did he expect? He hadn't exactly answered her question, after all.

His gaze flicked to the ceiling. She wasn't sure if he rolled his eyes out of exasperation or he was trying to point something out. So she rolled her head on her neck, stretching the strained muscles while she searched the ceiling. *Ee-gads*. The glow of the neon tubing in the floor reflected in a tiny surveillance camera nestled in the rock ceiling. Someone -- or the whole universe for all she knew -- had watched, possibly recorded, Ty and Kit fuck her!

And Ty knew they were being observed. Damn him! She hung her head and rubbed the back of her neck so whoever manned surveillance couldn't see the burn in her cheeks.

Okay, so now she knew they weren't alone. Was it Commander Cytra who watched them? Was this his private playground? She shook away the horrid thought. The man treated her like a daughter.

If whoever ran this place spied on everyone, they could probably hear them too. So she couldn't ask Ty outright what the hell was going on. How freaking frustrating. She took a deep breath and looked back up at Ty.

"No one is a prisoner here, Reeva. Visitors come and go at will."

She raised a brow at him.

"Okay, when they first arrive and learn what this place is, emotions run the gamut." He narrowed his eyes at her. "They can leave whenever they want, but everyone must agree to a short-term memory wipe."

"What!" She took a giant step backward. "No one is going to mess with my brain."

Ty dropped his gaze. "It's for the safety of all the crucial defenders gathered here." He took a slow, deep breath. "It's a risk having so many in one place." Closing the space between them, he glided his warm palm up her neck and cupped her jaw, not in a caress but in a firm hold. He looked hard into her eyes and spoke slowly and distinctly. "Can you imagine the chaos if an enemy gained control over our key people?"

A chill danced across her shoulders. Was he saying the enemy *had* infiltrated the place? No, he wouldn't be playing bondage games if that were the case. He'd be kicking their butt.

Unless he was stringing the bad guys along, playing on their side, until... what? He had powerful allies all around him. Why didn't he utilize them?

The more she tried to figure everything out, the more frustrated she became. He looked at her with purpose, as if he willed her to comprehend what was going on here. Hey, she wanted to understand just as badly.

"If you don't agree to the memory wipe, I'll have to put the blindfold back on. Orders," he said, apologetically.

Cytra's orders, she thought with a bad premonition about the commander. Well, she didn't care if Cytra was her boss or not, she wasn't going to agree to a memory wipe, and that blindfold was *not* going back on. "I'll cooperate with you, Ty." She hoped he understood her meaning.

"Good." He dropped his hand to her shoulder. "Now, are you staying or going?"

"Going..." The disappointment in his eyes squeezed her heart. "...to see the other fun rooms in this place. Will you give me a tour?"

In one swift move, he lifted her up onto her tiptoes and his mouth slammed down on her lips.

Reeva slipped her arms around his neck and pressed her breasts against his sweltering chest.

"Mmm. Mmm." Ty smacked kisses on her mouth, ending what could've been a hot make-out session. "Later, honey." He pulled her arms from his neck and winked at her. "As soon as we're done taking care of business." With a tilt of his head, he led her over to a metal chest pushed against the wall and opened the lid. "Get dressed," he said, scooping out her clothes. "There's a very special room I want to show you."

If he'd winked or given her a crooked smile, she would've prepared for another rousing bout of sex, but he looked too serious.

She watched him dress in his combat fatigues while she slipped on her snug, slash-proof shorts. His eyes shone with excitement and determination. She'd seen that look many times before when he prepared for combat... or sex. This time, she'd bet on a battle.

A burst of energy surged through her veins. "Is this room anything like the one on Jarvon Sector Six?" They'd demolished an enemy control center there.

"Hm. More like Sector Eight."

She raised her brows. Sector Eight contained an experimental med lab. "Wow. That place was intense." And scary.

"You understand, don't you?"

"Not much, but I'm with you all the way, Ty."

A huge grin lit his face. "Let's go," he urged.

She glanced down at her thigh holster on the floor. "My laser pistol is missing."

"I've got it." Ty held up her gun. "Visitors aren't allowed to carry weapons." He shook his head almost imperceptibly when she opened her mouth to argue, and then he tucked the weapon into his waistband at the small of his back. "You won't need it, Reeva."

Again that special look that spoke volumes. *You have Medusa power.*

Ill-prepared for whatever situation Ty was dragging her into, she trusted him nonetheless. For the first time since she'd arrived, Ty seemed like his old self -- confident and invincible.

She followed him up the stairs and down a long corridor. Ty shoved open a stairwell door with his shoulder and rushed up the circular steps.

Half way up, he spun around and pressed her against the curved wall in a full body slam.

"Wha --"

His mouth covered her lips in a hard kiss. One hand slipped beneath her shirt and roughly massaged her breast. He furrowed the fingers of his other hand through her curls. His pelvis ground against her.

Only problem -- he wasn't hard. Not much anyway. You'd think with this passionate display... Oh! He was putting on a show. His massive back hid her from prying eyes. His body, writhing in an apparent sexual frenzy, distracted spies from anything he said to her between kisses.

"Oh, Reeva." His voice dropped. "Cytra," he whispered between sporadic moans, "is a... traitor."

His proclamation shocked her. She responded by slipping her hands around his thick neck and groaning long and low.

"He sends visitors..." His voice dropped off, then came back strong. "Too bad you won't remember this." He pulled her leg around his and lifted his knee so she straddled his thigh.

"Mmm..." She couldn't resist sliding her crotch up and down his bent leg. The friction revved her up fast. "You're making me hot." His distraction was working too well. Something clicked in her brain about a mind scan. No, a memory wipe. Her mind raced to complete the puzzle. Cytra set up warriors to come here, and then someone -- Bujirians? -- erased the visitors' short-term memory. Why? What were they doing to the warriors here?

"Do you treat all the guests here so well?" she purred.

"No, just you. You're special." He pulled her hips closer so she rode higher on his thigh. His cock stiffened, probably against Ty's will, when it rubbed against the leg caught between his thighs. "Very, very special. No one can replace you, Reeva. I need you."

All right, she got it. He needed her special powers. Maybe there were volatile chemicals in the lab where he led her, or too many innocent bystanders. Whatever the reason, firepower was dangerous. Only a Medusa could put the enemy out of action without casualties.

A queasy feeling sank into her belly. Had everything between them been a farce in order for him to get her this far?

Suddenly, the damp spot on her shorts' crotch embarrassed her. "You're going to owe me, Tybirius West," she said, pushing him away, "after you show me this special room you're so fond of."

"Mmm. Right." He straightened up and adjusted himself with a grimace. "You've got to get a good look at the inside." He looked her over one last time, shaking his head with what looked like regret. "When we're through here, I'm taking you on a luxurious space cruise."

She blinked at him in confusion. "Honestly?"

"Oh, yeah." He grabbed her hand and led her up to the landing.

A red sign over the door ahead caught her eye. *Restricted Area. Authorized Personnel Only.*

His gaze roamed over her from head to toe. "I might even invite Kit on our next vacation."

Reeva swallowed, not sure how she felt about that.

Turning back to the door, he slapped his hand on a palm reader and the thick metal door slid open. Two guards roaming the corridor turned to scrutinize them. Reeva almost gasped aloud at the Bujirian insignia displayed on their uniform sleeves. Across the hall, a yellow light flashed above a solid gray door marked with the symbol for biohazards. A tight knot clinched in her belly.

Ty seized her arm. "Another visitor ready to check out."

"We'll take her from here," one of the Bujirian guards said, stepping forward to take her other arm.

"Yes, sir." Ty dropped his hold.

For a split second, panic seized her. Had he scammed her after all?

The fighter inside surged through her blood. Hell, she could take care of herself.

Just as the guard touched her wrist, Ty struck, hard and fast. His palm smashed into the guard's face, toppling him backward into an ungainly sprawl. The Bujirian's rifle skittered across the floor. Dark green blood oozed from the guard's broken nose.

The other guard raised his weapon.

With a high roundhouse kick, Reeva knocked it out of his hands. The guard glared at her and she glared back. The clueless alien froze in time.

Ty dragged the groaning, half-conscious, bleeding guard over to the entry panel and shoved the guard's face up to the biometric eye scan. When he scrunched his eyes closed, Ty grabbed the Bujirian's long eyelashes and yanked his eyelid open. After a quick scan, a white dot on the scanner blinked. A panel below the reader slid open. Ty punched in a series of numbers on the keypad and the lock on the biohazardous room door clicked open.

He dropped the guard with a quick bash to the head, making sure he'd stay down. Picking up the Bujirian rifle, he glanced back at Reeva, and tilted his head toward the entryway.

She led the way.

As soon as she stepped inside, Ty flicked the overhead lights. The room's standing occupants looked up at the ceiling in bewilderment, then over to the light panel by the doorway.

Reeva stared in shock at the pink glowing bands around so many familiar warriors' heads. Some of the patients' gazes slowly slid in her direction, but most stared straight ahead.

Once more, Ty's hand gripped her elbow, as if he owned her.

A med tech in a bright green lab coat approached them. "We hope you enjoyed your stay."

"Oh, yes," she said with a bright smile. "Especially this part." With a flutter of her lashes, she projected her hypnotic gaze out into the room, using the reflective glass surfaces of the lab tables and machines to bounce her Medusa power into a web that bound them in place.

She spun around with her back to the room, so she wouldn't be caught in her own immobilizing spell, grabbing Ty's arm as she turned. Unfortunately, he hadn't dodged her powers any better than the rest of the room. Clutching at his stiff body nearly knocked her off her feet.

"Oh, bother." She gave her spell a moment more to settle over the room before she turned around to assess the damage.

Deafening silence filled the room. She waited and watched, but nothing moved.

She practically jumped out of her skin when Kit crashed through the door, a laser pistol in each hand.

"Damn," he said, lowering his weapons. "I missed all the fun." He raised a brow at Ty's massive frame, frozen with his hand reaching for the pistol tucked into the back of his waistband.

Reeva followed Kit's gaze to Ty's face and then moved her head in synch with Kit's as they traced Ty's line of vision to a Bujirian crouched behind a patient's lab chair.

"He's blind!" she shouted, waving a hand in front of her face to emphasize her point. "Immune to my power!"

The med tech turned to the sound of her voice and with deadly accuracy, he fired a stun dart at her.

Kit knocked her aside and fired his pistol. *Direct hit!*

She rolled her eyes at Kit's body twitching on the floor, the dart stuck in his arm. She knelt down and pulled the barb free before it completely incapacitated him. Tearing open the standard warrior's med kit strapped around his biceps, she rubbed antidote onto the tiny wound.

While Kit groggily regained consciousness, she stood and turned her attention to Ty. By accelerating his heartbeat, she'd break her spell quickly. There were lots of fun ways to do that.

She placed her hand over his plump cock hanging loosely against his thigh inside his pants, and smiled at how hard it felt due to her enchantment. As the magic faded, his cock would revert to normal the fastest. Stimulation there would speed the process.

She stood on tiptoes and rubbed her lips over his smooth, solid mouth, warming his lips with her breath, slowly breathing life back into him. His cock began to soften against her palm. Soon she would wrap her fingers around it and then it wouldn't be so soft anymore.

By the time Kit gained full use of his faculties and stood on his feet, Ty held Reeva in a stiff, but strong embrace, his mouth now crushing hers.

"Shit!" Kit exclaimed. "Left in the dust again."

With a chuckle, Reeva pulled back from Ty's probing tongue. "Are all your parts back in working order, Ty?"

He growled and ground his hips against her belly, showing her exactly how well his parts worked.

"Come on," Kit groused. "We've got to shut down the memory probes and clean the scum from this place."

"We'll finish this later," Ty grumbled into her ear.

"We'll see," she said with a shrug.

He backed her against the nearby wall and nipped her earlobe. "No doubt about it, sweetheart."

Reeva just smiled.

Chapter Seven

Reeva stood at the picture window of her private cabin, a frown pinched between her brows, gazing at the stars rushing by.

"Will you stop worrying about Commander Cytra's trial?"

Reeva turned around and faced Ty. Her lover stretched out naked on the oversized bed, a muscular arm thrown above his head, his cock primed and ready as usual. She tugged her pink diaphanous dressing gown closed and wrapped her arms around her middle. The man wore her out. "How many times is the judicial council going to postpone it?"

"Until both sides are satisfied they have enough information for their day in court."

"Isn't it enough you witnessed the Bujirians interrogating our warriors for three weeks before I arrived? The information they obtained and sent to their leaders is on a microchip, for heaven's sake, along with a profile of each visitor that came straight from Cytra's files."

"But there's no proof Cytra sent those files to the Bujirians."

"He sent his personnel there! You saw the communiqués prior to each visitor's arrival. Surely, no jury is going to believe the New World Alliance tricks their warriors into a forced vacation at a sex retreat!"

Ty cocked an eyebrow at her. "There are hard copies of events."

Heat burned her neck and flared up into her cheeks. "There's proof of the interrogations too," she reiterated.

"Since none of the victims can remember the interrogation, it's a bit tricky. Hell, thanks to the short-term memory wipes, some can't recall their trip to the outpost at all. Plus, voices and conversations can be replicated electronically." He gave her a lopsided grin. "I'm a mercenary. Not the most reliable witness."

"Hmph! You're the most loyal man I know."

His smile broadened, and he patted the bed. "Come sit down and I'll rub the tension out of your shoulders."

"The last time you wanted to relieve my tension," she scoffed, "I was captured, blindfolded, and trussed up."

His cock twitched. "Did it work?"

"No." She turned her head away from his heated gaze and stared at the delicate glass flower bouquet he'd sent her.

"You're a horrid liar, Reeva."

"Am not." When she looked over at him again, his hand wrapped around his cock and he gave the hard length a few slow strokes.

"Kit's been after me to set up another threesome. He's infatuated with you, and mad I won't let him have you alone."

Reeva sighed. "You know I threw that threesome fantasy out in retaliation for your harem fantasy. There really isn't anything to it."

"Maybe." He didn't look convinced. "Regardless, your fantasy came in handy when I needed you at the Bujirian center. No one else could have gotten me into their lab without creating a blood bath of innocent, very important people. We certainly didn't want to fry any brain cells either in the process."

She cocked her head at him. "Any Medusa would've helped you immobilize them. We despise the Bujirians for their ruthless tactics."

Without warning, he sprung off the bed and tackled her to the floor, careful to avoid direct eye contact until he had her pinned down and she surrendered. "I didn't want to have sex with *any Medusa* during that mission. I wanted *you*, Reeva."

He kissed the sensitive spot on her neck just below her ear and passion roared to life. He rolled her over on top of him, settling her sex alongside the base of his stiff cock. "I waited a long time for you." His lips roamed lower, trailing kisses straight to a nipple tenting the thin, transparent material of her peignoir. "I'm not going to give you up easily."

The moist heat of his mouth dampened the fabric, creating a soft abrasion that rocketed desire to her core.

She clung to his biceps while he made her burn. "I'm crazy... about you... too."

"Glad... to... hear it," he said between the gentle tugs on her nipple.

She licked her top lip when he nudged aside her dressing gown with his nose and nuzzled toward the other nipple now unencumbered by material. Her back arched with each slow swirl of his tongue around her areola. She gently rocked against his erection, her pussy wet with desire.

A warm smile lit Ty's eyes. "Reeva, I'm in love with you."

A spasm of joy struck her in the heart. "Ty --" She leaned down and kissed him, her hand smoothing over his bald head, showing him how much she cared about him too.

His arms banded around her back, crushing her to him, as their tongues danced in a slow, sensuous celebration.

The flush of passionate heat rose into her cheeks with each slick, slithering slide of his tongue. Stars, he lit her fire fast. She squirmed on him and he loosened his killer hold.

"Ty --" she mumbled into his mouth.

Reluctantly ending the kiss, he framed her face with his big palms. "What?"

"I love you too." She planted a quick kiss on his mouth, and then pecked his chin.

He moaned as she shimmied down his torso tracing a salty drop of perspiration as it slid down between the hard contours of his pectorals. It rolled across his ribs and disappeared beneath him, so she continued her journey down his abs, wriggling backward until she swirled the tip of her tongue around his navel. She smiled when Ty sucked in his rock hard belly. Sensitive there, eh? She dragged her fingertips down his sides, loving how the pressure made him squirm. Her big, bad lover was ticklish -- how entertaining.

He reached out for her, his hands caressing her shoulders. His long cock twitched. The red-brown head bumped her chin, like a child vying for her attention.

She glanced up at him, laughter bubbling inside.

With an innocent expression, her lover shrugged.

Giddy, Reeva flipped her open dressing gown behind her and straddled his massive thighs. She might not be part of a harem, but she knew how to please Ty. She sat on his legs and grasped his veiny cock, stroking the hard length from balls to the tip and back down again, marveling how the soft skin floated over his rigid shaft.

His face stoic, Ty dropped his hands to his sides, seemingly relaxed, but a tiny spasm jerked his index finger.

She cupped his balls in her other hand, savoring the weight and wrinkled texture of his sac. Gently, she squeezed and stroked. All the while, she watched his eyes darken with desire.

A drop of pre-cum oozed out the tip and glinted in the soft overhead lights. The pungent smell of his sex set her pulse racing. Capturing his gaze, she leaned down and lapped up the salty drop. "Should I go on?" she asked breathlessly.

He rolled his eyes as if she'd asked the stupidest question in the universe. She supposed it was.

With parted lips, she bent lower, sliding her lips down the thick shaft with excruciating slowness, taking him as deep as she could.

Ty's chest heaved and his eyes glazed over with pleasure.

Taking her time, she slid her lips up his shaft, nibbling on it, tasting it, smelling his sexy musk. She rolled her tongue around the head, sucking gently, teasing him. When she sank down on him again, she sucked a little harder, and held his swollen cock in her mouth longer.

His fingers slipped through her curls, cupping her head in a gentle sling. "Gods, Reeva." Slowly, gently, he pumped his hips. His cock slid in and out of her mouth with loud wet slurps.

His belly quivered with the effort to hold back.

Well, he wasn't the only one who knew how to push a lover to the edge. Reeva grasped his hips and sucked him in earnest. She slid her mouth up and down, working the shaft between her lips, twisting her head from side to side.

He rewarded her with a loud groan. "Enough!" he roared, dragging her head up from his pulsing shaft. He pulled her forward and kissed her hard while his fingers dipped deep into her soft, moist center.

Low moans of pleasure rumbled between them. She supposed he was satisfied with her creamy entry because he lifted her up and speared his weeping cock into her.

One stroke and liquid heat flooded her sex.

"My sweet Reeva..." His breath hitched as he plunged in and out, filling her up with hot, throbbing cock. "You outshine the stars."

A piece of her filmy dressing gown caught in the juncture of her thigh and hampered the slick slide of his thrusts. "Get rid of this," he groused, practically tearing the fabric from her shoulders.

She shimmied down on his full length until he sank into her balls-deep, and then she wiggled out of her peignoir.

Desire smoldered beneath his drooping eyelids. As soon as she tossed the gown aside, he hissed through his teeth, grabbed her hips, and set her back into a sensual glide up and down his solid shaft.

Mmm. She could ride him like this all night long.

Moments later, he reached down and pulled some cream from her sopping pussy back to her puckered ass hole. As soon as his finger pressed inside, she clamped her muscles down and rode him harder. Ecstasy seized her with stunning force. Tears brimmed in her eyes. She'd never felt so complete in both body and soul.

"Tell me the truth," Ty demanded, sinking his finger in and out of her tight hole while he rocked against her vigorous thrusts. "You got a kick out of two males fucking you at once, didn't you?"

Holding on to his forearms, she threw her head back and panted. "Yes."

"More than you expected, eh?"

"Yes." Every nerve in her body grew taut and then quivered for release. "Yes!"

"Ah, my insatiable Reeva. I think Kit will be visiting us very soon."

The promise of more tempestuous sex pushed her into a black hole of throbbing arousal. She fell forward onto Ty's hard, damp chest and let him fuck her to completion. Holding his finger deep within her ass, he pummeled her pussy with hard, grinding thrusts of his cock.

She gritted her teeth against the throbbing ache in her clit, waiting, waiting…

The climax hit her with the force of an exploding star, bursting outward in rings of fire. She jerked with each pulsing contraction, milking Ty's deep-seated cock.

He groaned, grumbled, and trembled beneath her. And then his body stiffened, arching upward into her. Warm semen gushed deep inside.

Reeva collapsed bonelessly on top of him, breathing hard, her inner muscles pulsing around his stiff shaft.

Ty blew out a long breath. "Wow." He wiggled the finger in her buttocks.

Reeva gasped. "Stop that." She pressed her cheek against his chest and listened to the thunder of his heartbeat. Or was it her own pulse throbbing in her ear? Her brain was too mushy to tell the difference.

With a little laugh, Ty reached up to his shoulder with his free hand and clasped her fingers. "I want to make you happy, Reeva," he said, drawing her hand over to his lips.

She lifted her head and gazed into his eyes, surprised and confused. "You do."

He slipped his finger from her ass. "Do I?"

"Yes." Ah, back to the threesome again. "With or without Kit. With or without sex, Ty. Sometimes, holding your hand is enough," she said with a sigh.

He kissed her fingertips, relief shining in his eyes. "I'm so glad I waited for you, babe."

She settled back down on his warm body. "Me too, Ty. Now can I have at least a few hours' rest before we make love again?"

She felt him smile against her forehead. "Sure. It'll take me a while to think of something new." She began to fade into sleep when she heard him say, "Candles can be fun."

Reeva groaned, but a telltale squeeze around his softening cock gave away her excitement.

Ty brushed a curl away from her eyelid with a low chuckle. "Candles it is."

Elayne S. Venton

Like many authors, writing has always been a passion for Elayne S. Venton. After winning several writing contests, Elayne decided to bite the bullet and submit something. A friend recommended a new growing e-publisher, Changeling Press, and the rest is history. Elayne enjoys writing in several genres where the characters' passions hurl them together and love binds them throughout time.

Currently, she lives in the rural south with her wonderful, industrious husband, two teenagers, and a lovable golden retriever. In her spare time, she volunteers at the local historical society.

You can visit Elayne at www.esventon.com or email her at elayne@esventon.com.

BloodWolf

Sierra Dafoe

"The image of the lone wolf, while romantic, is essentially a myth. The solitary wolf, although capable of survival, is a pitiful creature. Isolated from his pack, or in search of a mate, he has remarkable powers of endurance and can... cover great distances in his search... Desperate for company, he will often become unstable or depressed..."

"My grandfather told me it was Wolf who first taught humans how to live in harmony. Wolf is the Great Parent, the Great Teacher who shows us the right way of living with each other... Wolf is the Healer, bringing wholeness to the wounded spirit and the divided clan."

Prologue

Two men faced each other across the poker table. One was enormously fat, his belly rising like a mountain above the green felt plain of the table's top. The other was lean, lean and tall, with hair so black and glossy it almost looked wet, making Cassie think of the thick, heavy oil forced from the sun-cracked earth of her native Rusk County, Texas.

There was something about that second man, something that made Cassie waggle her hips as she eased her way through the crowd, made her bend forward a little farther than was strictly necessary to set his drink -- an expensive French merlot -- by his hand. He had a scent to him, a tangy odor like pine trees -- or no, that wasn't it. Something wild, though. Outdoorsy. It contrasted strongly with his manicured nails and elegant appearance, and Cassie felt her nipples hardening beneath her bandeau top.

"There you are, sir." She hoped he'd look up, hoped his gaze might linger on her remarkable cleavage as so many men's did. She'd used her tits to great advantage over the years -- they'd gotten her out of the seedy trailer park she'd been raised in, out of Texas, out of poverty and into an exceedingly cushy job as a cocktail waitress at the Mandalay Bay Casino and Hotel. And sometimes, when a man's gaze fell to her bosom, Cassie would smile, and waggle her hips that extra bit. And the next day she'd have a new dress, or some jewelry. Once, even a car.

But when this man looked up, his gaze rose directly to her face.

He had the most remarkable eyes, Cassie thought as her lungs, which had forgotten for a moment how to breathe, fought to remember. Not brown, not hazel, they were amber, a clear, light-shot color like honey in a jar, with sunlight streaking through it. They looked at her, and the noise and the lights of the casino slid away.

So did her defenses. Cassie gulped, feeling exactly as she had when she first came to Vegas, a gawky knob-kneed kid with nothing but a knapsack and a big pair of boobs. All the poise, all the polish she'd learned over the past five years was gone, leaving her shaking and awkward, vulnerable in a way she hadn't allowed herself to be since the age of twelve, when her latest "uncle" had called her to him and held her between his knees. "Some nice titties you got growin' there, Cassie," he'd said.

Some nice titties you got growin' there.

The man's eyes changed as he watched her, becoming softer, somehow deeper. "Tell me your name." His voice was like his eyes -- deep, rich, gentle.

"Cassie. Cassie Smith."

His full lips curved in a small smile. Reaching for the pile of poker chips in front of him, he held one out to her. "Here. Find yourself a different job."

Blindly, she took it and started to turn away, but he grabbed her wrist, pulled her down toward him. His gaze was intent on her face, and a heat she'd never felt in all the nights she'd held a man in her bed, listening to the increasing pace of his breathing and counting the tiles in the ceiling above her, unfolded between her thighs.

"You're better than this, Cassie Smith," the man whispered. Tears sprang to her eyes, sharp and stinging. In the amber glow of his eyes she saw very clearly exactly what it was she'd been doing for the last five years.

But she saw something else, too. She saw that he was right. She was better than this.

He held her gaze till she nodded. Then he released her. Dazed, bewildered, Cassie walked back to the bar, teetering on four-inch heeled pumps that suddenly felt so precarious -- a narrow, treacherous height she might tumble from at any moment. Then she looked at the chip in her hand.

It was blue, with black, white and yellow checks running around the edge and the casino's logo in the center.

Ten thousand dollars. He had just given her ten thousand dollars.

No. What he'd really given her was a way out.

Cassie folded her fingers around it, feeling the hard edge digging into her palm, and started to cry.

Across the room, the man with amber eyes watched the girl dab at her quickly smearing mascara with a cocktail napkin, then, head held high, stride resolutely from the poker room, ignoring the bartender's disbelieving glare.

His name was Baudouin Delacor. He was almost a thousand years old. And he loved these frail, complex humans in a way he knew he could never explain.

Cassie Smith, for example. Delacor smiled slightly -- as with most things about him, the expression was tempered with grief. The girl was no one really -- a pretty young woman lost in a world that was too big, too wide. What her future would bring, who could tell? But at least for one brief moment, he had touched her life, and changed it.

It was such small things, the momentary connections like this that made his own life bearable.

Occasionally, in his wanderings he'd amuse himself by peering at the faces he passed, young or old, world-weary like himself or fresh as a new-picked peach, wondering whose life, whose story he might become entangled with next.

His own story bored him. It was the same -- always the same. Delacor turned back to the table, suddenly restless. It was time to end this charade. Time -- once again -- to move on. He laid down his cards.

"Full house," the dealer announced. "Nines over threes." He looked at the fat man, who simply folded his cards, and back to Delacor. "Well played, sir." A smattering of applause from the crowd, and they began to drift off. The dealer indicated the heap of chips in the center of the table. "Shall I have these taken up for you?"

"Please." Delacor rose.

* * *

"Here."

The cabbie stared into the rear view mirror. "Here, sir? But -_"

"Stop here."

The tires crunched to a stop on gritty sand. Handing a hundred dollar bill to the driver, Delacor got out. The thump of the cab door closing behind him was very loud in the silence.

He waited until the noise of the retreating cab had faded away. Then he tilted his head back, studying the smattering of stars just peeking through the darkening arch of the sky.

It had been a night very like this one that the *um al duwayce* had come for him. The stars had been different, half a world away, but the sand and the silence had been much the same.

He had smelled it first -- a whisper of sweetness on the warm desert wind, cloying and spicy, but somehow stale, cold, rotten with age. The scent had filled his mind like a madness, setting fire to his nerves and hazing the night with a veil of crimson. Then he'd seen it in the distance, gliding toward him across the sand. Even now, he could feel the heat that had burned in his loins at the demon's approach.

Closing his eyes, Delacor let himself remember...

* * *

It wore the shape of a woman, dusky and slim, draped in a silken robe that glimmered in the moonlight like cobwebs, so sheer and delicate it seemed it would shred at a single touch and float away. Her hair, black and glossy as onyx, fell in a straight, heavy line to her slender waist. Above it, her breasts curved, full and ripe. As she neared, he could see the darker brown of her areolae beneath the gauzy fabric.

Spellbound by lust, he stood, unaware of his sword sliding from his hands and tumbling to the sand below. His blood thundered in his ears as she studied him, her dark, secretive gaze finally coming to rest on the swell of his cock. She knelt before him in a whisper of silk, her long, clever fingers undoing his garments.

And then she took his throbbing shaft in her mouth.

* * *

Swallowing, Delacor tilted his head back, feeling his balls grow heavy. His cock pulsed, lengthening beneath the fabric of his pants. Groaning, he clenched his fists, refusing to touch himself, to relive the need that just the memory of the demon's touch could arouse.

The *um al duwayce*. The succubus. It was hunger incarnate, a searing, endless lust that fed off its victims, drawing their essence, their life force, into its primordial emptiness.

A light breeze skidded up from the south, blowing across the sparse vegetation of the Amargosa Desert and setting a clump of yucca to clacking softly. It brought with it the tang of sere, uninhabited spaces; rugged, rolling lands in which nothing but coyotes and rodents and scorpions moved. The scent filled his nostrils, sharpening the hunger that twisted inside him, the taint the *um al duwayce* had left in his blood.

It did not always kill its victims. No, some it merely changed, infecting them with its own insatiable desires. Beasts became feral, men became vampyr -- cannibals living off the blood of their own kind. And he, Baudouin Delacor, who had never been a man...

He hated this, hated what he was about to do. But already his hands were ripping at his cufflinks, dropping the pearl-tipped bits of metal behind him as he strode deeper into the Nevada night. His Cavellini suit jacket he left draped over the spindly limbs of a sagebrush, his belt near the base of a striated rock. Kicking off his shoes, he shed the rest of his clothes, retaining only the small waist pouch he habitually wore under his shirt. Cinching the pouch's strap tight around his lean waist, he narrowed his eyes, and waited.

To the east, above the horizon, a golden glow painted the sky -- the moon, just shy of full, hidden still behind the low-lying hills. It called to him -- a call that had once been the keenest of joys to answer.

Now the thought of what it meant sickened him.

Five, the old priest had told him. There are five aspects of the demon, representing each of the elements -- earth, air, water, fire... and spirit. For it is not truly flesh, Baudouin -- it is essence. An essence which can poison any living thing.

But these five -- they are its avatars, its manifestations. Destroy those, and perhaps...

Perhaps. It was the best Father Giovanni had been able to give him. The regret in the old man's eyes had not been feigned.

I am very sorry for you, my son.

Gone to dust centuries before, Father Giovanni, who had not cursed him or called him damned.

Delacor had already destroyed one, that first, beautiful, ethereal woman who had floated across sands the prophets themselves had trod. He had lain with her under the full Eastern moon, coupling again and again in an inhuman frenzy of lust -- until he'd felt her teeth on his neck.

She'd laughed, he remembered, even as he'd plunged his sword into her. Laughed and then stood before him, the wounds closing as he watched. Horrified, he'd stumbled back and she'd followed, her hands reaching out for his still rigid cock. Her scent -- the sickly-sweet odor of decayed spices and rotting flowers -- had surrounded him, making his head whirl.

Shrieking, torn between loathing and the desire to thrust her to the ground and split her open with his cock, Delacor had struck again and again, retreating before the thing that pursued him, remorseless, undying, until at last he'd severed its head with one great sweep of his sword, and the avatar of the succubus, the flesh in which it had clothed itself, had tumbled to the sand.

But the poison it had left in his blood still remained.

For eight months now he had suppressed it, hiding himself as the moon grew round, avoiding its light. Drinking himself into a stupor to try to silence the craving inside him, he'd sweated and shrieked inside sterile hotel rooms, holding himself back by sheer will from ripping open the curtains, letting the moonlight pour down...

He'd tried it before over the centuries, many times. Tried to starve the hunger into submission. Each time, he'd hoped he could outlast it, that without the blood his affliction demanded, he would die.

He didn't. The torment simply grew stronger with each passing moon till he could no longer fight against it, and must give in.

Bending down, he scooped up a handful of sand, letting it trickle slowly through his fingers. Moments passed, each one a grain of sand falling, falling... The moon cleared the horizon, and then there was no more sand, no more hand to hold it, no more Baudouin Delacor. A massive black wolf with eyes the color of amber stood in the desert, scenting the wind.

Breaking into a long, steady lope, the wolf headed north.

Chapter One

Petrified Forest National Park, Arizona

Spades bit into the dry earth, sending whorls of sand so fine it plumed like smoke into the air. Lauren Cole squatted at the edge of the square pit, shielding her eyes from the slanting early-morning sunlight, then raised her Nikon for another shot.

"Watch it!" Randy barked as Daniel, one of the three students, stepped back, fouling the thread stretched from peg to peg around the perimeter of the pit. As he stooped to disentangle himself, Randy hopped down into the four-foot deep excavation, squatted, and brushed carefully at the sand that had settled over the exposed find.

"What is it, Professor Anders?" Kelly, a lean-limbed sophomore with a cute little button of a nose, called from the opposite rim. Kelly Mapplethorpe. She'd tied her tee shirt up under her breasts, revealing a smooth, firm belly and taut back muscles. Her skin showed the telltale flush of incipient sunburn, and Lauren felt a certain grim satisfaction.

Flaunt those babies however you like, sweetheart, she thought uncharitably. *It's going to be damned uncomfortable sleeping for you tonight.*

It was, she suspected, more uncomfortable sleeping accommodations every night than Kelly had hoped when she'd signed on for the trip. Not that Randy would so much as look at one of his students. Hell, he hardly remembered to look at her half the time.

At that thought, Lauren sighed.

"Nicrosaurus," Randy replied. "Big one. Get a shot of this, honey, would you?" He smiled at Lauren, a gleam of excitement in his cornflower-blue eyes as she clambered into the pit and hunkered down beside him.

Dark Side

She was acutely aware of Randy's muscular thigh, deeply tanned and coated with soft gold hairs, brushing against hers. It wasn't hard to understand Kelly's attraction to her energetic, good-looking geology teacher, but it was damned annoying to have the girl shoving her tits at him every chance she got.

Adjusting the f-stop, Lauren decided against changing lenses -- the pit was dusty, and she wasn't spending another night cleaning sand out of the lens-mounts. Not if she could help it. She could think of far more pleasant ways to spend the short desert evenings -- if only Randy were more distractible.

He wasn't, she had to admit, the most exciting lover to begin with. Strictly your meat and potatoes kind of guy. He wasn't even that crazy about blowjobs, though he'd given up fighting her on that score at least. Lauren absolutely loved the taste of his thick, solid cock -- especially when he was all sweaty and salty from a dig. He tried to reciprocate every now and again, but his heart wasn't in it, and it showed.

Is there anything more of a turn-off, Lauren wondered, than being eaten by a guy who just doesn't like it? But after twelve years in L.A., Randy was like a fresh breath of air. Friendly, optimistic, almost naïve, full of a wholesome exuberance that still made her smile. It was that exuberance which had won her heart ten months ago. Jaded and exhausted by the cynicism of Los Angeles, where obscene wealth and unspeakable poverty lived almost cheek to jowl, she'd been more than happy to chuck in the towel when the University of Phoenix had offered her a position.

Those who can't do, teach. Lauren grimaced. No one had said it, but it had been there in everyone's eyes when she'd told them. Her editor, her friends -- hell, even her landlord. Why did everyone always equate having the goddamn sense to leave L.A. with failure? Hell, she'd won a Hearst for her piece on the ongoing fallout, a decade later, from the '92 riots. Not Beverly Hills: 90002, she'd called it. She'd been rather proud of the title.

How much proving did she have to do before she earned the right to leave with dignity? Shocked, Lauren realized she was still seething, even now. She had a sneaking suspicion that what had really been behind the lukewarm good wishes and thinly veiled sneers of her colleagues was jealousy -- not of her awards or her office (not a desk, an honest to God office) at the L.A. Times, but of the fact that, having worked so hard to achieve them, she'd had the courage (or sheer common sense) to give it all up.

Nodding to herself, she snapped another picture. That was it, she was certain. By choosing to leave, she'd confirmed what they already knew, deep in their hearts. Los Angeles was a rat race. A place where, as one extremely talented and alcoholic screenwriter she'd interviewed once had said, one didn't have friends, only business associates.

Randy was the absolute antithesis of L.A. And he certainly didn't have any qualms about teaching geology, even though his heart -- and his doctorate -- were both in paleontology, his interest restricted to summers and these work-study digs.

"Don't you resent it?" she'd asked him once. He'd glanced at her, his hands pausing over the bone fragments he'd been slowly assembling.

"Why should I?" he'd answered, his expression honestly puzzled.

That was Randy. Sweet, straightforward, what you see is what you get. With Randy there was no such thing as a hidden agenda. It was an incredibly soothing quality.

It was very, very hard to admit that it was also, well, dull.

Lauren shifted carefully to the other side of the fossil to catch the shadows better. Randy had unearthed the massive skull to a depth of four inches in places, revealing a perfect profile view of its three-foot long jaw and bristling teeth. "What a monster," she said admiringly.

"It's not actually a dinosaur," Randy replied, "it's a phytosaur."

"A what?"

Randy grinned. "Sloan?"

The gawky, black-haired geology major looked up from the square he was excavating. "Phytosaur. Late Triassic. Kind of a big crocodile cousin. I think I just found its back paw."

"How big?" Lauren glanced again at the teeth. Some of them were as long as her outstretched fingers.

Randy shrugged. "Oh, maybe eight meters."

"Twenty feet? That thing was over twenty feet long?" Lauren imagined a L.A. transit bus with fangs, and shuddered.

"Yup." He stood, brushed his hair back and glanced at the sky. The sun had shifted higher, and the morning softness had already burned from the air. "It's gonna be a busy day."

Lauren smiled as he reached down, helped her to her feet, and playfully brushed the dust off her butt. Kelly was scowling, watching them from the corner of her eye. Well, Kelly would just have to take her hormones elsewhere. Randy was hers.

He might be predictable. He might be -- okay, was -- a little monotonous in the sack. But these were drawbacks that, after twelve years in La-La Land, Lauren felt she could happily overlook.

Lauren spent the entire day taking pictures -- close ups of the fossil (Lyle, the students had already dubbed it), group shots, Randy and the three kids standing at the edge of the pit during lunch break, arms draped across each other's shoulders and grinning like idiots. Kelly, of course, had snuggled right up against him, her boobs brushing his chest as she pressed herself close. Lauren had gritted her teeth, and snapped the photo.

The sun had nearly set, and shadows stretched long from the base of the wind-sculpted buttes across the hard, reddish plain of the desert by the time the long arch of the spinal column finally started to emerge. Randy was squatting by the skull carefully brushing fixative over the exposed bone when Kelly called from the far side of the pit.

"Professor Anders? I think there's something else here."

* * *

Exhausted, heart-sore, Delacor stumbled down from the foothills of the Spring Mountain range as the sky slid toward twilight. Naked but for his waist pouch, he crouched by a tiny stream welling from between two boulders, and splashed the icy water over his face and arms.

There were two coarse black hairs trapped under his fingernails along with brownish clots of dried blood. At the sight of them, bile rose in Delacor's throat. He thrust his hands into the water, scooped sand from the bottom of the stream, and ground it between his fingers until his cuticles were shreds and his palms burned with abrasions.

It did no good to tell himself it had only been a dog.

His shoulders slumped dejectedly as Delacor leaned back against the rough boulder, letting his long-boned hands dangle between his knees. In the distance, the lights of Las Vegas glimmered, turning the horizon a poisonous yellow.

He was tired, so tired of this pointless existence. When the demon's madness came on him, it blotted out memory, conscience... everything. The *um al duwayce* had turned him into a beast for which there'd never before been a name. Not the *loup-garou*, the werewolf, but the *loup de sang*.

The BloodWolf.

Wolves, the beautiful, wild cousins of his kind, had all but disappeared from the world, a fact that was both a sorrow to him, and a relief.

But there were always dogs.

Remembering the two black hairs that had been trapped beneath his nails, Delacor dropped his face into his palms and howled his grief and fury.

Slowly, the sound of trickling water returned him to himself. It reminded him sharply of home, of the high craggy tors and deep, silent forests of the Languedoc. But the air here was heavy with a coppery stink that drifted down from the north -- from the barren, blasted wasteland that was the Nevada Test Site.

So many kinds of evil, in one tiny world.

Lifting his head, Delacor scented the breeze. Under the stench of Armageddon were smaller, softer smells -- the clean tang of running water, the cool bite of the pines, the earthy fragrance of rock and dirt. From Route 160, three miles east, came the reek of exhaust.

But there was something else, beyond all these. Something...

There. A tendril of odor, twisting through and underneath the closer, stronger aromas. A stink so faint it was almost undetectable. It was dry, sickly-sweet, vaguely erotic -- the scent of old perfumes, rotted by time. Miles away, maybe hundreds. But there.

The musty fragrance shuffled back the centuries like cards in a deck, and he saw it again in his mind's eye, gliding toward him like a mirage over saffron-colored sand. The *um al duwayce*.

It had awakened again.

For nine hundred years he had sought some trace of it, hoping to find the four remaining avatars, to destroy them and so remove one evil, at least, from this poor, tortured world. Then, perhaps, the corruption inside him would also be removed.

He was no longer sure he truly believed that. It was the *belle mensonge*, the beautiful lie. Without it, he might well have despaired long since, and let himself be overwhelmed by the poison inside him.

He knew, no one better, what the succubus could do. Whether he could ever free himself of its defilement or not, it had to be stopped.

It would seek prey, and quickly. Of that he had no doubt at all. Already Delacor was on his feet, moving cautiously through the scrub. Grimly, he smiled, wondering whose life he was about to become entangled with now.

But as he raised his head to the evening breeze, freshening now as night drew down, he felt a strange sensation prickle along his limbs. It took him much longer to identify the feeling than it did to find the direction.

Squatting, he concentrated. A moment later, all that could be seen at the edge of the bushes was a massive black wolf, staring down from the foothills over the flat, shallow bowl of the Las Vegas valley.

East. He'd have to go east now. And somehow he knew he had to go fast.

As he broke into the wolf's steady, ground-devouring run, for the first time in centuries Delacor felt a whisper of hope.

Chapter Two

It was almost completely dark, and Randy was still hunkered in the shadows of the pit, studying the knob of bone that protruded from the wall about eight inches above the base. The two boys and Kelly watched eagerly as he traced it lightly, following the small curve of exposed fossil with one finger.

"Well?" Lauren snapped. She was tired, and grimy from the day's exertions, and not at all amused by the way Kelly was leaning over Randy, even though he ignored the girl completely. "What is it?"

He looked up at her, excitement sparkling in his eyes. "I've no idea at all." His broad grin punctured her discontent, and Lauren couldn't help grinning back. But her expression changed as he straightened, a bit stiffly, and gave Kelly a look of beaming approval. "Good work. All right, let's cover them up."

Lauren had time for a quick wash behind the tent as Randy helped the students peg a heavy tarp over the dig, protecting the exposed fossils from the night winds of the desert. Then, freshly scrubbed and dressed, she started for the mess area, working her fingers through the tangles in her drying hair.

A soft evening breeze had begun stealing along the ground, bringing with it a faint, tangy scent that made Lauren think of cloves. She stopped abruptly. Food wasn't really what she was hungry for, was it? In the distance, she could see Randy, no more than a shadow against the dusky purple sky as he headed back from the pit. Twenty yards to her left, in front of the three pup tents where the students slept, a fire flickered brightly in the growing gloom.

Lauren smiled again, and headed back for the large tent at the base of the butte. It was almost completely dark inside, and she quickly shed her clean clothes and slipped under the sleeping bags on the mat. She caught the tang of spices again and tilted her head back, breathing it in, wondering briefly what late blooming plant produced it. The nylon of the sleeping bag rustled as it slid across her naked skin, teasing the small nubs of her nipples, and a familiar warmth stole through her groin.

Gods, it had been days since they had made love! Randy shied away from public displays in any case, and the close proximity of the students' tents had squelched any hopes Lauren had of getting laid. But tonight the very air seemed to whisper of carnality, and she could feel her body radiating a sensual heat in the darkness of the tent.

She heard the tent flap rustle as Randy entered. "Laur?" She chuckled softly in reply, and heard him pause just inside the tent. Then his footsteps approached, and she felt a sudden rush of irritation as a match scraped and the propane lantern flared into life on the small chest next to the mat.

Its greenish light fell over Randy's broad cheekbones, casting tiny shadows from the rough stubble on his cheeks and jaw. His hair, matted with sweat, stood out at odd angles as he glanced in her direction. Lauren, who had been about to toss back the sleeping bag, displaying her naked body before him, checked at the febrile excitement in his eyes.

She was used to his enthusiasm. Originally from Minnesota, with the strong-featured good looks and fair coloring of the Norwegian ancestors who had, by sheer perseverance, wrestled a living from that vast, untamed land, Randy had a placid but tenacious disposition that was admirably suited to the slow, painstaking excavations he loved. He'd wax rhapsodic over the tiniest thing -- a chip of bone, a fragment of petrified plant life, squirreling it away like some miniscule piece of a gigantic puzzle. Which, Lauren supposed, it was.

But the gleam in his eyes now was different. It was restless, unsettled, not at all like the sparkle of optimism she was used to seeing in them. "Randy?" He started, and Lauren realized that for all he'd been looking straight at her, he hadn't really been seeing her at all. "Randy, what's the matter?"

"Nothing. I don't know. I... We may have found something." His expression was oddly hollow, both excited and yet filled with a curious reluctance, as if he was afraid to give rein to the agitation inside him.

"Well, obviously," she replied, a teasing lilt in her voice. "Do you think there's more, then?"

"No. I mean, yes, I'm pretty sure there is, but..."

"But what?"

He ran a distracted hand through his hair, mussing it further. Really, Lauren thought, a few more days of this and he could play a mad scientist to perfection. Well, that is, if mad scientists were ever nicely muscled and handsome.

"I don't know, Laur," he repeated. "I just don't know."

"Any guesses, even?"

"I said I don't know!"

"Okay! Jesus." His vehemence surprised her. Briefly, she tried to remember if he'd ever spoken crossly to her before. "I was just asking."

"I'm sorry, hon. I didn't mean to snap."

"It's okay. C'mon. Come to bed." Tossing back the corner of her sleeping bag, she jerked her head in invitation. He hesitated, and she added, somewhat tartly, "Honestly, Randy! It'll still be there in the morning."

He chuckled at that, and the tension in him seemed to ease as he pulled off his boots and shirt, and stretched out on top of his sleeping bag. He really was excited, Lauren thought, if he'd let himself get that wound up. Reaching over, she turned off the lamp, then curled up beside him, her head pillowed on his broad chest, and lay listening to the wind scurry over the sand outside and the slow, steady beat of his heart.

She loved the way he smelled. Even after a long day's work in the sun, his odor was pleasantly musky rather than acrid. Snuggled close against him, she felt a renewed pulse of arousal at the feel of his warm, strong body next to hers. Turning her head, she let her cheek brush the smooth skin of his shoulder, and then licked it with her tongue lightly, enjoying the slight tang of salt.

Sliding tighter against him, she kissed the side of his neck, and let her hand drift down his abdomen to the front of his shorts. "You're not going to sleep with these on, are you?"

She felt his cheek curve in a smile and, encouraged, undid the snap at his waist and slid her hand inside. His cock wasn't especially long, but it was nice and thick. Solid, like Randy. Solid and comfortable. Curling her fingers around it, she felt it start to stiffen under her touch. She loved the way it filled her palm, the smooth, velvety skin of its head. The meaty curve of the lip brushed against the inside of her thumb as she worked her hand slowly up and down, tugging gently at the thinner skin of his shaft. Beneath her cheek, Randy's shoulder shifted as he turned slightly toward her, gathering her in his arms to kiss her.

His lips trailed lightly against her own -- dry, almost tickling. She squeezed his cock harder and he pressed his lips more firmly against hers in response. No tongue. Of course not. When she kissed him the way she wanted to -- mouths wide open, tongues intertwined -- he invariably complained she was suffocating him. Once he'd said it was like kissing a cow. Archly, she had inquired how, precisely, he'd know.

But it had hurt, all the same.

He moved again, and she withdrew her hand from his shorts. He tugged them off, then rolled her onto her back. Deep in her heart, Lauren sighed. Sometimes she couldn't help wondering if anyone had ever told him there were more than two positions for sex.

Well, at least tonight they could go for option number two. She didn't feel like being trapped under him, fighting for room to rub her own clit as he plunged himself into her. No, tonight she wanted freedom.

Pushing back, she shoved him away before he could mount her. "Uh-uh, loverboy. Tonight I'm in charge." In the darkness, she heard his exasperated sigh. But he rolled onto his back anyway, and curved his hands around her hips as she straddled his thighs.

Dark Side

Leaning forward, Lauren lowered her chest till one nipple grazed Randy's nose. Obligingly, he tilted his head back, catching it between his lips and suckling lightly. His shaft throbbed against the swell of her mons, and slowly, Lauren rocked against it, rubbing her clit against its hard ridge.

God, she was horny! She would never admit how many times she'd played with herself before he came to bed, working up enough lubrication to make intercourse pleasant. Tonight, that was definitely not going to be a problem -- she was sopping wet. She could feel her juices slicking his cock as she slid back and forth. Randy's breath was coming faster now, and his hands tightened on her hips. He was ready, she thought tartly. But tonight, she wanted more.

Arching her back, she pressed her breast against his mouth, willing him to suck it more firmly. Hell, even bite it. He had teeth, for God's sake -- why couldn't he ever use them? Squirming above him, she ground her cunt against him, mashing her clit against his cock as she leaned forward harder, feeling his grip tighten, tugging at her, trying to get her to let him inside.

Laughing, Lauren fought him, thrusting her breasts against his face, feeling a wild giddiness rush through her as he thrashed between her thighs, desperate to be inside her, to plunge his cock into her blazing hot cunt --

With one last flail, he shoved her off, and Lauren tumbled to the mat, gasping in shock. "Jesus, Lauren!" She heard him panting in the darkness, his breath rasping in his chest. "Are you fucking trying to smother me?"

Realization hit her, followed by sudden mortification. He hadn't been desperate to fuck her -- he'd been desperate to get her off him. She heard him sit up, heard the soft whisper as he ran a hand through his hair, trying to regain his composure. Biting her lip, she waited, unmoving, feeling her cunt throb with undiminished hunger. Finally she said, "Randy, I'm sorry."

He sighed heavily, and gathered her back in his arms. Lauren lay, her head pillowed on his shoulder, trying to ignore the aching points of her breasts, the slickness between the swollen lips of her cunt.

"Christ, Laur. I just can't... I'm not like that, you know that."

"I know," she whispered, so softly it was doubtful whether he even heard her. But he sighed again, in resignation. This time, when he rolled her onto her back, Lauren didn't protest.

His cock nudged against her, easing slowly into her. Lauren closed her eyes, feeling her cunt tighten around it, eager for all of him. Fighting back the urge to thrust herself upward, she slid her arms around his waist, hugging him close -- his breath warm and gentle against her neck. Turning her face toward him, she kissed his cheek.

Smoothly, like clockwork, he slid his shaft in fully, neither slow enough for her to savor the sensation nor quick enough to rouse her with a sense of his desire. With the same even rhythm, he withdrew. Lauren bit her lip again and wondered if he'd be offended if she worked her hand down between them to massage her clit. Instead, she cupped her hands around his buttocks, and concentrated on the feel of his cock moving inside her.

His balls, large and tight, brushed briefly against her ass with each stroke, and Lauren spread her legs wider, tilting her hips upward. She dug her fingers into his asscheeks, pulling him harder against her, feeling a novel, aching emptiness as his scrotum dragged against her asshole. Her jaw went slack as the heat in her cunt flared upward again, greedy, demanding, and her hands clamped down on his hipbones, shoving them back, then harder against her.

Harder, and faster. Oh, God, yes. His pubic bone slammed against her clit, igniting a bolt of lust that shot through her like lightning. She tossed her head, moaning incoherently, vaguely aware he was hissing at her, telling her to hush. Thrusting her hips upward, she sank her teeth into his shoulder even as she speared herself furiously on his thick, meaty cock...

With a wrench, Randy yanked himself away, and Lauren whimpered at the sudden emptiness inside her.

"Fuck." That one word was so laden with disgust that Lauren flinched as if he'd raised a hand to slap her. "Christ, Lauren."

She reached out vainly as he rose, her hands closing on nothing but empty air. She could feel him, in the darkness, standing over her. Then she heard the rustle of fabric as he pulled on his shorts, and a heavier thump as he tugged his work boots on. "Randy? Randy, I'm sorry…"

"You're really good at making me feel like a piece of meat, Laur, you know that? Sometimes I wonder if it's even really me you're fucking."

The tent flap opened, and for a moment she saw him, outlined against the sprinkle of stars outside. Then he was gone.

Biting her lip, Lauren listened to the fading crunch of his footsteps on sand. She threw herself back down on the mat and slammed her fists against it, feeling hot, bitter tears slide down her cheeks as she stared blindly into the darkness and waited.

* * *

Kelly had been seriously pissed when she'd seen Lauren loading her stuff into the back of the van. She had plans of her own for this trip, thank you very much, and they sure didn't include dealing with some bitch who was too uptight to even kiss her fiancé in public. C'mon, what kind of relationship was that?

Not that she'd ever let Daniel kiss her in public either -- but that wasn't a relationship. Hell, he wasn't even her boyfriend. He was just convenient.

He was a pretty good fuck for a college boy, though -- inventive, eager without being grabby, and enthusiastic, of course. He liked it bossy, she'd found -- most men did -- and she lay now on her back with his face buried in her cunt, his tongue dancing over and around her swollen clit, occasionally darting lower to flick at her wet folds. She'd kept him there for the past twenty minutes, clamping his head between her thighs when she came too close to coming.

Now, hearing a noise, Kelly swiveled her neck, tilting her head so she could peer out of the tent. She'd left the flap open, enjoying the cool, scented breeze, and now the ground outside was bathed in the glow of the rising moon. By its soft light she could see Professor Anders, stalking out of the shadows beneath the butte, obviously heading away from his tent.

She was right, then. Kelly smiled in triumph. She'd have bet twenty-to-one little Ms. Tight-ass wasn't putting out right. No wonder the professor (he was Randy only in the middle of the night when, her fingers working busily, she moaned his name into the privacy of her pillow) spent more time with a bunch of old bones than he did with his fiancée.

Well, Kelly was going to fix that. She might only be a sophomore, but she'd be willing to bet she knew more about pleasing a man than Lauren Cole had ever bothered to learn.

Arching her back, she slid one hand up to her firm, round tits and pinched at one nipple. She closed the other in Daniel's thick hair, forcing his face harder against her. Eagerly, he clamped his mouth around her aching clit, suckling it enthusiastically as she shoved him down harder, letting out little yips as the hunger inside her burst at last into waves of fire. They lashed through her body, again and again as she heard the frantic motion of Daniel's hand on his cock.

"Stop that!" she hissed sharply, and kicked downward. The noise ceased. "I'm on the pill, you dumb shit. Now come here and fuck me."

She loved the look on his face as he lowered himself above her -- slack-jawed and desperate for the feel of her cunt. "Fuck me hard, Daniel. Now!" Plunging into her, he slammed his cock home. Ow! Oh, yeah. He froze there, quivering, trying to hold back his peak. Fuck that shit.

Grabbing his ass, Kelly writhed against him, and heard him whimper with need. "Harder, baby," she commanded. "C'mon, is that all you got?" With a wild, snorting groan, he wrenched her thighs wide and pounded her cunt, ramming his cock into her with a frenzy she really quite liked. Snaking her hand down between them, she rubbed at her clit, sending sparks of lust jolting through her as she urged him on. "That's right, baby, fuck me hard, fuck me deeper. Oh yeah, give me all of it. Come for me, baby, c'mon..."

She could feel his cock swelling even further as he drilled her, his balls slapping against her ass, making it sound like he was spanking her. That thought tipped her over the edge again, and she shoved herself against him, her cunt gripping his shaft as hard as a fist as he bucked and shot into her, moaning hoarsely all the while.

Kelly dropped her head back, enjoying the slow, sharp aftershocks that still surged through her. Collapsed on top of her, Daniel blindly nuzzled her tits, suckling one dark, erect nipple as he squeezed the other. She liked the feel of him clinging to her, the knowledge that all she had to do was speak and he'd do anything she liked.

Take that, little Ms. Tight-ass, she thought lazily. She couldn't wait to have Professor Anders where Daniel was now. The idea stirred her, and she became aware of Daniel's mouth on her breast.

If he kept that up, she might have to let him fuck her again.

Chapter Three

Lauren opened her eyes to the sight of a ragged bouquet of desert mallow, resting beside her on the pillow. Tears stung her eyes, and gratefully she gathered them to her chest, snuggling deeper into the sleeping bag as she listened to the profound silence of early morning.

Not quite silent. She could hear the crackle of flames, not too far off. The scent of camp coffee, thick and acrid, reached her nostrils, and Lauren rolled over reluctantly. Then she heard the distinctive chunk of a spade biting into sandy earth, and sat up abruptly. The sound turned the guilt she'd felt as she lay, staring into the darkness and feeling horribly alone, into resentment.

This was his idea of reconciliation? Leave flowers on her pillow and go back to his damn bones?

Well, fuck the fucking flowers.

Soft pink blossoms tumbled to the floor as Lauren scrambled up and pulled on her jeans. Stomping from the tent, she saw Sloan hunkered near the fire. He held out a cup of coffee, and she sipped, hissing as it scalded her tongue.

"Yeah, it's pretty awful," Sloan said.

She grimaced agreement. "The others aren't up yet?" Sloan shrugged, his gaze sliding away from hers. He turned back to the pan of eggs he was scrambling, and Lauren looked around.

The sky still hadn't lost the last flush of dawn, and the warm, slanting light fell in streaks of pink and amber between the jagged, jutting hills. The camp was huddled at the base of one massive butte, near the mouth of an arroyo. Some forty yards distant, Lauren could see Randy's outline against the sky, dirt and sand flying behind him as he dug.

As she approached, she noticed the pegs had been moved, circumscribing a rectangle now about thirty feet long and twenty wide. "Jesus Christ, Randy, couldn't you at least wait till the sun was up?"

He stopped, leaned on his shovel, and took the cup from her hands, for all the world as if it were just another day in Randy-and-Laurenville. As she had, he grimaced at the taste of the coffee. "God, that's hideous. Which one of 'em made it?"

"Not Kelly, at least." Her voice was acerbic. "She's not up yet."

Randy grinned, looking so much like his usual self that Lauren wanted to slap him. "Neither is Daniel."

"Well, at least somebody's getting some," she replied tartly, then, as Randy's eyes darkened, immediately wished she hadn't. He looked like a remorseful puppy.

"Honey, I'm sorry. I --"

"Forget it. You were tense, and I was pushy."

"No, Lauren, I --"

"I said forget it, Randy!"

Turning away, she stared out at the desert, barely seeing it. She could feel Randy behind her, tense and uncertain. Almost to herself, she whispered, "It would have been nice to not wake up alone, though."

He came up behind her, slid his arms around her waist, holding her lightly. Lauren dropped her head back, resting it against his shoulder.

"I love you, Laur," he whispered. "But... sometimes I don't think I can give you what you want."

Tears prickled at the corner of her eyes, and she turned, burrowing into his embrace, hiding her face against his broad chest. "Don't say that. You are what I want, Randy."

Lifting her head, she gazed up at him until, gently, he kissed her, his mouth warm and reassuring. Even as a wave of relief washed through her, easing the momentary panic in her heart, Lauren felt a twinge of disappointment at that chaste, comforting kiss.

Why couldn't she be content with what she had? A fantastic guy, handsome, hard working, who wanted to marry her... And she wanted to marry him. She did -- even if his usual style of lovemaking left her grinding her teeth. And apparently he wasn't comfortable with any other kind.

Lauren sighed. Maybe she'd been too long in L.A. There were things one took for granted, living in a major city. Oral sex, for example.

It wasn't his fault.

He was studying her face earnestly, as if looking for a clue, a magic key to make it all better. Really, she was a fool if she couldn't learn to appreciate what she had.

"I'll make it up to you tonight."

"I'd like that." She leaned against him for a moment longer, enjoying the feel of his warm, strong arms around her. Then, cocking an eyebrow, she drew back and gazed at him challengingly. "Well? Aren't you going to show me your dino?"

He laughed, shaking his head at her quick shift of mood. "Sure. Just as soon as you help me dig it up."

Letting out a mock-groan, Lauren rolled her eyes and picked up a shovel. "Just show me where to plant this."

It had taken all five of them over ten hours to slowly scrape through the compacted clay and shale, working layer by layer down to Kelly's new find. For the final foot, they'd switched to hand trowels, painstakingly tagging soil samples as they cleared the last layers with delicate caution. Now Lauren watched, snapping pictures as Randy uncovered the slender bones of a forepaw, the wickedly hooked talons arched as if still seeking prey. The westerly sun seemed to tip them in blood.

"Jesus, Randy, what is it?"

Intent on his careful excavation, he shook his head -- whether in answer or a warning not to disturb him, Lauren wasn't sure. He started, almost dropping the dental pick he was using to unearth the delicate bones, as Kelly shrieked behind them.

"Help! Professor Anders!"

Spinning, Lauren saw that Kelly and Sloan had uncovered its skull. Playfully, the girl had stuck her hand deep inside the thing's jaw. She grinned impishly at Randy. "It's got me, Professor!"

"Kelly!"

At his barked reprimand, Kelly jerked her hand out -- too fast. One of the sharp, needle-like teeth caught her palm, gouging the skin. "Ouch!" Recoiling, she raised her hand to her mouth, sucking at the wound like a child. Randy gestured peremptorily, giving Kelly a stern look. Meekly, she extended her injured hand, and Lauren seethed inwardly as he examined it.

Oh, for God's sake! "It's just a scratch, Randy," she called. There wasn't even that much blood. Randy seemed almost to be caressing Kelly's hand, his thumbs stroking her palm...

No. Surely that was just her jealous imagination.

"It's not deep, but you'd better keep it out of the dirt. I'll bandage it later. Now..." Kneeling carefully to one side of the skull, Randy tilted his head, studying it. Sloan, behind him, stood tense with expectation. Daniel, big and blond -- he was a U of P halfback, desperately in need of the extra credit if he wanted to return the next fall -- whistled absently as he squatted at the rim of the pit, watching.

More cautiously than Kelly, Randy pressed the pad of a forefinger against one of its fangs, then withdrew his hand thoughtfully. Leaning forward, he peered into its empty eye sockets. Lauren half-fancied they gazed malevolently back.

"But what the hell is it?"

"No idea whatever," he replied. He glanced down at the tangle of bones protruding from the hard clay. "Almost looks as if he's about to bite Lyle's tail, doesn't it?"

Lauren scowled at the teasing tone in his voice. It wasn't funny. There was nothing amusing at all about that skull. The thing looked evil. "Well, whatever it is, you can't do much more tonight."

He glanced up at her, irritation flickering in his eyes. Lauren propped her fists on her hips. "Be sensible, Randy. Look at the light. Unless you're planning to work by flashlight, let's just cover the damn thing up."

Reluctantly, he pushed to his feet, dusting his hands off on the front of his jeans. "All right, folks. Put 'em to bed."

Without looking at her, he headed for the tents. Lauren paused for a moment, gazing out over the desert. The last streaks of crimson still hung in the sky, and the luminosity of dusk intensified the colors in the strata around her. Magenta, mauve, rust-red and brown, the Painted Desert stretched in all directions, breathtaking in its beauty.

Behind her, she heard the distinctive thwap of the tarp as Sloan and Daniel shook it out. The sound was loud in the twilight, and somehow it relieved her. The idea of that thing sitting there all night long, naked to the sky, its sharp teeth gleaming in the moonlight...

Lauren shuddered. Hastening her steps, she caught up to Randy and slid her hand through the crook of his warm, muscular arm.

* * *

Narrowing her eyes, Kelly watched Professor Anders head for the camp, arm in arm with her. Lauren Cole. Smug, flat-chested, superior bitch.

Complacently, Kelly smoothed her wrinkled shirt over the firm, lush curves of her chest. She was no fool, she'd seen the suspicious way Lauren watched her. And with good reason. It didn't exactly take Western Union to get the message Professor Anders was sending.

Kelly glanced down at her palm, smiling at the ragged gash in its surface. It didn't hurt much, just stung a bit, that's all. The memory of Professor Anders's touch was far more potent. She knew he'd felt the energy between them, the heat that had sparked in the depths of her cunt as he'd kneaded her palm.

Oh, yeah. He wanted it just as bad as she did. She hadn't been sure, not a hundred percent sure, before then.

Now she was.

Whistling, Kelly picked up a stray shovel and started to climb from the pit. On an impulse, she turned back, hunkered down by "her" fossil and whispered, "Thanks for the help, whatever you are. See you tomorrow." Whimsically, she patted the skull -- then hurriedly jerked back her hand.

The air had cooled rapidly as the sun sank behind the butte. And yet the fossil was warm -- still holding the sun's heat, she supposed, but it freaked her out just a bit, all the same. And the cut on her palm was burning again. Probably something in the clay dust still coating the skull.

Raising her hand to her mouth, Kelly sucked at the gash, remembering the feel of her forearm inside that cavernous mouth -- a toothpick, a pretzel. An insignificant snack. She shuddered, and forced herself to remember the feel of Professor Anders's arm around her instead -- warm, strong, and reassuring.

A fresh flare of heat pulsed inside her cunt -- her very experienced cunt, Ms. Suspicious Bitch. Stick that in your pipe and smoke it.

She would have Professor Anders. Soon. She could feel it.

And in the meantime, there was always meathead Daniel.

Backing away from the fossil (she didn't want to turn her back to it, for some reason), Kelly grinned to herself. One way or another, it was going to be an interesting night.

Chapter Four

In the dim gloom of the tent, Lauren bent to light the lamp. Randy entered behind her -- she could hear the rustle of the tent flap -- then he slid his hands around her waist and nuzzled her neck. "Leave it," he whispered.

Lauren protested as he caressed her sides. "Randy, I'm a mess, I haven't showered, I --"

"Leave it." Trailing his lips down the side of her throat, he pulled her back against him. The soft caress of his lips reawakened all the frustrations she'd repressed during the day, and Lauren sighed in remembered annoyance.

As if sensing her tension, Randy slid his hands to her shoulders, kneading the muscles until she slowly relaxed. Working downward, he massaged her back through her shirt, then eased it over her head and unsnapped her bra. Adding lips and tongue to the hands caressing her back, he continued the massage.

What had gotten into him? Not that she was about to argue. But for days, she'd barely been able to get him to touch her, and now...

Leaning forward, he whispered in her ear, "Do you like that?"

"Oh, yeah. Randy --"

"Sssh. Let me do this." Turning his attention to her neck, he worked both thumbs down the strong tendons, and her head lolled forward as she braced herself against the low table.

Usually he wasn't much into anything other than face-to-face fucking. It was wonderful, Lauren supposed, in a middle-America missionary-position kind of way, that he liked the visual connection so much, the ability to watch her reactions as they made love.

But there was something utterly erotic about the feel of him behind her, his cock pressed against her tailbone, his hands trailing over her skin. He could, she thought, be anyone -- anyone at all.

Kissing her shoulder, Randy reached forward, tracing the small, taut curves of her breasts. She could feel the pulse of his erection, snugged tight against her ass, as he ran his palms in circles over her nipples.

Lauren was almost shocked at how wet she was already. It was intoxicating, feeling him behind her, his chest against her back, his fingers tickling her nubs, his cock sliding against her ass cheeks. She arched her spine, pressing her ass harder against his shaft, and felt him respond with an answering pressure.

Exactly when during the course of the afternoon had he learned to make love like this?

"Professor Anders?"

God damn it! Lauren snatched for her shirt as Randy yanked himself away. Tugging it over her head, Lauren glowered at him. He grinned sheepishly and lit the propane lantern before opening the tent flap.

Kelly sidled in, all bashful and hesitant -- but Lauren wasn't fooled. Not for a second. The girl's big, innocent eyes flicked over Lauren's rumpled shirt, caught the flush on Randy's face, and positively glowed with a satisfaction she kept carefully from her other features.

"It's my hand, Professor. You said you'd look at it?"

Oh, give me a break! Lauren flung herself down on the sleeping bags and picked up a book, pretending to read it as Randy led the girl to the table and fetched the first aid kit. No way on earth was she going to leave the two of them alone in here, whatever the little minx might have hoped. Among other things, Lauren wouldn't put it past her to wreck Randy's career -- even if nothing had happened.

"Hmm. It looks like it might be infected. Does that hurt?"

"Ouch!" Kelly flinched, doing a marvelous job of looking helpless and needy. Lauren glared at her over the edge of the book. "It burns a bit, Professor."

Randy washed the wound thoroughly, sprayed it with disinfectant, then slathered on Neosporin and bandaged it carefully. Kelly propped her elbow on the table, holding her hand upright as he wrapped gauze around it so that Randy was practically forced to brush her breasts on each pass.

Lauren couldn't help noting the way he kept his gaze cautiously averted.

"There you go. All right and tight." He taped off the end, and Kelly looked up at him, startled.

"That's it?"

"Yup." He smiled, although his jaw looked rather tense. "Just keep it dry, and out of the dirt."

"Oh, okay. Well, thanks, Professor." The disappointment in her voice couldn't have been any clearer. Lauren suppressed a sneer as the girl headed for the tent flap, casting her a quick glance before looking back at Randy. "I'm sorry if I interrupted you."

Yeah. I just bet.

Randy puffed out his cheeks in a sigh as she left. "Teenagers."

"She's not," Lauren said tartly. "She's twenty."

"Same difference." Randy shrugged -- but his gaze sidled away from her. Or was that just imagination, too? Then he stretched and reached for his journal.

Rage flared inside her. "Oh, what? Kelly shows up and now you don't want to have sex?"

Randy gave her a look of pure disgust, then turned his back on her and opened the journal on the table before him.

That was it. She lost it. With a flick of her wrist, she flung the book at his back. When it hit him, he snapped his head around, staring in disbelief. His expression was closer to rage than she'd ever seen.

"Or is it just that you don't want to have sex with me?"

"God damn it, Lauren!" Randy slammed his fists down on the table. The first aid kit fell to the floor with a clatter. "What do you want from me? What is it that you want?"

"I want you to fuck me!"

Her screech punctuated the night. After it came a silence, broken only by the ragged sound of her panting and the rasp of Randy's breath. They stared at each other, shocked, mute with fury. The expression in Randy's eyes slowly changed, growing colder, distant.

He'd never looked at her like that before.

"What a lovely thing to scream in front of my students. Thanks, Lauren." Getting heavily to one knee, he started picking up the spilled items. Disinfectant. Ointment. Gauze bandages. She watched him wordlessly. What bandage, she wondered, could tape this night back together?

He finished reassembling the first aid kit, set it back in the corner. Then, grimly, he righted his stool, sat back down, and opened his journal.

Lauren laughed mirthlessly. "Oh, great. Get right back to your bones. God knows, it's not like they haven't been there for ten million years."

"Damn it, Lauren!" He slammed the journal shut. Pens rattled in the Mason jar on the table as he bumped it, turning to face her. "Do you know how important this is to me?"

"Fine," she said. "Maybe you can dig me up in another ten thousand years and we can have this conversation then."

"What conversation, Lauren? What, the fact that a nineteen-year-old student has a crush on me?"

"Twenty. She's twenty."

"So what? Lauren, I asked you to marry me. Or doesn't that mean anything, where you come from?"

Ouch.

Her reaction must have showed, because Randy's expression softened. He sighed gustily, and ran a hand through his sun-bleached hair. Then he pushed to his feet and crossed to sit beside her. He dropped his head, seeming to study the toes of his hiking boots. Lauren stared blankly at the wall of the tent. After a moment she groped blindly for his hand, felt his fingers close around hers.

"I guess I haven't been very good company this trip." His voice was bleak.

Lauren glanced at him. "Not especially, no."

"It's just that… Ah jeez, Laur, it's what I love."

Lauren nodded. But she withdrew her hand from his clasp. "I know."

He looked at her, an earnest, yearning question in his eyes. Randy. Safe, loving, reliable Randy. Lauren nodded again. "Yeah. Go ahead."

He leaned forward, kissed her forehead. He even fetched the book she'd flung, sliding it into her hands with a sad little smile. "I'll make it up to you, honey."

"Yeah, yeah, yeah." Irritably, she waved him away.

Reassured, he returned to the table, reopened his journal. Lauren could hear the scratch of the pen as he jotted down notes. After a few minutes, he chuckled.

"What's so damn funny?" she asked.

Without turning his head, he replied, "I think I'll name it the Laurenus Hornysaurus." Then he glanced back at her, his eyes dancing with mischief.

Lauren stuck her tongue out at him and rolled onto her side.

* * *

Sitting in the cab of an eighteen-wheeler, Baudouin Delacor listened impatiently to its idling engine. Beyond the glow of the truckstop lights, the night spread out, velvet black and seemingly endless. Cars whizzed past along Route 40, their taillights like staring red eyes in the darkness.

Ever since sunrise, he'd felt a tension in his gut, a hideous sense that time was running short. Loping through the Hualapai Indian Reservation, he'd noted the sun sinking rapidly toward the horizon and had changed direction, veering southeast to Seligman where he'd pilfered a tee shirt and jeans from a backyard washline without being seen by anything larger than a slat-sided cat.

Leaving a hundred dollar bill pinned in their place, he'd hiked to Route 40 and stuck out his thumb.

As the driver, a fat, aging fellow with arms covered in faded tattoos, heaved himself back up into the cab, Delacor said, "I'd better get off here."

"You sure? Ain't nothing past here till you get to Pinta."

Delacor nodded. Yes, he was sure. The scent was thick here, almost overwhelming, a stench like the foul decay of a tomb. It was close now, very close.

The trucker regarded him for a moment, then reached for his wallet and took out a twenty. "Here. Take it." Surprised, Delacor looked at the rumpled bill. "Go on, take it. Ain't gonna get far with no shoes on your feet." As he closed his hand over it, the old man grinned at him, showing pink gums where his front teeth had once been.

Delacor stood on the asphalt of the service station's parking lot, watching as the truck pulled back out. Slowly, it disappeared into the distance, blending with the traffic, just one more eighteen-wheeler, anonymous and unremarkable.

Clutching the rumpled bill in his fist, Delacor looked toward the small distant town, its lights twinkling in the vast darkness. There was an ache in his throat, compounded by pain and estrangement and the beauty of innocence. For they were beautiful, these humans. Even in the midst of their frailties and pettiness there was love and generosity and kindness. What he would give to go down among those lights, slide into a life as ephemeral and nameless as the old trucker's, to be one of them.

He had never been one of them. Never. No matter how much he'd tried. And now --

Delacor paused, his black hair blowing in the wind. Turning his face away from the lights, he walked into darkness. As he went, he folded the bill the trucker had given him and put it carefully into his pouch. Then he peeled off the purloined shirt and left the jeans hanging from the branch of a tree and turned east, toward the moon.

Toward the moon and his enemy.

Chapter Five

Down the dark maze of the arroyo, a cool wind twisted, skittering through the dry vegetation and out over the sand. An unsecured tent flap fluttered in its passing, first revealing, then hiding the empty sleeping bag inside.

Forty yards away, Kelly stood at the edge of the pit, staring down at the blank gray surface of the tarp. The desert stretched before her, a vast silver landscape filled with twisted shadows and the torturous outlines of wind-sculpted rock. The fury, which had boiled inside her at Professor Anders's bland dismissal had evaporated entirely at Lauren's piercing screech.

Now she felt only restless, expectant, vaguely aroused. An electric tension filled her, oppressive and yet exhilarating like the air before a storm. It was as if the night was whispering to her, calling her. She wanted something... something...

Like being hungry, but you're not sure what for. Like that.

The scrape on her palm throbbed, itchy beneath its bandage. Moved by some impulse, Kelly reached for the tarp. She had to tug it quite hard before it came free of the pegs. It made a heavy, flapping, slithering sound as she dragged it aside.

The moon, just rising, flooded the pit with slanting light. In the low illumination, the fossils stood out like x-rays. She could see the curve of Lyle's spinal column, his long pointed snout. Behind him, her fossil seemed to be leaning forward, its head and forearms straining as if trying to break free of the covering clay. Professor Anders was right -- it did look very much like it was about to eat Lyle. For some reason, the idea made her giggle.

It also made her hungry.

The empty eye sockets seemed to stare up at her, their shadows filled with an unspoken message. Restive, impatient, she turned from the pit and shuffled back toward the tents.

Professor Anders's was set a bit away from the others. Inside, a lamp still burned, and she could see his shadow on the wall of the tent. That blurred outline fascinated her, and she stood in the night, her bandaged hand cradled against her chest, tilting her head back and forth idly, studying it.

Finally, she turned away, headed toward the three pup tents pitched near the fire pit. The flap of the middle tent, which was hers, still hung open, gaping slightly. Contemptuously, Kelly ignored it, walked past to the third, and squatted outside.

She could almost smell the heat of Daniel's body inside -- like the meat inside a nut, or a candy in its wrapper. A regular all-American red-blooded boy. Kelly laughed softly, the sound murmuring deep in her throat. She heard motion, then Daniel's sleepy whisper. "Kelly? That you?"

She giggled again. Everything seemed to amuse her tonight. The moonlight. His question. It all seemed so surreal. "Do you know," she whispered back, "I'm really not sure."

The pup tent was cramped. There was barely room for her to squirm in alongside Daniel. The cool, sticky canvas thwapped against her back, and she fumbled impatiently at the sleeping bag's zipper. "C'mon, goddammit," she hissed, tugging at the metal tongue.

Daniel fidgeted inside. "Just let me get it." His hands closed over hers, pulled the zipper down. He tossed back the top half and dragged her against him.

His skin was hot after the chill of the air outside, and Kelly slid on top of him, her thighs gripping his waist. He pulled her down to kiss her, but she turned her head aside, nuzzling the soft declivity beneath his ear.

The skin there was thin, almost delicate. Kelly trailed her lips along it, feeling the pulse of blood just beneath the surface, breathing in the scent of his hair, his warm flesh. She let her eyes fall closed as his hands slid to her ass, pinning her tighter against his erection. She could feel it through the fabric of her jeans, hard and hot, pressing against the nub of her clit. Rocking her hips, she rubbed herself against it, mashing her clit against its pulsing ridge. "Oh yeah," she breathed, and ground harder.

"Ow!" Daniel's hands clamped on her asscheeks, holding her still. At the interruption of her pleasure, Kelly felt a momentary spurt of rage. "Kelly, I'm gonna have no skin left! Here, hang on."

Fumbling at her jeans, he tumbled her off him. The sleeping bag twisted, entangling them, and Kelly thrashed as the canvas of the tent again brushed against her. Daniel was tugging at her pants, trying to remove them. They fouled on her sneakers, and Kelly kicked out, annoyed. "Jesus, Daniel! Oh, fuck it. Just quit it!"

Scrambling out of the tent, she yanked her jeans up. Something made her glance at the first tent, on the far side of the firepit. Sloan's tent. She narrowed her eyes. How much had he heard?

"Kelly!" Daniel was crouched in the opening of his tent, beckoning her back inside.

No. No fucking way. Besides, she had a better idea.

Slitting her eyes at him, she smiled and jerked her head toward the desert. Turning, she walked away, confident he'd follow.

Yes, much better. The night air was cool against her itchy, overheated skin, soothing her restlessness to a kind of expectant certainty. The desert stretched out before her, glimmering in the moonlight. Its torturous landscape looked alien, otherworldly, adding to her weird, dreamlike mood.

It felt as if she were moving through water, as if every step she took was both buoyant and deliberate, predetermined. Ahead, the pit gaped, a flat, rectangular blackness, a hole in the surface of the eerie, glowing night, a portal, a door.

Yes. The word whispered around her, as if it were an exhalation of the night itself. And she responded, deep inside her, with a silent, absolute sureness.

Yes.

There was a rustling sound behind her -- Daniel, with the sleeping bag. She could hear it dragging along the ground. Her lips curving again in a slow, secretive smile, Kelly peeled off her shirt, feeling the stretch of her back muscles, the play of air over the flat span of her stomach. Standing at the rim of the pit, she dropped it, watched it flutter down into the shadows.

"Ah shit. What happened to the tarp?" Daniel came up beside her, and she glanced at him, irritated. What did it matter? Then she jumped lightly into the pit. "Kelly! Get out of there. C'mon, if the prof sees you…"

He trailed off as Kelly, turning to face him, reached behind her and unsnapped her bra. The expression seemed to drain from his face as her breasts spilled out, firm and large and almost perfectly round. Holding his gaze, she caressed them, playing with the nipples, then squeezing them together. She watched his eyes grow huge, his face going slack, suffused with arousal. His cock strained from the waistband of the cutoffs he'd pulled on.

"Don't you want it, Daniel?" Cupping her tits, Kelly reveled in the weight of them, the way they overflowed her hands, seeming to swell out into the night. "Don't you want these?"

Teasingly, she trailed her fingers over their lush curves, working up to the tips, then circled her nipples. The areolae were contracted into furrows, the nubs darkening further as she pinched them lightly. Looking down, she admired them, letting the sight of her fingers tugging at their points turn her on even more. She heard the sleeping bag slide from Daniel's nerveless grasp, the hoarse sound of his breathing, the soft scrape of his zipper. Glancing up, she smiled at the intensity of his gaze. His eyes were fixed on her tits, on her hands moving over them. She wondered if he was even aware he was gripping his cock, his fist dragging the skin up and down the swollen shaft.

She stepped back further into the pit, opened her mouth, licked her lips. "Come and get it then, tiger."

"Ah jeez," Daniel muttered. "Kelly, he's gonna kill us." Nevertheless, he slid his shorts off and followed her down.

The low, slanting moonlight left the base of the pit in shadows. Daniel trod carefully, coming toward her, avoiding the tangle of fossils in the center. She moved to the far side and leaned her back against the pit wall, stretching her arms out along the lip and leaning her head back. The stars, far overhead, twinkled coldly, and the Milky Way stretched, breathtaking in its clarity, across the arch of the sky.

She closed her eyes as Daniel leaned against her, his mouth warm on her neck as he kissed it. His hands closed on her breasts with adolescent urgency. She let him paw at them a while, enjoying the stimulation, and didn't object when he sank to his knees, squeezing her breasts together as he flicked his tongue over the nipples.

Lazily, she reached down, toyed with his hair awhile, then closed her fist in it, yanking his face tight against her. In response, he moaned and clamped his mouth around one nipple, sucking it in a delirium of voracious greed. Kelly arched into the sensation, enjoying the frantic tugging of his mouth, the way he pulled at her nipple while his hand raked over his cock. Tilting her head to one side, she watched him pinch the very tip, closing his fingers into a vise as he pumped his hips, trying to force the head deeper into his grip. All the while, his mouth sucked her tit, his tongue laving the nipple to a sharp, burning point.

Oh, yeah.

Pulling his hair, Kelly dragged his head away from her breast. He whimpered in longing, his tongue stretching forward, trying to get one last taste. His eyes were half-closed, clouded with lust. She shoved his head downward, toward the crotch of her jeans. "Take them off, cowboy," she whispered, "and eat me."

He fumbled her sneakers off, unsnapped her pants. Sliding them down over her ass, he paused a moment to fondle her round cheeks, digging his fingers into them as he dragged her hips forward and licked the smooth curve of her belly. Then he slid her jeans down to her ankles, the crown of his head brushing her mons, and held the fabric as she stepped out.

Burying his face between the v of her thighs, he darted his tongue over her dripping folds. Kelly could feel the motion of his shoulder muscles as he rubbed his cock. Lifting her head, she gazed blankly, her vision blurred with arousal, and found herself staring into the eye sockets of the skull.

They were hollow, black, endlessly deep. Shadows moved within them, and Kelly felt as if it were watching as they coupled before it, like some ancient god observing the primitive rites of its worshipers. It loomed from the earth, not ten feet away, and under its gaze her body seemed to glow, incandescent with a power she'd never before felt. Her nipples ached, and she arched her back, lewdly thrusting her breasts into the moonlight, displaying them before the empty eyes of the skull.

It wanted something, she fancied, something she wanted, too. She was close to the edge, so close... but she wanted more. Her clit throbbed as she pulled her cunt out of the reach of Daniel's tongue and shoved him away, tumbling him backward to the dirt.

"What? Kelly --"

Grinning, she pushed him back down with her foot as he started to rise. He sprawled before her, his knees bent, his balls heavy and full between his thick athlete's thighs. Trailing her foot down his torso, Kelly rubbed her sole over his erection, then slid her toes down to the crack of his ass and nudged lightly. Panting, he stared up at her, his eyes wide and slightly frightened. That small gleam of fear pleased her. The sensation of power was almost overwhelming as she realized he was hers, hers to do whatever she liked with.

She stalked around him, studying him as he lay passive and aroused on the dusty earth. Perhaps she should turn him over, put him on his hands and knees, find something to fuck him with. Such an idea had never occurred to her before. She toyed with it, imagining penetrating that round, perfect ass, fucking him till he came, screaming in mingled pain and desire. Oh, she liked that idea -- or something inside of her did -- very much.

Kneeling down, she straddled his face, grabbed his chin, and yanked his mouth up to her crotch. Electricity exploded inside her as his tongue found her clit, flickering over its swollen length. She stared avidly as his hand moved over his shaft, smearing the clear fluid already leaking from the tip down its length. Moonlight glimmered in the slickness, and she could see every twitch, every gape of his slit as he raked his fist downward, then back up to the head.

"Squeeze it again," she whispered. He did, his hand gripping the head so tight he whimpered. The sound vibrated against the lips of her cunt. *Oh, very nice. What would more sound feel like?*

His left hand was curved around her thigh. She took it and, leaning forward, led it to his crotch, pushed it between his legs till his fingers brushed his balls. "Now squeeze them," she commanded, and felt him gulp.

She stared down, watching as his fingers caressed his balls. His other hand rubbed his cock with short, eager strokes. Kelly sat back, pressing her cunt more firmly against his face. She felt his tongue slide inside her. "Now, Daniel."

The muscles of his forearm flexed and bunched as he dragged his balls up against the base of his cock and clamped them, hard. His back arched, and he screamed, the sound muffled by her body.

Kelly tilted her hips, shoving her clit into his mouth, and he sucked it frantically, moaning as he squeezed his testicles again and again, the strokes of his fist on his cock becoming harder, faster, almost vicious. Kelly watched, transfixed, as he savaged his cock, letting go of his balls now to wrap both hands around the shaft, pumping it with a mindless, wanton abandon. The tip swelled, rigid and shiny, almost purple in the moonlight, and his hands flew up and down in a headlong, spastic rhythm as the slit gaped open and spurted milky-white jets of semen onto the taut, smooth ripples of his abs.

Running her fingers through it, she smeared it across his chest, leaning forward as he suckled her clit in frenzied urgency, his cock still spilling come across his sticky fingers. His throat muscles worked repeatedly as he swallowed her juices. The night seemed to whirl around her, and the hunger inside her roared in anticipation.

Scrambling to her feet, she shifted around and straddled his thighs, grasping his cock in one hand and impaling herself on it, shoving it deep inside her with one hard thrust. Grabbing his wrists, she dragged his hands to her breasts, and moaned as he clenched his fingers around them. "That's right, cowboy. As hard as you like. Make me pay for hurting you."

She watched his eyes change as the fear faded from them. Something different and darker shone in its place. His face looked older, harder, suffused with a desire most men never admitted to. Viciously, he grabbed her nipples and twisted. Kelly's head snapped back as pain flared through her, driving the hunger inside her up another notch. *Yes.*

Yes.

"Do it again." Leaning forward, she braced her arms on either side of his shoulders, positioning her tits directly above his face. He stared at them ravenously as his fingers worked over them, pinching, squeezing, punishingly rough. His cock throbbed inside her, swollen and stiff, hard as rock. He thrust upward with his hips, jabbing deep inside her, and Kelly gasped. "Oh, yeah, baby. That's right. Fuck me hard."

She could hear the pound of his heart as he strained below her, could practically see the blood surging through his veins, pulsing in his arteries, darkening his features as he drilled himself up into her with a deep, primal fury. Kelly rocked her hips back, egging him on.

His heartbeat seemed to throb through the night like a drum. The sound was intoxicating, maddening. It teased the craving inside her into a snarling, feral beast. Raising her head, Kelly gazed directly into the sockets of the skull. Her palm itched, under its bandages. She felt her limbs tensing, the muscles quivering, overflowing with strength. Her fingers dug into the dirt like claws.

Daniel stiffened below her, his hands cramping on her tits as his orgasm took him. His head rocked back and he groaned into the night as he exploded inside her, his come flooding her cunt. She arched her back, her cunt gripping him tighter, sucking him deep into the fire that burst within her womb, pouring outward in a flood of delirious sensation.

Now, something whispered, deep in her mind.

Do it now, Kelly.

She looked down at the white, exposed flesh of Daniel's neck. His head was still tilted back, his breath rasping through his throat. Need, voracious and undeniable, flooded through her, and Kelly plunged her head down, her jaw open, her teeth ripping. A second orgasm ripped through her like lightning, and Daniel's screams cut off abruptly.

A satiation so complete it felt almost like drowning stole along Kelly's limbs, and she rolled off Daniel's body and sprawled luxuriously on her back, staring up at the stars. Lazily, she drew her fingers up her belly, leaving dark, wet trails across the soft skin.

Something still tugged at her, a nagging, pulsing ache deep in her mind. There was something more, wasn't there? Something else to be done.

Tilting her head back, Kelly glanced at the skull, glimmering in the moonlight. It sat silent now, waiting. She sensed it wouldn't wait long. Not happily, at least.

Sighing like a child ordered to clean up her room, she climbed heavily to her feet, reached down, and closed a fist sticky with blood in Daniel's hair. "C'mon, you," she said amiably, and tugged.

Spastically, jerk by jerk, Daniel's body slid through the dust toward the gleaming white skull.

* * *

Sloan had very nearly stopped them when Kelly jumped into the pit. Okay, sure, they liked fucking -- and he liked watching them do it. It wasn't the first time he'd spied on them, his hand surreptitiously pressing his cock as they thrashed and groaned. But Jesus Christ! Those fossils were priceless.

When Kelly had removed her bra though, all thought of stopping them, of rousing the professor if he had to, fled. Man, what he wouldn't give to get his hands on those tits. He'd wrapped them around his hard-on instead, peering from behind the pile of dirt from yesterday's digging. They were far too involved to hear his hoarse breathing.

Watching the muscle-bound stud squeeze his balls at Kelly's command almost tipped Sloan over the edge, but he held back, watching avidly as Kelly switched positions, mounting Daniel and offering her tits to his grasp. Sloan bit back a moan as Daniel twisted her nipples, and his hand moved faster over his throbbing shaft.

He was right on the edge when Daniel arched below Kelly, throwing his head back in ecstasy as he shot his wad into her. Sloan felt the first pulse in his own balls as she plunged her head down.

Then the screaming started.

Stumbling backward, his shorts around his ankles, Sloan fell to the sand, scraping his ass raw. Yanking his shorts up, he scrambled to his feet and ran, feeling the fabric of his cutoffs tug at his erection with each stride. He sobbed in horror as the screams faded, sliding into a last wet burble of sound. He wasn't running for the tents, now far behind, he wasn't running for help -- he was simply running, as fast and far as his legs could take him.

He staggered as his shorts, pressing and scraping across his still throbbing cock, pushed him over the edge. Dropping heavily to his knees, he moaned as his cock jerked and spasmed, spurting hot, sticky fluid. Leaning forward, Sloan vomited onto the sand.

Chapter Six

Lauren thrashed once, felt the book slide from her chest to the floor of the tent, and sat up.

Something had disturbed her -- a noise, perhaps. Whatever it was, it was gone now. The camp was silent around her, the kiddies long since all tucked in their beds. A light breeze gusted outside, moaning between the buttes. The propane lantern hissed, casting harsh shadows in the tent's corners.

She didn't know what the time was, but it felt late. She'd been so deeply asleep she'd been drooling, Lauren realized. Brushing the slick dampness from her cheek, she looked around for Randy.

He was still where he'd been when she fell asleep, hunched over the small table like a man possessed, a book open before him. He didn't seem to be reading, just staring blankly, almost as if he were in a trance. She watched for a while. He didn't move.

Finally, she chucked her pillow at him. He looked up, startled, and Lauren recoiled. In the greenish light of the lantern, his face looked like a death's head -- the eye sockets no more than shadowy pits, the cheeks hollowed, the skin white with exhaustion. Then he shifted, shaking himself like a dog shedding water, and the impression faded.

"Sorry, is the light keeping you awake, hon?"

"No," she replied. "Just making sure you're still breathing."

He smiled wanly, still looking dazed, and Lauren flipped the edge of the sleeping bag back. Crossing to the bed, he flopped down on his stomach, sighing heavily as he collapsed. Lauren smiled and stroked his hair softly. "So have you figured out what it is yet?"

He hesitated, then rolled onto his back. "I don't know, Lauren. I just don't know. I've never seen anything even vaguely like it. The nasal cavities, the cranial dimensions... it's all wrong."

"What do you mean, wrong?" Reaching over, Lauren ran her hand idly over the warm, bronzed expanse of his chest. He shifted restlessly, and she withdrew her hand, pulling herself up into a sitting position with her arms wrapped around her legs.

"Look, I... It's nothing. Just a feeling, I guess. The hairs on my neck..."

Playfully, she slid her hand around the back of his neck. "They feel fine to me."

"God damn it, Lauren!" He jerked his head away. Lauren froze in surprise, a sliver of hurt piercing her chest. Distractedly, he ran a hand through his hair, making the shaggy mess worse. "I'm sorry, hon. I didn't mean to snap."

"It's okay," she replied -- too quickly. "You just need some sleep."

He sighed, rose, and turned off the lantern. When he lay back down, Lauren curled up on her side, keeping a thin strip of distance between them. Outside the tent, the wind scurried over the sand. Heat radiated off him in waves, and Lauren wondered for a moment if he was ill.

After a few minutes, she felt him shift closer, rolling onto his side so they faced one another in the darkness. Then he slid his hands beneath her tee shirt and cupped her breasts.

Finally, she thought, and leaned into his touch, hoping against hope that whatever had gotten into him earlier would still be there. No such luck. He was stroking her now with his usual hesitant delicacy, as if she were a doll or -- God forbid -- a virgin. She had to bite back a sigh of exasperated disappointment.

But the feathery touch of his work-callused hands was slowly drawing a first, tentative tendril of warmth from between her thighs. She could hear his heart pounding with arousal, feel his breath growing quicker as he kissed her, his tongue probing modestly between her lips. Once, just once, though, she wished he'd be a little less diffident, a little more --

Oh.

Her spine seemed to melt as Randy, with an uncharacteristic roughness, squeezed her breasts -- hard. Ducking his head, he tongued her nipples through the fabric of her shirt, and Lauren felt her cotton panties growing distinctly damp. "Mmm," she murmured, and wrapped her arms around his neck, wanting to hold him there. But with an impatience that both surprised and delighted her, he tossed his head like a bull, freeing it from her clasp, then yanked her shirt upward, exposing her breasts to the cool night air.

Immediately, her nipples contracted, and Randy lowered his head again, closing his lips around one taut nub while he rolled the other between his rough fingers. Moaning slightly, Lauren arched her back, urging him on. Whatever had gotten into him, she was loving it.

Fumbling, she felt for his crotch, found the thick swell of his erection, and caressed it through his boxers. He rocked his hips forward, pressing himself more deeply into her grasp, and at the same time tightened his own, pinching her nipple fiercely.

Ouch! Lauren jerked back. "Hey, not so hard!" He didn't answer. He just lay on his side, unmoving, as if waiting for her to roll back toward him, bring her breasts back within reach of his mouth.

What the hell? Usually he was a talker, murmuring in her ear as he caressed her, lifting her chin to gaze into her eyes. This silent, fiercely intent Randy was a little... well, weird.

Still, it was definitely an improvement over his usual so-soft-it-tickled approach. She moved back into his arms, lifted his hand and placed it again on her breast. "Just a touch gentler, honey, okay?"

His tongue snaked out, brushed her bruised nipple. Lauren jumped, and then held herself still as he devoured her breasts, crushing them in his grip as he sucked at them greedily, first one, then the other. She tried to relax into the sensation, but it seemed like every time she started to enjoy it, his teeth would catch her nipple, jarring her out of the experience.

For once, she wished she could see his expression.

She was actually relieved when he slid his hands down to her hips. Firmly, he pulled her toward him, his erection jabbing her stomach as he shoved it against her. He thrust a hand between her legs, probing her crotch, but the moisture that had slicked her cunt was gone, evaporated like mist.

"Randy, I --"

Suddenly, he shoved her onto her back, his hands pawing at her underwear, his thighs already between her own, forcing them open. The heat pouring off his body was fiery in its intensity. What the hell?

"Randy. Randy!"

He froze, one hand closed on the crotch of her undies, the other God knew where -- on his dick, she suspected. It was too dark to see. "Randy, could we please slow down just a bit?"

There was a pause. Then he said, "Sure," rolled off her, and lay motionless on his sleeping bag.

Lauren stared at the ceiling, her stomach knotted with rage. Rage, and a certain nebulous fear. Of Randy? Ridiculous. Coldly, she said, "I didn't say stop, you know." He didn't respond.

None of this was like him in the least.

And what was going on here, anyway? Out of all the times she'd tried to get him to be a little more passionate, a little more forceful...

Ah.

Suddenly Lauren felt awfully dumb.

She'd asked him for this, so many times. Well, not this, exactly, but a little more force, a little more passion. At least he'd been trying. She could hear his breathing, heavy and tense in the darkness. She was glad, actually, that she couldn't see his face, couldn't see the hurt and disappointment in it.

How many times, she wondered, had it been like this? How many times had he been being perfectly wonderful, and she simply hadn't noticed? If she felt he'd been slighting her over the past few weeks, wouldn't it be just as fair to say she'd been taking him for granted?

No more of that. From now on, she was going to appreciate everything she had. If she didn't, she might as well go right back to L.A., back to her condo and a cat that really did ignore her, and the whole damned rat race.

"Randy, I'm sorry." Lauren snuggled against him apologetically, raised one hand and traced the line of his jaw. It was tight, the muscles bunched as if he were clenching his teeth. "We can try it again, if you like."

She felt him shrug. "Go ahead, if you want."

It was something at least. Tentatively, she slid her hand down his chest, the utter lack of sight making her doubly aware of the texture of his skin, the swell of his pectorals, the slight indentations between his ribs. The fine blond hairs that dusted his chest tickled her palm, and she smiled.

Playfully, she circled one of his nipples with her finger, teasing the tight nub. She liked his nipples, tanned a deep ruddy bronze, found them incredibly sexy. But when he flinched, she immediately moved her hand, and continued her tactile exploration.

There was something so soothing about this, so intimate and comfortable. Even though she'd said yes when he'd asked her, this was the first time she'd been actually able to imagine being married to him, sharing a bed, a home, a life. And what business had she had, saying yes in the first place, when deep in her heart she hadn't been sure at all? Had she been so desperate to prove that she wasn't a failure, that she wasn't throwing her life away by leaving L.A., that she'd made the right choice? Had the sneers and jibes and unspoken judgments affected her so profoundly?

Was she really that insecure?

Yes, she supposed she was. And Randy, steadfast, loving Randy, had borne the brunt of it. Lauren blushed, grateful for the concealing darkness, as she remembered how she'd bridled at Kelly's transparent attempts at seduction. As if Randy would ever stoop to such bait!

Really, she'd been completely, utterly, and totally an ass. Well, she would make it up to him, damn it.

Starting right now.

"Turn over," she whispered. After a brief hesitation, he did. Smiling into the darkness, Lauren swung her leg over his thighs and straddled him, rubbing the warm, heavy muscles of his back. He really was hot. Perhaps it was just too much sun. He shifted slightly below her, and she paused until he lay still again.

Working slowly down the corded columns on either side of his spine, she reached his tailbone and pressed her thumbs firmly against it. He groaned slightly, and encouraged, she lifted his hips slightly and slid his boxers off. Then she kneaded the firm, smooth curves of his ass, digging her fingers into the muscle. He flinched - - not with pain, though. Arousal? She hoped so.

Lowering her head, she kissed his back, then licked the velvety skin between his shoulder blades before sitting back up and sliding her hands down the outside of his thighs, intensely aware of his hard, rounded ass cheeks brushing her mons.

Her breath was shallow, a little shaky, and Lauren realized she was nervous. Shifting off him, she gripped his hips and tugged him up into a kneeling position. Then, before she lost her nerve entirely, she reached around and closed her hand on his cock.

It pulsed in her grip, hot and hard against her palm. Oh, thank God. She'd been terrified that he was hating it, silently suffering through her unwanted attentions. More confidently, she snuggled against him, pressing her breasts beneath her thin tee shirt against his back as she caressed his shaft, trailing her fingers over it, tickling the fleshy lip of its head. He sighed and leaned back into her.

Better and better.

Then he closed his hand over hers, squeezing it tight around his cock. Holding it firmly, he moved it up and down, using her hand to masturbate himself with. Lauren's cunt throbbed at the sensation.

His skin was like velvet, sliding between her fingers. It grew thicker, stiffening further as he worked her hand over it. His head rested against her shoulder, his strong neck inches from her lips.

Lauren ran her tongue down it, enjoying the clean, slightly salty taste.

His breathing grew harsher, and his hand clamped down on hers, moving it faster. His hips flexed as he bucked up into her grasp. Her fingers were beginning to ache and, with a tentative jerk, Lauren tried to extricate her hand. His fingers tightened, mashing her fingers beneath his grip as he raked her hand up and down.

"Ow! Jesus, Randy!" This wasn't funny, it wasn't okay, and it sure wasn't arousing. "Randy, quit it!"

Yanking her hand free, Lauren glared into the darkness. Which was, she supposed, pretty ridiculous. She shoved to her feet, meaning to light the lamp and have this out with him once and for all, but Randy grabbed her wrist, jarring her shoulder as he tumbled her to the floor of the tent.

Dear sweet Jesus, what was wrong with him? Fury shot through her, but behind it, the question burned at her mind. Randy scrabbled at her thighs, and she felt the first trickle of fear as he forced them apart. Kicking out, she felt her heel connect with something, and he tumbled sideways.

Lunging to her hands and knees, she scrambled toward the tent flap. In the darkness behind her, something growled -- and for one crucial second, Lauren froze.

That's not Randy.

With the thought, an icy certainty filled her. Oh, she knew the traps women laid for themselves. He'd never act like that, really. He doesn't mean it. He's not being himself. She knew them *ad nauseum*; as a journalist she'd heard them over and over. But this... this was different.

That's not Randy. That's not even human.

She threw herself toward the flap, but a hand clamped around her ankle. Twisting desperately, she locked her fists together and swung with the entire weight of her torso. Pain screamed through her knuckles as the blow connected, but his hand fell away. Thrusting herself forward blindly, Lauren ignored the silence behind her. He could be dead, he could be knocked out -- she didn't care. She tore at the tent flap and fled into the night.

* * *

On hands and knees, Kelly stroked the skull with long, firm motions, almost like a woman scrubbing a floor. Blood coated her arms to the elbows, glimmering wetly in the moonlight. Pausing, she reached down into the open cavity of Daniel's abdomen, scooped out a mass of spongy, blood-soaked tissue, and rubbed it over the exposed bone.

"There, there, you greedy thing." Her tone was indulgent, vaguely maternal. Blood soaked into the bone like water into a desert, leaving no trace. Tugging at the rubbery rope of Daniel's intestines, she pulled them out, wrung them, foot by foot, like a dishcloth. Blood spattered down onto the fossil beneath.

Slowly, slowly, the gleam of bone faded. A thin haze of flesh formed over the skull. Plunging her hand up under Daniel's ribs, Kelly yanked out his heart, held it aloft like a trophy. Then she squeezed it, laughing as the blood gushed out.

The blood slowed to a trickle. She nudged the corpse with her toe. "All gone," she said sadly, and looked at the skull.

It wasn't a skull any more, not really. Tendons laced the massive hinge of its jaw. Pink, suppurating gums lined the needle-like teeth. Where the eye sockets had been, a milky film now stretched, almost like cataracts.

It was still hungry. She could feel its appetite beating against her, as tangible as hot sunlight or ocean waves.

"I told you already. It's all gone!"

A fierce stab of pain shot through her skull, and Kelly grabbed at her forehead. "Don't do that!" She kicked at it and heard a wet, squelching thump.

A flutter of movement in the distance caught her eye. Kelly crouched down quickly and watched as Lauren stumbled from Professor Anders's tent and fled, her white cotton panties catching the moonlight like a rabbit's tail.

That's right, little bunny, run. Run into the hills. Kelly nearly laughed aloud, but she stifled it, cupping a sticky hand over her blood-smeared mouth. She glanced around slyly. All else was still.

Then a light bloomed inside the professor's tent, warm and amber. The skull seemed to whisper behind her, but she ignored it.

He wanted her. Randy. Could it be any clearer? He was calling to her, his light like a beacon to guide her to him. She felt a flare of longing, deep in her cunt. How she'd waited for this moment!

And oh, how very hungry she was.

Like a moth drawn by a candle, Kelly glided across the pit and climbed out onto the sand.

Chapter Seven

"Laur?" Blinking, Randy pushed himself up, and groaned. His head was throbbing so hard he saw splashes of light against the darkness. Cupping his forehead, he sat, trying to push through the sense of dislocation.

He was in the tent. On the floor. There was a sleeping bag under his thigh, tangled into a ball -- and empty. The whole tent felt empty, abandoned.

Why did his head hurt so much?

He'd been dreaming, something about the fossil, something... He couldn't recall...

Had they fought? His head swam, trying to remember. It was a safe guess, though -- they were always fighting these days, and he was never sure why. He couldn't seem to make any sense of her, of her moods, her sudden outbursts -- but at the same time, that was what had attracted him to her. He liked her unexpectedness, her passions, the way he'd manage, sometimes, to do or say the right thing and her face would fill with light like the sun breaking free of a thundercloud.

It was a sight more precious to him than he'd ever found words to tell her.

The eastern wall of the tent was beginning to glow as the moon cleared the top of the butte outside, but it wasn't enough light to see by. Carefully, Randy felt through the darkness till his hand brushed the table. Sliding his palm along its surface, he located the lantern and lit it.

His books and journals littered the table. Looking at them, he vaguely remembered paging through them, half in a trace. Then Lauren had -- what? Made him go to bed, that was right, he remembered that much. Had he had a fever?

His head ached. Sunstroke, maybe.

Randy stared blankly at the twisted sleeping bags, feeling the first stirrings of alarm. The mats were askew, the pillows flung violently about. But where was Lauren? Surely she wouldn't have gone wandering off in the middle of the night. Most likely she was just taking a piss.

The wreckage of their bed seemed to mock that possibility.

He knew she'd been unhappy, and she had some right to be, he supposed. He did get awfully wrapped up in his work but he only got out here twice a year, if that. It wasn't too much to ask, was it?

Kelly.

Remembering, he groaned and sank down onto the campstool. What on earth had possessed him to let the girl come? It was ridiculous though -- Lauren had no reason to feel jealous. Student or not, Kelly was hardly the sort of girl to interest him. Her overt sensuality was disturbing, to put it mildly. Rather like being stalked by a tigress in heat.

Disturbing, and okay, a little arousing. It wasn't like he was ever going to do anything about it.

The feel of her breasts brushing the back of his hand as he'd bandaged her palm... Randy flushed.

How could he have been so stupid?

There was a rustle of movement, outside the tent. Lifting his head, he called hopefully, "Lauren?" His voice, he realized, was little more than a croak.

But it was Kelly who twitched aside the flap and slid out of the night.

The girl was naked, spattered in blood, and Randy's first panicked thought was that she was hurt, badly. Shit! It was a twenty mile drive before he'd even reach a paved road, and another thirty to a hospital...

Then she came toward him, one hand tracing a lazy design on her torso -- up the belly, around her nipples, down again to the thatch of her sex. Randy's feet tangled in the stool as he lurched to his feet, and he stumbled as he backed away till he hit the wall of the tent. She smiled at him blandly, as if completely unconscious of the blood coating her. "I saw your light, Randy."

At the use of his name, the hairs stood up on the back of his neck. Her eyes were oddly unfocused, seeming both to study him and hardly notice him at all. And still her hand kept tracing that triangle on her body -- crotch to nipple to nipple to crotch. It mesmerized him, drawing his gaze again and again to exactly those places he didn't want to look. Swallowing hard, he forced his head up.

"Are you hurt, Kelly?"

She laughed, low and long. The sound sent a shiver through him -- not of fear, or not only of fear. There was a thrill of risk in it, a dangerous carnality that seemed to mock him. *If you're man enough*, that laughter taunted. *If you're man enough...*

The challenge in it roused him. Without conscious volition, his gaze slid again to her blood-spattered body. She was short, compact, with breasts that thrust forward, large and round as cantaloupes. Her waist tucked in nicely before flaring out again to lush, curvy hips. He'd caught himself more than once staring at her ass in the halls, and she turned now, displaying it before him. Full, taut ass cheeks above sturdy, muscular thighs, tapering down to slim ankles. Kelly reached back, grabbed her cheeks in both hands, spreading them slightly as she tilted her hips. Randy swallowed again, realizing for the first time that he was stark naked -- and painfully erect.

"Oh, you like that, Professor Anders." Smiling at him over her shoulder, she wiggled her butt. He could see the swollen, glistening lips of her sex, the small pink rosebud of her tight asshole. "Doesn't your bitch let you put it up her ass?"

"She's not my -- don't talk that way, Kelly!" But his cock twitched against his belly. *Doesn't your bitch let you put it up her...*

Jesus.

"Get out. Now."

She smiled again.

"I mean it."

Pouting, Kelly moved as if to leave, and Randy breathed a sigh of relief. Shit, if Lauren came back now...

As if by accident, Kelly stumbled over the stool, crying out as she fell. Automatically, he moved toward her, reaching to help her up -- but she hadn't tripped. She'd draped herself purposefully over the stool, her ass tilted up toward him, her thighs spread wide. He yanked his hand back from her shoulder. Her skin had been so hot, almost burning...

What would it feel like, to be inside her?

Ah, Christ. "Kelly, no. Please. Come on, get up."

Reluctantly, her full lips curved in a sulky droop, she rolled over on the stool. For a moment her head hung off one side, her back arched over the seat, her huge, perfect tits thrust directly up at him. His hands quivered at his sides, aching to squeeze them, torment them as he had Lauren's --

What? When did I --

His head whirled, his blood pounding at his temples. The tent seemed suddenly stifling, the air thick as if filled with incense.

Randy gasped, flailing backward gracelessly. It took all his will to thrust himself away from Kelly's offered body. Blood roared in his ears, sounding like a cyclone, a whirlwind. The tent spun like a vortex, sucking him toward that hot, waiting cunt. Eyes wide, he watched as she slid forward onto her knees, trapping his cock in her mouth in one smooth motion. She pumped her head downward, once, twice, her tongue flicking over his shaft, scalding him. His balls swelled in anguish, and Randy shut his eyes.

Please, God, make her stop. I can't. I can't stop her...

He didn't want to stop her. The sensation was intoxicating, driving away all thought of Lauren, his job, his reputation... Nothing mattered but her lips tugging at him, stretching around the thick, sensitive head, plunging down till he felt himself enter her throat. A sound that was almost a whimper escaped him as he fought to hold himself still, to resist the urge to fuck her mouth till he came in great, spurting wads...

Ah, shit.

When she pulled back, he didn't jerk himself away, as some tiny part of his mind still knew he should. He stood motionless, waiting, as she licked her lips and looked up at him, a satisfied smirk on her catlike features.

"Now," she murmured, "tell me you want it."

Her lips whispered against his swollen, aching cockhead. His balls contracted, heavy as lead, and his legs felt like they'd been turned to jelly.

"I want it, Kelly."

He pushed his hips forward slightly, and she licked just the very tip of his cock. "Say it again."

More fervently, he repeated, "I want it. I want my cock in your mouth."

"More." She opened her lips, dragged her little white teeth over the velvety skin. A rush of saliva flooded his mouth, and Randy swallowed again. He could feel his body quivering, senseless with desire.

"I want to fuck your mouth, Kelly. I want to fuck it hard. "

"Louder."

That light tickle again, spreading her lips open, teasing the tip before she pulled back. Randy's balls throbbed. "Suck me, damn you. Put my cock in your mouth. Come on, damn it! Suck me!"

Clamping his hands in her hair, he forced her head downward, and Kelly barely had time to wrap her lips over her teeth before he was shoving his cock into her. He jerked himself back out, and Kelly eagerly gobbled the tip, sliding her tongue around its meaty lip before he slammed it in, rocking her head back.

She wanted him to fuck her? Oh, he'd fuck her all right. He'd fuck her in every hole she possessed till she trembled beneath him, begging for mercy.

The night swirled around him, the air intoxicating, heavy with scent. It was thick, cloying, not entirely pleasant. It made him think of altars on which incense was burned -- incense and other, darker, sacrifices.

Reeling, delirious, he fucked Kelly's mouth. She squirmed, fighting his hold, and he grabbed her hair harder, pounding his cock deep into her throat. At the satisfied gleam in her eyes, he realized that was exactly what she'd wanted. Sobbing with mingled lust and despair, Randy felt his balls swell, aching for release.

* * *

Deep in the twisting cleft of the arroyo, Lauren crouched, shivering in nothing but her tee shirt and panties. Hard rock scraped against her butt where she hunkered beside a boulder, and her bare feet against the rough stones were chilled to the bone.

The night had gotten cooler as the moon rose, shrinking as it neared its zenith. Now cold white light poured down the steep sides of the chasm, giving every rock, every pebble, every outcrop and ledge its own, distinct shadow. It picked out her shape like a floodlight, making her feel hideously exposed, and she shrank closer to the boulder, trying to hide in the thin sliver of black the moon cast at its feet.

There was an eye in the night, watching her. An amused, malevolent eye.

Oh, ridiculous!

Lauren clenched her chattering teeth. Inside her, fury warred with shock and dismay. What the hell had happened in the past twenty-four hours that she was suddenly squatting behind a rock, freezing her ass off in the middle of the desert?

The night hung around her, preternaturally silent. Something breathed at the edge of her awareness, like a great, hungry, invisible beast. She could almost smell its foul stink on the air, the sweet, sickly odor of carrion, rotting meat...

Scowling, Lauren jabbed her toes into the sand, felt the scrape of pebbles against her cold skin. That was real. That was solid, not these vapors of her imagination. Randy, a rapist?

C'mon! She knew him, knew him inside and out. He was levelheaded, straightforward, just plain decent. It was impossible.

Another part of her was keenly aware of the throb in her knuckles, the bruises on her knees.

Oh yeah, it's possible, Lauren. You just don't want to believe it.

True enough -- and yet it didn't feel quite like that, like a dismaying truth she was trying to avoid. It felt more like being told the earth really was flat, or that what she'd thought were her hands were actually a kind of fleshy spider that had crawled onto her arms and taken up residence. Impossible, of course... but you'd stare at them, wouldn't you, feeling your world slide treacherously around you? You'd scoff -- but wouldn't there also be just that faint trace of doubt?

Moonlight coated the landscape, making solid stone seem shadowy and unreal.

No, Lauren decided abruptly, there wouldn't. The idea was insanity. Shivering in the moonlight, she called up the image of Randy's face, just that morning, tilted up toward her with his eyes gleaming in excitement. She thought of the way he'd looked, so serious and hopeful, as he'd proposed, three months ago, sliding the stunning one carat solitaire that was really far more than he could afford onto her finger with a look of such pride...

No. It didn't add up. Something about the whole thing -- Lauren smiled grimly -- stank.

It was very hard to stride purposefully over gritty, shifting sand, especially barefoot. The jagged edge of a rock caught her heel and she hissed, but kept her head firmly erect as she stumbled her way back out of the arroyo, acutely conscious of the black spaces beneath boulders, the shadowed cracks between stones. There were snakes out here, scorpions... Her heart thudded in her chest, but she didn't slow down.

Something was wrong here. Something was horribly, horribly wrong. And damn it, she was going to find out what.

Right now.

Chapter Eight

Lowering his head, the BloodWolf sniffed at the uneven tracks in the sand. They were recent, headlong. A scent of panic clung to them. But they led north, away from the stink of corruption ahead. Whoever the ragged tracks belonged to was safe for the moment. Delacor turned away, lifted his muzzle -- and caught the smell of blood on the wind.

No. Oh, no.

It had already killed. Once, at least. How many more had it infected?

Lunging forward into the night, the BloodWolf ran, a shadow on the desert, a familiar fear growing in his breast.

Late. Too late.

Snarling, the wolf ran faster.

* * *

At the sight of the lantern's glow inside the tent, Lauren sighed with relief. He'd probably been waiting up, worried sick. At any rate, she was grateful she wouldn't have to wake him. Pushing back the tent flap, she walked in, and stopped short.

Kelly crouched on the ground, naked, her massive breasts brushing Randy's thighs as she sucked his cock. No -- Lauren stared -- as Randy fucked her mouth. His knees were bent, his legs spread slightly, and Lauren could see Kelly fondling his balls as he rocked his hips forward, driving himself between her stretched lips. His hands were fisted in her hair, yanking her to him, his eyes half-closed in ecstasy as he watched every stroke.

Lauren felt her heart crack into bitter shards as she watched him pounding Kelly's mouth with a greedy intensity he'd never shown her -- no. He had. Once.

Tonight.

It was true, then. It was all true. The man she'd been so sure she knew had never existed.

Randy hadn't even looked up as she'd entered. He hadn't even done that. She meant so little to him that he wasn't even ashamed.

A sob burst from her as she whirled away, shoving back through the tent flap. She was running again -- she didn't care. This time, she wasn't coming back.

As she scrambled into the Jeep, she heard a shout behind her. Too late -- it had already been too late when she'd walked into the tent, saw him fucking Kelly's mouth, his face lax and heavy with the urgency of lust... Viciously, Lauren twisted the keys in the ignition, slammed the Jeep into gear, furious at the tears that coated her cheeks and doubly furious at the throb of arousal in her cunt.

Tires spun in the silence as she peeled out, barely seeing the rough track in the headlights before her. All she saw was Randy, his eyelids dropping, his mouth hanging open in carnal rapture as his hips pumped and pumped and...

She jammed the Jeep into third. It bucked below her, slithered across the sand toward the ditch at the side. Tromping the gas, Lauren spun the wheel, dragging the vehicle back under control.

Her breath hitched in her chest as the track straightened ahead of her. With grim determination, Lauren floored the pedal. Thirty... forty... fifty... The engine whined. She shifted up into fourth.

Sixty...

Something gleamed for a moment, at the edge of her vision. A long black shadow dashed out of the night, into the headlights. The brakes squealed as she slammed them down -- far, far too late. There was a heavy, meaty thud, and a shape flew through the air.

"Jesus!" Lauren spun the wheel, trying to stop. The tires hit the embankment, rode up and over. The Jeep lurched and almost toppled as it thumped into the ditch and came to a stop, its axle hung up on the embankment, the back tires spinning free. Leaping out, Lauren ran back up the track.

Moonlight glimmered on the compacted sand. The track stretched, empty. But...

No, that thump had been all too dismally real. She hadn't imagined that.

She sprinted down the track, her head swinging from side to side, her gaze sweeping the roadsides. A shadow, off to her left. Something in the ditch? She dashed toward it, then stopped abruptly.

Ah, shit.

Not a dog, as she'd thought. A man, his limbs skewed at impossible angles.

Shit, oh shit.

Sobbing, she crawled down the slope, her limbs shaking with reaction. He was naked, she realized with a dull sort of wonderment. No, not quite -- there was what looked like a leather fanny pack cinched tight around his waist.

What was a naked man doing in the middle of the desert?

His profile in the moonlight seemed carved from white marble. Square, strong jaw. High, beautiful cheekbones. Thick brows arched low above a proud Gallic nose, with black, tousled hair shading his broad forehead. His lips, slightly parted, were full, classically curved... and very, very pale.

He was the most beautiful man she had ever seen. And he was dead.

Her tears spattered in the sand as she reached for the fanny pack. Maybe there'd be a driver's license, identification, something...

Her fingers brushed the supple leather, and a hand grabbed her arm.

Lauren shrieked and scrambled backward. She tripped, fell to the sand, and huddled, shuddering, as the man slowly sat up. He blinked twice, then jerked his head, his black curls tossing as he did so. Lauren heard the grind of vertebrae as his spine cracked, straightening. He stood carefully, as if feeling to make sure all his limbs were still there. Then he looked down at her.

His eyes were the color of fresh-minted gold. They seemed to glow in the moonlight, like an animal's. The shape she'd seen dashing in front of the Jeep...

Lauren shook her head mutely, pushing herself back away from him, scooting up the slope of the ditch on her butt. He'd been dead. Dead! She'd seen the angle of his neck, the way his body was twisted...

He looked at her calmly, almost coolly, and said, "There isn't time for this. Please." Taking her wrist, he pulled her upright. He was tall, she realized, tall and lean, with muscles like a swimmer's or a long-distance runner's. His fingers around her wrist were long, supple, the tips slightly spatulate. An artist's fingers, or a lover's.

Trembling, she yanked her hand from his grasp. "You were dead!"

He shook his head. "No."

"Yes! I saw you! You weren't even breathing!"

He ignored her entirely, climbed up the embankment, and glanced down the track in the direction she'd come. "You found something today. Yes?"

She stared at him. How did he know? He glanced back at her, his dark face full of a sudden impatience. "What was it?"

She shrugged. "A fossil. Just bones. Randy --" Her jaw clenched on his name, and bitter tears spilled down her cheeks. The man lifted her chin, studying her face. Through her tears, his face seemed to glow with watery light. The face of an angel, or a saint.

He was so beautiful.

The entire situation was utterly surreal.

"Tell me your name," he said.

"Lauren. Lauren Cole."

"Lauren." His voice had a softness to it, a cadence that made her think of foreign films. The accent was light, barely discernible. She couldn't place it -- but she loved the sound of him saying her name. "Lauren, whatever happened tonight, whatever you saw -- it's not Randy's fault."

Laughing cynically, Lauren yanked her chin away. "Not his fault. Yeah. Sure."

"You must understand --"

"Understand what? He was fucking her!"

"If he hadn't, he'd already be dead."

What? Lauren stared.

"Come on." Grabbing her hand again, he strode toward her Jeep.

"Come on where? Look, Mister --" Lauren jerked free of his grasp. "That Jeep's not going anywhere," she said caustically. "It's stuck."

He just glanced at her sidelong, those golden eyes gleaming down, and pushed her forward, impelling her toward the Jeep. "Get in."

Lauren caught herself against the fender, whirled around. "Fuck you."

The look he shot her was almost contemptuous. "If we don't get there soon, your Randy will die. Now get in."

He was insane. She was stuck in the desert with a dead, naked, insane Frenchman. "Are you deaf? I told you -- the fucking thing's stuck!"

"Not for long." He walked to the front of the Jeep, bent his shoulder against it.

"Fine." Lauren clambered into the driver's seat, flinching as the Jeep shifted below her, sliding deeper into the ditch. Slamming the door, she hunched behind the steering wheel, staring skeptically at the naked man.

"Start the motor and put it in reverse."

She sneered. "It won't help."

"Just do it!"

Fine. She jammed the key over, ground the clutch, spun the wheels. If he did actually manage to get the stupid thing free, she'd leave him so far in the dust...

The Jeep bucked, and she felt the front wheels spin, digging themselves deeper into the sand. Then Lauren stiffened in shock as she felt the vehicle moving upward. In the headlights she could

Dark Side

see the man's -- Delacor's -- shoulder muscles bunching as he pushed it up the slope. *That's not possible. Even with the front wheels helping, it's not --*

The rear end slid higher, jutting out over the embankment. Lauren's teeth snapped together as it tumbled back, the rear wheels thumping onto the track. Stunned, forgetting her intention to speed away and leave him there, she stared as he leapt into the passenger seat, not even breathing hard. "Drive," he said tersely. "Head back to your camp."

"How did you do that?" she demanded.

He shook his head as if to say it wasn't important, and gestured imperiously at the steering wheel.

"Mister, the only thing you're going to find back there is my fiancé fucking one of his students."

"Let us pray you're right." His voice was grim. "And the name is Delacor. Now drive." She glanced at him uncertainly, then, catching his tension, threw the Jeep into first. The tires spat sand and gravel as she peeled out, racing her sudden fear back to the site.

Chapter Nine

He'd lost her. Even as he'd shouted after the departing Jeep, Randy had known it was hopeless. She was gone, forever. He'd never get her back.

He stood in the center of the dark, silent camp as the sounds of the Jeep faded into the distance. He felt literally petrified, turned into stone. Everything he'd done, every choice he'd made, had led only to this.

What in hell had he been thinking? It was like he'd been hypnotized -- one moment, he'd been trying to get Kelly out of the tent, the next, he'd looked down to see his cock in her mouth, and Lauren whirling away, a shattered expression on her face.

What had happened, in between? Why couldn't he remember? Was it simply that he didn't want to?

No, he supposed he didn't.

He felt a hand touch his back, feather-light, and spun, his hand swinging out of its own accord. Black, pounding fury welled up inside him, and he wanted to smash Kelly's face in, wanted to grind her into the dirt for what she'd done...

There was nobody there. His fist whipped through empty air, fell uselessly to his side. From somewhere, he would have sworn he heard laughter, a low, scathing, feminine chuckle.

"Who's there?" he shouted. "Kelly?"

Nothing. Not even the laughter. But a phantom hand brushed his shoulder again.

"God damn it, who's there?"

Randy.

The voice seemed to sigh out of nowhere. Randy froze. A breeze clacked through the spiny brush, and faded. For a moment, he caught a whiff of scent -- rancid cinnamon, or mildewed spices. Then it was gone.

"Randy?"

He whirled. Kelly was standing before him, her breasts gleaming in the moonlight. The blood smearing her body had dried, leaving dark, leprous looking splotches across her belly and thighs.

Where the hell did all that blood come from? Randy was appalled. How had he even brought himself to touch her, let alone --

Randy...

He jerked his head up, his gaze wildly raking the darkness.

"Randy, what's wrong?" Child-like, Kelly reached for him, her fingers outspread. He stared in horrified fascination at the blood caked under her nails.

"Don't touch me." Holding his hands up protectively, he backed away.

"But Randy, don't you want me?" Her wide eyes peered up at him, innocent, bewildered -- but her mouth was curved in a knowing smile.

"Stay away from me! Just... stay away..." He stumbled backward, blundered into the firepit. Dead cinders crunched under his bare feet, and ash plumed around him. He bent over, coughing.

Still she came toward him, her arms outstretched, beseeching. "I know you want me, Randy. Please, just touch me."

"No!"

Randyyyy...

A warm, invisible hand brushed past his ankle, slid up the inside of his thigh. The aroma of incense filled his nostrils.

No, Please, God, no...

He felt it stroke his balls. His cock twitched. Kelly reached for him. "Just let me touch you..."

He broke and ran.

The world shimmered in silver, shallow, unreal. His breath rasped in his ears, and his heartbeat thudded through his chest. His lungs burned. But the smell, the damnable smell, only got stronger. As he ran, his cock thickened, flopping before him. His head spun with the charnel smell of rotting flowers.

Suddenly he lurched, his left foot slipping down into darkness. Randy flailed, his arms windmilling, fighting for balance as the dirt under his feet crumbled.

Staggering back, he stared down into the pit. Blackness smeared the bottom, not shadows, but...

His stomach heaved as he saw Daniel's mangled corpse, the guts strewn across the ground. But it wasn't till he saw the thing behind it that Randy started screaming. He never even heard Kelly as she slid up beside him and pushed him over the crumbling edge of the pit.

* * *

Lauren rode the clutch, shifting gears with a clash. She didn't dare spare a glance at the man sitting beside her. The headlights swept over the curves of the track, glared off the U of P utility van parked near the camp, and came to rest on the wall of the butte. Almost before the Jeep had stopped rolling, she leaped out and rushed to the tent. Getting out behind her, Delacor paused, sniffing the air.

"He's not here!" Panicked, she burst back out, dashed for the pup tents. "There's nobody here!"

"There." Delacor nodded toward the distant pit. Immediately, Lauren broke into a run.

In four loping strides, he caught up to her and grabbed her arm. "Softly, Lauren." His strange amber eyes caught hers, held her gaze till she nodded. Then he led the way, sinking low to the earth twenty yards from the pit and gliding forward silently. Lauren followed as quietly as she could.

She should have been prepared, she thought in some bleak, cynical part of her mind. She shouldn't have been so shocked by the sight of Randy, straddling Kelly's torso, his hands squeezing her tits together as he pumped his cock in between them. The two were facing away from her, at an angle, giving her an outstanding view of his shaft sliding in and out between her huge, luscious mounds.

It hurt. God, how it hurt! Forgetting Delacor's words, she started to rise -- though whether she was intending to stalk down there in fury or slink away in pain, she never found out. Delacor placed his hand on her back, holding her down, and nodded past them, toward the far end of the pit.

Lauren stiffened, suppressing a scream. Turning her face away, she caught Delacor watching her, his expression willing her to silence. She clung to his gaze as if to a lifeline, till the whirling nausea that gripped her started to ease. He shifted close, and once again she became conscious that, other than the pouch on a strap around his waist, the man beside her was completely naked. She was keenly aware of the feel of his skin against hers, his lips brushing her ear as he whispered, almost silently, "I will get her away. He will want to go to her. Do not let him."

She turned toward him, her eyes asking the question -- how? Gently, as gently as a mother or a priest, he pressed his lips to her forehead. "Remember, he loves you. And be brave, Lauren Cole."

Delacor slid down into the pit. Quickly, he moved to his left, and saw Lauren, from the corner of his eye, shrinking back into the shadows. *Good girl.* It was better she stay hidden for as long as possible.

Warily, he eyed the half-buried thing. It pulsed now, the veins and arteries lacing the half-formed flesh. *Um al duwayce.* Succubus. Akhkharu. Skatene. It was the nameless monstrosity behind a thousand legends, reaching back into the dawn of man's earliest existence -- and further, Delacor realized, as he studied the thing protruding from the clay which had held it for millennia. Already he could feel its power beating against him. It was hunger incarnate; the desire to suck, to devour, to consume. None could approach it and not feel its influence.

Its attention, he could tell, was all on its captives. The lust that beat in his loins, the merest effect of its nearness, was nothing to the torment he'd feel when it sensed his presence.

The two victims writhed, coupling wantonly before the half-reanimated thing like savages performing at the feet of some ancient god. The girl's face contorted in eager pleasure as the man above her squeezed her breasts, twisting her dark, engorged nipples as he worked his cock back and forth between her huge mounds. Her mouth was open, her tongue lapping the juices from Randy's hard, swollen tip with each stroke. It took all the strength of Delacor's formidable will not to sink to his knees between her parted thighs, plunge his shaft into her ripe, waiting flesh...

No. He must not go to her. He must make her come to him.

Averting his gaze, he tilted his head back, let the tendril of awareness emanating from the monster touch him. It seemed to hesitate, uncertain. Delacor opened his eyes and looked up at the moon, now hard and bright as a coin overhead. The blood lust sprang up within him, a deep, greedy howl of need. He fought it back, holding it like a ravening beast on a leash -- but the *um al duwayce* sensed its presence. With a sudden, eager rush, the succubus's power flowed into him, reinforcing the blood lust till it flared up like a bonfire.

Kelly strained forward now, eagerly wrapping her lips around Randy's cock. Delacor saw the flush in her cheeks, the white gleam of her teeth. If she bit the man, if she so much as punctured his skin...

He would have to hurry.

Gritting his teeth, he struggled for control. His entire body burned, filled to overflowing with febrile lust. The fever of the succubus pulsed in his testicles, in his manhood, till his shaft jutted out before him, hard as if it were cast of iron. Through half-lidded eyes he saw Kelly lift her head, as if scenting the air.

That's right, you can feel me. You can feel the poison inside me. It is stronger in me than in that one. You want me. You want this.

Squirming from under Randy, she slid to her feet. Randy lunged for her, but she raked her nails at him, hissing, and evaded his grasp. Delacor heard a rattle of sand and pebbles behind him as Lauren sprung into the pit. *Yes. Go to him. Keep him from her.* He circled the pit, drawing Kelly after him.

Come for me, then. You can smell it, can't you? Yes.

He could feel power flowing from the half-reanimated avatar behind him, stronger now, this close to it. Hunger roared through him, and he could no longer completely suppress it. He must not lose control!

Panting heavily, he waited for the girl. She approached slowly, her eyes unfocused, her lips parted with lust. Her head wavered, swinging as mindlessly as a compass needle back toward Randy, and Delacor realized he must touch her, now, before he lost her attention.

There was nothing she could do to him. He had already been tainted. But at all costs, he must keep her from Randy.

Running his hands down the curve of her hips, he stooped and trailed his tongue up the side of her neck. Her gaze shifted back to his face as Delacor drew back, studying her. Her eyes were blue, blue and clear as forget-me-nots, the eyes of a child or a doll. Innocent.

There was no innocence left in her, Delacor reminded himself. This close, the heat of her body was overwhelming. He could feel it against his chest, his thighs, the hard shaft of his cock. Lauren screamed in fury, somewhere behind him, but the sound was distant, unimportant. He brushed his hands over the swell of Kelly's breasts, teasing the nipples, and smiled as she shuddered.

"Do you like that, *ma chérie*? Do you want me to touch you?" Wordlessly, she nodded. Delacor leaned closer, letting his cock rub against her firm belly. "Do you want me to fuck you?"

She said nothing, but her open, panting mouth and heavy lidded eyes answered for her.

"Then, my darling, get on your knees."

The urgency inside him leapt up another notch as she knelt before him, wrapping her lips around his cock. Her fingers trailed across the strap of his waist pouch, seeking the buckle, but he brushed her hand away. She slid it instead to his hard, swollen balls.

Delacor closed his eyes, swallowing. How long had it been since he'd allowed a woman to touch him so intimately?

He knew the answer. It was branded forever in his soul.

Looking down again, Delacor studied Kelly's face, her little button of a nose, and found nothing inside himself but grief. She was innocent, truly. She had not asked for this. But she had been marked by the *um al duwayce*. He could see the tattered bandage on her right hand.

The girl was no longer human -- she was vampyr, and would prey on her own kind forever -- unless she was destroyed.

Kelly's lips moved greedily over his shaft, and Delacor watched her, feeling an ironic despair. Was there no end to the pain life could bring? Lovely, flawed, undoubtedly selfish, nevertheless she had been human.

And now she must die.

With a deep self-loathing, he felt his balls tightening, heavy with come. In another moment, he would spill his seed in her mouth. The urgency in his loins roared in anticipation, and he struggled against the impulse to knot his hands in her hair, drag her hard against him as he pounded her throat...

His face twisted into a grimace as he pulled his cock gently from the warm, wet embrace of her lips. A sound that was both growl and whimper burst from her as she writhed, trying to reclaim his shaft.

"No, *chérie*," Delacor whispered. Bending down over her, he cupped her face in his hands, effortlessly holding her away from his body despite her furious struggles. Lightly, tenderly, he kissed her feverish forehead. She hissed at him and snapped, trying to sink her teeth into his forearm.

Delacor tightened his grip, feeling her cheekbones creak beneath his palms. Closing his eyes, he murmured briefly, a prayer so old he thought he'd forgotten it.

Then, with a horrifying, inhuman strength, he snapped her head hard to the left, and watched as the light in those doll-like blue eyes flickered, froze, and died away.

Chapter Ten

As soon as Kelly -- or the thing that had been Kelly -- slid out from under Randy, Lauren leaped down into the pit. The sickly sense of betrayal that had rocked her when she'd first seen them together was gone. She could see the glazed look in his eyes, the terrifying absence of personality.

That's not Randy. She remembered her reaction, back in the darkened tent. No, it wasn't. Torn between terror and hysteria, Lauren glanced at the shape in the corner of the pit. Ten hours before, it had been nothing but petrified bone. Now the skinless flesh oozed pus, and she could see the beat of its pulse through its veins.

None of this was possible. But the moment she'd entered the pit, she had felt it -- a wall of carnal energy that beat at her like sunlight, or gusts of wind. Had it been there all along, earlier, and she, already sexually frustrated on her own account, simply hadn't noticed?

I want you to fuck me!

Remembering, Lauren blushed. Yes, she rather suspected it had.

Now she felt her body glowing, as if she had stepped into an inferno. An arousal so intense it was agony throbbed in her groin. Her swollen clit chafed with the tiniest shift of position, and for a moment she gave into the urge to thrust her hand into her panties and rub it. Saliva seemed to explode in her mouth as she pressed her fingers against the hot, aching point of her need.

Before her, as if drawn by a magnet, Kelly turned to follow Delacor. Lauren saw Randy reach after her clumsily, stupefied by lust. For a moment she felt nothing but a vague irritation -- she wanted to watch them as she rubbed herself -- but then Kelly spun, hissing at Randy. The sound shocked Lauren, for a moment, back to rationality -- it reminded her of the way Randy had growled at her, earlier. Impelled by a sudden terror, Lauren ran to him, grabbing his arm.

Please, please let him still be free of whatever has possessed her! Staring into his eyes, she couldn't tell. His handsome, boyish features were twisted with bestial rage as Kelly slipped after Delacor. He lunged after them, and desperately, Lauren hung on. Feeling the lust-maddened strength that propelled him, she realized she couldn't possibly hold him back.

Remember, he loves you. Delacor's voice rang in her ears and, biting her lip, she raged at herself. *Do you love him, Lauren? Do you really?*

Then what are you willing to do to keep him alive?

The way he'd glanced up at her, just this past morning, his eyes alight with excitement, and vibrancy, and joy...

Anything, she realized. Anything at all.

Sprinting in front of him, she tore off her tee shirt. Grabbing his hand, she plunged it between her thighs. Like a dog scenting a rabbit, his head turned, his nostrils flaring.

This time, at least, being wet wasn't a problem. At the touch of his fingers, the heat in her cunt swelled to a fire. God, how she wanted him! She wanted him to fuck her, viciously, ruthlessly. With a thrust of her hips, she drove his hand deeper, his fingers sliding between the dripping folds of her cunt.

For a moment, he wavered. Then with his other hand, he ripped off her panties. The elastic snapped, catching her across the ass, and the sudden sensation made her gasp in anticipation.

She was no longer anything like in control of herself. Reduced to an animal, a lust-maddened beast, she wanted to fuck, God damn it, wanted to feel a hard, stiff cock plunging into her. Writhing against Randy's hand, she lifted her ribcage, let her breasts press against him as she wrapped her arms around his neck, and felt his fingers slide into her wet, waiting cunt.

Yes. Her eyes closed as she savored the feel of his hard cock prodding her belly. But then, like sand being sucked from a beach by the retreating tide, she sensed his attention wandering away from her. Glancing over her shoulder, Lauren saw Kelly looking back at them, her wide, glazed eyes glittering in the moonlight, beckoning.

Lauren screamed in fury as Randy slid from her grasp. Enraged, she pounced after him, throwing herself onto his back. Wrapping her legs around his waist, she clung as he roared, spinning, trying to dislodge her. She clung tighter, her fingernails raking his chest, until he reached back and grabbed her arm, almost wrenching it from its socket as he hauled her off and slammed her to the floor of the pit.

She lay, trying to draw breath back into her lungs, staring up as he towered over her, blotting out the moon. For a moment she thought she saw a flicker of confusion in his eyes. Confusion, and fear.

"Randy?" she whispered.

There was no way to tell if he'd heard her, but it was enough, it was hope. Before he could look away, she spread her legs, letting the moonlight shine on her wet, hungry cunt. Trailing a hand down her stomach, she pressed her clit lightly, gasping at the sensation, then slid her fingers lower.

His gaze was fixed intently on her hand, and Lauren smiled to herself, feeling her own excitement heighten as he toyed with his cock. She loved his cock, she loved the shape of it; the head that was as thick and firm and fleshy as a plum; the thick, solid shaft that filled her so nicely. Spreading the inner folds of her cunt with one hand, she slipped a finger deep inside her, and saw him grab the swollen tip of his cock and squeeze.

Working her finger in and out, feeling it slide easily through her juices, Lauren was amused to notice that Randy's hand kept time with her strokes. Playfully, she sped up, and watched his grip tighten as his face flushed with the telltale signs of incipient orgasm.

Enough. She wanted him in her. Now.

Rolling to one side, she pushed herself onto all fours, and smiled in triumph as he dropped to his knees behind her. The heavy odor of incense floated around them, increasing her need.

Tilting her ass high, she rocked her hips backward, and felt Randy grab them as he rammed his cock in.

Ruthlessly, he dragged her against him, his hips slamming her ass as he drove into her with a frenzy that made her squirm with delight. He slid one hand from her hips to the dripping folds of her cunt, and then -- Lauren's eyes widened even as she thrust back to meet him -- she felt his finger pressing firmly against her asshole.

Slick with her own juices, it slid easily past the tight ring of muscle, and Lauren moaned with ecstasy as he pumped his hips forward, shoving both his cock and his finger deep into her. In tandem, he slid them out, only to plunge in again, fucking her cunt and her ass simultaneously.

Delacor and Kelly were both long forgotten. Nothing existed but the feel of Randy fucking her, his cock stretching her wide, his finger violating her in a way she'd never known she wanted. She barely noticed the scent like spoiled cinnamon in the air, or the sand under the palms of her hands as she pushed back to meet his thrusts, feeling his pace increase.

The double fullness was intoxicating beyond anything she'd ever known. She could feel the lips of her cunt swell further, and her rectum gaped and quivered, seeking to draw him deeper. As if reading her mind, Randy obliged, ramming himself inside her, and then pressing deeper still.

Reaching down, Lauren stroked her clit once. That was all it took, and then she was tumbling, inside herself, down into a vast molten ocean of hot, pounding waves. They swept through her, seizing her body, making her howl aloud as her cunt and asshole clamped and released. Randy's cock flexed inside her, swelling even further as he hammered it, spurting, as deep as he could. At the feel of his cock splitting her open, Lauren came again, moaning in ecstasy as he clung to her hips, quivering, his pulsing balls sending wave after wave of come shooting into her.

Groaning, he dragged his cock almost all the way out, only to shove it home again. "Lauren..."

He was still completely erect. Lauren felt a fresh shiver of desire go through her and wiggled her hips.

"Lauren, I can't stop."

She started to reply, but a hideous, ripping sound made him jerk himself away. Lauren whipped her head around just as the earth trembled beneath them, and she scrambled back, screaming, from the thing tearing itself loose from the ground.

Even as he snapped the girl's neck, Delacor felt it -- a pulse of fury that seared through his mind, jabbing behind his eyeballs like a white-hot spike. Groaning, he stumbled backward, clasping his skull, staring in horror as skinless muscle flexed, tearing the wedge-shaped head free of the clay. The massive jaws snapped, seizing Kelly's body as it tumbled, and the razor-like teeth sheared through her neck. Her head tumbled to the ground, bounced, and rolled a few feet away.

Delacor's stomach heaved. Blood gushed from the stump of her neck, and a gray, slab-like tongue flickered out, licking at it. The jaws worked once, twice. And then Kelly was gone.

Like green furze spreading over a stagnant pond, heavy, mottled hide spread over the raw flesh. The film evaporated from the monster's eyes, and it turned its head, gazing directly at him. The neck muscles bunched. The hard clay encasing it shattered as it ripped itself from the ancient grasp of the earth.

Lauren screamed again, a high, terrified shrill, but Delacor had no time to turn, no time to warn them. Closing his eyes, he let his body shift…

Lauren's scream choked off in a dumbfounded squeak. She realized, distantly, that Randy was dragging her back, but her body was too numbed by shock to feel it.

She had seen him -- Delacor -- standing there, and then…

No. Impossible. As impossible as the thing prying itself loose from the ground. It was dead, dead! Two hundred million years ago. But as she watched, it yanked a forearm free and tried to scrabble at the enormous black wolf which had leapt to its back and was now gnawing frantically at the base of its skull.

He could taste the poison flooding his mouth. But what matter? He was already poisoned. The monster's blood was like acid, burning as it flowed down the neck from the wound.

What would it do to him? Already he could feel its venom pulsing through his veins, reawakening the bloodlust. It would be stronger now, he feared. But still he bit deeper, tearing at the thing's flesh. Its shrieks split the night as it thrashed below him, and a gash opened in the earth, widening as it struggled.

Grimly, Delacor dug in his claws, somehow hung on.

Thrusting his jaws deep, he located hard bone, thick as a tree limb. Desperately, he worried at the cartilage between. The monster bucked, trying to dislodge him. Then, with a heave, it ripped its hindquarters free.

It would roll now, crush him. And that would be the end.

It would not be such a bad thing, to die -- he'd prayed for death so many times. But Lauren would die with him, and her Randy -- and how many others, with the *um al duwayce* again free to roam the earth?

Snarling, Delacor bore down with all his might, feeling tendons shred beneath his sharp fangs. The monster tossed its head, roaring. As it did, he thrust his jaws into the sudden gap in the vertebrae and clamped down.

Something snapped, deep in the thing's neck. The huge head lolled forward, tearing free of its own weight. As the enormous body tilted, Delacor lifted his head. The two humans, clinging to each other, were staring at him, their faces dumb with horror.

Run! Delacor shouted inside his mind.

The carcass below him pitched forward and crashed to the ground. Under the impact, the crack widened, gaping suddenly in the night. He fought for a grip, his claws scrabbling against the blood-slicked skin, as the monstrous carcass slid slowly downward.

Flinging himself frantically, Delacor leaped, his forepaws catching the crumbling edge of the crack, his hind paws scrabbling for purchase. He saw Randy drag Lauren, screaming, out of the pit. She was fighting him, clawing at his arms, trying to climb back down in.

Why?

Her face was slicked with tears as she struggled furiously to get loose. She wanted --

Cher Dieu!

She wanted to save him.

The night roared, and the avatar of the *um al duwayce* tumbled finally into the chasm it had itself created. Clinging by his claws, Delacor found he had no regrets. Perhaps it was best this way -- no goodbyes, no explanations. It would be hard enough for them to live with what they'd just seen.

He could see Lauren sobbing as Randy hauled her to safety. She had wanted to save him. She had seen what he was, and still she'd wanted to save him.

That was enough, he thought with a small inward smile. For him, perhaps, the story finally ended here.

Satisfied, at peace, the BloodWolf let himself fall.

Epilogue

Boulder, Colorado

Watching in the bathroom mirror, she slowly removed the daisies braided into her hair. She was nervous, she realized, and was surprised.

You'd think that would have been earlier, wouldn't you? Lauren thought wryly. But she hadn't been. She'd felt nothing but a proud, solemn happiness at the sight of Randy, looking very handsome and earnest, waiting for her at the stone they'd chosen for an altar beside the crystalline waters of Wonderland Lake.

Both of them had felt it'd be better to leave Arizona. They didn't talk about it often, the things that had happened that night. Sloan, when they'd found him, had been more than happy to keep his mouth shut and forget the whole thing ever happened. The small, localized earth tremor had puzzled seismologists, but with funding tight, no one had pursued it very far.

The memorial services, though, had been ghastly. Randy had sat through them ashen-faced and frozen. Afterward, he'd clung to her with a need she knew she'd never be able to refuse.

Lauren picked up one of the daisies she'd removed, carefully unfolding the petals that had gotten bent. Before they'd left for Colorado, she'd insisted on going back. Leaving the unhitched U-Haul in the visitor's parking lot, they'd driven out to the abandoned site, silent for the entire twenty-minute ride. When they'd gotten there, they still hadn't said much as they walked over the ground that had fallen in on itself, burying Lyle -- and whatever had been unearthed with him -- under forty metric tons of sand, rock, and clay.

They'd stood for a long time, listening to the sound of the wind skittering over the desert, unable to find any words of comfort to offer each other until the sun bathed the rocks around them in harlequin hues of lavender and orange. But Randy had held her as she'd wiped at the tears streaming down her cheeks.

He was teaching at Colorado College now, very excited to be a part of its famous natural sciences department. And Lauren found she loved Denver. Her editor at the Denver Post had thrown her an impromptu bridal shower, and then offered her a weekly column -- one that people actually read.

In short, their life was better than either of them could have imagined, eight short months ago.

So why, as she struggled out of the frothy white dress Randy had insisted she wear (of all the stupid things -- she'd had to hike in to the lake in jeans and then change) did she suddenly feel such dread?

Because it's your wedding night, silly.

Wedding afternoon, actually. But on the other side of the hotel bathroom door was a bed, and in that bed was Randy.

She shouldn't have let him make them wait. They should have leaped this hurdle months ago, not waited till now when the expectations were so high.

They hadn't slept apart since the first night they'd returned to Phoenix. Lauren could no longer imagine a life in which Randy was not a constant, the daily touchstone of her existence. But not once in all that time had they made love.

For a long time, it hadn't mattered in the least. But finally, as the months passed and the shock and grief slowly diminished, she'd begun to feel again the first stirrings of desire.

Wait, Randy had said, *let's wait. Lauren, I want to do this right.*

And so they had.

Now Lauren stood in the bathroom of their honeymoon suite, almost as frozen with terror as she'd been that night in the desert. She gazed out the window at the steep, wooded slopes of a mountain, not a hundred yards away. In the crisp air the aspens had already turned, coating the massive ridges with gold.

What if it didn't go right? What if she couldn't respond? What if --

"Laur? You still alive in there?"

"Coming," she called. Quickly, she slid out of her bra and panties, and turned toward the door. Then, checked by a sudden impulse, she picked the daisy back up. Sliding open the window, she tossed the flower into the cool breeze, watching it tumble as it fell out of sight.

She would never forget him, she swore, raising her eyes to the towering mountains. They were so enormous it was almost incomprehensible. But their beauty pierced her heart.

"Laur?"

Smiling, she opened the door. Randy was in the bed, sitting up, the heavy linen sheet modestly draped over him. He looked at her standing there, utterly naked, and tossed the sheet back.

He was beautiful too, in his own way, Lauren thought. His long, powerful body was still tan from the summer, contrasting nicely with the white of the sheet. She loved looking at him, at the play of muscles in his torso, the firm bulges in his arms...

"If you're done ogling the merchandise," Randy interrupted her reverie, grinning. When she didn't return his grin, his gaze softened, and as the playful sparkle died from his eyes she saw the desire behind it, smoldering deep in their clear, intense blue. "Lauren..."

"I just... Randy, I can't forget."

"I wouldn't want you to. Come here." Gently, he reached for her hand, drawing her to the edge of the bed. His hand stroked her back as she sat, breathing deeply, trying to relax. She turned to him, meaning to ask a question -- something -- but the words fled from her mind as his mouth came down on hers, warm and firm and gently insistent. Slowly, he prodded past the barrier of her teeth, and sighed into her open mouth as she met his questing tongue with her own.

His tongue tasted sweet and warm, and she sucked it lightly, waiting for him to pull back. Instead he opened his mouth wider, hungrily flicking his tongue against hers. Saliva flooded her mouth -- and his too, she realized. She heard small, mewling noises, almost whimpers, and realized they were coming from her own throat.

Dark Side

His hands were buried in her hair, pulling her mouth more firmly against his, and Lauren pressed herself closer, mashing her breasts against his broad chest. Suddenly, a hunger which was all her own, which had no taint of that thing about it, flared inside her, and they tumbled backward, their mouths still locked together, their limbs winding around each other as if they couldn't get close enough, couldn't squeeze tight enough...

Or maybe, she thought distractedly as Randy moved his head downward, nuzzling and nipping at her aching breasts, *maybe it was there all along, and I couldn't see it, couldn't feel it, couldn't --*

She gasped as Randy drew one nipple between his lips, suckling at it as if he was starving. Wetness burst between her thighs, and she became aware of his cock, nudging insistently against her hip. Reaching down, she wrapped her hand around it, marveling again at its hard velvet thickness. It pulsed eagerly against her palm, and suddenly Lauren felt she would die if she couldn't have him inside her now, right now. Tugging at his shoulders, she pulled him back up above her as she spread her thighs. He hesitated.

"Oh please, Randy. We've waited far too long."

"With you," he murmured, a chuckle lacing through his words, "five minutes is too long."

She started to expostulate, then saw the merry gleam in his eyes. Giving him an evil smirk, she tilted her hips, and saw his eyes darken with desire as his cockhead slipped inside her. "Oh, Jesus, Laur," he breathed. "You feel just like velvet."

"Funny, I was just thinking the very same thing."

Flexing his hips, he slid into her smoothly, and Lauren felt the familiar pressure against the walls of her passage as his cock prodded deeper, spreading her open. Wrapping her hands around the back of his neck, she pulled his face down to hers, wanting all of him inside her -- his tongue, his cock. Randy happily obliged, rocking her steadily to a peak that was as gentle and slow as snow falling on a hillside. He held her close as she orgasmed, her cunt tightening around him, crying out lightly as her body quivered beneath him.

Opening her eyes, she found him still looking down at her. She raised a hand to touch his cheek and he turned his head, placing a kiss in her palm. "Is it so bad this way, Lauren?"

"This?" Her eyes widened. "Was this what you wanted, all those times you…"

He nodded, his gaze never leaving her face.

"Oh, Randy," she breathed. "No. No, it's wonderful."

"Good." He yanked himself out of her, and grinned at her gasp. "Now turn over."

"What? Randy!"

"You heard me, wife. Flip."

She stared at him, astounded, till he seized her hips and bodily rolled her beneath him. At his tug, she lifted her ass in the air, feeling him rise to his knees behind her. "Randy, are you sure…"

His fingers slid through the sodden folds of her cunt, flicking lightly at her clit. Lauren gasped again, and bucked lightly. Then she froze as his hand was removed, feeling his fingers a moment later spreading her slick juices over her exposed rectum. At the same time he bent low over her, his cock rubbing against her opening, and whispered, "Oh yeah, I'm sure. Or did you want to tell me it was only that thing that made you enjoy this?"

And on that word, he rocked his hips forward, burying his shaft in her hot, waiting cunt, sliding first one finger, then two, past the resistance of her sphincter. Lauren panted, swept away by the sensation, feeling herself laid open below his probing touch. Reaching down, she slid her hand between her thighs, found the heavy weight of his swollen balls, and caressed them gently. He responded with a groan, and thrust harder inside her, pounding her cunt with an undeniable craving as his fingers slid more gently but firmly in and out of her willing ass.

"Oh, Lauren," he moaned, "the things you make me feel…"

"Like what?" she whispered, floating on the delirious edge of orgasm. Her nipples dragged against the smooth linen sheet, sending another flare of heat through her groin.

"Like I want to fuck you. I want to come in your mouth."

Lauren felt her breath catch, and her cunt pulsed with need.

"I want to lie beneath you and let you ride me. I want to squeeze your breasts till they ache. I want to watch you touch yourself till it drives me crazy and I'd do anything, anything you asked me, just for you to let me inside your cunt."

Lauren's head swam as she listened, feeling her breath grow hoarse as his cock jabbed her harder, keeping time with his words. Was this Randy, saying these things? She couldn't believe it. But if he said six words more, she was going to come. Right now.

His free hand slid from her hip to her thigh, trailed slowly up it till his fingers brushed the spot where their two bodies joined. She felt him buck at the feel of his fingers rubbing his cock, even as it plunged into her. Then he reared back above her, his thumb flicking her clit as he pounded her cunt, his breath hissing between his clenched teeth. "Oh, Jesus, Lauren. I'm going to --"

Yup. Six words. She beat him to it.

* * *

Later, when something like thought had finally returned, she rolled to him lazily, tracing circles on his broad, sweaty chest. "Well, well," she chuckled. "I think that calls for champagne, don't you?"

"Oh!" Randy sat up. Outside the sliding glass door leading to their balcony, the sky was growing dim in the quick twilight of the mountains. "I put it outside to keep cool. Hang on half a sec."

Lauren lay back, stretching luxuriantly. If life got any better than this, she thought it might kill her. She heard the rumble as the glass door slid open, then a pause.

"Laur?"

She sat up. Outside, she could still see the champagne sitting in its bucket, the two glasses forgotten beside it. Instead, Randy held a battered old leather pack, turning it over and over curiously in his hands. "Do you know where this came from?"

But already she was on her feet, dashing out to the balcony. "Huh," she heard Randy say behind her. "There's a note."

Leaning against the rail, she strained her gaze upward. For a second, she thought she caught a shadow in the twilight, a flicker of movement as some animal slipped from the ridge above.

Then it was gone -- if it had ever even been there at all. She stood naked in the wind that gusted down from the mountains, shivering as she unfolded the note Randy held out to her. It was written in an elegant hand on a torn piece of hotel stationery, and as she scanned it, suddenly Lauren didn't feel the cold at all.

Be gentle with each other. And always remember -- there is more of good in this world than evil.
-- Baudouin Delacor

Sierra Dafoe

Sierra Dafoe published her first erotic romance with Changeling Press in May of 2006, and hasn't stopped since! Named a Rising Star of Romance in July 2006 by Love Romances and More, she received three 2006 CAPA nominations including Favorite Erotic Author (a fact which still has her stunned!).

Sierra lives in northern New Hampshire's White Mountains with her incredibly tolerant hubby, her thoroughly obnoxious cat, and her twelve-year-old puppy. Visit her at www.sierradafoe.com for free stories and monthly contests, and join her yahoogroup at http://groups.yahoo.com/The_Sierra_Club -- she loves hearing from her readers!

Night Creatures

Elisa Adams

Chapter 1

Thick layers of mist swirled up from the ground, wrapping its clammy fingers around Juliana's ankles. She quickened her pace. The heels of her sandals clacked against the uneven stone floor, the only noise echoing through the otherwise silent tunnel. The sharp, staccato beats mimicked the pounding of her heart. Monstrous wrought iron sconces held burning white candles, their flames painting flickering shadows on the walls.

She shivered and glanced at her surroundings -- unknown, yet at the same time strangely familiar. She'd seen this place before.

In her nightmares.

Nightmares she spent every waking minute trying to forget. A chill hung in the damp air, thick and humid, a living entity invisible in the dim lighting. It danced across her skin like ghosts flitting through the night. Goose bumps rose in its wake. The rancid scents of putrid salt water and rotting seaweed coated her nostrils, getting stronger the deeper she went into the bowels of the tunnel. Bile burned her throat, as much from the stench as from the terror that raced through her bloodstream and made her pulse pound in her ears. Still, she pushed onward. What choice did she have? In front of her or behind her, the tunnel led to the same place.

To hell.

The ground slanted suddenly beneath her feet, angling to take her deeper underground. She wobbled and pitched forward. Her arms shot out to catch her, but it was too late. She hit the ground with a sickening thud, the tender skin on her knees tearing as they connected with the rough stones.

A cold sweat peppered her forehead. She swiped it away with her palm, coating her skin with the slimy filth that covered the floor. Algae, rotten seaweed, and who knew what else. Her stomach turned. She pushed up to her feet and glanced behind her. Nothing but darkness greeted her. Something had extinguished all the candles she'd passed. There was no way for her to return, even if she'd been brave enough to face what awaited her at the mouth of the tunnel. Her only choice was to press on and pray that nothing deadly met her at the end.

A few dozen feet ahead of her, a soft yellow glow filtered through the thick air. The proverbial light at the end of the tunnel? Somehow she doubted it would be that easy. Still, what more could she do than follow it? It would be better than stumbling back through the dark unknown. Part of her knew what she'd face when she reached the end, but her mind had blocked it from her memory.

As she stepped closer, the soft sounds of chanting reached her ears. Unintelligible words, spoken in harsh murmurs, many voices speaking together as one. She swallowed hard against the lump of ice clogging her throat. There were people there, at least. Whether or not they would help her remained to be seen.

When Juliana reached the end of the tunnel, the uneven ground gave way to a steep, narrow staircase cutting harshly through the stone. She hesitated only a moment before descending, instinct urging her forward and at the same time, warning her away.

The chanting grew louder, the light brighter, as she made her way down the slippery steps. When she finally reached the bottom, the stairway emptied into a cavernous stone room that smelled of the sea. And blood. The coppery tang filled the air and she nearly gagged on its intensity. But a brief search of the room produced no sign of the red liquid.

Her gaze fell on a group of people, clad in black cloaks, gathered in the center of the roughly circular stone room. They knelt in a circle around a granite platform draped in red cloth. An altar, of sorts. A woman lay on top, every inch of her fair skin exposed to the eyes of all kneeling around her. Her eyes were closed, her body unmoving. Was she dead?

Dark Side

Fear drove a jagged spike through Juliana's heart. Whatever awaited her at the mouth of the tunnel had to be better than this. She backed up a step, but not before they noticed her presence. The chanting stopped and a sea of faces, gaunt and watery with eyes that glowed an angry red, turned toward her. A scream pierced the air. It took her a moment to realize the scream was her own.

One of the cloaked ones stood and moved away from the group, walking toward her with such fluid grace it appeared to be floating above the ground. It reached one bony gray hand out to her, its open mouth a gaping chasm surrounded by two rows of pointed teeth. She screamed again, scrambled backward in a desperate attempt to get away. Her heel caught on a step and she lost her balance, her legs falling out from under her. Her muscles tensed, waiting for the hard smack of the stone against her ass, but it never came. The bony hand grabbed her arm and yanked her upright before she made it all the way to the ground. The touch of its moist skin against hers made her stomach roil.

"Let me go!" She struggled to get out of its grasp, but the thing wouldn't release her. She closed her eyes, shivering. Her whole body was ready to collapse. And then the touch turned warm, dry and solid.

"Remember." The voice that spoke to her was deep and masculine. Familiar and alien at the same time.

"What?" Juliana's eyelids snapped open and she glanced up into the warm, dark eyes of a tall man with fair skin and long blond hair peeking out of the hood of his cloak. His expression was gentle and kind, though some hidden part of her mind told her he was anything but. Her gaze scanned the room, her heart beating a frantic rhythm against the wall of her chest. Where was the creature who'd grabbed for her? Had she imagined the whole thing?

"Remember. You know this place. You've visited us before." His smile displayed a perfect row of human teeth, white and gleaming. "Join us, Juliana. Take part in what we offer tonight."

"Who are you?" She darted furtive glances around the room. The people had all risen and were stripping out of their cloaks. They were nude, male and female, young and slim, their skin a variety of shades from the palest alabaster to the deepest cocoa brown.

"You know who we are. You just have to remember." With that he walked back across the room to the platform and ran his hand down the woman's body. She writhed and moaned. "Come in, Juliana. Join us."

She stepped forward, her gait slow and hesitant, her gaze focused on the woman lying on the platform. At first Juliana had thought the woman was a sacrifice of some sort, but now doubt crept into her mind. The naked woman, fair and freckled with flowing red hair, seemed to get pleasure rather than pain out of being touched by the blond man. He stroked her breasts, rolled her nipples between his thumbs and forefingers, before he trailed a hand down and buried it between her parted legs.

He turned to Juliana, the smile on his face taking on a sensual edge. "Would you like to take her place tonight? I'm sure she wouldn't mind waiting. I could give you so much pleasure. Bring you to a release like none you've ever felt."

"No." Even as she said the words, her cunt muscles fluttered at the thought of those strong hands on her, those long fingers stroking inside her. Her nipples beaded against the lace of her bra. "*No.*"

He gave her a succinct nod, though the hunger in his eyes didn't dim at all. "All right. Then you may watch instead. But we need to get you comfortable first."

He waved a hand in the air and several people rushed toward her. In a frenzy of activity, they tore at her clothes and ripped them from her body. Their sharp nails scratched her skin, their rough movements sucking the breath from her lungs. She thrashed and tried to move away, but they wouldn't let her. One of them, a man, held her in place while the other ones finished the job that had been assigned to them. Once they'd stripped her of everything, including her shoes, they walked back toward the center of the room. The man behind her remained.

The cool air brushing against Juliana's body made her skin crawl. She tried to cover herself, but the one holding her wouldn't allow it. "No," he whispered into her ear. "You're beautiful. Don't feel embarrassed. Let us all enjoy looking at your body."

It was then that she remembered. She *had* been there before, to the underground room reeking of the sea and sacrifice. Many times. They beckoned to her, their voices a siren's call that lured her out of sleep in the middle of the night and brought her to where they gathered. But there was one voice in particular that drew her in. *His* voice. The one holding her.

Max.

Juliana twisted around, tried to get a good look at his face, but it only caused him to hold her tighter against him. She didn't need to see his features to know what he looked like. His face had been burned into her memory too long ago to recall. Eyes of the deepest, warmest green. Full lips and a strong, straight nose. Features that would have bordered on pretty had they not been paired with a tall, strong body and chestnut brown hair that fell past his shoulders. No, she didn't need to see to remember. Long ago, Max had been her first love. Her only love. And now, for some reason unknown to her, he was part of her worst nightmare.

The hard press of his cock against her bare lower back made her body flame. He leaned closer, his breath a heated whisper against her ear. "Watch, Juli. Watch her. Watch them together."

She could do nothing but obey. She stared at the couple in the center of the room. The blond man -- Lane, she remembered -- stroked his fingers in and out of the woman's cunt, the pink folds of her labia glistening in the soft candlelight that lit the room. He spread her legs further, giving them all a better view of the sensual torture he was inflicting upon the redheaded woman. His other hand squeezed and plumped her breasts with harsh, gripping strokes, drawing moans and half-screams from the woman's lips.

All of Juliana's weight rested against Max's body. She wouldn't have been able to stand if he let her go. Her cunt ached to be filled, like the other woman's. Her breasts begged to be touched. Soft, rough, she didn't care. She just needed... *something.* She wriggled against Max.

Soon the chanting began again, a pagan language she didn't understand. The others joined in the sexual play, pairing off into small groups to fondle and tease each other while they watched Lane fuck the woman with his fingers. The chanting grew louder, more urgent, as did the movements of the people around her. Most of them had given up the pretense of watching and now had moved on to fucking or sucking each other. Juliana whimpered, the sight almost too much to take. She throbbed so much it would take only one stroke of a finger across her clit to push her off the edge. A trickle of her juices seeped from her cunt.

"What do you need, Juli?" Max asked in hushed tones, his hands lowering until he held her hips in his palms. "Tell me what you need."

Lane spun around and gave Juliana a seductive smile. "She needs this. Me. *Us.*"

"No." Max's grip tightened on her hips to just before the point of pain. She cried out, a soft sound lost among the chants.

Lane's smile only widened at Max's denial. "Come play with us, Max. You want to. I know you do. I see it in your eyes. She'll be fine alone for a little while. You don't belong with her. You belong with us. *To us.*"

"*No.*"

The force of the single word shook Juliana and her knees buckled. She pressed an open palm to her lips. She struggled to get away from Max, to leave the twisted orgy and run away as fast as she could, but his strong arms still wouldn't let her go.

She grunted and writhed in his arms. "Max, please. Something isn't right here."

"I know. You'll be safe with me. But you have to trust me, Juli. It's the only way I can protect you." He released her long enough to take her hand. "Come with me."

He led her to a red velvet couch tucked into the corner of the room. The vantage point gave them a perfect view of what Lane was doing to the woman on the altar. Max sat down and settled her into his lap, his cock bobbing between her legs and brushing along her slit. She moaned, ground herself against him. "Max, please."

He leaned in and kissed her bare shoulder. "We can't. Not yet. You watch instead, and let me play."

His fingers found her clit, rubbing and stroking, alternating the gentle touches between hard, deep thrusts of his fingers into her cunt. She leaned back against him, spreading her legs as wide as she could. A long, ragged moan escaped her lips. Max stroked his fingers into her in time with Lane's thrusts into the other woman. When Lane flicked a finger across the other woman's clit, Max did the same. Max's free hand came up to cup one of her breasts, rolling the nipple between his thumb and forefinger in a way that made her shudder inside. The tactile sensations coupled with the visuals in front of her brought her to the edge of orgasm, her nerves tingling with unspent release.

Lane turned to her and gave her a knowing smile, a wink, before he focused his attention back on the other woman. A sound akin to a growl rumbled in Max's chest. She couldn't take it anymore. The tempo of the chanting, the sight of the groups of people fucking on the ground, the feel of Max behind her, all around her, sent her over the edge. She screamed as her orgasm ripped through her, her body bucking wildly in Max's arms. When he leaned down and sank his teeth into the tender skin where her shoulder met her neck, another scream tore loose from her throat. She understood his action. Something deep inside her, the basest level of her mind, knew what he'd done. It was a sign of possession, marking her as his for everyone around them to know. A shiver raced down the length of her spine and her tremors amplified. All the while Max was there, holding her close, pressing his thumb down on her clit to milk the last of the spasms from her spent body.

It took until her breathing had returned to normal and her body had stilled for her to realize things on the altar had changed. Lane's sensual expression had morphed into a hunger that went beyond lust, beyond sex, into something that sent a bolt of fear arcing through her body. He raised his hand to the woman's chest and dragged a finger from her breastbone down to her pelvis. A small, thin line of blood bubbled up from the skin where he'd touched.

Juliana tensed, her muscles on high alert, but Max held her still. Wouldn't let her move even an inch off his lap.

The others, seeing the blood seeping from the writhing woman's body, converged. The chanting reached a frantic pace and the candlelight seemed to swirl and dip around them. They leaned over the woman, suckling and licking, fighting for a position around the altar. It was a frenzy she could make no sense of and it only heightened her fear.

"What are they doing?" Juliana asked.

Lane swung his head around, a murderous expression on his face. "This one's joining us tonight. You'll be next."

One of the others turned to Juliana, a slight blond woman with icy blue eyes. Blood dripped from the corners of her mouth. "Join us, Juliana."

Several more spoke. "Join us. Join us," they chanted over and over, their voices mingling into a single harsh whisper. They stalked toward her. As they moved, their bodies hunched over, the skin turning a pale, waxy gray. Their eyes sunk into their heads and their lips puckered around teeth that elongated and multiplied. Their eyes glowed red in the dim lighting. "Join us."

Max pushed her to her feet and turned her toward the exit. "Go."

"I can't. I have to help the woman before they kill her."

"It's already too late for her. You're not safe anymore. You need to leave. Now."

"What about you?" She grabbed for his hand, but he set her away.

"I'm fine. But you aren't. You need to get out before it's too late."

Too late.

The words echoed in her head, spinning round and round. *It's already too late.* Her vision grayed around the edges, her hands and feet going numb. Just before the creatures reached her, everything went black. She held her hands out, searching for Max, but even he had disappeared into the darkness. The sights and sounds of the room faded, leaving behind nothing but the salty scent of the ocean.

And the breaking of waves against the shore. Her eyes snapped open and she glanced around, disoriented. Several things registered at once. The soft blue glow of the moon washing the night in pale color. The ocean surf breaking against the cool sand under her feet and the rocks twenty feet to her left.

Her breath left her lungs in a heavy whoosh. She'd been sleepwalking again. Sleepwalking and dreaming. And somewhere along the way, she'd stripped out of her clothes.

She rubbed her hands down her arms to warm them, but it was no use. It would be hours before the chill left her body. It wouldn't matter how many layers of clothing she put on once she was back in the safety of her house. What she'd seen, though logic told her it wasn't real, made her stomach twist into a painful knot. Time would make the dreams better, her aunt had always said. But they hadn't gotten better. They'd only gotten worse.

She'd been living with the dreams for the past ten years. At first they'd been not much more than twisted, demented visions of the nightmare creatures taunting her --visions she'd been able to put out of her mind come morning. But over time, they'd intensified, turning more disturbing and sexual in nature in the past few years.

And Max... he'd shown up in them in the past few weeks, since she'd moved back to Davenport. His presence, though, baffled her more than the dreams themselves. In the ten years since she'd been away, she'd never really been able to get him out of her mind. Now that she was back in the town they'd grown up in, living less than half a mile from the house he'd built on the beach, he was never far from her thoughts. But that didn't explain why she would insert him into what amounted to a twisted, sensual dream.

The sleepwalking was a new development too. A dangerous one. She always ended up in the same spot -- a darkened stretch of private beach that belonged to the man who had pushed her out of the dream before the creatures had reached her. He'd saved her tonight, as he had every other night this week. But with each night, each new dream, he waited a little longer to push her away. They were getting closer. It wouldn't be long before Max wouldn't be able to get her out in time. And the dreams wouldn't stop. She'd been living with them long enough to know.

The nightmare creatures would never leave her alone.

With a shuddering breath, she turned to walk back up the path cutting through the tall grass that flanked the beach and head home. But a dark, hulking figure blocked her way.

"Don't you know better than to wander around alone at night?"

Chapter 2

Juliana's heart leapt into her throat and her pulse pounded in her ears over the sound of the breaking surf. Instinct kicked in and she bolted, rushing through the beach grass where it met the sand. Her bare feet pounded on the ground, catching on the occasional rock or twig. She winced at the pain, but didn't dare slow her pace. If she did, he would catch her. Whoever he was. She wouldn't wait around long enough to find out. Footsteps sounded behind her, dull thuds on the soft sand. If she stopped, he'd catch her.

An arm snaked out and wrapped around her waist, dragging her back against a hard chest covered in soft flannel. "Juli, stop. I'm sorry. I didn't mean to scare you."

She froze, her mouth going dry. Her heart beat so hard against her ribs she could hear the sound echoing in her ears. "Max?"

"Yeah. I thought you knew it was me." His warm palm splayed across her bare stomach, sending a rush of tingles through her belly. "What are you doing out here? It's three o'clock in the morning. And why on earth do you have no clothes on?"

That was all it took for the dam to crumble. Tears streamed from her eyes, burning wet paths down her cheeks to drip on her breasts. The spring night air cooled them immediately, making her shiver even more. The sobs racked her body, Max her only source of warmth.

"Hey, take it easy." He stroked her damp hair away from her face and brushed a kiss across her cheek. "Don't cry. God, it kills me to see a woman cry. Hold on a second."

He let her go and her body wept from the loss of contact. Soft rustling sounds came from behind her, but she refused to turn around in her vulnerable state to find out what he was doing. Within seconds he wrapped her in something warm and soft. His shirt. Juliana cuddled her cheek against the flannel, inhaled his clean, strong scent.

"Thank you."

"It's nothing. Really. Let's get you inside where it's warm. After you relax a little, I'll drive you home."

She turned and blinked up at him, her stomach clenching at the thought of going into his house. Of having to sit with him while she *relaxed*. Every inch of her skin flamed. He'd just found her naked, wandering around on private property. *His* private property. The last thing she wanted was to spend any more time with him than necessary. She'd rather go home and lick her wounds in peace.

"I'm fine. If you don't mind, I think I'll just walk home now and save you the trouble."

"I don't think so."

He crossed his arms over his chest, now naked. He wore only a pair of loose, dark sweatpants, his feet as bare as the skin of his upper body. She swallowed hard. The sight of him standing before her made a curl of arousal rise in her core, but at the same time guilt gnawed at her insides. He hadn't even taken the time to put on shoes. "Did I wake you up?"

"Your screams did. When I heard the first one, I figured I should check out what was going on."

She said nothing, not sure of how to explain her actions.

"You wanna tell me what's going on or do I have to drag it out of you?" There was a slight thread of amusement in his voice, but concern overshadowed it.

"No. There's really nothing to talk about. I just want to go home and get some sleep."

She started to walk away, but his hand on her arm pulled her to a stop. Max spun her around to face him again. "Bullshit. I can see the fear in your eyes. Tell me what happened. Did someone hurt you?"

The set of his jaw as he glanced around the surrounding area told her he was ready to kill her assailant. How could she tell him that the assailant had been him, along with a group of creatures only her nightmares could create?

"No. No one hurt me. I'm fine. I'm sorry I woke you."

Max let out a harsh laugh. "Like I'm going to believe that? You know me better than to lie to me, Juli. Come inside. I'll make some decaf to warm you up."

Without allowing her time to protest his command, he put his arm over her shoulders and led her up the lawn to his house. He opened the side door and stepped back, letting her walk into the cozy warmth of his kitchen. He came in after her, the hollow click of the lock echoing the traces of earlier terror still racing through her bloodstream. She jumped.

His hand immediately came to rest on her shoulder. "What happened that has you so nervous? And don't even try to lie to me. Remember, you were trespassing on my property. I think you owe me an explanation."

She spun around and gaped at him, her hands clutching the sides of his shirt tight together. "You wouldn't dare press charges."

A single dark eyebrow shot up, and one side of his mouth curled in a sexy half-smile. "Wanna risk it?"

She let out a breath, returned the smile with a genuine one of her own. This was the Max she knew. Sexy, playful, a bad boy with a heart of gold who always knew how to pull her from despair and make her feel human again. Even tonight he was doing his best to calm her. "No. I definitely don't want to risk it."

"Then sit down." He pulled out a high-backed oak chair, one of the four that surrounded the small, square table. "I'll make the coffee. You can tell me all about why you were sleepwalking."

She dropped into the chair, her pulse kicking up a few beats and her palms breaking out in a sweat. "How did you know I was sleepwalking?"

He froze in the act of pulling a green can of decaf from an upper cabinet, the muscles of his back bunching under smooth, tanned skin. The pose lasted a beat too long before he moved again. "You just told me."

"Max?"

He filled the carafe with water and poured the water into the coffee pot, filled the basket with grounds and started the machine. Still he refused to look at her. "What?"

"How did you know?"

His shoulders heaved in a sigh and he turned, leaning back against the counter. His gaze trailed down her body to her uncovered knees. "Did you fall?"

Yeah, in my dream. "No, I don't think so."

"You must have. You scraped up your knees pretty well. Let me get something for that."

He walked out of the room, leaving her alone with thoughts she wished would go away. She glanced down at her knees and let out a shaky breath. He'd been telling her the truth. Her knees were skinned raw and caked with dried blood.

And some sort of strange, green grime that could only have come from the tunnel in her dreams.

* * *

Max dug through the medicine cabinet until he found the supplies he needed to clean Juliana's wounds, the whole time cursing himself for bringing her into his home. And cursing himself again for not trying to keep her safe sooner. It had gone bad so quickly. The whole situation was now slipping from his control and there was nothing he could do to stop it.

He ran a hand through his hair and let out a soft curse. Why had he ever thought he could let Juliana go?

They wanted her. Would stop at nothing to get her. Though he didn't understand all the reasons why, their intent was clear enough. They planned to bring Juliana into their fold.

He'd be damned if he was going to let that happen.

Hell, he was already damned. But that wouldn't stop him from protecting her. She was the only one involved who was innocent, and he wouldn't let them take her. They didn't need her.

He did.

"No," he whispered into the stillness of the room. He didn't need her. Couldn't let himself get attached to her all over again.

When her father had sent her away years ago, it was, in part, because of Max. James McGovern had wanted his precious only child as far away from the boy from the wrong side of the tracks as he could get her. It didn't matter that they were in love. It didn't matter that Max, despite his parentage, had had a bright future ahead of him. Max still fumed inside. He'd been good enough for her, damn it. Why hadn't her parents seen that?

He'd been good enough for her then, but he wasn't now. He was no longer worthy of her attention.

There were other reasons James sent his daughter away, reasons that Juliana wasn't aware of. Reasons that had gotten James and his wife killed. The same reasons that, several years after Juliana had left town, had caused Max's life to make a downward spiral into the bowels of hell.

He picked up the items he needed and carried them down the short hallway to the kitchen. He should have stayed away from her. Let them take her, as her destiny apparently dictated. He'd tried, but he hadn't been able to. And now that he'd held her close to him again, awake rather than just in her dreams, he wouldn't be able to let go. Let them try to come for her. They'd have to get through him first.

He dumped the supplies onto the table -- a box of bandages, a few squares of gauze, and a small bottle of antiseptic liquid. Then he dropped to his knees in front of her.

"Just relax for a second. I'll have you cleaned up in no time."

"Thanks, Max."

He opened the bottle of antiseptic and squirted a stream onto one of the gauze pads. "You don't need to thank me."

She wouldn't want to if she knew the truth. If she learned even half of the terrible truths that surrounded his life, she'd run away screaming like she had earlier on the beach. He went to work cleaning her wounds, his gaze making the occasional trip up her body and back again. She looked so sexy, wearing nothing but his red plaid shirt. Her chocolate brown hair hung in tangles to her elbows and her blue eyes held a lingering hint of fear. Since she'd been back, he'd seen her only from a distance. Being this close to her took his breath away, even with the time and distance that had stretched between them.

She smelled so soft, so feminine, a light floral perfume she'd worn even then. Back when they'd been barely eighteen and he hadn't been able to keep his hands off her. The feelings hadn't faded. Not even a little bit. Max dropped the gauze to the table and clenched his hands into fists.

"What's the matter?" Her fingers sifted through his hair, stroking his scalp. He leaned into her touch -- for a second, before he remembered it was the wrong thing to do.

"*Nothing*." His tone was harsh. Harsher than he ever wanted to use with her. Juliana didn't deserve his anger. She was the only one who didn't. "Nothing. I need to get these fixed up for you."

He untangled her hand from his hair and went to work bandaging the scrapes. When he was finished, he should have stood up and walked away from her. That would have been the right thing to do. But he'd never been one to play by the rules. He stayed on his knees and looked into her eyes.

Big mistake. For the few weeks she'd been back in town, he'd avoided her for one specific reason. The look she was giving him now. He couldn't resist it. Had never been able to. And now he was in deep, deep trouble. Her expression was a mix of lust, tenderness… and love. The same things he felt for her. Had never stopped feeling in the ten years they'd been separated. There had been other women, but none of them had earned a place in his heart like Juliana had.

How ironic. She was also the cause of his downfall.

"Max?" Her tone held a host of questions. Questions he had no easy answers for.

And so he said nothing as she leaned down, her palm cupping his jaw, and brushed her lips against his.

All it took was that one soft kiss for his resolve to crumble and disappear into the night. Fuck being gallant. Fuck being the gentleman she deserved. Right now he wanted to taste her. And he never wanted to stop.

Max knelt up, bringing his body closer to hers, and fit himself between her parted legs. Her breasts brushed his chest through the thin material of his shirt, her nipples hard points against his skin. He put one hand on the small of her back and threaded the other through her hair, angling her head to deepen the kiss.

She parted her lips on a soft sigh and he slipped his tongue into her mouth. Immediately it all came rushing back. The taste of her, the feel of her soft skin under his as he stroked her, kissed her. Loved her. Her flavor exploded on his tongue, hot and intense and all Juliana. No woman had ever made him feel this needy, this ready to burst. The dreams didn't help relieve the pain. They only increased the tension boiling inside him.

The dreams were what would keep them apart.

Once she knew, she'd never want to see him again. And if he told her there was a way to end those horrible nightmares, it could very well bring an end to his own life. This couldn't go on. Pretending wouldn't help either of them.

Max broke the kiss and stood. Though it ate him up inside to walk away from her, he had to do what would be best for her. He went over to the counter and grabbed two mugs from the dish drainer. "Do you still like milk, no sugar?" he asked without turning around.

Her cool hand on the small of his back made him jump. He hadn't even heard her walk across the room.

"Max? What's wrong?"

How was he supposed to explain it to her without scaring her away? He couldn't. Trying would be a wasted effort. "Nothing. Go sit down. I'll bring you your coffee. Milk, no sugar, right?"

Juliana's hand dropped away, leaving his entire body cold. "Yes. Milk, no sugar. Thank you."

He fixed the two mugs of coffee and brought them to the table, taking a seat across from her. "So tell me about the sleepwalking. Is that something new?"

Dark Side

"Yes." She took a sip from her mug, not meeting his eyes. "Since I've been back in Davenport."

Worry twisted his gut into a knot. They were closer than he thought. They'd almost drawn her in. She wouldn't even know it until they'd snared her, and by then it would be too late to save her. There had to be some other way.

"I'm surprised it didn't wake you up when you fell."

"Me, too. I..." Her voice trailed off, her hand touching her cheek. "It was strange. I fell in my dream, but not on sand. On some slimy tunnel leading underground. This just doesn't make any sense."

"Sometimes when a person is sleeping, things that happen in the environment around them can be perceived as part of the dream." He tried to smile, to make light of an impossibly bad situation, but he couldn't quite manage. "What were the dreams about?"

She pushed away from the table and wandered to the rear window overlooking the beach. "I don't want to talk about them. I just want to go home. I need to be alone for a while, okay?"

Hurt laced her tone and her shoulders slumped inward. His rejection bothered her, but what was he supposed to do? He had two choices -- either comfort her, or send her away. If he sent her away, she'd never speak to him again. He couldn't do that. She needed comfort.

He needed, too. But his needs had nothing to do with comfort. They had everything to do with Juliana. With sex. His cock had been semi-hard for most of the night.

He followed her to the window and wrapped his arms around her from behind. "I don't think you really want to be alone tonight."

"No, I don't. But I can't be around you and not want you. I've tried, but it just isn't possible."

The same emotions churned and twisted inside him, so strong they threatened to overwhelm Max's common sense. "Then maybe we both need to stop trying so hard to deny this."

Juliana spun around and leaned back against the window, her eyes flashing fire. "What are you suggesting?"

A way to alleviate the burden of his guilt, at least for a little while. And a way for both of them to forget about... *them*. For tonight. "What if I don't take you home just yet?"

Relief washed away the tension etching her beautiful face. "Do you really want me to stay?"

"Juli, I've never wanted anything more in my life."

Before she had a chance to change her mind, he pulled her close and crushed his lips down over hers. This might be the worst mistake he'd ever made, but he no longer cared. Having Juliana was worth it, whatever the risk.

Chapter 3

Something about Max had changed. Juliana knew it the second he pulled her into his arms. His touch had a rough, demanding edge that fit more with the make-believe Max in her dreams than the real one she'd been so in love with years ago. The change scared her, yet at the same time made her cunt heat and her nipples bead, her whole body begging for his touch.

He devoured her with his kiss, possessing her with his lips and tongue. One of his hands tangled in her hair, anchoring her to him, as the other snaked beneath the shirt she wore to rest on her bare hip. Her body responded to him on a carnal level, her cunt dripping with her juices, her inner muscles fluttering in anticipation. Her mind threatened to shut down while her body fought to control the situation.

His mouth left hers to trail moist kisses down her throat. His tongue darted out to lick back up the path his lips had made. He ended the sensual kiss with a soft bite to the skin where her chin met her throat. Her knees nearly buckled. It had never been like this.

He pushed her back against the window, his hands everywhere at once. Spreading the sides of his shirt, stroking and cupping her breasts, splaying across her ass to drag her even closer. She arched toward him, craving more of his touch. He pulled her hard against him, the unmistakable ridge of his erection pressing against her belly. She whimpered and a gush of her juices drenched her cunt. She was more than ready for him, and she'd been waiting far too long. The only thing that separated them now was his sweatpants. And they wouldn't be in the way for much longer.

She reached between them and slid her hand past the waistband of his pants, her fingers encircling his cock. She squeezed gently and stroked from base to tip one time before he broke the kiss. His breath puffed from his lungs. His gaze held a warning that made her gulp.

"Don't."

She ignored the warning, ignored everything except the instinct that urged her forward, and dragged her free hand down his chest. "You don't like it when I touch you?"

"I love it. That's the problem. You've been driving me crazy for the past two weeks."

Juliana laughed. "I haven't even spoken to you in the past two weeks."

"Not while you've been --" Max's gaze turned hard for a second, a darkness flashing through his irises, but it was gone before she could make sense of it. "No. You haven't. And it's had my cock as hard as stone just thinking about you."

She stroked the length of him again, teasing the tip with her thumb. "Then why not let me touch you now?"

"Because if you keep this up, you're going to end up bent over the kitchen table."

His blunt words sent a tremor through her cunt. She closed her eyes and drew a deep breath. *Oh, my God.* When she opened her eyes her gaze locked with Max's and the intensity there nearly knocked her off her feet. He was so beautiful, so amazing and sexy with his lips parted and his eyes heavy-lidded. She darted her tongue out to wet her lips, wanting instead to lick every inch of his body.

"Fuck, Juli. Stop looking at me like that. If you don't cut it out, I can't be held responsible for my actions."

"Sounds fine to me." She stroked his cock again, harder and slower this time. His harsh indrawn breath made her smile in triumph. "You want me, Max. Why don't you take me?"

"You don't want it that way. You won't like who I am now." He closed his eyes and balled his hands into fists. "I'm not the same man I was before."

She cupped his jaw in her hand, leaning up to kiss his stubble-covered chin. "Don't tell me what I do and don't want. I think I know myself better than you do. I want you right now.

Dark Side

Hard and fast. Slow and easy. I don't care. I want it however you want to give it to me."

Max's eyes flew open, his gaze flashing fire. He spun her around and pushed her against the window, his body so close behind her she felt the heat radiating from his skin. "Don't forget, you asked for it."

"I won't." Her voice sounded too small and weak to belong to her. Her breasts mashed against the glass, the cool smooth surface a contrast to her heated skin. She trembled, as much from the cold as his sudden action. It shouldn't have turned her on as much as it did.

"You'd better not." He used his knee to push her legs apart. His hand dipped between her thighs, stroking along the slick folds of her labia to spread her moisture everywhere. He leaned in and nipped at her earlobe, sending a shock of heat from her neck down to her cunt. "You're so wet. So fucking wet. You're mine, Juli."

She moaned in answer. She'd always been his. Always would be. Nothing could change that.

He thrust a finger into her cunt, stroking and twisting in a rhythm designed to drive her mad. She thrust back against him, yearning for the touch of his fingers against her clit. But he didn't even slow the thrusts of his finger inside her. He pushed another finger into her, stretching her, readying her for his cock.

His thumb pressed against the rosebud of her anus, pushing in just a little. Enough to make a jolt of pleasure race up her spine. She moaned and writhed, her body craving more than he was giving her. His touch wasn't enough. She needed his cock pounding into her. He'd touched her in her dream. Made her come. That was foreplay enough. "Please, Max."

"What's the matter? Don't like to be teased?" He found her clit with his finger and stroked along the sensitive nub. Her body bucked hard against him. "You like that though, don't you?"

"Yes." *God, yes.* And she needed so much more. She'd been dying for him since the first brush of their lips. As soon as he'd wrapped her in his shirt.

He continued to play and stroke, every brush of his finger driving her closer and closer to the edge. Until she finally toppled, his name on her lips, a sob wrenching from her throat.

His finger stroked her still, drawing out every shudder and thrash, pressing her tight between him and the glass. It seemed to go on and on until the tremors finally stopped and he stepped back, his hands on her hips. His lips grazed her shoulder, and then his teeth nipped the same spot.

"You're amazing, Juli."

She only smiled, not trusting her voice.

"I have to tell you, this isn't going to be slow."

She leaned back against him, tilting her head to look in his eyes. "I know."

"Good." He pulled back and led her to the table, bending her over the chair she'd been sitting in. "Put your hands on the seat."

Juliana shivered, licked her lips again. Her body spent, she was helpless to do anything but obey. She bent forward at the waist. She was drenched by now, a trickle of her juices running down her thigh. Her hands hit the chair seat with a soft smack, and then he was behind her. His cock prodded her pulsing entrance before driving inside.

She cried out, loving the feeling of being filled by him. Finally. She'd waited so long. The figment of her imagination had only teased her in her dreams. The real Max was anything but a tease.

Max didn't thrust at first. Instead he ran his hand down the center of her back, pressing down lightly just above her tailbone. Her back arched, bringing him even deeper inside. She dug her nails into the wood under her hands, unable to get enough leverage to brace herself. His hand stroked her ass with a reverence that nearly brought tears to her eyes.

"God, Juli. I don't want to hurt you."

"You won't," she assured him, breathless. "You won't."

He drew back until his cock almost left her cunt. And then he slammed back into her. The momentum of the thrust pushed her forward, her head nearly banging against the chair back. She didn't care. He felt so good, after all this time, that she'd let him do anything.

After a few more hard, measured thrusts, his strokes grew more erratic. His hands gripped her hips, pulling her back to meet him thrust for thrust. Soft moans flew from her lips as a series of soft, quivering orgasms rocked her cunt. Her inner muscles gripped him tight, trying to draw him deeper each time he thrust inside her. Her arms nearly gave out, her elbows buckling. It took all of her strength to remain upright as he pounded his cock inside her.

He was close. She felt it in his unsteady rhythm, in the tight grip of his hands on her hips. Heard it in his ragged breathing and low groans. With one final, hard thrust he let go and groaned out her name as he came. Nothing had ever felt so right.

He pulled out and reached a hand between her legs, his fingers brushing her shuddering cunt, collecting their mingled fluids. He brought the hand up and rubbed the sticky wetness into the small of her back. Once he'd coated her skin, he gave her ass a light swat and helped her upright. "Stay tonight."

She could only nod.

* * *

Max lay on his side, watching Juliana snore softly as she slept. She'd been overwhelmed with stress, and he'd worn her out. Almost as soon as her head had hit the mattress, she'd been asleep. He smiled, though guilt still plagued him. He'd ignored instinct for lust, and now it would be hell to not have her in his arms every night when he went to bed.

She wouldn't be with him forever. He wasn't stupid enough to believe in that myth -- at least not for him. She wouldn't want him anywhere near her once she knew the truth. But for now, he'd take what he could get and be thankful for every day he had with her. Damned men didn't usually get such a tempting opportunity, and he'd be a fool to pass it up.

A scraping sound on the bedroom window drew his attention. He bolted upright and jumped out of bed, adjusting his sweats as he left the room and headed for the side door. He had to take care of a few issues before they got worse. No way were *they* going to disturb Juli now. Not even in her dreams. Not if he had anything to say about it.

He stepped out into the cool night and closed the door softly behind him. "Where are you?"

A figure appeared out of nowhere, clad in a black cloak. Red eyes glowed from a gray face. A single bony hand reached out as if in a wave, but then dropped to the creature's side. "She's with you."

"Yes." The breeze whipped his hair around his face. He clenched his hands into fists, rage tightening a knot in his gut and bile rising in his throat. She thought they were scary in her dreams. She'd better hope she never came face to face with one in real life. A shiver raced down the length of his spine. "You can't have her."

"You have no say in the matter. I'll have her, and I'll have you too." The creature cackled, a sound that chilled Max to the bone.

"No. You can't have her. Not anymore. She's with me now, and I won't let you take her. *Not ever.*" He stepped toward the creature, his hands raised into fists even though he knew physical violence would bring no harm to the thing. He'd learned that lesson the hard way. "Leave here. Now. You're not welcome."

"You belong with us. You enjoy what we do. I've seen you watching our rituals from darkened corners of the room. You'd be so happy. And you could have her too."

"No." Joining them wasn't an option. The curse that made them what they were was worse than death. Juliana may have been promised to them years ago, but Max was going to find a way to see that the promise was never fulfilled. Whatever it took, he'd do it. She didn't deserve to live an eternity as a monster. "I'm not going to say it again. Leave now. Don't ever come back."

It was an empty threat, and they both knew it. The creature, all of the cloaked ones, would be back. But the threat served another purpose, one the creature didn't miss. It was a challenge, and the being accepted with an unholy smile.

The creature whispered a single, terrifying sentence before it faded into the night. "Let the battle begin."

Chapter 4

Juliana bolted upright in bed, her heart thumping wildly against her ribcage. Her breath wheezed from her lungs. Sweat poured from her body, the sheets tangled in damp masses around her. Glowing red eyes danced like specters in the quiet room for a few moments before they faded into the shadows, along with the remnants of the night's dream.

She glanced around her at the sparse oak furniture barely visible through the darkness -- a tall dresser, full-length mirror tucked into the corner, hope chest at the foot of the bed, nightstand next to her. The décor in the room was plain, dark bedding and matching curtains. Plain and comfortable. Max's bedroom.

She let out a breath and flopped back on the mattress, pulling the covers up over her bare breasts. For three nights now, Max had insisted she stay with him. For three nights he'd told her he wanted to be with her, couldn't stand to be apart from her for any longer. But his eyes had told a different story. He wanted to be with her, yes, but there was a deeper reason for him asking her to stay. A reason that had nothing to do with lust, or love, or whatever was developing between them.

It had everything to do with her nightmares.

She ran a hand through the tangled mass of her hair, darting her tongue out to wet her lips. For three days and three nights the truth had hung between them, silent but persistent, threatening to take her world and shatter it all around her. Max knew about her nightmare creatures. Every time she mentioned them, she saw the understanding in his eyes. If he knew, that would make them... No. She wouldn't even contemplate the possibility.

She had her own reasons for staying with Max. Selfish reasons. Since she'd started sleeping in his bed, she hadn't once walked in her sleep. And the dreams. She'd still had them every night, but the intensity had faded, returned to the way it had been before she moved back to Davenport. She had moved back to the position of a spectator now, watching their rituals from the sidelines. They hadn't seen her, hadn't called to her to join them. She'd watched the proceedings through a fine red haze, as if a chiffon veil separated her from the group. Maybe, given time, they would finally start to fade and leave her in peace.

Or, more likely, Max had somehow caused a temporary reprieve.

Max. He'd been absent from her nightmares since that first night she'd spent in his bed. Though, on that particular night, he hadn't let her have much sleep. Juliana laughed softly to herself. She hadn't really wanted much, anyway.

She got out of bed and pulled on her robe -- one of many items she'd retrieved from her own house after her first night with Max. After cinching the belt around her waist, she walked to the window and pushed the curtains aside. Bright sunlight streamed into the room. She blinked, glanced down at the slender gold watch on her wrist. *Noon.* Why had he let her sleep that long? Had he gotten too involved in his work again to notice the time?

It wouldn't surprise her. The past two mornings she'd woken up late to find him in the spacious office in the back of the house. It brought another smile to her face. The hazards of working at home. She knew them well. She dealt with them on a daily basis herself -- though she hadn't become a regionally renowned architect. She'd chosen freelance journalism. She had yet to make a name for herself in her field, and that was fine with her. She preferred to stay as far away from the spotlight as she could get.

Max, too, seemed to live like a recluse. He'd been outgoing before, when they'd first been together. She'd grown up with him, been in the same grade in school. She'd always been jealous of his numerous friends, and of his ability to adapt to any situation. By the time they'd reached high school, the jealousy had morphed into something else, but he'd still had to be the one to approach her first. She'd never seen him like this --distant, cautious, and secretive. Worry gnawed at her gut. There were still too many things he had yet to tell her.

She'd let it slide over the past few days, hadn't pushed him for answers he wasn't ready to give and she wasn't ready to hear, but that needed to change. She was in danger. Instinct warned her of that fact as much as the anxiety in Max's eyes did. Now Juliana wanted to know where the danger was coming from. In order to protect herself, she needed the information he'd so far refused to give.

He wouldn't be refusing her for long.

She wouldn't let him.

* * *

Fifteen minutes later, after a long, hot shower, Juliana stood in Max's kitchen staring at the note he'd left her.

Had to run into town for a few things. Be back soon. Wait for me. Do not leave the house.

She rolled her eyes. It wasn't that he was afraid of her walking away from him while he was gone. The short, concise words and the heavy, dark scrawl told her otherwise. It was an order. Her eyes narrowed and her face went hot. Whatever was going on with him, she wasn't sure she liked it. He could take his order and shove it. She wouldn't be bossed around by anyone.

Fresh air would do her stressed body and mind wonders. She headed for the side door and opened it. And ran straight into Max's broad chest.

He gripped her arms and lifted her off her feet, moving her back into the house. He set her down, kicked the door shut with his heel, and faced her with a stormy expression. His aggravation hung so thick between them it almost took on a life of its own. "Where do you think you're going?"

"Outside. I just wanted a little fresh air. Though I don't particularly care for your attitude. I don't owe you any explanations."

"A little bit defensive, huh?" His expression relaxed and a grin quirked one corner of his mouth. "Why were you sneaking out, Juli?"

"I told you. Fresh air. I'm sick of being inside all the time. You have that amazing yard and incredible beach. Why is it you seem to never spend any time out there?"

"Just fresh air. That's all?" The grin widened even more, but then it faded almost as quickly as it had appeared. "You're scared of me."

"No." *Liar.* Max had changed. He wasn't the same gentle boy she'd known. A host of questions popped into her head. "Where did you go?"

His gaze slid away. "I had some things to do."

"Max?"

"Have you had a chance to eat yet? I could make you some breakfast."

"Don't change the subject."

He let out a breath, turned his attention back to her. The weariness in his eyes made her stomach clench. What had he seen? What had he done that had shaped him into the dark, mysterious man who stood before her? A decade wasn't that long, but at the same time an entire lifetime had passed since they'd parted.

"I had to do some personal stuff, okay?" His tone brooked no argument, his jaw set in stone. "Just leave it alone for now. It isn't important. If it was, I would have told you. Why don't I make you some pancakes?"

She shook her head, her heart beating a steady pace against her ribs. Her mouth had gone dry and her legs weakened. What was going on with him? "I'm not hungry."

All the darkness bled out of his expression, leaving him looking world-weary and pale. He reached out to pull her into his arms, but she dug her heels in and crossed her arms over her chest.

Max's hand cupped her chin and tilted her gaze up to his. "What's the matter, Juliana? You really are afraid of me, aren't you?"

"No." To admit that would be to admit weakness -- and she'd already done enough of that when she had confessed her nightmares to him. "Why would I be afraid of you?"

"That's what I'm trying to figure out." Pain replaced the ever-present anxiety in his eyes. "Don't you know by now that I would never do anything to hurt you?"

She stared at him for a long time, her mind turning over and over everything that had happened in the past couple of days. The emotions inside her were raw, open and honest. Fear. Lust. Happiness. *Love.* She wanted to hold him close, assure him that she knew he'd never do anything to hurt her, but she didn't. Her mind warned caution. She'd gotten involved, deeply, in just a few short days. It was time to pull back a little bit and put some much-needed distance between them until she could make sense of the chaos her world had become. So she offered him a bright smile instead of reassurances she couldn't, in good conscience, make.

"I don't want pancakes. It's noon."

The grin came back full force, and for the first time in days most of the darkness left his eyes. "If you want to eat, you do. I don't know how to make much else."

* * *

"Max? Can I ask you something?"

Max turned to Juliana, taking in her anxious gaze, pale face, and parted lips. This had to be hell on her. And he had yet to find a way to stop it. He muttered a curse, ran a shaky hand through his hair. In the early hours of the morning, while she'd been sleeping, he'd been sitting in front of his computer. In this age of technology, it was amazing, the information one could find online. But his search, the second one since she'd come back into his life, had proved fruitless. He still had no idea what to do to fix her situation.

But he did have one advantage. He had a secret weapon. Something *they* wanted even more than they wanted Juliana. He'd retrieved that *something* from his safety deposit box that morning. He might be able to bargain with them. The item for Juliana's soul. But only after he exhausted all other possibilities.

An hour had passed since lunchtime and they'd spent the better portion of it in companionable silence. Now they walked along the length of the beach, as close as they could be without touching, enjoying each other's company. Until she'd broken the silence.

"Sure. What do you want to know?" He braced himself for her questions, more of her relentless badgering about the things plaguing her dreams, but what she asked took him by surprise.

"Did I hurt you when I left?"

Hell, yes. Max's knees threatened to buckle. Why did she have to ask that, of all questions? There was no easy answer to it. At least not one he was free to give. He let out a heavy breath, something dark and vile turning in his gut. The question was so deeply personal he couldn't manage to come up with an answer.

"What do you want me to say to that?" Almost of its own volition his gait sped up, his mind intent on only one thing. Escape. Escape from her questions, escape from the past that would forever hold him in its grip, keeping him teetering on the edge between human sanity and eternal madness.

Juliana grabbed his hand and pulled him to a stop. "Don't run away from me, from this. I just want the truth. In the past three days you've said nothing about what happened before. We can't just go back to the way things were. Not until I know the truth. Please, Max. Talk to me."

He glanced away, his lips curling into an involuntary sneer. The truth was the last thing she wanted. It would tear her into a million pieces. Pieces that would leave her scattered in the wind. He'd never be able to pick them all up, and he'd never be able to put her back together. Yet she asked him for the truth, *a* truth, an honest answer about the past he'd rather forget. He was helpless to deny her that one small thing.

"Yes, you hurt me." He closed his eyes for a brief second as if the action would ward off the memories. "It fucking killed me inside."

"But you went on with your life. Went to college and got your degree. You're a successful architect now. It doesn't seem like it affected you that much."

He nodded. On the outside, he might appear unchanged. But it wasn't the outward appearance that counted. Not in this case.

"You haven't said a word about the past since we've been together this time," she continued, her voice low and quiet. "Not a single hint that it even meant anything to you. The chemistry is still there between us, you can't deny that, but for some reason you seem intent on denying the history we share."

Max glanced down at her. He'd never meant to hurt her. He'd promised her he wouldn't. But now it seemed that despite his best intentions, he'd done it anyway. He took her hand in his, reveling in the feel of his fingers enveloping the smallness of hers.

"I'm not trying to deny it. Here we are, starting over. Sometimes I think the past is better left where it belongs. Behind us. I'd rather concentrate on the here and now." He spared her a brief glance before looking away, his gaze trained on the expanse of deep blue ocean in front of them.

"I don't agree." The pain in her voice wrenched his gaze back to hers. Juliana gave him a sad smile. "I think the past, what happened between us and what happened after we were separated, might pull us apart if we don't talk through it."

"We're going to need to work up to that slowly then," he told her, the most truthful answer he could give. Though he doubted they'd ever reach that point in their relationship. One way or another, very soon they'd be ripped apart.

"I'm sure there were other women." She cast her eyes down to the sand, her bare toes drawing swirls and shapes in the granules. "I'm not foolish enough to believe I was the only one."

Shit. She was going to kill him with her uncertainty. "Don't tell me there haven't been any men in your life since me."

A short burst of laughter escaped her. "I won't lie to you. But I've never loved anyone but you."

Her gaze turned watery, her cheeks flushing. What could he say to that, other than what he was feeling inside? She'd given him a gift just then, and she deserved one in return.

"There have been other women. No one for a while after you left, and no one in a few months now." He leaned down and brushed a kiss across her soft lips. "But I never loved any of them. Never loved anyone but you."

A fat tear rolled down her cheek. He caught it with his thumb.

The action brought a smile to her face. "I'm so sorry. I wish I'd been able to control what happened, but my father... you know what he was like."

"You were eighteen. You could have said no." As soon as the words left his mouth, he wanted to pull them back. He muttered a curse. For a man who claimed he didn't want to hurt her, he was doing an excellent job making a liar of himself.

"I tried. But he told me my life was in danger. That there were people after him who would hurt me, too. I was young. Stupid. I believed him. But he lied. He only wanted to keep us apart."

Max closed his eyes and pinched the bridge of his nose. James McGovern hadn't lied. Someone *had* been after him. And they *would* hurt her. But he'd left out an important detail in his story to his daughter.

Running away wouldn't help.

They were strong. They'd drawn her back to Davenport after all this time. Back to them. And this time they planned to keep her.

"I knew what he was doing," Max answered. He'd known, and he'd tried to stop it from happening.

That mistake had cost him, for all intents and purposes, his life. Now there was no going back. Not for him. But there was still hope for Juliana. He just had to keep her safe for a few more days. Until he could work out the solution to her problem.

"And you didn't follow me?"

"I couldn't." At the time he'd been... indisposed. Recovering, in a way, though he'd never truly been able to accomplish that. "I wanted to, but I wasn't able."

Her eyes flashed, her lips drawing into a thin line. "Did he do something to you? Did he hurt you?"

A bitter laugh clogged Max's throat. *Yeah, baby. He hurt me. Tried to kill me, even.* What would she say if she knew he'd just about succeeded? Since that fateful night, Max had been one step away from the grave. He had to fight daily not to slip into the void. Just being with her again was killing him slowly, but if he didn't keep her close, they'd kill *her.* "What he did doesn't matter. Right now, the only thing I'm concerned with is keeping you safe."

"From what? You?"

"No. The things in your dreams." With that answer, he'd opened the air between them for more questions. Juliana might not be ready for the answers, and he wasn't ready to give them. But there were things she needed to know. It would be easier to keep her safe if she knew what they were dealing with. Maybe then she wouldn't fight him so much on every little thing.

Her gaze told him the moment the weight of his words had sunk in. "But they aren't real. Those are just figments of my imagination."

"No. They're real."

He expected anger, panic. Hatred. But he got none of that. The only thing she gave him was silence. She turned away, walked a few feet down the strip of sand and sat on a large rock protruding from the shore. The wind whipped the long, rich strands of her hair around her face. She leaned forward and propped her forearms on her thighs. "What is it you're keeping from me?"

So, so much. I'm so sorry. "What do you want to know?"

"I want to know everything you do. There are things you aren't telling me. I've put up with it for a few days now, and I'm not going to any longer. What are they, those things in my nightmares?"

A small smile nudged at the corners of his lips. The strong, independent streak he'd always admired hadn't gone anywhere. But then he thought about her question and the smile faded away. "Ashnori. The living dead."

"Vampires?"

"No. Ancient lore often confused the two, but in essence, they aren't the same. The Ashnori are far worse than vampires. Far more dangerous. And seductive. You've witnessed that firsthand."

"Why are they haunting my dreams?"

"Because you have something they want."

A frown dipped her lips, her brow creasing. "What could I possibly have that would appeal to them?"

"Your soul."

Chapter 5

Max's words echoed inside Juliana's head until she was afraid it might burst. Her heart pounded against her chest, her blood rushing through her ears so loud it drowned out the ocean sounds around them. *Her soul.* Why? How was that possible?

"Why me?"

He shrugged. "I don't know all the details. I just know what they want."

"How?" Tears formed in her eyes, fat and hot, blurring her vision. "How do you know that? How do you know so much about what haunts *my* nightmares?"

A terrifying possibility struck her in the silent moment before he spoke. Did he seem to have all the answers because he'd been a cause of the problem?

No. It couldn't be that. She wouldn't accept that as an answer. But his reaction didn't instill faith.

"Don't ask a question you're not ready to hear the answer to," Max said simply before he turned and started back up the beach.

No way in hell was she letting him walk away. Not when he'd just increased the turmoil in her mind tenfold. Now determination filled her, even stronger and steadier than before. She *would* have her answers. He wouldn't hide anything from her anymore. She jumped up from the rock and chased after him. "Max, stop!"

He turned, his expression hesitant. "What?"

"What about you? You were in the dreams too. Does that mean they're after you too?"

He barked a laugh. "No."

"How do you know? How can you be so damned sure?"

"They don't want my soul, honey. They already have it."

He didn't give her a chance to respond to his alarming comment. He turned away from her again and continued up the path that would lead back to his house.

Her blood ran cold, icy anxiety tightening around her heart. She clenched her hands into fists, watching his retreating back. How could he drop something so huge on her and then walk away? She'd just sunk into the bowels of hell. He'd put her there and he'd damned well better offer up a reasonable explanation.

She chased after him, her feet pounding along the sandy path. "Max, slow down. Talk to me."

"There's nothing to talk about." His gaze searched the yard, carefully avoiding her eyes. "Let's get up to the house and get you inside. It's going to rain. I don't want you to get sick."

She glanced up at the cloudless sky, squinting into the bright sunlight. The least he could do was find a feasible excuse. "It doesn't look like it to me."

"Trust me. It is." He waved a hand in front of him. A frown marred his handsome features. "The wind is picking up."

Another lousy excuse. New England weather was famous for changing drastically from minute to minute, but usually they had a little warning first. She needed to find something to crack the walls he'd built around himself so he'd let her in. They couldn't help each other with so many things standing between them. "What's the real problem here, Max? What is it you're trying so hard to hide?"

"Just get inside, okay?"

He opened the door and nudged her through. Once inside he grabbed a glass from the dish drainer, filled it with water, and gulped the whole thing down. When he finished, he set the glass down on the counter with a thump. "Do you want something to drink? Something to eat? You didn't have much at lunch."

"I don't want food, Max. This is bullshit. What I want, *right now*, is answers."

"There's nothing more I can tell you. Just don't go outside without me. I know it's daytime, but the clouds will cover the sun soon and it won't be safe."

"What does that have to do with anything?" The Max she'd loved before had been blunt, always saying exactly what was on his mind. The man he'd become spoke in disturbing riddles.

"The Ashnori don't usually come out in bright sunlight. It hurts them."

She shook her head. This had to be some kind of sick, twisted joke. None of this could be real. Yet the name resonated in her head. She'd heard it spoken before. Many years ago.

From her father.

At the time she'd been much younger and hadn't been able to make sense of the word. She'd been a teenager, eavesdropping on a conversation he'd had with her mother. Now she wanted nothing more than to talk to one of her parents and ask them what was going on, but she couldn't. They'd both been killed not long after she'd left town. A car accident. Or so she'd been told. Now doubts about their demise crept into her mind.

Juliana wrapped her arms around herself and squeezed. Juliana's aunt, who she'd been living with in New York while she attended college, had brought her home for the funerals. That was the last time she'd seen Davenport until just a few weeks ago. Up until then, she'd had no reason to return. No reason besides Max, and at the time she hadn't thought he'd want anything to do with her after the way she'd cut all ties when she'd walked away.

But a month ago everything had changed. The cousin who'd been renting her parents' house from her had moved out, and she'd seen that as the perfect opportunity to come home again. If only she'd known what a mistake that would turn out to be.

"I've been here for two weeks, and I've been outside at all hours of the day and night. No one's tried to hurt me yet." At least not while she'd been awake.

"Things are different now. They're closer. Ready to move in and claim what they think is theirs."

A chill raced down her spine. This could *not* be happening. "I can't deal with this right now. I just want my life back." She stalked out of the kitchen, down the hall into the living room and flopped down on the navy blue couch. Juliana rested her head against the back and closed her eyes. The tears threatened again as she tried to hold on to her crumbling sanity. What was she supposed to do? This was just too much.

She sat alone in the quiet for what felt like an eternity before warm hands settled on her shoulders. She opened her eyes and found Max looking down at her.

"Are you okay?"

"Yes." Determination filled her voice. She would be. She'd have to be. There was no other way.

"What can I do to help you?"

"Help me get rid of those things. The Ashnori. Get them out of my nightmares. Out of my life."

"I'm working on it."

As he said the words, a clap of thunder tore through the air. Her gaze flew to the window to find the day had turned overcast, just as he'd predicted. Seconds later, a flash of lightning streaked across the now-purple sky. She gulped and pushed up from the couch, rushing to the window. The sky opened and rain began to pour down.

She spun on him, her hands on her hips. "How the hell did you know it would rain?"

He walked over to her, stopped just a few inches in front of her. He pressed his lips to her forehead. "Bad knees," he whispered. "Old football injuries. They act up every time we're going to get a storm."

His hands came up to her waist, brushing bare skin under the cropped hem of her T-shirt. She shivered. Her body still responded to him though her mind had doubts. But instinct told her she could trust him. No matter what else happened in this mess her life had become, she could trust Max.

She let out a breath. "You never played football."

Instead of responding, he leaned in and kissed her.

* * *

Max's world damned near exploded the second his lips touched hers. It had always been like that between them. Hot. Intense in a way he couldn't describe, could only feel. He cupped her face in his palms, holding onto Juliana when she would have pulled away. This time he wasn't letting her go. He wasn't ever letting her go. Not without a fight.

And a fight it would be, when it all came down to it. As much had already been promised.

Max's tongue played at the seam of her lips, first asking then demanding entry. Her lips parted and he delved his tongue inside, hungry for her in a way he'd never experienced. He wanted to memorize the taste of her, the feel of her. Every last detail about the only woman he'd ever love. He was no longer free to give her that love, but he couldn't ignore the emotions twisting and turning inside him.

One way or another he was going to lose her. Either she'd walk away, or he'd... No. Now wasn't the time to think about that. Now was the time to think about Juli, and everything she was to him. He loved her. Nothing would change that. He wouldn't let it. She was too important. She loved him, too. He knew it without her having to say it. It wouldn't matter in the end, but it mattered now. More than anything ever had.

So for now, he vowed to take all he could, and give as much of himself to her as he was able. He might not be able to offer her forever, but he could offer her now. He could offer her safety, protection. And a way to sate the heat that burned between them.

Now, more than ever, he needed that satisfaction. His whole body throbbed, his cock pressing hard against the zipper of his jeans. It was always like this now -- the intense reaction to the scent of a woman, the need to bury himself deep inside her. It kept him in isolation most of the time, and was the reason the women who came after Juliana had been few and far between. The beast inside him always fought to break free, and each time it got harder and harder to contain. It was an overwhelming urge, almost impossible to resist.

He deepened the kiss, cupping her breasts in his palms and kneading them. His thumbs grazed her peaked nipples and a growl rose in his chest. She was *his* woman. He'd prove that to her over and over for whatever time they had left. She broke free of his lips, her breath ragged and her face flushed a becoming pink. "How can you manage to make me need you this much, so quickly?"

It was a part of who he was now. But she'd never understand. "It's us. This chemistry. I feel the same way."

It was the truth, or at least part of it. The chemistry between them did incite some pretty powerful reactions. Max leaned down and pressed an open-mouthed kiss to Juliana's nipple through the fabric of her shirt. He pulled back and inhaled the scent of her arousal faint in the air. Juliana's pussy would be wet for him, the bud of her clit hard and begging for his touch. Max's cock hardened even more, his balls drawing up a little closer to his body. Something inside him snapped. Urgency replaced common sense, as it always did when he got so close to her.

"I need you now, Juli."

She just nodded in reply, her eyes glazed with lust and her lips parted, revealing the tip of her pink tongue.

He stripped her out of her clothes and removed his own, taking her down to the floor with him. She lay on her back on the dark red oriental rug, looking for all the world like a sexual offering to some forgotten pagan god. Her legs splayed across the rug, her knees bent slightly as if offering him to look his fill of her glistening cunt. Her breasts rose and fell with each breath, their hardened tips calling for him to suckle her. And her face... her expression begged him to take her in the way he had before -- all the times they'd been together in the past three days. The wanton need he saw in her eyes beckoned him, a siren's call he was helpless to ignore.

He bent over her and buried his face in her cunt.

The warm, musky taste of her made his gut clench hard. The beast rattled its cage, harder than ever this time. He should pull back, if for no other reason than to protect her, but the beast wouldn't let him. That fateful night so long in the past had turned him into an animal. A man Juli wouldn't recognize. But so far, she hadn't uttered a single complaint. Maybe the incidents of the past had changed her, too, and she had yet to figure it out.

Max ran his tongue down the length of her slit and pressed a kiss to her clit, reveling in the slick juices that coated his lips. Juliana writhed against him, arching her back to put her pussy in closer contact with his mouth. He smiled against her skin. Nothing could be more perfect than this single moment in time. He wanted to hold onto it forever. There might not be other moments like this, because soon the time would come to tell her the truth.

The smile faded and he pushed the thoughts away. When the time came, he'd deal with it appropriately. Now was not that time.

He stroked his tongue in and out of the wet heat of her cunt, delighting in every pant and moan that escaped from her lips. His thumb found her clit and brushed back and forth across it, using the exact amount of pressure she responded to. He'd learned her body all over again in the past three days, and knew just what it would take to make her scream. And scream she would. He intended to make her feel every sensation with as much intensity as she could take.

Her writhing became short bucks of her hips, the moans as regular as her jagged breaths. Her hands gripped his hair, holding him in place while he licked and sucked and stroked her body into oblivion. The scent of her passion filled the air, wrapping around his neck, seducing and enticing. Her fingers tightened in his hair until he worried she might tear it out at the roots. Small tremors ran through her cunt, her muscles clenching and releasing against his tongue as he rammed it into her. And then she came with a scream, her juices gushing from her pussy. He lapped them up, continued to lap at her until her bucking stopped and she lay still below him, whimpering softly.

He moved up her body with slow precision, kissing every exposed inch of flesh between her pussy and her mouth. He pressed a soft kiss to her lips and looked up to stare into her eyes.

The heat he found caught him by surprise.

"I want to be on top this time," she told him in a tone that brooked no argument.

The beast responded to her comment, sending a surge of fire through his cock. Who was he to turn her down? Max lay back on the rug and reached his arms out to her. "By all means, Juli."

With a sensual smile that sent a spike of lust through his gut, she straddled him, held his cock in one hand, and slid her hot, slick cunt down over the length of him. Her inner muscles still pulsed and trembled, milking shudders from his body. Her hands came to rest on his chest, her thumbs playing across the flat disks of his nipples. He groaned, arched his hips toward her to get her to move.

"A little impatient?" she asked, her tone filled with amusement.

"Yeah. I have a reason to be. You feel so damned good." Juliana pinched his nipples between her forefingers and thumbs and he groaned again. "Jesus, Juli. Are you trying to kill me?"

She smiled down at him. "No. I'm just trying to make you come."

"You have no idea how close you are to accomplishing that goal."

She laughed, a husky, sexy sound that reverberated through his whole body. She licked her lips and raised herself up before dropping down again on his cock. Her pace was slow, measured, and driving him insane.

"I need more than this right now. Please." He gripped her hips, squeezing them in his palms and guiding her into a faster rhythm that matched the need boiling inside him.

She slammed down on him over and over, her hips moving in small circles that ground her against him even more. His grip on her hips tightened, the skin around his fingers whitening. She threw her head back and moaned, a sound that echoed deep inside him.

It was then that the world around him started to change.

A haze clouded his vision, misty and tinted red. He closed his eyes and tried to shake off the odd sensation, but when he opened them it was still there, painting everything around him in a harsh but oddly sensual light.

The red began to fade, the colors around him brightening to a strange intensity. Juliana, still moving above him, took on the form of a sensual, alabaster-skinned goddess with gleaming hair and eyes so bright they appeared to glow. His heart beat a steady rhythm against his ribcage. His pulse whooshed in his ears like the sound of chanting.

No. The chanting wasn't inside him. It was inside the room.

He squeezed his eyes shut again, determined to drive it all away. This couldn't be happening. Not now. But it was. The beast had escaped and there was nothing he could do but go along for the ride.

The soft rug under him became velvet-coated granite, the scents and sounds of the ocean filling the air. Dampness stole over his skin, prickling goose bumps wherever it touched.

His eyes flew open, his gaze scanning their surroundings. Not his house. The Ashnori's secret room. The breath left his lungs in a whoosh.

The Ashnori surrounded the altar, in human form, pleasuring each other while they watched the people on the altar. Juliana slammed down on him over and over, her lips red and parted, her eyes half-closed. It was in that moment that he gave in to the beast. Let go of all his inhibitions and emotions and concentrated on what the inner beast wanted. To fuck. A roar tore from his chest and he lifted her, dislodging his cock from her cunt with a wet pop.

Max flipped Juliana to her back and sank back into her, his strokes fierce and unrelenting. Every muscle in his body strained, reaching toward her, reaching toward the ultimate fulfillment.

He was savage, untamed, and she was too. Her nails gouged his back, her legs coming around his waist and her heels digging into his ass. She met him thrust for thrust, her fingernails cutting through his skin. The blood that seeped from the wounds burned, trailed in hot paths down his back, and made him pound into her even harder. Heated little moans flew from Juliana's lips, her head thrashing from side to side, the look in her eyes one of pure ecstasy.

The Ashnori echoed her moans, their bodies writhing and bucking on the floor. The chants grew until they overwhelmed his senses. His mind threatened to shut down, his body fighting for complete control. Juliana's legs tightened around his hips, her body arching toward him as her orgasm took her over the edge. She convulsed beneath him, the bite of her nails against the skin of his back growing even harder. The pain only urged him on until he tumbled over the edge with her, finding release inside her quivering cunt. His whole body shook from the incredible pleasure of the act. When the last hot jet of semen bathed her inner walls, he leaned in and sank his teeth into her shoulder.

His name ripped from her throat on a scream was enough to send the beast back into hiding and bring Max back to himself. The stone walls vanished, as did the Ashnori writhing on the floor. The scents of the ocean faded into nothingness and the chanting ceased. They were back in his living room, away from the horrible, sensual world of the living dead. He glanced down and saw Juliana looking up at him, apprehension in her eyes.

"Are you okay?"

She nodded, bit her lower lip. "What was that?"

There were no easy answers to her question. He closed his eyes for a brief second, swallowed hard. When his eyelids snapped open, his gaze focused on the angry red teeth marks on Juliana's shoulder. The blood rushed from his head. He'd come too close this time. If he'd broken the skin, gotten a taste of her blood... in that moment, it would have been over for both of them. He couldn't make love to her again. Not until he'd found a way to banish the Ashnori from her life. The price was too steep, the risk too high. This had to end, one way or another. He'd kept her safe this time, but he knew deep inside the next time neither of them would be as lucky.

But what killed him was that he still couldn't let her out of his sight. He'd have to keep her with him, and find a way to keep his hands to himself. He leaned down and kissed her softly on the lips.

"Stay with me again tonight," he said. "Let me keep you safe while we work this thing out."

She let out a strained laugh. "Do I have much choice?"

"No. I'll chain you to the bed if I have to."

"Then I guess it's settled." She said the words with determination, but a look of weary defeat had begun to creep into her gaze.

Sometime later, Max curled Juliana in his arms and held her close. It was enough, for tonight, to hold her and listen to the slow, steady sound of her breathing. The quiet beat of her heart.

"Are you awake?" she asked in a voice barely above a whisper.

"Yeah."

"Good." Her hand brushed his cheek, her fingers skimming his jaw. "How are we supposed to get them? Is there really a way to stop them or are they going to kill me anyway?"

Though she'd never admit it, fear tinged her voice. It showed in the way her muscles had tensed, the way she held him tight over the past few days, even in sleep. The same fear was what had kept him up for the past few nights, desperate to find a way to break her out of their spell. But he'd come up empty. There was nothing he could do -- save for the one thing that might well end his life. He'd been hesitant before, but now that he knew there was no other way he saw he had no choice. He had to tell her.

"You need to be looking a little closer to home. Didn't your father keep journals?"

She nodded.

"Where are they?"

"I don't know. I never really wanted to go through their personal stuff. It was too painful. But there are some boxes in the basement. My aunt packed up the house and put anything down there that she thought I might want to have later. They're probably down there somewhere."

If they were, she'd find them. And she'd learn what it would take to finally be able to free herself from the nightmare. He sighed. He'd miss her when she was gone.

If he even remembered her at all.

"Good. Check there. I have a feeling the answers we're looking for are closer than we first thought."

Chapter 6

Juliana sat cross-legged on the dusty cement floor of the basement, searching through box after box to find the journals Max had mentioned. The musty smell that hung in the air filled her lungs and made her cough. The desolation that had been stealing up on her in the past few weeks now swelled inside her stomach. Only three boxes left and she had yet to find what she was looking for. She lifted the lid of a smaller box that had been tucked into the corner and a smile crept up on her lips. *Finally.* Inside the box was a small set of brown, leather bound notebooks. The journals her father, an antiques exporter, had kept, detailing his travels around the world.

Max thought the answers they searched for would be somewhere inside the volumes. At this point she'd try just about anything to get rid of her nightmares. To get rid of the Ashnori. She pulled out the first journal, opened the front cover, and began to read.

Several hours later, she'd finished the volume, along with the two that had come before it. Tears blurred her vision and an ache had formed in her chest. She'd found the answers she had been looking for, but they'd only intensified the pain inside her. Max had been right. Her father was the key to stopping the Ashnori.

Because he was the cause of them visiting her nightmares.

On one of his trips to Egypt, he'd brought back a souvenir. She remembered it well even now -- a golden sun pendant with a red jewel in the center, hanging from a thick, box-link gold chain. The jewel had reminded her of a ruby in color, but it had a strange quality that brought to mind warm, flowing liquid. It had been a stunning piece, captivating, even to her young mind. She'd wanted it for herself, but he'd insisted on hiding it away instead of displaying or selling the beautiful jewelry. Now she understood the reason why he'd hidden his treasure. It belonged to the Ashnori. He'd bought the piece from a street vendor, not knowing anything about its history -- or the curse it carried. All who touched the jewel in the center were cursed to become one of the Ashnori, or die if they refused to join the living dead.

There was a way to break the curse, and her father had detailed it in his journal. He'd apparently sought help before he died, but it had been too late for him. There was still hope for her, though it was a hope that faded a little more as each second passed. It was an impossible task, one she'd never be able to complete. In order to banish the Ashnori, she would have to find the sun and break the flame-red jewel in the center. And then pour Ashnori blood on the pieces.

She leaned back against the wall. How the hell was she supposed to do that?

Fear and hopelessness warred inside her. She hadn't seen the pendant in years. Her aunt had cleaned out the house and moved the boxes to the basement, but when Juliana had asked about the piece, along with the rest of her father's treasures, her aunt claimed that the sun pendant hadn't been among his possessions.

And the Ashnori blood... she couldn't even spare a thought for that right now. First she had to find the sun.

"I see you found the journals."

Juliana snapped her head up to find Max standing by the basement stairs, his arms crossed over his chest and a dark expression on his face. She gulped. Had he set her up somehow? He had blocked her only exit.

No. She took a deep, calming breath. Max wouldn't do anything to hurt her. He'd been trying to help, and, in his own way, he had.

"Yes. I found them." She explained to him what she'd read. "But I don't know where the sun is. I haven't seen it in so many years. When my aunt packed up the house, she didn't find it either."

He pulled something out of his pocket and tossed it to her. She caught it, a small package wrapped in white tissue paper. She carefully pulled apart the tissue and found herself staring down at a fire-red jewel set in gold. The sun. She brought her gaze back to Max's, confusion clouding her mind. "How did you get this?"

"Your father gave it to me before he died. Said I should keep it safe for you."

"But he really just wanted it away from him so the Ashnori couldn't find it."

Max shook his head. "No. He just wanted me dead. He knew they'd come after me like they were after all of you."

She gulped, her heart skittering. "But you're alive."

He didn't answer. He walked over to her and helped her to her feet. "We have to get to the underground room before daylight ends."

She stared up at him for a long time, unable to voice the words tumbling around in her head. The room from her nightmares… the room she'd visited so many times over the years in dreams she just wanted to forget. Her stomach bottomed out and her heart lurched to her throat. "It's a real place?"

He nodded again.

"How far is it?"

"Nearby. The big rocks along the edge of my beach -- the entrance is there."

He turned and started up the stairs. She grabbed the back of his shirt to halt his progress. "Don't even think about running away yet. How long have you known where to find them?"

"For a couple of days. Since you've been back, they've… set up shop. Waiting for you. I found the entrance that first night we… the night I found you wandering my beach. I went back out later, after you fell asleep."

Her stomach clenched, the sting of betrayal washing over her as she looked at him. "Why didn't you tell me?"

"I'm sorry." What looked like remorse flashed in his eyes, followed by a sliver of fear. "I really am. But we can't dwell on this right now. You have the pendant. We can get rid of them."

Dark Side

"But I need blood." She cringed. "Their blood."

"I know." He didn't wait for her to follow. He took the steps two at a time and disappeared into the house. She clutched the pendant tight in her fist and followed.

* * *

"This place is even worse than it looked in my dreams." Juliana shuddered as Max led her down the slippery stone tunnel, the beam from his flashlight the only light to guide their way. The stench of decay filled the air. The walls glistened with a green slimy tinge of something she didn't even want to contemplate. The dampness wrapped around her, chilling her straight through.

She tightened her grip around the pendant and kept her eyes on Max. It wasn't long before they reached the cavernous room where she'd seen the altar. It looked innocuous now, with sunlight streaming in through windows carved high up in the rocks. Waves broke just below the openings, sending sprays of water into the room and creating a fine mist in the air.

Except for the waves, the room was silent. No gray monsters with red eyes greeted them. No one tried to stop them as Max grabbed her hand and pulled her over to the altar. "Put the sun on there," he told her, the urgency in his voice coupled with the way his gaze seemed to continually scan the room making the anxiety double inside her.

It was *too* quiet. It couldn't be this easy.

"Where is everyone?"

"They're coming. Trust me. Just do it." He rushed across the room into a dark hollow nearly hidden by rocks.

She shivered, dropping the pendant onto the altar and wrapping her arms around herself. Even as she stood there waiting for him to return, the atmosphere in the room shifted. The coldness intensified and the hair on the back of her neck rose. Max was right. They were coming. She could feel them with every fiber of her being. Her stomach roiled and she just about doubled over. What if it didn't work? How would she get blood from one of them without them grabbing her and pulling her into their world?

A shuffling noise in one corner of the room caught her attention. She swung her gaze in that direction. The shadows there had begun to move and sway, separating into dozens of singular forms.

"Max!"

He rushed out of the alcove and headed straight for her. In his hand, he held a long, thin-bladed knife with an ornate carved handle. Her gaze flew from the weapon to the forms in the corner, now moving closer and taking shape. Black cloaks. Gaping mouths. Glowing red eyes. She fought against the urge to squeeze her own eyes shut.

"Is that going to protect us from them?" she asked him. Bile rose in her throat and her pulse rushed in her ears.

"No. This isn't for them." He lifted the knife above his head and brought the butt of it down in the center of the pendant with a sharp crack. The jewel split down the center, the cracks spidering off into dozens of little hairline fractures. He glanced at her, the darkness in his eyes making her legs turn to mush.

"Now what?" she asked, her voice barely above a whisper.

The shapes in the corner had become the cloaked ones, gliding toward them, their bodies hunched and their mouths tipped in hideous smiles. They started chanting, and their hands rose in front of them, palms together, in a sick mockery of prayer.

"Now you need the blood of the Ashnori. It needs to flow over the pieces." Max waved his hand over the altar. "Then you'll be free of the curse."

"Okay. Give me the knife." She started toward him, her hand outstretched, but he shook his head.

"They won't give you their blood willingly. They'll kill you first."

The cloaked one in the front of the pack started to morph into human form. Blond hair flew free from the hood of the cloak and he reached a hand out to her. Lane.

Max stepped in front of her.

"Leave her alone," he said, his voice rough and commanding.

"No. She belongs with us. To us."

"Bullshit." Juliana ducked around Max and tried to wrestle the knife from his grasp. He wouldn't let go. He set her behind him again.

"Stop, Juli. I'm serious. He will kill you." There was an edge of panic to his voice that sent a spike of fear through her gut.

The chanting grew seductive as more of the Ashnori morphed into their human forms. They smiled at her, their eyes warm and kind. Inviting. "Join us, Juliana."

Even with the knowledge that they would kill her, something inside her begged to answer their call. She took a step back, then another, trying to break out of their spell. But it was no use. They were too strong, and the nightmares had worn her down. She wouldn't be able to resist them much longer.

"I need their blood," she whispered to Max. "Like *now*."

"Not theirs." He turned to her, his expression grave. "You can have mine."

For just a moment in time, her world stopped spinning. When it started again with a jerking motion, the axis had tilted. She fell against the altar.

She glanced at the Ashnori as the chanting reached a fevered pitch. The candles in the sconces burst to life in a sea of orange flame. Red eyes glowed now from human faces, long, bony fingers tipped human hands. "What did you say?"

"My blood. You can have it." Max touched his hand to her cheek before it slid away. "They didn't kill me, but they cursed me. For the past ten years, I've been hovering between your world and theirs. I'm as much what they are as I am human, and every day I feel a little more of that humanity slipping away."

His words hit her hard, square in the chest. She sucked in a breath, a throbbing ache claiming her temples. "Then if we kill them, won't it kill you too?"

"I don't know. It might." His expression was one of grim acceptance, and it nearly stopped her heart.

"Max, don't do it."

"I don't have a choice. I *won't* let them take you. There's nothing, *nothing*, else we can do. It's either this, or you go with them. That isn't going to happen. Not as long as I'm alive."

He turned away from her then. She could only watch, helpless, as he lifted his wrist over the pendant and slashed the knife blade across his skin.

Blood flowed from the wound, dripping onto the pendant. The jewel started to glow, red like the eyes of the Ashnori, orange like the glow of the candle flames. The creatures stopped moving, though the seductive chanting didn't cease. Their faces bubbled and moved as their bodies shifted back into their true form.

Soon the chanting turned into wails and screams. The bubbling of their skin continued, their eyes, noses, and mouths leaking dark rivulets of blood. Pieces of their flesh fell off in chunks, hitting the floor with popping and sizzling sounds. They collapsed to the floor one by one amid a chorus of keening moans.

Smoke rose from the pile of black cloaks, now rotting threadbare fabric rather than the rich velvet they'd first appeared to be. She walked over to the mass of bodies and kicked at one with the tip of her shoe. No movement. The acrid odor of burnt flesh hovered in the air.

A huge smile spread over her face. She was finally free. "Max, it worked." She turned to him, ready to jump into his arms.

But he lay in an unmoving heap on the ground in front of the altar.

Epilogue

Juliana swirled her fingers over Max's bare stomach and leaned in to kiss his hot skin lightly. "You're going to get a sunburn if you don't cover up."

He laughed. "Whatever. I don't even care."

"Well, then, neither do I. Just don't complain to me if you get sunburned." She pinched his side. "Of course, there's always skin cancer to think about."

He rolled onto his side on the towel and smiled at her. "Another few minutes, okay?"

She shook her head. In the months since the Ashnori had been destroyed, Max had spent an inordinate amount of time outside in the sunshine. Breaking the curse had nearly killed him, but the human part of him had managed to cling to life as his body and spirit healed. At first he'd been too weak to do more than recline in a chaise lounge on the deck, but lately his strength had started returning.

Today he'd suggested walking down to the beach for the afternoon, and she'd reluctantly agreed. Now she was glad she'd relented. Every day he got stronger -- and every day he smiled more. The old Max, the one she'd first fallen in love with, had started to return.

"Okay, fine. Another few minutes." For the first time in more than ten years, the nightmares were gone. She'd slept soundly for months. In Max's arms. Her broken life had finally started to heal.

Just that morning, she'd signed the closing papers on the house she'd grown up in. Keeping something that had so many bad memories attached to it wouldn't be healthy for her or for Max. And right now, she needed to take care of him. He'd been willing to give his life for her, and she'd be grateful to him for as long as she lived.

She hadn't used the house in months anyway. She'd been living with him since that night he'd found her on the beach, and had made the move official to help him with his recovery. As far as she saw it, they'd hit the bottom together and there wasn't anywhere to go but up.

"What are you thinking?" Max asked, his playful expression growing serious.

"Just that I love you."

He leaned up and kissed her softly on the lips. "I love you, too."

"Thank you." She glanced away. "You know… for saving me."

"Juli," he warned on a sigh of mock-annoyance. "Am I going to have to hear that same thing for the rest of my life?"

She looked out at the water, rippling blue and gold as the bright sunlight shined down on it. "Of course. I wouldn't have it any other way."

Elisa Adams

Born in Gloucester, Massachusetts, Elisa Adams has lived most of her life on the East Coast. Formerly a nursing assistant and phlebotomist, writing has been a longtime hobby for Elisa. Now a full time writer, she lives on the New Hampshire border with her three children.

Changeling Press E-Books
Quality Erotic Adventures Designed For Today's Media

More Sci-Fi, Fantasy, Paranormal, and BDSM adventures available in E-Book format for immediate download at www.ChangelingPress.com -- Werewolves, Vampires, Dragons, Shapeshifters and more -- Erotic Tales from the edge of your imagination.

What are E-Books?

E-Books, or Electronic Books, are books designed to be read in digital format -- on your computer or PDA device.

What do I need to read an E-Book?

If you've got a computer and Internet access, you've got it already!

Your web browser, such as Internet Explorer or Netscape, will read any HTML E-Book. You can also read E-Books in Adobe Acrobat format and Microsoft Reader, either on your computer or on most PDAs. Visit our Web site to learn about other options.

What reviewers are saying about Changeling Press E-Books

Shelby Morgen -- Troll's Blog: Troll Under The Bridge

"Not only does the sexual tension between the troll and the cop begin immediately, it's also thick enough to cut with a knife... The steaming sex and unexpected ending will keep you smiling long after you finish The Troll Under The Bridge."

-- Trang, Fallen Angel Reviews

Alice Gaines -- Driven to Justice

"The plot is tense, the dialogue tight and the characters are heart winning. Ms. Gaines has again written a winning story that is creative and different."

-- Valerie, Love Romances and More

Camille Anthony -- Women of Steel 4: Strawberry Daiquiri

"I am once again amazed at Camille's talent for world-building. She's a master storyteller, crafting characters for readers to fall in love with... Strawberry Daiquiri is amazing and a must read!"

-- Sharyn McGinty, In the Library Reviews

Elizabeth Jewell -- Black Tie and Hot Tails

"This is a great m/m love story that I enjoyed reading very much! The sex scenes are hot, sensual, and graphic."

-- Regina, Coffeetime Romance Reviews

Aubrey Ross -- AWU3: Price of Passage

"Price of Passage is a magnificent book. Aubrey Ross has a great talent for weaving an exciting tale of passion, mystery and intrigue."

-- Julianne, Two Lips Reviews

Changeling Press, LLC

www.ChangelingPress.com

LaVergne, TN USA
16 October 2009
161136LV00002B/8/A